BLACKOUT

MIRA GRANT

orbit

www.orbitbooks.net

ORBIT

First published in Great Britain in 2012 by Orbit

7 9 11 12 10 8

All characters and events in this publication, other than those clearly in the public domain, are fictitious and any resemblance to real persons, living or dead, is purely coincidental.

A CIP catalogue record for this book
is available from the British Library.

ISBN 978-1-84149-900-0

Typeset in Garamond by M Rules.
Printed and bound by CPI Group (UK) Ltd, Croydon, CR0 4YY

Papers used by Orbit are from well-managed forests
and other responsible sources.

FSC www.fsc.org MIX Paper from responsible sources FSC® C104740

Orbit
An imprint of
Little, Brown Book Group
Carmelite House
50 Victoria Embankment
London EC4Y 0DZ

An Hachette UK Company
www.hachette.co.uk

www.orbitbooks.net

This book is dedicated to
Kathleen Secor,
Diana Fox,
and
Sunil Patel.
Without their efforts, I would never have made it this far.

Book I

From the Dead

People say things like "it wasn't supposed to go this way" and "this isn't what I wanted." They're just making noise. There's no such thing as "supposed to," and what you want doesn't matter. All that matters is what happened.

—Georgia Mason

I honestly have no idea what's going on anymore. I just need to find something I can hit.

—Shaun Mason

My name is Georgia Carolyn Mason. I am one of the Orphans of the Rising, the class of people who were under two years of age when the dead first started to walk. My biological family is presumably listed somewhere on The Wall, an anonymous footnote of a dead world. Their world died in the Rising. They didn't live to see the new one.

My adoptive parents have raised me to ask questions, understand the realities of my situation, and, in times of necessity, to shoot first. They have equipped me with the tools I need to survive, and I am grateful. Through this blog, I will do my best to share my experiences and opinions as openly and honestly as I can. It is the best way to honor the family that raised me; it is the only way I have to honor the family that lost me.

I'm going to tell you the truth as I understand it. You can take it from there.

—From *Images May Disturb You*, the blog of Georgia Mason, June 20, 2035.

So George says I have to write a "mission statement," because our contract with Bridge Supporters says I will. I am personally opposed to mission statements, since they're basically one more way of sucking the fun out of everything. I tried telling George this. She told me that it's her job to suck the fun out of everything. She then threatened physical violence of a type I will not describe in detail, as it might unsettle and upset my theoretical readership. Suffice to say that I am writing a mission statement. Here it is:

I, Shaun Phillip Mason, being of sound mind and body, do hereby swear to poke dead things with sticks, do stupid shit for your amusement, and put it all on the Internet where you can watch it over and over again. Because that's what you want, right?

Glad to oblige.

—From *Hail to the King*, the blog of Shaun Mason, June 20, 2035.

One

My story ended where so many stories have ended since the Rising: with a man—in this case, my adoptive brother and best friend, Shaun—holding a gun to the base of my skull as the virus in my blood betrayed me, transforming me from a thinking human being into something better suited to a horror movie.

My story ended, but I remember everything. I remember the cold dread as I watched the lights on the blood test unit turn red, one by one, until my infection was confirmed. I remember the look on Shaun's face when he realized this was it—it was really happening, and there wasn't going to be any clever third act solution that got me out of the van alive.

I remember the barrel of the gun against my skin. It was cool, and it was soothing, because it meant Shaun would do what he had to do. No one else would get hurt because of me.

No one but Shaun.

This was something we'd never planned for. I always knew that one day he'd push his luck too far, and I'd lose him. We never dreamed that he would be the one losing me. I wanted to tell him it would be okay. I wanted to lie to him. I remember that: I wanted to lie to him. And I couldn't. There wasn't time, and even then, I didn't have it in me.

I remember starting to write. I remember thinking this was it; this was my last chance to say anything I wanted to say to the world. This was the thing I was going to be judged on, now and forever. I remember feeling my mind start to go. I remember the fear.

I remember the sound of Shaun pulling the trigger.

I shouldn't remember anything after that. That's where my story ended. Curtain down, save file, that's a wrap. Once the bullet hits your spinal cord, you're done; you don't have to worry about this shit anymore. You definitely shouldn't wake up in a windowless, practically barren room that looks suspiciously like a CDC holding facility, with no one to talk to but some unidentified voice on the other side of a one-way mirror.

The bed where I'd woken up was bolted to the floor, and so was the matching bedside table. It wouldn't do to have the mysteriously resurrected dead journalist throwing things at the mirror that took up most of one wall. Naturally, the wall with the mirror was the only wall with a door—a door that refused to open. I'd tried waving my hands in front of every place that might hold a motion sensor, and then I'd searched for a test panel in the vain hope that checking out clean would make the locks let go and release me.

There were no test panels, or screens, or ocular scanners. There wasn't anything inside that seemed designed to let me out. That was chilling all by itself. I grew up in a post-Rising world, one where blood tests and the threat of infection are a part of daily life. I'm sure I'd been in sealed rooms without testing units before. I just couldn't remember any.

The room lacked something else: clocks. There was nothing to let me know how much time had passed since I woke up, much less how much time had passed *before* I woke up. There'd been a voice from the speaker above the mirror, an unfamiliar voice asking my name and what the last thing I remembered was. I'd answered him—"My name is Georgia Mason. What the *fuck* is going on here?"—and he'd gone away without answering my question. That might have been ten minutes ago. It might have been ten hours ago. The lights overhead glared steady and white, not so much as flickering as the seconds went slipping past.

That was another thing. The overhead lights were industrial fluorescents, the sort that have been popular in medical facilities since long before the Rising. They should have been burning my eyes like acid . . . and they weren't.

I was diagnosed with retinal Kellis-Amberlee when I was a kid, meaning that the same disease that causes the dead to rise had taken up permanent residence in my eyeballs. It didn't turn me into a zombie—retinal KA is a reservoir condition, one where the live virus is somehow contained inside the body. Retinal KA gave me extreme light sensitivity, excellent night vision, and a tendency to get sickening migraines if I did anything without my sunglasses on.

Well, I wasn't wearing sunglasses, and it wasn't like I could dim the lights, but my eyes still didn't hurt. All I felt was thirst, and a vague, gnawing hunger in the pit of my stomach, like lunch might be a good idea sometime soon. There was no headache. I honestly couldn't decide whether or not that was a good sign.

Anxiety was making my palms sweat. I scrubbed them against the legs of my unfamiliar white cotton pajamas. *Everything* in the room was unfamiliar . . . even me. I've never been heavy—a life spent running after stories and away from zombies doesn't encourage putting on weight—but the girl in the one-way mirror was thin to the point of being scrawny. She looked like she'd be easy to break. Her hair was as dark as mine. It was also too long, falling past her shoulders. I've never allowed my hair to get that long. Hair like that is a passive form of suicide when you do what I do for a living. And her eyes . . .

Her eyes were brown. That, more than anything else, made it impossible to think of her face as my own. I don't *have* visible irises. I have pupils that fill all the space not occupied by sclera, giving me a black, almost emotionless stare. Those weren't my eyes. But my eyes didn't hurt. Which meant either those *were* my eyes, and my retinal KA had somehow been cured, or Buffy was right when she said the afterlife existed, and this was hell.

I shuddered, looking away from my reflection, and resumed what was currently my main activity: pacing back and forth and trying to think. Until I knew whether I was being watched, I had to think quietly, and that made it a hell of a lot harder. I've always thought better when I do it out loud, and this was the first time in my adult life that I'd been anywhere without at least one recorder running. I'm an accredited journalist. When I talk to myself, it's not a sign of insanity; it's just my way of making sure I don't lose important material before I can write it down.

None of this was right. Even if there was some sort of experimental treatment to reverse amplification, someone would have been there to explain things to me. *Shaun* would have been there. And there it was, the reason I couldn't believe any of this was right: I remembered him pulling the trigger. Even assuming it was a false memory, even assuming it never happened, *why wasn't he here?* Shaun would move Heaven and Earth to reach me.

I briefly entertained the idea that he was somewhere in the building, forcing the voice from the intercom to tell him where I was. Regretfully, I dismissed it. Something would have exploded by now if that were true.

"Goddammit." I scowled at the wall, turned, and started in the other direction. The hunger was getting worse, and it was accompanied by a new, more frustrating sensation. I needed to pee. If someone didn't let me out soon, I was going to have a whole new set of problems to contend with.

"Run the timeline, George," I said, taking some comfort in the sound of my voice. Everything else might have changed, but not that. "You were in Sacramento with Rick and Shaun, running for the van. Something hit you in the arm. One of those syringes like they used at the Ryman farm. The test came back positive. Rick left. And then . . . then . . . " I faltered, having trouble finding the words, even if there was no one else to hear them.

Everyone who grew up after the Rising knows what happens when you come into contact with the live form of Kellis-Amberlee. You become a zombie, one of the infected, and you do what every zombie exists to do. You bite. You infect. You kill. You feed. You don't wake up in a white room, wearing white pajamas and wondering how your brother was able to shoot you in the neck without even leaving a scar.

Scars. I wheeled and stalked back to the mirror, pulling the lid on my right eye open wide. I learned how to look at my own eyes when I was eleven. That's when I got my first pair of protective contacts. That's also when I got my first visible retinal scarring, little patches of tissue scorched beyond recovery by the sun. We caught it in time to prevent major vision loss, and I got a lot more careful. The scarring created small blind spots at the center of my vision. Nothing major. Nothing that interfered with fieldwork. Just little spots.

My pupil contracted to almost nothing as the light hit it. The spots weren't there. I could see clearly, without any gaps.

"Oh." I lowered my hand. "I guess that makes sense."

I paused, feeling suddenly stupid as that realization led to another. When I first woke up, the voice from the intercom told me all I had to do was speak, and someone would hear me. I looked up at the speaker. "A little help here?" I said. "I need to pee really bad."

There was no response.

"Hello?"

There was still no response. I showed my middle finger to the mirror before turning and walking back to the bed. Once there, I sat and settled into a cross-legged position, closing my eyes. And then I started waiting. If anyone was watching me—and someone *had* to be watching me—this might be a big enough change in my behavior to get their attention. I wanted their attention. I wanted their attention really, really badly. Almost as badly as I wanted a personal recorder, an Internet connection, and a bathroom.

The need for a bathroom crept slowly higher on the list, accompanied by the need for a drink of water. I was beginning to consider the possibility that I might need to use a corner of the room as a lavatory when the intercom clicked on. A moment later, a new voice, male, like the first one, spoke: "Miss Mason? Are you awake?"

"Yes." I opened my eyes. "Do I get a name to call you by?"

He ignored my question like it didn't matter. Maybe it didn't, to him. "I apologize for the silence. We'd expected a longer period of disorientation, and I had to be recalled from elsewhere in the building."

"Sorry to disappoint you."

"Oh, we weren't disappointed," said the voice. He had the faintest trace of a Midwestern accent. I couldn't place the state. "I promise, we're thrilled to see you up and coherent so quickly. It's a wonderful indicator for your recovery."

"A glass of water and a trip to the ladies' room would do more to help my recovery than apologies and evasions."

Now the voice sounded faintly abashed. "I'm sorry, Miss Mason. We didn't think . . . just a moment." The intercom clicked off, leaving me in silence once again. I stayed where I was, and kept waiting.

The sound of a hydraulic lock unsealing broke the quiet. I turned to see a small panel slide open above the door, revealing a red light. It turned green and the door slid smoothly open, revealing a skinny, nervous-looking man in a white lab coat, eyes wide behind his glasses. He was clutching his clipboard to his chest like he thought it afforded him some sort of protection.

"Miss Mason? If you'd like to come with me, I'd be happy to escort you to the restroom."

"Thank you." I unfolded my legs, ignoring pins and needles in my calves, and walked toward the doorway. The man didn't quite cringe as I approached, but he definitely shied back, looking more uneasy with every step I took. Interesting.

"We apologize for making you wait," he said. His words had the distinct cadence of something recited by rote, like telephone tech support asking for your ID and computer serial number. "There were a few things that had to be taken care of before we could proceed."

"Let's worry about that *after* I get to the bathroom, okay?" I sidestepped around him, out into the hall, and found myself looking at three hospital orderlies in blue scrubs, each of them pointing a pistol in my direction. I stopped where I was. "Okay, I can wait for my escort."

"That's for the best, Miss Mason," said the nervous man, whose voice I now recognized from the intercom. It just took a moment without the filtering speakers between us. "Just a necessary precaution. I'm sure you understand."

"Yeah. Sure." I fell into step behind him. The orderlies followed us, their aim never wavering. I did my best not to make any sudden moves. Having just returned to the land of the living, I was in no mood to exit it again. "Am I ever going to get something I can call you?"

"Ah . . ." His mouth worked soundlessly for a moment before he said, "I'm Dr. Thomas. I've been one of your personal physicians since you arrived at this facility. I'm not surprised you don't remember me. You've been sleeping for some time."

"Is that what the kids are calling it these days?" The hall was built on the model I've come to expect from CDC facilities, with nothing breaking the sterile white walls but the occasional door and the associated one-way mirrors looking into patient holding rooms. All the rooms were empty.

"You're walking well."

"It's a skill."

"How's your head? Any disorientation, blurred vision, confusion?"

"Yes." He tensed. I ignored it, continuing. "I'm confused about what I'm doing here. I don't know about you, but I get twitchy when I wake up in strange places with no idea how I got there. Will I be getting some answers soon?"

"Soon enough, Miss Mason." He stopped in front of a door with no mirror next to it. That implied that it wasn't a patient room. Better yet, there was a blood test unit to one side. I never thought I'd be so happy for the chance to be jabbed with a needle. "We'll give you a few minutes. If you need anything—"

"Using the bathroom, also a skill." I slapped my palm down on the test panel. Needles promptly bit into the heel of my hand and the tips of my fingers. The light over the door flashed between red and green before settling on the latter. Uninfected. The door swung open. I stepped through, only to stop and scowl at the one-way mirror taking up most of the opposite wall. The door swung shut behind me.

"Cute," I muttered. The need to pee was getting bad enough that I didn't protest the situation. I glared at the mirror the entire time I was using the facilities, all but daring someone to watch me. See? I can pee whether you're spying on me or not, you sick bastards.

Other than the mirror—or maybe because of the mirror—the bathroom was as standard-issue CDC as the hallway outside, with white walls, a white tile floor, and white porcelain fixtures. Everything was automatic, including the soap dispenser, and there were no towels; instead, I dried my hands by sticking them into a jet of hot air. It was one big exercise in minimizing contact with any surface. When I turned back to the door, the only things I'd touched were the toilet seat and the floor, and I was willing to bet that they were in the process of self-sterilization by the time I started washing my hands.

The blood test required to exit the bathroom was set into the door itself, just above the knob. It didn't unlock until I checked out clean.

The three orderlies were waiting in the hall, with an unhappy Dr. Thomas between them and me. If I did anything bad enough to make them pull those triggers, the odds were good that he'd be treated as collateral damage.

"Wow," I said. "Who did you piss off to get this gig?"

He flinched, looking at me guiltily. "I'm sure I don't know what you mean."

"Of course not. Thank you for bringing me to the bathroom. Now, could I get that water?" Better yet, a can of Coke. The thought of its acid sweetness was enough to make my mouth water. It's good to know that some things never change.

"If you'd come this way?"

I gave the orderlies a pointed look. "I don't think I have much of a choice, do you?"

"No, I suppose you don't," he said. "As I said, a precaution. You understand."

"Not really, no. I'm unarmed. I've just passed two blood tests. I *don't* understand why I need three men with guns covering my every move." The CDC has been paranoid for years, but this was taking it to a new extreme.

Dr. Thomas's reply didn't help: "Security."

"Why do people always say that when they don't feel like giving a straight answer?" I shook my head. "I'm not going to make trouble. Please, just take me to the water."

"Right this way," he said, and started back the way we'd come.

There was a tray waiting for us on the bolted-down table in the room where I'd woken up. It held a plate with two pieces of buttered toast, a tumbler full of water, and wonder of wonders, miracle of miracles, a can of Coke with condensation beading on the sides. I made for the tray without pausing to consider how the orderlies might react to my moving faster than a stroll. None of them shot me in the back. That was something.

The first bite of toast was the best thing I'd ever tasted, at least until I took the second bite, and then the third. Finally, I crammed most of the slice into my mouth, barely chewing. I managed to resist the siren song of the Coke long enough to drink half the water. It tasted as good as the toast. I put down the glass, popped the tab on the can of soda, and took my first post-death sip of Coke. I was smart enough not to gulp it; even that tiny amount was enough to make my knees weak. That, and the caffeine rush that followed, provided the last missing piece.

Slowly, I turned to face Dr. Thomas. He was standing in the doorway, making notes on his clipboard. There were probably a few dozen video and audio recorders running, catching every move I made, but any good reporter will tell you that there's nothing like real field experience. I guess the same thing applies to scientists. He lowered his pen when he saw me looking.

"How do you feel?" he asked. "Dizzy? Are you full? Did you want something besides toast? It's a bit early for anything complicated, but I might be able to arrange for some soup, if you'd prefer that . . ."

"Mostly, what I'd prefer is having some questions answered." I shifted the Coke from one hand to the other. If I couldn't have my sunglasses, I guess a can of soda would have to do. "I think I've been pretty cooperative up to now. I also think that could change."

Dr. Thomas looked uncomfortable. "Well, I suppose that will depend on what sort of questions you want to ask."

"This one should be pretty easy. I mean, it's definitely within your skill set."

"All right. I can't promise to know the answer, but I'm happy to try. We want you to be comfortable."

"Good." I looked at him levelly, missing my black-eyed gaze. It always made people so uncomfortable. I got more honest answers out of those eyes . . . "You said you were my personal physician."

"That's correct."

"So tell me: How long have I been a clone?"

Dr. Thomas dropped his pen.

Still watching him, I raised my Coke, took a sip, and waited for his reply.

Subject 139b was bitten on the evening of June 24, 2041. The exact time of the bite was not recorded, but a period of no less than twenty minutes elapsed between exposure and initial testing. The infected individual responsible for delivering the bite was retrieved from the road. Posthumous analysis confirmed that the individual was heavily contagious, and had been so for at least six days, as the virus had amplified through all parts of the body.

Blood samples were taken from the outside of Subject 139b's hand and sequenced to prove that they belonged to the subject. Analysis of these samples confirmed the infection. (For proof of live viral bodies in Subject 139b's blood, see the attached file.) Amplification appears to have begun normally, and followed the established progression toward full loss of cognitive functionality. Samples taken from Subject 139b's clothing confirm this diagnosis.

Subject 139b was given a blood test shortly after arriving at this facility, and tested clean of all live viral particles. Subject 139b was given a second test, using a more sensitive unit, and once again tested clean. After forty-eight hours of isolation, following standard Kellis-Amberlee quarantine procedures, it is my professional opinion that the subject is not now infected, and does not represent a danger to himself or others.

With God as my witness, Joey, I swear to you that Shaun Mason is *not* infected with the live state of Kellis-Amberlee. He should be. He's not. He started to amplify, and he somehow fought the infection off. This could change everything . . . if we had the slightest fucking clue how he did it.

—Taken from an e-mail sent by Dr. Shannon Abbey to Dr. Joseph Shoji at the Kauai Institute of Virology, June 27, 2041.

Times like this make me think my mother was right when she told me I should aspire to be a trophy wife. At least that would have reduced the odds of my winding up hiding in a renegade virology lab, hunting zombies for a certifiable mad scientist.

Then again, maybe not.

—From *Charming Not Sincere*, the blog of Rebecca Atherton, July 16, 2041. Unpublished.

Two

"Shaun! Look out!"

Alaric's shout came through my headset half a second before a hand grabbed my elbow, bearing down with that weird mixture of strength and clumsiness characteristic of the fully amplified. I yanked free, whirling to smack my assailant upside the head with my high-powered cattle prod.

A look of almost comic surprise crossed the zombie's face as the electrified end of the cattle prod hit its temple. Then it fell. I kicked the body. It didn't move. I hit it in the solar plexus with my cattle prod, just to be sure. Electricity has always been useful against zombies, since it confuses the virus that motivates them, but it turns out that when you amp the juice enough you can actually shut them down for short periods of time.

"Thanks for the heads-up," I said, trusting the headset to pick me up. "I've got another dead boy down. Send the retrieval team to my coordinates." I was already starting to scan the trees, looking for signs of movement—looking for something else that I could hit.

"Shaun . . ." There was a wary note in Alaric's voice. I could practically see him sitting at his console, knotting his hands in his hair and trying not to let his irritation come through the microphone. I *was* his boss, after all, which meant he had to at least pretend to be respectful. Once in a while. "That's your fourth catch of the night. I think that's enough, don't you?"

"I'm going for the record."

There was a click as Becks plugged her own channel into the connection and snapped peevishly, "You've already *got* the record. Four catches in a night is twice what anyone else has managed, ever. Now please, *please*, come back to the lab."

"What will you do if I don't?" I asked. Nothing seemed to be moving, except for my infected friend, who twitched. I zapped him with the cattle prod again. The movement stopped.

"Two words, Shaun: tranquilizer darts. Now come back to the lab."

I whistled. "That's not playing fair. How about you promise to bake me chocolate chip cookies if I come back? That seems like a much better incentive."

"How about you stop screwing around before you make me angry? Immune doesn't mean immortal, you know. Now please." The peevishness faded, replaced by pleading. "Just come home."

She's right, said George—or the ghost of George, anyway, the little voice at the back of my head that's all I have left of my adopted sister. Some people say I have issues. I say those people need to expand their horizons, because I don't have issues, I have the Library of Congress. *You need to go back. This isn't doing anybody any good.*

"I don't know," I said. I used to be circumspect about talking to George. That was before I decided to go all the way insane. Madness is surprisingly freeing. "I mean, *I'm* having fun. Aren't you the one who used to nag me to get my butt back into the field? Is this field enough for you?"

Shaun. Please.

My smile faded. "Fine. Whatever. If you want me to go back to the stupid lab, I'll go back to the stupid lab. Happy now?"

No, said George. *But it's going to have to do.*

I poked my latest catch one last time with the cattle prod. It didn't react. I turned to stalk back through the trees to the ripped-up side road where the bike was parked. Gunshots sounded from the forest to my left. I paused. Silence followed them, rather than screaming. I nodded and started walking again. Maybe that seems callous, but I wasn't the only one collecting virtual corpses for Dr. Abbey, the crazy renegade virologist who'd been sheltering us since we were forced off the grid. Most of her lab technicians were either ex-military or trained marksmen. They could take care of themselves, at least in the "killing stuff" department. I was less sure about bringing the zombies home alive. Fortunately for me, that was their problem, not mine.

Alaric's sigh of relief made me jump. I'd almost forgotten that he and Becks were listening in from their cozy spot in the main lab. "Thank you for seeing sense."

"Don't thank me," I said. "Thank George."

Neither of them had anything to say to that. I hadn't expected them to. I tapped the button on the side of my headset, killing the connection, and kept walking.

It had been just under a month since the world turned upside down. Some days, I was almost grateful to be waking up in an underground virology lab. Sure, most of the things it contained could kill me—including the head virologist, who I suspected of having fantasies about dissecting me so she could analyze my organs—but at least we knew what was going on. We had a place, if not a fully functional plan. That put us way ahead of the surviving denizens of North America's Gulf Coast, who were still contending with something we'd never anticipated: an insect vector for Kellis-Amberlee.

A tropical storm had blown some brand-new strain of mosquito over from Cuba, one with a big enough bite to transmit the live virus to humans. No one had heard of an insect vector for Kellis-Amberlee before that day. The entire world had heard of it on the day after, as every place Tropical Storm Fiona touched discovered the true meaning of "storm damage." The virus spread initially with the storm, and then started spreading on its own as the winds died down and the mosquitoes went looking for something to munch on. It was a genuine apocalypse scenario, the sort of thing that makes trained medical personnel shit their pants and call for their mommies. And it was really happening, and there wasn't a damn thing we could do about it.

The worst part? Even if no one wanted to say it out loud, when you looked at the timing of everything going wrong—the way it all happened just as we started really prodding at the CDC's sore spots—I thought there was a pretty good chance it wasn't an accident. And that would mean it was our fault.

There was no one standing watch over the vehicles. That was sloppy; even if we cleared out the human infected, there was always the chance a zombie raccoon or something could take refuge under one of the collection vans and go for somebody's ankles when they came back with the evening's haul. I made a mental note to talk to Dr. Abbey about her tactical setup as I swung a leg over the bike. Then I put on my helmet—Becks was right, immune doesn't mean immortal—and took off down the road.

See, here's the thing. My name is Shaun Mason; I'm a journalist, I guess, even though right now all my posts are staying unpublished for security's sake. I'm not technically wanted for anything. It's just that places where I show up have a nasty tendency to get wiped off the map shortly after I get there, and that makes me a little gun-shy when it comes to telling people where I am. I think that's understandable. Then again, I also think my dead sister talks to me, so what do I know?

About a year and a half ago—which feels like yesterday and an eternity at the same time—George and I applied to blog for Senator Peter Ryman's presidential campaign, along with our friend Georgette "Buffy" Meissonier. Before that, I was your average gentleman Irwin, wanting nothing beyond a few dead things to poke with sticks and the opportunity to write up my adventures for an adoring populace. Pretty simple, right? The three of us had everything we needed to be happy. Only we didn't know that, so when the chance to grab for glory came, we took it. We wanted to make history.

We made it, all right. We made it, Buffy and George *became* it, and I wound up as the last man standing, the one who has to avenge the glorious dead. All I know is that part wasn't in the brochure.

The road smoothed as I got closer to our current home-sweet-home. Shady Cove, Oregon, has been deserted since the Rising, when the infected left the tiny community officially uninhabitable. We had to be careful about how visible we were, but Dr. Abbey had been sending her interns—interning for what, I didn't know, since most universities don't offer a degree in mad science—out at night to patch the worst of the potholes with a homebrewed asphalt substitute that looked just like the real thing.

Fixing the road was a mixed blessing. It could give away our location if someone came looking. In the meantime, it made it easier for supply runs to get through, even if no one seemed to know how we were getting those supplies, and it would make it easier for us to evacuate the lab when the time came. Dr. Abbey didn't care how many of us died, as long as her equipment made it out. I had to admire that sort of single-minded approach. It reminded me of George.

Everything reminds you of me, George said.

I snorted but didn't answer. The roar of the wind in my ears was too loud for me to hear my own voice, and I like to pretend that we're having real conversations. It helps. With what, I can't quite say, but . . . it helps.

Barely visible sensors in the underbrush tracked my approach as I came around the final curve and entered the parking lot of the Shady Cove Forestry Center. The building was dark, its vast pre-Rising windows like blind eyes staring into the trees. It looked empty. It wasn't. I drove around to the back, where the old employee parking garage had been restored and strengthened to provide cover for our vehicles.

[redacted] [redacted]

Since it was a pre-Rising design, I didn't need to pass a blood test to get inside, and was able to just drive straight to my assigned slot, shutting off the bike. I removed my helmet and slung it over the handlebars, leaving it there in case I needed to leave in a hurry. I approach everything as a potential evacuation these days. I've got good reason.

Cameras tracked my progress toward the door. "Hello, Shaun," said the lab computer. It was pleasant and female, with a Canadian accent. Maybe it reminded Dr. Abbey of home. I didn't know.

What I *did* know was that I don't like computers pretending to be human. It creeps me out. "Can I come in?" I asked.

"Please place your palm on the testing panel." An amber light came on above the test unit, helpfully indicating where I needed to put my hand. Like any kid who lives long enough to go to kindergarten doesn't know how to operate a basic blood testing panel? You learn, or you die.

"I don't see the point of this." I slapped my hand down on the metal. Cooling foam sprayed my skin a bare second before needles started biting into my flesh. I hate blood tests. "You know I'm not infected. I *can't* be infected. So why don't you stop fucking around and let me inside?"

"All personnel must be tested when returning from the field, Shaun. There are no exceptions." The amber light blinked off, replaced by two more lights, one red, one green. They began flashing.

"I liked this place a lot better before Dr. Abbey got you online," I said.

"Thank you for your cooperation," replied the computer blithely. The red light winked off as the green one stabilized, confirming my uninfected status. Again. "Welcome home."

The door into the main lab unlocked, sliding open. I flipped off the nearest camera and walked inside.

Dr. Abbey's people have had lots of practice converting formerly abandoned buildings into functional scientific research centers. The

Shady Cove Forestry Center was practically tailor-made for them, being large, constructed to withstand the elements, and best of all, in the middle of fucking nowhere. Entering from the parking garage put me in the main room—originally the Visitor's Welcome Lobby, according to the brass sign by the door. That explained the brightly colored mural of cheerful woodland creatures on the wall. People used to romanticize the natural world, before the Rising. These days, we mostly just run away from it.

Interns and technicians were everywhere, all rushing around on weird science errands. I don't understand most of what Dr. Abbey's people do, and that's probably a good thing. Mahir understands a lot more than I do, and he says it makes it hard for him to sleep at night.

Speaking of Mahir, the man himself was storming across the room, a look of profound irritation on his face. "Are you *trying* to get yourself killed?" he demanded.

"That's an interesting philosophical question, and one that would be better discussed over a can of Coke," I replied amiably. "It's good to see you, too."

"I have half a mind to punch your face in, you bloody idiot," Mahir said, still scowling.

Mahir used to be George's second in command. Since she can't run a third of the staff as a voice in my head, Mahir took over the Newsies when she died. I sometimes think he's angry with me for not being angrier with him over taking her place. What he never seems to quite understand is that he's one of the only people in this world who loved George the way I did, and having him on my side makes me feel a little better.

Besides, it's funny as hell when he gets pissed. "But you won't," I said. "What's our status?"

Mahir's glare faded, replaced by weariness. "Alaric is still attempting to find out what keeps happening to our mirror sites. We've put up six new reports from the junior bloggers in the past hour, none of which touch on the Gulf Coast tragedy, and three of them have vanished into thin air. I think he's going to start pulling his hair out before much longer."

"This is what happens when you piss off a government conspiracy." I started walking toward the kitchen. "How's Becks doing on the extraction plan?"

Mahir answered with a small shake of his head.

"Aw, damn." Alaric's little sister, Alisa, was in Florida when Tropical Storm Fiona made landfall. She managed to survive the first wave of infections, through a combination of quick thinking and dumb luck. After that... Alaric was unable to step forward to claim her, since Dr. Abbey said that if one of us left, all of us left. We thought Alisa might wind up placed with a foster family, but things in Florida were too bad for that. She wound up in a government-sponsored refugee camp. She was sending regular updates and had managed to stay mostly out of trouble. Still, it was clear that if we didn't find a way to get her out of there soon, Alaric was going to do something stupid. I understood his motivation. Family's the most important thing there is.

"Yes, well. It is what it is." Mahir paced me easily. He wasn't always a field man, but he'd been working out since we arrived at Dr. Abbey's—something about not wanting to die the next time we wound up running for our lives. "Dr. Abbey requests the pleasure of your company once you've had the opportunity to clean yourself up."

I groaned. I couldn't help it. "More blood tests?"

"More blood tests," he confirmed.

"Motherfucker." I scowled at nothing in particular. "Immunity is more trouble than it's worth."

"Yes, absolutely, being mysteriously immune to the zombie plague which has devastated the world is a terrible cross to bear," said Mahir, deadpan.

"Hey, you try giving blood on a daily basis and see how you feel about it."

"No, thank you."

I sighed. "Is this another of those 'no caffeine before donating' days? Did she say?"

"I believe it's not."

"Thank God for that." Don't get me wrong. No one knows why I seem to be immune to Kellis-Amberlee amplification—something the CDC has been telling us is impossible since the Rising, by the way. You get bitten, you amplify, simple as that. Only it turns out that with me, it actually goes "you get bitten; you get annoyed; you have to take a lot of antibiotics, because human mouths are incredibly dirty and dying of a bacterial infection would suck; you get better." I understood why Dr. Abbey needed blood almost every day. It was just a *lot* of needles.

Becks was in the kitchen when we arrived. She was sitting on the counter, holding a can of Coke. "Looking for this?" she asked.

"My savior." I walked toward her, making grabbing motions. "Gimme. Gimme sweet, sweet caffeine."

"The word is 'please,' Mason. Look it up." She tossed me the can, a gentle underhand lob that wouldn't shake the contents up too much. The team does that a lot these days—throws me things to double-check my manual dexterity. My recovery after being bitten was too miraculous to believe. We're all waiting for it to wear off and for me to go rampaging through the lab.

I made the catch and cracked the tab, taking a long, cold drink before putting the can down on the nearest table and asking, "Have any of the new guys made it in yet?"

"The first batch is in processing now," Becks replied. "We managed to net twenty-four infected tonight, including your four."

"Cool." Our lovely hostess needed a constant supply of fresh subjects, since her experiments required a couple dozen at any given time, and her lab protocols didn't leave many of them alive past the three-day mark. Snatch-and-grab patrols were going out twice a week, minimum, and at the rate they were working, Shady Cove was going to be free of the infected in under three months.

"I guess." Becks slid off the counter, giving me a calculating look. "What were you doing out there tonight, Mason? You could have been killed."

"That wasn't my first solo in these woods."

"It was your first one at night." She shook her head. "You're starting to scare me."

"And me," said Mahir.

And me, said George.

"You don't get a say in this," I muttered. Mahir didn't look offended. He knew I wasn't talking to him. In a more normal tone, I asked, "So what do you want me to do, Becks? I don't speak science. I barely speak research. Things are a mess out there, and we're stuck in here, spinning our wheels."

"So maybe it's time you stopped spinning." The three of us turned toward Dr. Abbey's voice. Like the lab computer, it was pleasant and Canadian-accented. Unlike the lab computer, it was coming from a short, curvy scientist with bleached streaks in her shaggy brown hair. Her lab coat was open, exposing a bright orange Cephalopods Union #462 T-shirt.

I raised an eyebrow. "Okay, I'm listening. What have you got in mind?"

Dr. Abbey held up a thumb drive. "Get your team and meet me in the screening room. It's time we had a little talk about what's going on in Florida." She quirked a small smile. "You can bring popcorn."

"Science and snacks, the perfect combination," I said. "We'll be there."

"Good," said Dr. Abbey, and left.

Mahir stepped up next to me. "Do you have any idea what that's all about?"

"Nope." I shrugged, picking up my Coke again. The second drink was just as good as the first had been. "But hey. We may as well get started. What's the worst that can happen?"

Managing things without Georgia has never been what I would term "easy," but it's never been harder than in the past few months. The devastation wreaked by Tropical Storm Fiona would have been terrible even without the additional horror of a newly discovered insect vector for Kellis-Amberlee infection. The loss of life would have been appalling even if so many of the lost had not gone on to attack and infect their fellow men. I find myself watching the news feeds and wishing, more than ever before, that Georgia Mason were with us today.

Georgia had a gift for reporting the news without letting sentiment color her impressions: She saw the world in black and white, no shades of gray allowed. It could have been a crippling disability in any other profession, but she made it her greatest strength. If she were here, she would be the one reducing bodies to statistics, rendering disasters into history. But she's not here. She, too, has been reduced to a statistic, has been rendered into history. All of which means that I, unprepared as I am, have been forced to do her job.

May posterity show mercy when it looks back upon the work we do today. We did what we could with what we had.

—From *Fish and Clips*, the blog of Mahir Gowda,
July 16, 2041.

Subject 7c is awake, responsive, and self-aware. Subject has asked several conditionally relevant questions, and does not appear to suffer any visual or cognitive disorders. Subject self-identifies as

"Georgia Mason," and is able to recount events up to the point of physical death (see *Georgia C. Mason, autopsy file* for details of injury).

We are prepared to continue with this subject for the time being. Full medical files are being transmitted under a secure encryption key.

—Taken from an e-mail sent by Dr. Matthew Thomas, July 16, 2041.

Georgia Mason Lives.

—Graffiti from inside the Florida disaster zone, picture published under Creative Commons license.

Three

I have to give Dr. Thomas this: He recovered quickly from the question I obviously wasn't supposed to be asking yet. "I don't think you understand what you're saying." He retrieved his pen from the floor. "Maybe you need to sit down."

"My eyes are wrong. I could possibly be convinced to believe in a regenerative treatment that erased my scars. I could even accept that it was a deep enough dermal renewal to remove my licensing tattoo." I raised my wrist, showing him the spot where my personal information should have been permanently scribed. "But there's nothing that could have repaired my eyes. So I ask again: How long have I been a clone?"

Dr. Thomas narrowed his eyes. I stood up a little straighter, trying to look imposing. It wasn't easy to do in a pair of CDC-issue pajamas.

"This is highly irregular . . ." Dr. Thomas began.

"So is cloning reporters." I took a final sip of Coke before forcing myself to put it down. The caffeine was already starting to make me jittery. The last thing I wanted to do was finish the can and have my hands start shaking. "Come on. Who am I going to tell? I'm assuming you're not planning on giving me a connection to the outside world anytime soon."

Dr. Thomas gave me a calculating look. I looked back, wishing I had the slightest idea of how to look earnest and well meaning with my strange new eyes. Living life behind a pair of sunglasses was so much easier.

Finally, he nodded, a familiar expression flickering across his face. I'd seen it worn by a hundred interview subjects, all of whom thought they were about to pull one over on me. None of them ever seemed to realize that maybe my degree in journalism included one or two classes in human psychology. I may not be good at lying, but oh, I know a lie when I hear one.

"As I said before, this is highly irregular," he said in a lower, warmer tone of voice.

Trying to win my trust through confession. Pretty standard stuff, even if the situation was anything but standard. "I know, but please. I just want to know what's going on." I've never done "vulnerable" well. It wasn't on the final exam.

Maybe the fact that I was actually feeling vulnerable behind my facade of journalistic calm was showing through, because Dr. Thomas said, "I understand. You must be very confused."

"Also frightened, disoriented, and a little bit trying to convince myself this isn't a dream," I replied. I picked up my Coke again, not to drink, but to feel it in my hand. It was a poor substitute for the things I really wanted—my sunglasses, a gun, Shaun—but it would have to do.

"You have to understand that this is an experimental procedure. There was no way we could predict success, or even be sure that you would be yourself when you woke up." Dr. Thomas watched me as he spoke. He was telling the truth, or at least the truth as he understood it. "To be honest with you, we're still not sure how stable you are."

"I guess that explains the men with the guns, huh?" I took a sip of Coke without thinking about it, and decided against putting the can back down. I deserved a little comfort. Resurrection turns out to be really hard on a person. "So you're waiting for me to flip out and . . . what, exactly?"

"Cloning is a complicated process," said Dr. Thomas. "Modern generations are infected with the Kellis-Amberlee virus while in the womb. Their bodies grow up handling the infection, coming to . . . an agreement with it, if you will. Adult infections have been rare since the Rising."

"But cloned tissue is grown under clean-room conditions," I said. "How did you introduce the infection?"

"Aerosol exposure when the . . ." He stuttered to a stop, obviously unsure how to proceed. Their reports probably referred to me as "the subject" or "the body" at that stage of the process. Using a proper pronoun would involve giving too much identity to something he'd been treating as a lab experiment.

The temptation to point that out was there. I let it pass. I needed an ally, even one who thought he was getting me to cooperate, more than I needed to score a few points just to make myself feel better. "How far along in the growth cycle was the tissue?" I asked.

"Halfway," he said, visibly relieved. "We used techniques developed for organ cloning to accelerate the growth of the entire body. The immune and nervous systems were fully mature. We even used a blood sample on file at the Memphis installation, to be sure the exposure involved the strain of Kellis-Amberlee with which you were originally infected. It seemed the most likely to be compatible with your system. For all that we work with this virus every day, things like this, well, they aren't precisely an exact science . . ."

Things like this absolutely *are* an exact science. They're exactly what the Fictionals tell us to expect once mad science gets involved. I decided that was something else that didn't need to be pointed out. Instead, I seized on the thing he was doing his best to avoid saying. "The men with guns are here because there's a chance I'm going to spontaneously amplify, aren't they?"

"Yes," said Dr. Thomas. He looked genuinely sorry as he continued.

"It will take a few days to be sure your system has properly adjusted to the infection. Until then, I'm afraid your movements will be carefully monitored. You can use the intercom to request food or drinks, and there will always be an escort ready if you need to visit the sanitary facilities. Showers will be available to you on a regular basis."

"Can I ask for an Internet connection?" I asked.

He looked away as he answered. "That isn't a good idea yet. We're still running tests, and we don't want to stress you more than is absolutely necessary. Hard copy reading material can be provided, if there are specific subjects you're interested in."

"Carefully censored, so as not to 'stress' me?" He had the good grace to look embarrassed. That didn't make me feel any better. "If you're trying to avoid stress, you should know that isolation stresses me."

"That may be, but you're going to have to live with it for a little while longer. I'm sorry. It's necessary for your health."

Something about the way he said that made my throat close up. A dozen nightmare scenarios flashed through my mind, all of them beginning in the dangerous seconds following the gunshot that killed me. I took a long drink of Coke to steady myself, and asked, "Is Shaun okay? Did he make it out of Sacramento? Please. Just tell me if he made it out of Sacramento."

"It's July of 2041. It's taken us a little over eight months to get you to the point of being both awake and aware of your surroundings," said Dr. Thomas. He delivered this apparent non sequitur in a hurried almost-monotone, like he wanted to get what he was about to say out of the way as quickly as possible. "A great deal has changed during that time."

"You didn't answer my question."

"I know."

"Why aren't you answering me? What are you trying to—"

"Miss Mason, I can't give you the answers you're asking me for. But I am truly and sincerely sorry for your loss."

I gaped at him, openmouthed. I was still gaping when he stepped out of the room, the door closing behind him. I didn't move. Not until my Coke hit the floor with a metallic *clink*, so much like the sound of a bullet casing being dropped. My knees went weak, and I sank into a kneeling position, my eyes fixed on the blank white door.

My cheeks were wet. I reached up with one hand, touching my right cheek. My fingertips came away damp. "I'm crying?" I said numbly. Retinal Kellis-Amberlee robs its victims of the ability to cry. Somehow, the idea that I could cry now was even more unbelievable than the idea that I was a CDC science project.

I staggered to my feet and stumbled over to the bed, where I collapsed atop the covers and curled into a ball, hugging my knees to my chest. The tears came hard after that, leaving me shaking and barely able to breathe. Somewhere in the middle of all that, I fell asleep.

I dreamed of funerals. Sometimes they were mine, and Shaun was standing in front of a room full of people, awkwardly trying to pretend he knew what he was doing. Those were the good dreams. Those were the dreams that reflected life as I knew it. Other times—most of the times—it was his face on the picture in front of the funereal urn, and either I was delivering a eulogy in a robotic monotone, or Alaric was standing there, explaining how it was only a matter of time. Once I was gone, no one really expected anything else.

The room was dark when I opened my eyes. They ached in a totally unfamiliar way. I shifted enough to free a hand to rub them, and discovered that my eyelids were puffy and slightly tender. I considered getting upset about it, but dismissed the idea. Either this was a normal side effect of crying, or Dr. Thomas had been right to be concerned, and I was starting to amplify. If it was the first, I needed to learn to live with it. If it was the second, well. It might be somebody's problem. It wasn't going to be mine.

I sat up on the bed, squinting to make out shapes in the darkened room. Even with the retinal Kellis-Amberlee, I probably couldn't have seen in a room this dark. Still, dwelling on it gave me something to do for a few seconds, while I waited for my eyes to stop aching and let my thoughts settle down into something resembling normal. I wasn't usually this scattered. Then again, I hadn't usually just come back from the dead. Maybe I needed to cut myself a little slack.

Minutes slipped by me almost unnoticed. It wasn't until my butt started going numb that I realized how long I'd been sitting there, paralyzed by the simple reality of the dark. "Fuck that," I muttered, and slid off the bed, only stumbling a little as my feet hit the floor. There. Step one had been successfully taken: I was standing up. Everything else could come from there.

If I remembered correctly, the wall with the door would be about six feet in front of me. I started forward, holding my hands out in a vain effort to keep myself from walking face-first into anything solid. I felt a little better with every step. I was *up*. I was *doing something*. Sure, what I was doing was basically creeping my way across a dark room like a heroine from one of Maggie's pre-Rising horror movies, but it was *something*, and that was a big improvement over what I'd been doing before.

It's amazing how effective simple disorientation is as a mechanism for controlling people. Reporters use it whenever we think we can get away with it. We try to be the ones in control of the environment, using everything from props and street noise to temperature to keep people either completely relaxed or totally on edge, depending on the needs of the piece. Well, the CDC was trying to disorient me, and I'd been playing right into their hands. Who cared if I was a clone of myself, being kept under lock and key in a secret facility somewhere? I was still Georgia Mason—call it "identity until proven otherwise." And if I was going to be Georgia Mason, I couldn't sit around feeling sorry for myself. I needed to do something.

My hands hit the one-way mirror. I stopped, leaning forward until my forehead grazed the surface of the glass. If I squinted, I could make out the hallway on the other side. It was like trying to look through a thick layer of fog; if the lights in the hall hadn't been on, I wouldn't have been able to see anything at all. As it was, I was only getting outlines. The walls. The equally deceptive "windows" looking in on those other, empty rooms. Were they waiting for their own secretly cloned residents? Was I the first, the last, or somewhere in the middle?

"Stop it," I muttered, wrenching my way out of that line of thought. It was something I needed to think about—probably at great length, and potentially as part of an exposé on illegal human cloning being conducted by the CDC—but this wasn't the time. Here and now, it didn't matter if they had a damn *army* of clones. I was the only clone I cared about.

I was the only . . .

I stepped away from the mirror, staring into the darkness in front of me. If the CDC was monitoring me on a hidden video feed—and I had absolute faith that the CDC was monitoring me on a hidden video feed, that's what hidden video feeds are *for*—they'd probably think I was having a seizure. Let them think what they wanted. My frozen stare was as close as I could allow myself to come to cheering and punching the air in raw triumph.

They'd almost managed to catch me in their little logic puzzle, I had to give them that, but I've spent my entire life pursuing the truth ahead of all other things, and I know a lie when I don't hear one. Dr. Thomas tried so very hard not to give me any firm answers . . . and that was the problem. He said he was sorry for my loss. He wouldn't let me have an Internet connection, not even one that wasn't capable of transmitting, only receiving. And he never, not once, went so far as to say that Shaun was dead. Why wouldn't he tell me Shaun was dead?

Because he didn't have any proof. The old Internet rallying cry: pics or it didn't happen. There was no way he could invent a believable story that I wouldn't be able to poke holes in, and if he'd been telling the truth, he would have been happy to prove it.

Shaun was alive.

I could be a clone, up could be down, and black could be white, but Shaun had to be alive. If I were in their shoes, the only thing that would have convinced me to clone a potentially recalcitrant reporter—and let's face it, I was renowned for my stubbornness, especially when people were trying to tell me what to do—was the need to have that *specific* reporter on my side. The CDC wouldn't have brought me back unless they needed me to do something for them. And there was only one thing I could do that no one else could.

I could make Shaun stop.

Shaun was alive, and he was doing something they didn't approve of. Shaun was doing something they wanted stopped. But this was the CDC—they were the good guys. Whatever he was doing had to be something I would support stopping, right? Shaun was always good at making trouble, and I was usually the one in charge of stopping him. Take me out of the picture, and well . . .

For a moment, I lost myself in the pleasant fantasy of the CDC telling me that they were done processing me, everything was fine, and I could go. They'd hand me a pair of sunglasses and show me the door, sending me out into the world to find Shaun and give him a brisk smack upside the head. I was the only one he'd listen to, after all.

Regretfully, I set that pretty daydream aside. If they just wanted to make Shaun settle down, they'd hit him with a tranquilizer dart or something. Cloning a single sterile organ for a transplant patient cost millions of dollars. My shiny new factory-issue body probably came with a price tag somewhere in the billions. Shaun could cause a lot of trouble if he wanted to, but he wasn't capable of *that* much trouble—certainly not enough to justify the cost of resurrecting me.

So what had he done that justified it? What did they want from me that they couldn't get from him? My fingertips brushed the edge of the door. I stopped, turned, and paced in the opposite direction, letting the fingers of my other hand whisk along the wall. Fine; so they hadn't brought me back from the dead for purely altruistic reasons. I knew that when I woke up. I represented too much money and too much time to be a purely scientific exercise. If this had happened before the Rising, human cloning might have been seen as a way to enhance and extend life. Worn out your body? Get a new one! Every cosmetic procedure imaginable in one easy step. Well, assuming you considered having your brain—whatever it was they did to my brain—having your brain somehow extracted and inserted into a whole new body "easy."

That was before the Rising. Our modern zombie-phobic society would never embrace something that brought people back from the dead, even if they came back without all those antisocial cannibalistic urges. When I got out of here—if I got out of here—I was going to have a lot of extremely fast explaining to do, unless I wanted to find myself getting shot dead for the second time in my life.

There was something wrong with that phrase. I reached the wall, turned, and continued pacing.

Shaun was alive, Shaun was causing trouble, and they weren't willing to risk getting caught in a lie if they told me he was dead. That might mean they were planning to use me against him somehow, convince me to spill private information about where we hid our network keys and offsite backup drives. That idea felt thin, like there was something I was missing, but it was a start. Every article begins with a line that can be twisted, somehow, into a hook.

Fine: The CDC brought me back so they could use me as a weapon against the only person in the world I loved more than I loved the truth. How they were planning to do that, I had no idea. Shaun knew I was dead. If anyone in the world knew, without question, that I was dead, it was Shaun; he's the one who pulled the trigger. Seeing a woman who looked like me might make him pause for a second, but it wouldn't be enough to bring him running.

Would it?

The door opened abruptly, sending light flooding into my

absolute darkness. I recoiled, more from the expectation of pain than anything else, stumbling to a stop and catching myself against the wall.

The light didn't hurt my eyes the way it would have before my resurrection, but it still made them sting, blinding me for a few disorienting seconds. I raised a hand to shield them, squinting through the brightness at the man standing in the doorway. He wasn't moving, and hadn't moved, as far as I could tell, since he opened the door.

I dropped my hand. "Hello?" I hated the uncertainty in my voice. I was still unsteady, and the CDC was controlling too damn much of my environment. I hate being controlled.

Having two things to hate actually helped. I stood up straighter, frowning at the man silhouetted in the doorway. Being in pajamas should probably have made me feel vulnerable. Instead, it just made me angrier, like it was one element of control too many. Let them take away my connection to the outside world, my autonomy, and hell, even my body, but they weren't allowed to *dress* me.

"I said hello," I said, more sharply. I took a step forward. "Who are you? What are you doing in here?" Belatedly, it occurred to me that maybe walking toward a man I couldn't really see was a bad idea. Human cloning was illegal, after all, and it was entirely possible that there might be people at the CDC who didn't want me up and walking around.

"I saw you on the monitors," said the man. He had a low, pleasant voice, with just a hint of a Midwestern accent. He stepped out of the doorway, moving back into the hall, and giving me my first real look at his face. His skin was a medium brown with reddish undertones, a few shades lighter than Mahir, a few shades darker than Alaric, with a bone structure I thought might be Native American. He had straight, dark hair, worn loose and almost as long as mine. It grazed his shoulders, tucked behind his ears to keep it from getting in his face. I'd have to remember that trick, at least until I could get my hands on a pair of scissors. He was smiling cautiously in my direction, like a man facing a snake that could decide to bite at any second.

I'd never seen him before in my life. But he was wearing hospital scrubs, with a CDC nametag pinned to his chest. That made him, if not an ally, at least a vaguely known quantity.

"Who are you?" I asked, taking another step forward. "Did Dr. Thomas send you to check up on me?"

"No," he said, with careful patience. "Like I said before, I saw you on the monitors. You looked unsettled. I thought I'd come down and see if you needed anything. A glass of water, another blanket . . ."

"What if I wanted to go to the bathroom?"

He didn't miss a beat. "I'd call for guards to escort us there, so I didn't get fired. But I'd be happy to get you some water and an extra blanket first." He took the clipboard from under his arm, flipping back the top sheet. "Are you having trouble sleeping? This says you had some caffeine earlier. I know that when I have too much coffee, I can't sleep for love or money."

"I was sleeping just fine," I said. "Then I woke up. My internal clock is all messed up. It might help if I knew what time zone we were in."

"Yeah, it probably would," he agreed. "I'm Gregory, by the way, Miss Mason. It's a pleasure to see you up and about." He turned his clipboard as he spoke, holding it against his chest with the paper facing me. "You had everyone concerned for a while there."

I've had a lifetime of experience in the fine art of not reacting to things. Still, I froze as my eyes found the block letters on the top sheet of Gregory's clipboard, clearly intended for me to see.

YOU ARE NOT SAFE HERE.

Gregory's expression begged me not to react, like he knew he was taking a risk, but had gauged it a worthwhile one. I managed to school my face into something close to neutrality, tilting my chin slightly upward to hide the unavoidable wideness of my eyes. I would have killed for my sunglasses in that moment, if someone had offered me the opportunity.

"I'm not sure you can blame me for that. I was technically dead at the time."

Relief flooded Gregory's expression. He nodded, turning his clipboard around like he was reading from it, and said, "That's true. You weren't legally alive until you started breathing independently."

"That's interesting. Who got to make that fun call?"

"It's part of the international agreement concerning the use of human cloning technology for medical research," Gregory said, flipping over another page. "As long as the clone never breathes independently of the life-support machines, it's not a living entity. It's just meat."

"So you're allowed to call me a clone?"

"Dr. Thomas said you'd reached that conclusion on your own, and that we were allowed to reinforce it, if it came up. Said it would make you more confident in your own identity." Gregory glanced up from his clipboard and smiled. "I don't think anyone expected you to figure it out so soon."

"That's me, refusing to meet expectations," I said, struggling to keep my tone neutral. This man said I wasn't safe. Did I trust him? *Could* I trust him?

Did I have a choice?

"All we expect from you now is that you keep getting better," said Gregory, with the sort of firm, bland sternness I'd been getting from medical authority figures since I was seven years old. He turned his clipboard around again, showing me the second sheet of paper.

I AM WITH THE EIS. WE ARE GOING TO GET YOU OUT OF HERE. GO ALONG WITH EVERYTHING THEY ASK YOU TO DO. DO NOT ATTRACT ATTENTION.

I nodded. "I'll do my best," I said, replying to both what he'd said aloud, and to what he'd written down for me to see. "Thanks for stopping by."

"Well, you'll be seeing a lot of me. I'm one of your night attendants. Now, are you sure I can't get you anything?"

"Not just yet," I said, and paused, suddenly alarmed by the idea of being left alone, again, in the dark. "Actually . . . I don't know if this is something you can do, but can you turn the lights back on? Please? It's so dark in here with the door shut that I'm not sure I'll be able to get back to sleep."

"I can turn the lights back on," Gregory assured me. "I can even turn them up halfway, if you'd like, so that you're not trying to sleep with things lit too bright."

"That would be great," I said. Tomorrow, I'd have to start trying to talk Dr. Thomas into giving me a lamp.

"I'll do it as soon as I get back to the monitoring station," said Gregory, putting a subtle stress on the word "soon." "If you decide you need anything else, all you need to do is say the word. The monitors will alert me immediately."

"Got it," I said, suddenly glad I didn't talk in my sleep. "It was nice meeting you."

"Likewise, Miss Mason," said Gregory. He turned his clipboard around one final time, hiding the message written there, and took another step back. The door slid shut almost instantly—too fast for me to have rushed out of the room after him, even if I'd been inclined to try—and I was plunged back into darkness.

I stayed where I was, counting silently. The lights came on as I reached a hundred and forty-five. The monitoring station, wherever it was, was approximately two and a half minutes away for a man walking at normal speed. That was good to know. That meant it would take at least thirty seconds for someone to run from there to here. There's a lot you can do in thirty seconds, if you're really committed.

I walked back over to the bed and climbed under the covers, stretching out with my hands tucked under my head as I stared up at the ceiling. So the EIS was getting involved . . . and they weren't on the side of the CDC. That was interesting. Interesting, and potentially bad.

The EIS—the Epidemic Intelligence Service—was founded in 1951 to answer concerns about biological warfare in the wake of World War II. EIS agents were responsible for a lot of the earliest efforts against infectious pandemics. Without them, smallpox, wild polio, and malaria would never have been eliminated . . . and if they'd been aware of the Marburg Amberlee and Kellis flu trials, the accidents that led to the creation of Kellis-Amberlee might never have occurred. They've always had a reputation for ruthlessness, focus, and getting the job done. It's too bad the Rising put an end to most of what they did. In a world where there's only one disease making headlines, what are a bunch of disease detectives good for?

But the branch held on. No matter how much the CDC restructured, no matter how the funding shifted, the EIS endured. Every time there was a whisper of corruption from inside the CDC, the EIS was there, dispelling the rumors, cleaning up the mess. Most people wrote them off as a bunch of spooks who refused to admit they weren't necessary anymore. I'd always been one of those people.

Maybe it was time for me to reevaluate my position.

Gregory came from the EIS; the EIS was part of the CDC; the CDC brought me back to life. Gregory said I wasn't safe here; Gregory spoke to me on his own, without barriers or guards. Dr. Thomas wouldn't come near me without an armed guard. Dr. Thomas was willing to let me believe Shaun was dead. I probably couldn't actually afford to trust either one of them. But given a choice between the two . . .

If the EIS was willing to get me out of here, I was willing to bank on my ability to escape from the EIS. I let my eyes drift closed, rolling onto my side. It was time to start playing along and find out what was going on, because when Gregory and his friends broke me out I was going to break the whole thing open.

I didn't dream of funerals this time. Instead, I dreamed of me and Shaun, walking hand in hand through the empty hall where the Republican National Convention was held, and nothing was trying to kill us. Nothing was trying to kill us at all.

The difficulty with knowing what something is and how it operates is that you're likely to be wrong, and just as likely to be incapable of admitting it. We form preconceptions about the world, and we cling to them, unwilling to be challenged, unwilling to change. That's why so many pre-Rising structures remain standing. Our generation may be willing to identify them as useless, archaic, and potentially deadly. The generations that came before us regard them as normal parts of life rendered temporarily unavailable, like toys put on a high shelf. They think someday we'll have those things again. I think they know they're wrong. They just can't admit it, and so they wait to die and leave the world to us, the ones who will tear all those death traps down.

Sometimes the hardest thing about the truth is putting down the misassumptions, falsehoods, and half-truths that stand between it and you. Sometimes that's the last thing that anybody wants to do. And sometimes, it's the only thing we *can* do.

—From *Postcards from the Wall*, the unpublished files of Georgia Mason, originally posted on July 16, 2041.

I keep writing letters to my parents. Letters that explain what happened, where I went, why I ran. Letters that tell them how much I love them, and how sorry I am that I may never see them again. Letters about how much I miss my house, and my dogs, and my bad-movie parties, and my freedom. I sometimes think this must be what it was like for everyone in the months right after the Rising, only the threat of the infected was never personal. They didn't kill all those people because they wanted to, or because their victims knew some inconvenient truth. They did it because they were hungry and because the people were there. So maybe this isn't like the Rising at all. With us, it's personal. We asked the wrong questions, opened the wrong doors, and Alaric will try to say that it was never *my* fault, it was never *my* idea, but he's wrong.

I always knew there was an element of danger in what we did, and I went along with it willingly because these people are my heart's family, and this is what I wanted. So I keep writing letters to my parents, saying I'm sorry, and I miss them, and I may not make it home.

So far, I haven't sent any of my letters. I don't know if I ever will.

—From *Dandelion Mine*, the blog of Magdalene Grace Garcia, July 16, 2041. Unpublished.

Four

Dr. Abbey's screening room was originally the Shady Cove Forestry Center's private movie theater, intended for teaching bored tourists and wide-eyed school groups about safely interacting with the woods. I've watched a few old DVDs that Alaric dug out of the room's back closet. Most of them said "safely interacting with the woods" meant being respectful of the wildlife, and backing away slowly if you saw a bear. Personally, I think "safely interacting with the woods" means carrying a crossbow and a sniper rifle whenever you have to go out alone. I'll never understand the pre-Rising generation . . . but sometimes I wish I could. It must have been nice to live in a world that didn't constantly try to kill you.

The screening room was in disarray when we started crashing with Dr. Abbey. Now, barely a month later, it was as close to state-of-the-art as could be achieved with secondhand parts and cobbled-together wiring. That was Alaric's doing. I'm sure Dr. Abbey's people could have handled everything eventually—this wasn't the first time she'd uprooted her entire lab with little warning—but Maggie got uncomfortable when she didn't have access to a big-ass screen. So she batted her eyes at our last surviving tech genius, and Alaric, who was probably glad to have something to distract him from his sister's situation, started flipping switches. The result was something even Buffy might have been proud of, if she hadn't been, you know, dead.

The room was set up theater style, with gently curved rows of chairs descending toward the hardwood floor. Dr. Abbey was standing in front of the screen with her arms crossed, leaning against the built-in podium.

"Sorry we took so long." I held up my bowl of popcorn as I descended the steps, shaking it so she could hear the kernels rattle. "You said we could stop for snacks."

"That's true; I did. One day you'll figure out how to tell when I'm serious." There was no actual rancor in Dr. Abbey's tone. I stopped being able to really piss her off the day she learned that I couldn't amplify. I guess there are some advantages to being a human pincushion.

"Did you bring me any?" Maggie was sitting in the middle of the front row. She turned to look over the back of her seat. Her curly brown-and-blonde hair—brown from nature, blonde from decontamination and bleaching—half hid her face. She was one of the only women I knew who managed to make that combination look natural, largely on account of having a Hispanic father, a Caucasian mother, and really good skin.

"Sure." I started down the steps. Becks and Alaric followed me.

"Hey, Dr. Abbey," said Becks.

"Hello, Rebecca," said Dr. Abbey.

"Gimme popcorn," said Maggie. I leaned over to hand her the bowl. She beamed, blew me a kiss, and started munching.

Out of all of us, Maggie was the one who didn't have to be here. Alaric, Becks, and I were the ones who broke into the CDC facility in Memphis. While we were there, a man we thought was our ally showed his true colors, and the newest member of our team was killed. Her name was Kelly Connolly. She worked for the CDC, and she wanted to do the right thing more than almost anyone else I knew. The fact that her name will never go up on The Wall is a crime and a sin, and there's nothing I can do about it. There's nothing anyone can do about it.

Maggie wasn't there for any of that. Maggie could have said, "It's been fun; see you later," and left the rest of us to carry on without her. I wouldn't have blamed her. She had a life, one that didn't involve becoming a fugitive, or sleeping on an army cot in an abandoned park building. When her house was rendered unsafe, she could have just asked her parents to buy her a new one. She was the heir to the Garcia family fortune, possibly the richest blogger in the world, and she had absolutely no reason to be standing by us. But she *was* standing by us, and that meant she could have all the popcorn she wanted.

Dr. Abbey straightened, taking the remote control from the podium. "If you're all settled, I've got a few things to show you."

"We're good," I said, dropping into a seat.

Behave, said George. *You could learn something.*

"You mean *you* could learn something, and explain it to me later," I said, making only a cursory effort to keep my voice down. The others ignored me. After everything we've had to deal with, I guess knowing the boss is crazy isn't such a big deal anymore. That's fine by me. I have no particular interest in ever being sane again.

Becks and Alaric took the seats to either side of me. Maggie got up and moved to sit next to Alaric, bringing the popcorn with her. Becks smiled at them a little wistfully. I tried not to let my discomfort show. Becks and I slept together once—just once—before she realized exactly how crazy I really was. I hurt her pretty badly over that. I didn't mean to, but that doesn't excuse it, as both she and George were happy to point out. Sometimes I regret the fact that I'm probably never going to have a normal adult relationship with a woman who has a pulse of her own. And then I remember how deep the shit we're in already is, and I'm just glad I don't have anyone left for them to take away from me.

"Finally," said Dr. Abbey, and pointed her remote at the back of the room. The projector came on, filling the screen with an outline of the Florida coast. "Florida," said Dr. Abbey needlessly. She pressed a button. The image pulled back to show the entire Gulf Coast. A red splash was overlaid across the characteristic shape of Florida itself, covering almost two-thirds of the landmass.

Alaric winced, fingers tightening around a handful of popcorn with an audible crunch. That was the only sound in the screening room. That, and the sound of George swearing in the back of my head, inaudible to anyone but me.

Dr. Abbey gave us a moment to study the image before she said, "This is the most recent map showing the airborne infection following Tropical Storm Fiona. I know of six labs that are currently trying to sequence the genetic structure of the mosquitoes involved."

"Why?" asked Becks. "What does that matter?"

"This isn't a new strain of virus, which means it has to be a new strain of mosquito. If we know what species they were derived from, we'll know what temperature range they can tolerate."

A voice spoke from the back of the theater: "Derived from?"

"Mr. Gowda. Glad you could join us. And yes, derived from. Surely you don't think this happened naturally?" Dr. Abbey shook her head. "Mosquitoes can't spread Kellis-Amberlee because the virus is too large. You can't make it smaller; it would become unstable. That means you need a larger mosquito if you want an insect vector."

"Yeah, because who wouldn't want *that*," muttered Becks.

"Who made it?" asked Mahir. I turned in my seat to see him descending the stairs. He was frowning deeply. That was nothing new. I honestly couldn't remember the last time I'd seen him smile.

"Good question," said Dr. Abbey. "Now, as I was saying, if we know what species the mosquitoes are derived from, we'll know what temperature range they can tolerate. If we're looking at *Aedes aegypti*—the mosquito responsible for the American yellow fever outbreaks—then we're dealing with a mosquito confined to warm climates. Like so." She pressed another button. The image progressed, printing an orange zone on top of the red. "That's the maximum projected range for *Aedes aegypti*. They won't be able to get a foothold on the colder parts of the country, although it's doubtful we'll be cleaning them out of the Gulf Coast anytime soon."

"What are our other options?" asked Mahir.

"We have about a dozen possible candidates, although some are more likely than others. If you want to see the doomsday option, look no farther than *Aedes albopictus*, the Asian tiger mosquito. It's been nominated for the title of 'most invasive species in the world,' in part because the damn thing can survive anywhere. It sets up housekeeping, and that's the end of that. Reach for your bug spray and kiss your ass good-bye." Dr. Abbey clicked her remote again. The image pulled back, showing the entire continental United States. A third band of color appeared around the first two. This one was yellow, and extended almost all the way to the Canadian border. "Good night, North America. Thank you for playing."

"Isn't there anything we can do?" asked Maggie.

Becks leaned forward in her seat. "I have a better question. Why are you telling us this? We already knew things were bad. You could have just given us a written report."

"Because I wanted you to understand exactly *how* bad things are out there." Dr. Abbey pressed a different button. The map was replaced by a slideshow of pictures out of the flooded streets of Florida—still flooded, for the most part, even this long after the storm, because no one had been able to get past the ranks of the infected long enough to clear out the drains.

Mobs of blank-eyed, bloody-lipped zombies waded through the dirty water, their arms raised in instinctive fury as they closed ranks on the rare remaining uninfected humans. Their numbers were great enough that they clearly weren't trying to infect anymore; they had the critical mass the virus always seemed to be striving for. There was nothing left of the people they'd been before the storm touched down. All that remained was a single, undeniable command: feed.

Maggie gasped as a still picture of a young boy with his abdomen ripped completely open flashed across the screen. She twisted and buried her face against Alaric's shoulder. He raised one hand to stroke her hair, his own eyes never leaving the screen.

This is horrific, said George.

"Yeah," I whispered. "It is."

We knew how bad things were—there was no way we could avoid knowing—but the government had been doing a surprisingly good job of suppressing images from the infection zones. Something about the way journalists who tried to sneak into the cordoned areas kept winding up infected, shot, or both was doing a lot to discourage the curious. Most of the pictures that made it out were fuzzy things, shot from a distance or using cameras attached to remote-controlled drones. These pictures weren't fuzzy. These pictures were crystal clear, and the story they told was brutal.

"Where did you get these?" asked Mahir. He seemed to remember that he should be descending the stairs. He trotted quickly down the last few tiers, settling at the end of our row.

"I have my sources," said Dr. Abbey. "Most of these were taken in the last week. Since then, the body count has continued rising. We're looking at a death toll in the millions."

"I heard a rumor that the government is going to declare Florida officially lost," said Becks.

"It's not a rumor. They're making the announcement next week." Dr. Abbey pressed another button. The still pictures were replaced with a video, clearly shot by someone with a back-mounted camera as they were running for their life. A mob of infected pursued the unseen filmmaker down the flooded, debris-choked street, and they were gaining. Maggie glanced up, hearing the change in the room. As soon as she saw the screen, she moaned again, and pressed her face back into Alaric's shoulder.

"They can't do that," said Becks.

Yes, they can, said George.

"Yes, they can," I said. The others looked at me, even Maggie, who raised her head and stared at me with wounded, shell-shocked eyes. "Alaska. Remember? As long as they can prove they've made every effort to preserve the greater civilian population, the government is not only allowed to lock down a hazard zone, they're *required*." Shutting down a state would mean proving they'd done it to save the nation. Somehow, I didn't think that would be all that hard of a sell. Things were too bad, and people were too frightened.

"We have to go to Florida," said Alaric abruptly. "We need to get Alisa." He sat up in his seat, almost dislodging Maggie. "The refugee camp is inside the state borders. When they closed Alaska, they didn't evacuate all the camps."

Becks, Maggie, and Alaric started talking at once, all of them raising their voices to be heard. Even George got in on the action, although I wasn't relaying her comments to the others—yet. If they didn't settle down quickly, I'd probably start.

Mahir beat me to it. "*Quiet*!" he roared, standing. He walked over to the rest of us, focusing his attention on Alaric. "I'm sorry, Alaric, but there's no way. Going into Florida would be suicide."

"I don't care." Alaric stood, stepping forward so that he and Mahir were almost nose to nose. Mahir was easily four inches taller. At the moment, that didn't seem to matter. "Alisa is the last family I have left. I'm not letting them abandon her in a hazard zone."

"And as your immediate superior, I'm not letting you throw your life away running *into* a hazard zone."

"Does he really think that's going to work?" asked Becks.

"Would you have done it for *his* sister?" Alaric thrust out his arm, pointing at me. "If it were George in that hazard zone, would you have stopped *him*? Or would you have been putting on your protective gear and saying it was an honor to die trying to save her?"

"Hey, guys, let's settle down, okay?" Maggie cast a nervous look in my direction as she stood and tried to push her way between them. "Inciting Shaun to kill us all isn't anybody's idea of a good time."

"I don't know," said Dr. Abbey. "It might take care of a few problems. It would definitely cut down on the grocery bills."

She's really not fond of helping, is she? asked George.

"No, she's not," I replied, and stood. Becks, who was now the only one still sitting, gave me a worried look, like she wasn't sure whether I was about to try defusing the situation or start punching people. I couldn't blame her. Before Memphis, I wouldn't have been sure either, and it wasn't like I'd been exactly stable since then.

But the one thing I learned in Memphis—the one thing I was sure of now, even if I hadn't been sure of it before—was that my team was the only thing I had, and if I didn't want to lose them, I needed to take care of them. Somehow.

"Okay, everybody," I said. "Settle down."

"Shaun—" Alaric began.

"You're part of everybody. So shut up. Mahir? We're not abandoning Alaric's sister. We wouldn't abandon yours, we're not abandoning his."

"I don't have a sister," said Mahir.

"Yeah, well, join the club. Alaric?" I took a step toward him, letting my anger show in my eyes for a fraction of a second. Alaric paled. I might not be willing to lose my team, but that didn't mean I was willing to let certain things go. "Calm down. We'll figure this out. And don't you ever, *ever* use George against any of us, ever again. Do I make myself clear?"

Alaric nodded, pushing his glasses back up the bridge of his nose. "Extremely."

"Good. Thanks for trying to calm things down, Maggie."

She didn't say anything. But she smiled wanly, and I knew the comment was appreciated.

Good job, said George.

"Thanks," I replied. I looked to Dr. Abbey and asked, "Why are you telling us this? It's like Becks said—you would have just left a note on the refrigerator, if all you wanted to do was make us aware that things are shitty. Everyone knows things are shitty. This isn't news."

"Not that it's stopping 'everything in Florida is shitty' from dominating the news cycles right now," said Becks. "What impresses me is the way it's dominating them without most people actually knowing anything."

"Welcome to the modern media world," said Alaric.

Dr. Abbey had been waiting while we got the last of the nervous chatter out of the way. Not saying a word—not yet—she pressed a button on her remote. The video froze and vanished, replaced by an atlas-style road map. It could have been anywhere in the world, if not for the label identifying the thickest line as the border between Florida and Alabama. A small red star popped up on the Florida side of the line.

"The Ferry Pass Refugee Center," said Dr. Abbey serenely. She'd been setting us up for this moment. I would have been impressed, if I hadn't wanted to punch her. "The middle school has been turned into a holding area for people who were evacuated from the primary outbreak zones before evacuations ceased."

"You know where Alisa is?" Alaric's voice was suddenly small. We'd been getting updates from his sister since she was transferred to the camp, but she'd never been able to tell us where that camp was located. Alaric thought it was because things were too hectic, and the rest of us were willing to let him keep thinking that until we had something better to tell him. Because in my experience, when people are kept isolated "for their own safety" and not told where they are, those people are probably never going to be seen or heard from again.

"Camps were established in Florida, Georgia, and Alabama after Tropical Storm Fiona hit. People were assigned to them supposedly at random, although the Florida camps received a higher than average percentage of the poor, children without surviving parents, and journalists who'd been arrested inside the quarantine zone. The

Georgia camps were evacuated last week. They're evacuating the Alabama camps tomorrow."

"And the Florida camps?" asked Mahir.

"Are considered a lower priority, due to the chance that they've already been contaminated. Luck of the draw, I suppose." Her tone was blackly amused, like it was that or start breaking things. "One more tragedy for a summer already packed chock-full of tragedies."

"They can't do this," said Becks.

"It's already done. The only question is whether they're going to get caught, and so far, the answer's been 'no.' Things are chaotic. No one knows exactly what's going on, and the people carrying out the orders aren't the ones giving them. As long as no one ever gives the order that says 'let those people die, they don't matter,' nothing illegal is being done." A small, bitter smile twisted the edges of Dr. Abbey's lips. "Trust me. I'm a scientist. We know all about the art of skirting ethics."

"We have to go to Florida," said Alaric. He grabbed my sleeve, eyes wild. "We have to! They're going to let her die! Shaun, you have to help me; you can't let my sister die!"

He's right; you can't, said George. *You can't go to Florida, either. So what are you going to do?*

The answer was obvious, at least to me. I gave Alaric's hand a reassuring pat before removing it from my sleeve, folding my arms, and focusing on Dr. Abbey. "What do you want us to do?"

She lifted her eyebrows. "What do you mean?"

"You made a big production out of telling us things suck in Florida. We knew things sucked. You just wanted us to really *believe* it. So you've got us. We believe." I let my smile mirror hers. "It's classic media manipulation. Present the facts in the scariest way possible, and wait for your audience to sell their souls for whatever you think they need."

"And what could I possibly have that you would need?"

"Beyond the whole 'shelter and hiding us' thing, which we already have, you know where Alaric's sister is. That means you know someone who's involved with the camps in Florida. Can you get her out?"

Alaric's eyes widened, and he focused on Dr. Abbey with new hope. "Is that why you told us all this? Can you get Alisa out of Florida?"

"It's possible," said Dr. Abbey, putting her remote back on the podium. "I could pull a few strings."

"Thought so." I looked at her appraisingly. "Now I know you don't want to cut me open, because I'm a better test subject alive than I'd be dead. And I know you don't want to kick us out for basically the same reason. So what do you want?"

"I do want you to leave, actually. I just don't want you to stay gone." Dr. Abbey shook her head. "Remember what I said about the mosquitoes?"

"Which part?" asked Maggie. "The scary part, the really scary part, the legitimately terrifying part, or the part that makes suicide sound like an awesome way to spend an evening?"

"That last one, probably. As I said before, there *are* labs working to sequence the genetic code of the mosquitoes. But they're working with inherently damaged data, because they're working with dead specimens."

Becks stared at her. "You want us to go out and catch mosquitoes for you?"

"Not all of you. Just him." Dr. Abbey pointed at me. "If you can get into one of the infection zones and catch some live specimens, we may be able to determine their base species—or at least make a better, more educated guess—without needing to wait for the gene sequencers to finish running. Plus, we can study their behavioral patterns, maybe come up with ways to avoid being bitten."

"This is all assuming I survive the bug hunt," I said dryly.

"You've survived everything else you've run up against, even when there's no way you should have. I'm willing to take the chance." Dr. Abbey sighed, raking her brown and bleach-yellow curls back with one hand. "Look. I realize this isn't exactly the nicest thing I've ever done to you people."

"You're a mad scientist," said Maggie, in what may well have been intended as a reassuring tone. "We don't expect you to be nice. We just go to bed every night hoping you won't mutate us before we wake up."

Dr. Abbey blinked at her. "That's . . . almost sweet. In a disturbing sort of a way."

"Maggie's good at sweet-but-disturbing," said Mahir. "Are you genuinely telling us you have the capacity to extract Alaric's sister from danger, and will not do so unless we agree to your request?"

"I'm telling you I have the capacity to *try*." Dr. Abbey shook her head. "Please don't misunderstand what I'm offering here. I can't guarantee anything. The mosquitoes haven't reached Ferry Pass, but that doesn't mean they won't. It also doesn't mean there won't be another form of outbreak before we can get there. All I'm offering is a chance, and yes, sometimes, chances have to be paid for."

Alaric gave me a pleading look. The others followed suit, even Dr. Abbey, all looking at me with varying degrees of hope, or reluctance, or resignation. In that instant, I knew that what came next was entirely my decision. Maybe I was the crazy one, maybe I was the one who felt like he had nothing left to lose, but I was also their leader, and the only one my team had left. They needed someone to tell them what to do. Even Mahir, for all that half the time it seemed like *he* was the one who was actually in charge, needed me to be the one to pull the trigger.

"I didn't sign up for this shit," I muttered, as quietly as I could.

Good thing you're such a natural, then, isn't it?

I managed to bite back my laughter before it could escape. The team might be used to me talking to myself, but that didn't mean they'd forgive me for laughing at a time like this. I turned my laugh into a smile, calling up all the old tricks I'd been forced to learn back when I was a working Irwin and needed to smile despite pain, or terror, or just plain not wanting to be the dancing monkey for a little while.

"You know we can't all go, right, Doc?" I asked.

Dr. Abbey nodded. "I know."

"Alisa's going to need ID, papers, everything. There's no way she can use her real name. It wouldn't hurt for the rest of us to have a fall-back plan, either. I want to send Mahir and Maggie up the coast. There's an ID fixer there who comes pretty highly recommended."

"The Monkey," said Alaric.

"I've heard of him. He's supposedly the best, and things *are* going to get worse before they get better," said Dr. Abbey, apparently unperturbed by my desire to split the team. "I'm even willing to supply an unmarked car, to help them get there."

"And someone's staying with you, to coordinate."

"I wouldn't have it any other way."

"I'm going with you," Becks said, stepping up next to me before Alaric could speak. She raised a warning finger in his direction. "*Don't* argue. You aren't good at fieldwork, you don't like being away from your computer, and if Dr. Abbey can get Alisa out of Florida, your sister will want to know that you're safe. We won't be."

Alaric deflated slightly, looking ashamed. I couldn't blame him. He was clearly relieved not to be the one going, and just as clearly felt like he should have insisted on it.

"Hey," I said. He didn't look at me. "*Hey*."

This time Alaric's attention swung my way. "What?"

"Becks is right. Alisa needs you more than we do. Stay with Dr. Abbey. Keep the crazy science lady happy, or at least non-homicidal. We'll be back as soon as we can. Okay?"

For a moment, I didn't think Alaric was going to give in. Finally, he nodded. "Okay," he said. "If that's the best way."

"It is." I looked to Dr. Abbey. "Well? What are we waiting for? Let's get this show on the road."

She smiled. "I thought you'd never ask."

But I'm scared a lot, too. There are ten girls sleeping in the classroom with me, and also our chaperone, Ms. Hyland. I don't think anyone here realizes my e-diary can also transmit. They're not supposed to be able to do that. That's why the people let me keep it. I don't know what I'd do if they took it away from me. Thank you, thank you, thank you for giving me this for last Christmas. I think it's saving my life.

They're starting to say scary things when they think none of us are listening—or maybe they don't care anymore whether we're listening or not, and that's scary, too. Please come get me. Please find a way to come and get me. I don't know what's going to happen next, but I'm really scared, and I need my brother.

Please come.

—Taken from an e-mail sent by Alisa Kwong to Alaric Kwong, July 19, 2041.

This morning I woke up, and for almost ten minutes, I forgot that George was dead. I could hear her in the bathroom, getting her clothes on and waiting for her painkillers to kick in. I could even see the indent her head left in the pillow. And then I turned to get something from my bag, and when I looked back, the indent was gone. No one was in the bathroom. I was alone, and George was dead again.

It's been happening more and more often. Just those little moments where something slips, and it becomes possible, for one beautiful, horrible moment, to lie to myself about the world. I won't pretend that I mind them, or that I'm not sorry when they end. I also won't pretend that I'm not afraid.

The last big break with reality is coming. I can practically hear it knocking at the door. And I'm terrified I won't have time to finish everything I need to do before it gets here.

I'm sorry, George. But I'm afraid I might want you back so much that I'm willing to let myself let you down.

—From *Adaptive Immunities*, the blog of Shaun Mason, July 17, 2041. Unpublished.

Five

I barely glanced up from my book when the door slid open. It was an outdated sociology text written when people still lived in the middle of Canada, but it was a *book*, and in the absence of access to the Internet, I was so starved for data that I'd take what I could get. They still wouldn't let me have anything but hard copy, for fear that I'd somehow figure out a way to hopscotch off the local wireless network. As if. Techie tricks were Buffy's forte, and Buffy had left the building.

The door slid closed. I kept reading. Dr. Thomas cleared his throat. The sound was a dead giveaway. After a week with nothing to distract me, I'd learned to recognize my regular visitors by the things they couldn't help, like the way they breathed—or, in Dr. Thomas's case, the annoying way he cleared his throat. I turned a page. Dr. Thomas cleared his throat again.

"I can keep this up all day," I said pleasantly, even though the fact that I was the first one to speak proved I couldn't actually stand spending any more time sitting silently and pretending I wasn't bothered by Dr. Thomas standing there, watching me. "You know what you need to do."

"I think you're being unreasonable."

"I think that I legally became a human being as soon as you

detached me from your crazy mad science clone incubator, which means I'm entitled to basic human courtesy." I turned another page. "It's up to you." Gregory wanted me to play along. Well, I was playing, but that also included a certain amount of understandable resistance. A totally complacent Georgia Mason would never have been believable, to anyone.

Dr. Thomas sighed. Finally, he said, "Hello, Georgia. May I come in?"

"Why, hello, Dr. Thomas." I looked up, dog-earing the top of the page to keep my place. "Would it make any difference if I said you couldn't?"

"No," he said curtly. I was starting to learn the limits of his patience. It was difficult, more so than learning to tell his footsteps from the footsteps of the guards who usually accompanied him. If I pushed him too far, they'd gas the room, and I'd wake up to find that whatever tests I'd been balking at had been run while I was unconscious.

When I finished with my exposé of this place, the CDC was going to wish they'd been willing to leave me dead. I kept that thought firmly in mind as I plastered a smile across my face and said, "Well, then, come on in. What can I do for you?" I paused, something else about the situation registering. I'd only heard one set of footsteps. "Where are your guards?"

"That's part of why I'm visiting. We've been reviewing your test results, and we've decided I don't need them in your quarters." Dr. Thomas's smile looked as real as mine. Whoever made the decision to send him into my room without protection had done it without asking how he felt about it. And clearly, how he felt wasn't good.

"Does that mean they've also decided I'm not a danger to society?"

"Don't be too hasty, Georgia. It simply means they've decided that spontaneous amplification is not an immediate danger. We still have a lot to do before we can be confident your body is prepared to function outside a laboratory setting." Dr. Thomas adjusted his glasses with one hand, something I'd learned to read as a nervous tic. "You may not feel particularly protected, but I assure you, this is the cleanest, most secure environment you have ever been in."

"It's definitely the most boring," I agreed, twisting around to face him. I'd been sitting cross-legged on my bed for long enough that my thighs ached when I moved. That was good. It looked like I wasn't doing anything. I was actually tensing and relaxing the muscles of my core, strengthening them as best I could without a better means of using them. I'd asked a few times about getting access to an exercise room, or at least a treadmill. So far, I'd had no luck. That meant I was getting my exercise where I could, and through whatever means available.

I never thought I'd be so grateful to Buffy for making me and Shaun sign up for that stupid virtual Pilates class.

The thought of Shaun, even that briefly, was painful. I pushed it away. I was still holding tightly to the belief that he was alive, but it was hard, and getting harder as Dr. Thomas continued not giving me anything to work with. I had to believe Shaun was alive. If I didn't, I was going to go insane.

Assuming the CDC didn't drive me crazy first.

"I thought you'd been provided with reading material?" Dr. Thomas gave my book a meaningful look. "That was what you requested, wasn't it?"

"'Something to read' was on the list, yes, but I provided authors and titles, and nothing I've been given has been remotely like the things I asked for." I blew a wayward strand of hair out of my face. "I've been asking for a haircut, too. Any idea when I might be able to get one? If it's too hard to find someone on your staff who's cut hair before, you can give me a pair of scissors and I can do it myself."

"No, I'm afraid I *can't* give you a pair of scissors, Georgia, and I'll thank you not to make a suggestion like that again, unless you'd like to have your silverware privileges revoked." Dr. Thomas frowned in what I'm sure was intended to be a paternal manner. He'd been trying that a lot recently, acting like he had a fatherly interest in my welfare. Maybe if my own father had ever shown that sort of interest, I would have believed it. As it was, all he'd managed to do was get on my nerves. "Asking for potential weapons is not a sign of mental stability."

"Pardon me for arguing, Dr. Thomas, but I'm a clone living in a post-zombie America. I'm pretty sure *not* asking for potential weapons would be a much worse sign. Besides, I'm not asking for weapons, I'm asking for a haircut, and giving options if there's no way to get me someone willing to do it." I kept smiling. It was better than screaming.

Dr. Thomas sighed. "I'll see what I can do. In the meanwhile, you're going to need to do something for me."

I stiffened. "What kind of something?" I asked carefully.

"We need to run some special tests tomorrow, in addition to the ones on your usual schedule. There's some concern about your internal organs. These tests won't be quite the noninvasive sort that you've become accustomed to, I'm afraid. They'll be rather painful, and unfortunately, the nature of the needed data requires you to be awake during the process."

"And they're dealing with my internal organs?" I raised my eyebrows. It was a sign of how numb I was becoming to their endless tests that I couldn't even work up a mild level of concern over the idea of my kidneys shutting down. "Are my internal organs doing something they're not supposed to be doing?"

"No, no, not at all. We just want to be sure they're not going to *start* doing something they're not supposed to be doing. They're much younger than you look, after all, and there's always a chance for biological error."

"I don't really have a choice about this, do I?"

"Not really," said Dr. Thomas. "I hoped you'd be accommodating, since we're only concerned about your health."

"If I don't fight you on this, can I get some of the books from my list?"

"I'll see what I can do."

"How about that haircut?"

Dr. Thomas shook his head. "All things in good time, Georgia. For now, don't push it. I'm going to need you to go on an all-liquid diet for the next twelve hours, and then we'll be taking some fluid and tissue samples in the morning."

That was one of the first indicators I'd had of the actual time. I perked up a little. "If the tests are being run in the morning, that makes it, what, four in the afternoon? Five?"

"Don't push it," Dr. Thomas repeated, and withdrew a pair of clear plastic handcuffs from his pocket. "It's time for today's tests."

"This is really unnecessary," I said, and presented my wrists.

"Hopefully, we won't have to go through this for much longer." Dr. Thomas snapped the cuffs into place, careful not to touch my skin. He never touched me when he could help it. The few times that I'd "tripped" and touched him with my bare hands, he'd practically injured himself lunging away from me. It was a funny response, but it wasn't useful, especially not when I was trying to convince him that I was harmless.

"That would be nice," I said, and stood, pausing a moment as my rubber-soled socks found traction on the hard tile floor. I would have preferred shoes—even slippers—but the orderlies responsible for my clothing wouldn't let me have anything but socks. At least the rubber treads made it easier for me to walk with my hands restrained.

The cuffs didn't come out until the third time they took me out of my room. They'd been a constant reality since then. If I left the room to go anywhere but the bathroom, I left it in handcuffs. Presumably, whoever was actually in charge of my care—and it wasn't Dr. Thomas; if he'd been in charge of me, he would never have come near me—wanted to be sure I wasn't going to make some sort of daring escape. I was never sure whether I should be flattered by their apparent faith in my ingenuity or insulted by the fact that they thought handcuffs would stop me. That was the sort of thing I had a lot of time to think about these days. Solitary confinement punctuated only by intrusive medical testing will do that for a person.

The guards were waiting in the hallway. I recognized both. Not surprising, but reassuring in its own way. If I was starting to know the guards on sight, that meant they didn't have an infinite number of them. Eventually, they'd start thinking of me as a person, rather than as a test subject, and that would make them easier to get around when the day finally came for me to escape. Assuming I didn't spontaneously amplify or suffer acute organ failure before then. Also assuming Gregory didn't find a way to smuggle me out with the laundry, or do something else out of a bad pre-Rising heist movie.

Also, if the guards had never been repeated, I would have started to worry that they were being taken out back and shot after their shifts were finished. Call me sentimental, but I'd really rather not be the human equivalent of a death sentence.

One of the guards led us down the empty hall, while the other walked behind us. In the time since I woke up, I hadn't seen anyone aside from Dr. Thomas, Gregory, the constantly shifting crew of guards, and the lab technicians who were waiting at the end of this little journey. If there were any other patients in the building, my handlers were doing an excellent job of keeping me away from them. Whether that was for my protection or for theirs, I couldn't say.

We reached the end of the hall. The first guard pressed his hand against a blood test panel, waiting for the light over the door to go from red to green. The door opened, and the guard stepped through. Dr. Thomas repeated the process. The second guard gestured for me to do the same, not saying a word. None of the guards liked to talk to me. I'm pretty sure I made them nervous.

Dr. Thomas and the first guard were waiting on the other side. Dr.

Thomas motioned for me to start walking, not waiting for the second guard. "Come along. The faster we get this done, the faster we can get you back to your room."

"Yes, empty rooms without Internet are absolutely the sort of place I yearn to get back to." This hall was colder. I shivered. This was a negative-pressure zone, and whoever was responsible for the environmental controls kept them turned lower than was strictly necessary.

"It's for your own good," said Dr. Thomas. There was no conviction in his words. He was parroting the argument we'd been having almost constantly since we met, and somehow, the thought of having it one more time was enough to make me tired.

"Right," I said, and kept plodding steadily along.

Dr. Thomas stopped at a door that looked like every other door in the vicinity. "Here we are. I don't have to remind you again how important it is that you cooperate with the technicians, do I?"

"No, Dr. Thomas, you do not," I replied blandly. "I'm going to be a good girl today. I'd like you to make note of that in my file, since maybe it can help me get Internet privileges faster. How would that be?"

Dr. Thomas smiled, the expression not quite managing to mask the fact that he was grinding his teeth. "We'll see," he said, and opened the door.

I was becoming quite the expert in CDC labs, at least as they were configured locally; like the guards, they seemed to rotate, with every battery of tests conducted in a different place. Even when I saw the same rooms, they'd been rearranged, equipment swapped around until my head spun. I couldn't tell whether they were intentionally trying to disorient me or just doing a really good job by mistake. Either way, I'd started making note of the things they couldn't rearrange—or wouldn't, anyway, unless those things were pointed out to them. I glanced up as I entered the room, making note of the pattern of holes on the ceiling. This was the one I called lab three, then. The last time I'd been in lab three, my afternoon test array included a bone marrow sample.

"Won't this be fun," I muttered.

Lab three was about the size of every other lab I'd been in at the CDC: twice the size of my current bedroom, and roughly the size of a large living room. It just seemed small because it was so packed. My stomach sank as I realized I didn't know what half of the machines were for. Technicians in lab coats bustled around the room, making tweaks and adjusting settings.

I used to try guessing which technicians would be running my tests. That was before I realized the person in charge was never one of the people operating the machines. Operating machines was beneath anyone chosen to supervise testing on a real live clone of a dead journalist. This session was no different. As soon as the door closed behind us, another door opened on the opposite side of the lab, revealing a small office. A tall, Nordic-looking woman with ice-blonde hair scraped into a tight bun stepped out, offering a chilly smile in our direction.

She was beautiful, in a "touch me and get frostbite" sort of way. Her lab coat was the normal white, but she had accessorized it with an indecently red silk shirt the color of the lights on a testing unit. Her shoes matched her blouse. I found myself envying them, despite their three-inch heels. I hate high heels. Having actual shoes would have been enough to make up for my dislike. Besides, in a pinch, high-heeled shoes can make good improvised weapons. Sure, that gets you right back to barefoot, but at least then you're armed.

"Ah, Dr. Thomas," she said, directing her words at my escort, even as her gaze settled firmly on me. "You're just in time. Thank you for bringing the subject to see me."

"It was no trouble, really, Dr. Shaw. If there's anything I can do to assist—"

"There's nothing you can help me with," she said, still not looking in his direction. She was studying my face avidly, like she expected it to provide the answer to some question she hadn't told me anything about. "I'll have you contacted when it's time to return her to her holding cell. Thank you."

"Dr. Shaw, I'm not sure—"

Annoyance flashed across her features as she looked away from me for the first time. "I have tests to perform, Dr. Thomas, and as you have made so abundantly clear, we are on a schedule, one that required me to jump through a ludicrous number of hoops in order to get even this much access. I refuse to waste any of my allotted time in shepherding you around my equipment. You may go, and take your trained monkeys with you. I will send one of my assistants to collect you when I'm prepared to remand the subject to your care."

Dr. Thomas hesitated, looking like he was going to argue. Dr. Shaw narrowed her eyes very slightly, and took a single half step forward. The heel of her shoe hit the floor with a loud snapping sound, like a pencil being broken in half.

That seemed to decide the matter. "Georgia, Dr. Shaw is in charge until I return," he said. "Cooperate with whatever she requests." He turned and stepped quickly out of the room, gesturing for the guards to follow him. Looking uncertain about the whole situation, they did.

Dr. Shaw waited for the door to shut before returning her attention to me. Something about her expression made me want to squirm, which just annoyed me even more. I stood up a little straighter, narrowing my eyes, and met her stare for stare.

Finally, surprisingly, she laughed. "Oh, *very* good! They really did bring you back, didn't they? Or good as, one supposes. If you would be so kind as to step behind the screen there and remove your clothing, we can begin."

"Sorry. Can't." I held up my hands, showing her the cuffs. "I'm too much of a threat to run around without restraints."

"I see." Dr. Shaw reached into her pocket, producing a key. She smiled at my startled expression. "They're standard CDC issue, for control of troublesome subjects. It wouldn't do to have someone require the services of a locksmith simply because their primary physician was unavailable when their cuffs needed to be removed."

I kept still as she unlocked me, waiting until the cuffs had vanished into her pocket before I asked, "Does the CDC make a practice of handcuffing patients?"

"Only the potentially dangerous ones." Her amusement vanished as quickly as it had come. "Now please. Behind the screen, and remove your clothing. Kathleen will supply a robe once you're done."

"Why is it that you people always try to get me naked first thing? It's not like I have any weapons to hide in my pajama pants." I rubbed my wrists as I walked to the indicated screen and stepped behind it. Then I stopped, my heart jumping up into my throat as I saw what the screen had been concealing from the rest of the room.

"Go ahead, Georgia," said Dr. Shaw's voice from the main room. "We really must get started as quickly as possible."

I stepped slowly forward, barely breathing as I picked up the tiny pistol that was sitting on the stool, almost like it was waiting for me. I revised that thought to remove the "almost" as I felt the way the gun fit into my palm, vanishing behind my fingers. Firearms this small were usually mass-manufactured, but this was a custom job. There was no other way to explain the rightness of it sliding into my hand. It felt like it was made for me because it *was* made for me.

It was made of hardened ceramic and heat-resistant plastic polymer. All the metal detectors in the world wouldn't be able to catch the fact that I was carrying it, and the guards' reluctance to touch me when they didn't have to meant I was pretty much safe from a pat down. It was mine. They wouldn't take it away from me, because they wouldn't know I had it. Not until I needed them to.

The gun had been holding down a piece of folded paper. I picked it up with my free hand, unfolding it, and read.

Georgia—

This is all the protection we can give you right now. We're still working on an exit plan. Trust Dr. Shaw. She's been working with me for a long time. Keep cooperating. They can't know you're planning to escape. You have to keep trusting me.

The gun was enough to buy a *lot* of trust. I kept reading, and stopped breathing for the second time in as many minutes as I saw the second part of his message:

I have received confirmation from my West Coast contact: Shaun Phillip Mason is alive. I repeat: Shaun is alive. He's been off the grid for a little while, for reasons I hope to have the opportunity to explain soon, but he is alive, and he will be waiting when we get you out of here. Whatever they say, whatever lies they try to make you believe, believe me: Shaun is alive. All we have to do now is keep you that way long enough to get you back to him.

Yours—G.

I sank onto the stool, staring at the letter. My fingers were creasing the paper, rendering some of the words almost illegible, but that didn't matter. I knew what they said. They were burning behind my eyes, lighting up a darkness that I hadn't even realized was there.

Shaun was alive. I wasn't making educated guesses. I wasn't just telling myself something I wanted to believe: Shaun was actually and genuinely alive. That, or the CDC had planted Gregory to earn my trust . . . But the gun nixed that line of thinking. I paused, turning my attention from the paper to the pistol just long enough to eject the clip and check that it was loaded. It was. Those tiny bullets made all the difference, because no matter how hard the CDC was trying to make me believe them, they weren't going to give me a gun.

"There you are." Dr. Shaw stepped around the screen, moving with a silence that made it plain how much she'd been exaggerating the sound of her footsteps before. She plucked the paper from my hand, not seeming to mind when she ripped it in the process. "Thank you for cleaning up the lab, Georgia. I'll just go feed this through the shredder while you finish undressing. You can leave your clothing here. No one will disturb it."

My eyes widened as I glanced from her to the gun and back again. Dr. Shaw followed my gaze and nodded understandingly.

"I appreciate that you have little privacy in your current circumstances, but I assure you, no one will touch your things while you're here. I take privacy concerns *very* seriously." Her smile was thin and cold, briefly recalling the way she'd first presented herself. "You have my word."

Gregory said I could trust her, and she wasn't sounding the alarm over my possession of a weapon. I swallowed to clear my throat, and nodded. "I'll get ready."

"Thank you. Call for Kathleen when you want the robe." She paused, as if one more thing had just occurred to her, and added, "You may keep your underwear."

"I appreciate that."

"I thought you might." Dr. Shaw walked away, her heels clacking on the floor, as if to illustrate that outside this small, screened-in space, we were playing by the CDC's rules.

I may not enjoy playing by other people's rules, but I've had enough experience to be good at it. I slid off the stool, putting the pistol back where I originally found it, and disrobed, piling my white pajamas over the gun. If any of Dr. Shaw's technicians weren't in on things—and I had no real reason to believe that *any* of them were in on things—they'd need to actively look before they found anything awry.

While I stripped, I heard the oddly reassuring sound of a shredder coming from the main room. Dr. Shaw had been telling the truth about disposing of Gregory's message. I just hoped she'd have the sense to take the trash with her when she left.

Kathleen was waiting when I stuck my head around the screen. She held a plain white robe out to me, smiling pleasantly. "Dr. Shaw is ready for you now."

"Tell Dr. Shaw I'm almost ready for her," I said, and ducked back behind the screen to shrug into the robe. With one last, regretful glance toward the pile of clothing concealing my new gun, I turned to head out into the room.

Kathleen was still waiting. Her smile brightened as she saw that I was dressed. "This way," she said, beckoning. "We're going to begin by measuring your basic neurological responses."

"Meaning what?" I asked, following her.

"Meaning we'll be applying electrodes to your scalp, asking you neutral questions and watching to see how your brain waves change as you respond. Dr. Shaw has been petitioning for permission to do a sleep study, but so far, they've refused." Kathleen frowned, like the refusal was somehow a personal insult. She led me toward a complicated-looking machine where Dr. Shaw and two of the technicians were waiting. "I'm sure she'll be granted permission sooner or later. For the moment, conscious brain wave studies will have to do."

"For *today*," said Dr. Shaw, snapping a connector into place. "Georgia. So glad you could join us. If you would be so kind as to take a seat, we can begin getting you ready. Please remove the robe."

I froze. "Please *what*?"

"Remove the robe."

"Why did you give it to me if—?"

"Modesty and science are not always compatible," said Dr. Shaw. "Kathleen?"

"Yes, Dr. Shaw," said Kathleen, and took hold of my robe's collar, tugging just hard enough to make sure I knew she was there. "If you would be so kind?"

I bit back a sigh. I've never been the most modest person in the world, and my time as the CDC's favorite new lab rat was rapidly eroding what little modesty I possessed. I undid the belt, letting Kathleen peel the robe away, and took a seat in the indicated chair. It was covered in clear plastic that made little crunching noises as I slid myself into position. Worse, it was cold.

So was the greenish gel that Dr. Shaw's technicians began applying to my throat, shoulders, and stomach. I frowned. "I thought this was going to be a brain wave test?"

"Yes, but since we have limited time, and you're going to be immobilized anyway, I'm taking this opportunity to get a clear picture of your vital signs." Dr. Shaw smiled. "I'm very fond of efficiency."

"I'm beginning to see that." The technicians, including Kathleen, were taping sensor pads to my front.

"There's just one more thing that you might object to. I apologize, but I assure you, it's necessary to ensure the accuracy of my tests."

I gritted my teeth, steeling myself for something I wasn't going to enjoy. "What's that?" I asked. "You need me to sing Christmas carols while you measure my brain activity?"

"That could be entertaining, and you should feel free if it helps you relax, but no." Dr. Shaw produced a pair of scissors from her pocket, holding them up for me to see. "Your hair will interfere with the placement of the sensors on your scalp. I'm afraid I'm going to have to cut most of it off if we're going to get a clear result."

For a moment, I simply stared at her. Then I started to laugh. I was still laughing when she began cutting my hair, and barely got myself under control in time for the testing to begin. The real test—the test of whether or not I could survive the CDC—was still ongoing. But I was starting to feel like I might actually stand a chance.

Subject 7c continues to respond to stimulus, and has begun questioning the conditions of her containment. She—and it truly is impossible to avoid assigning a gender, and even an identity, to a subject that has been awake and interactive for this length of time—continues to adhere closely to the registered template. Her responses are well within the allowable parameters. Perhaps too well within the allowable parameters; early concerns about cooperation and biddability were not unfounded.

It may be necessary to begin preparing the 8 line for release. I will continue to observe and study 7c, but do not believe that 7d would offer any substantial improvement in the problem areas.

—Taken from an e-mail sent by Dr. Matthew Thomas, July 23, 2041.

Preparations to separate the members of our group are nearly complete. Maggie keeps saying we shouldn't split the party. Privately, I agree with her. This is madness. We will separate, and we will each of us die alone. And yet . . .

Something must be done. If Shaun's paranoid ravings are correct, and the mosquitoes were engineered for release when a news cycle truly needed to be buried—one such as the cycle we were prepared to unleash when we left Memphis—then it is our responsibility to find a way to save the world from them. How arrogant that looks! "Save the world." I'm not in the world saving business. I'm a journalist.

But it seems the world has other ideas. Maggie and I leave for Seattle tomorrow. I'm terrified that I will never see London, or my wife, again. And a small, traitorous part of me is elated. I thought we no longer lived in an age of heroes.

I was wrong.

—From *Fish and Clips*, the blog of Mahir Gowda, July 23, 2041. Unpublished.

Six

Deciding to hit the road took only a few seconds—the amount of time necessary for a thought to travel from my brain to my big mouth. Actually leaving took longer. Dr. Abbey wasn't sending us out to die; if anything, she was sending us out *not* to die, something she took great pains to make sure I understood.

"This isn't just about the mosquitoes, Shaun," she'd said, while running yet another blood test and getting yet another negative result. "I wasn't exaggerating when I showed you those distribution maps, or when I talked about the number of lives you could save by bringing me some live specimens. But it was never just about the mosquitoes."

George had sighed in the back of my head then, sounding so tired it made my chest ache. She was dead. She shouldn't have been tired anymore. But she was, and it was my fault, for refusing to let her go. *She wants you to get exposed again.*

"Are you fucking kidding?" I'd asked, too startled to remember to keep my voice down.

And Dr. Abbey had smiled, that bitter half twist of her lips that I normally saw only when she thought no one was looking, or when she murmured endearments to her huge black dog, the one with her dead husband's name.

"Someday you're going to have to explain how it is you've managed to create a subconscious echo that's smarter than you are." Still smiling, Dr. Abbey had looked me squarely in the eye and said, "I need to know if you can shrug off the infection a second time, outside lab conditions. If you can, that changes everything."

Swell.

The next four days rushed past in a blur, with all of us preparing to do the one thing I'd sworn I'd die to prevent: We were getting ready to go our separate ways. After everything I'd done to keep us together, to keep us alive, I was going to scatter us to the winds, and pray everyone came home again. We started as a news site. Somewhere along the line, we became a family. Me, and George, and After the End Times. That was all I needed. I'd already lost George. Did I have to lose everyone else, too?

Alaric would be staying with Dr. Abbey; that hadn't changed. He was our best technician. If it became necessary for the lab to move while we were still on the road, he'd be too useful for Dr. Abbey to just ditch, and he'd be able to keep the rest of us aware of its location. Besides, I didn't trust him in the field when his sister's safety was on the line. He was likely to do something impulsive and get himself hurt, and I wasn't sure I'd be able to force myself to stay on the road instead of running straight back to Dr. Abbey and her advanced medical facilities. Especially since by "advanced," I meant "better than a first aid kit." We were still off the grid. If one of us got messed up, the hospital wasn't going to be an option.

Maggie and Mahir, meanwhile, were going to head farther up the coast, leaving the wilds of Oregon for the dubious safety of Seattle. Maggie's plan was to go back *on* the grid as soon as possible, reclaiming her position as heir to the Garcia family fortune, and presenting Mahir as her latest boy toy. "People like their circuses when the news gets bad," she'd said, a perverse twinkle in her eyes. "I'm a Fictional, remember? I'm going to tell them a story so flashy they won't even think to ask where I've been." Alaric wasn't thrilled about the "boy toy" part, but it was solid. They would use her celebrity as a cover while they made contact with the Seattle underground, and located the man everyone called "the Monkey." He could cook new IDs for my whole team, IDs that were good enough to let us disappear forever, if things came to that.

Most of us, anyway. Maggie came to see me on the fifth day after we began planning our departure. I was clearing my things out of the van. I'd been sleeping there most nights, preferring the illusory privacy of its familiar walls to the dubious comforts of the dormlike sleeping arrangements inside the Forestry Center. The garage wasn't secure, but the van was, once the doors were locked.

She knocked once on the open rear door, and then just stood there, waiting.

I looked up. "Yeah?"

"You know we're not getting me an ID from the Monkey, don't you?" Her expression was a mixture of resignation and resolve. She looked like a heroine from one of the horror movies she loved so much, and in that moment, I really understood what Dave—one of the many teammates I'd buried since this whole thing started—and Alaric saw in her. She was beautiful.

And she was right. "Yeah, I do." I put down the toolbox I was holding, moving to take a seat on the bumper. "You can't disappear."

"If it weren't for the fact that my bio-tracker is still registering with my parents, I wouldn't even be able to stay underground for this long." Maggie touched the skin above her collarbone. Her parents had implanted a subdermal bio-tracker beneath the bone when she was still in diapers. It didn't come with a "trace" function—Maggie's misguided teenage years before she discovered journalism were proof that they'd been telling her the truth about that—but it enabled them to sleep soundly at night, serene in the knowledge that their only child was still alive.

"We could have it removed."

"If *anything* would switch this thing from transmitting my vitals to actively giving them a location, that would do it." Maggie sat down next to me. "It's too risky."

I looked at her levelly. "It's too risky, and you don't really want to disappear, do you?"

"It's not that! It's just . . . it's . . . " She took a breath, stopping herself before she could go any further. Finally, reluctantly, she nodded. "You're right. I don't want to disappear. I don't want to do that to my parents, and I miss my house. I miss my dogs. I miss my Fictionals. They have to be so worried. I've never done this to them before, not once. Alaric and I talked about this. He's not happy, but . . . it's what has to happen."

Tell her you understand, said George.

"I understand," I said, and even if I had to be prompted into the words, I meant them. Maggie had already given up a lot to stay with us this long, more than any of my team members except for maybe Mahir. Alaric's family would have been in Florida no matter where he worked. Becks hadn't spoken to her family in years. She was a lot like Georgia that way; both of them found the news and ran for it with open arms, not caring what got left behind in the process. But Maggie wasn't like that. Maggie was different.

Maggie was looking at me hopefully, like she could barely bring herself to believe I was really saying the words she was hearing. "I know I'm letting you down."

"You're not." I'm not a huggy person. I used to be more physically affectionate—not excessively so, but enough that I didn't seem standoffish. That was George's job. I took the hugs that were aimed at her. I haven't felt like hugging people very often since she died. I still leaned over and put my arm around Maggie's shoulders, giving her a brief squeeze. The situation seemed to call for it.

"Really?" she whispered.

"Really. Your parents would tear down the world trying to find you if you stayed gone too long. That's cool. That's sort of awesome, if you think about it. Becks's family hates her. Alaric's family is dead. Mahir's family is in England, and they probably think he's insane. And the Masons . . . " I stopped, the sentence coming to a halt.

"It's not your fault," said Maggie, filling the space with the words she assumed I needed to hear. "They were broken a long time before you came to live with them. It's not your fault you couldn't fix them."

"The flat-drop."

"What?"

"The flat-drop!" I turned to face her, grabbing her shoulders in my excitement. "We sent them a copy of our files when we were on the run from Memphis. I mean, we were going to die, so *someone* needed to have the data, right? Only I told Alaric he could encrypt the fuck out of them if he wanted to, and since the Masons haven't suddenly started 'discovering' lots of corruption inside the CDC, I guess he must have used a pretty damn good encryption."

"You're not making any sense," said Maggie, eyes wide.

"No, see, this is *perfect*! I was worried about how Becks and I were going to get into the hazard zone without getting caught, but the Masons practically invented breaking into hazard zones! They're pioneers in the field!" I laughed, mainly from relief. "All we have to do is show up on their doorstep and offer to crack those files in exchange for a low-risk route into Florida, and they'll jump at it. They'll have to."

"What if they don't?"

"Then I'll shoot their kneecaps out." I didn't realize I meant it until the words were said. The Masons raised me. The Masons gave me the greatest gift anyone has ever given me: George. But they were never really my parents, because they never wanted to be, and if they were what stood between me and what I needed to do, then they needed to be moved.

"Um," said Maggie. She pulled away from me and stood. "Well, okay, if that's what works. Really, though. Thank you for understanding."

"Thank you for being willing to go to Seattle with Mahir," I replied. "You heading back inside?"

"Yeah. Will you be out here long?"

"Not too long."

"If you're not inside by dinner, I'll send someone to get you." She walked away, her long brown braid swaying with every step. It was hard to believe that she was planning to use "bored heiress" as her cover during the trip up the coast. It was harder to believe that the news media would probably buy it.

"You need to be careful what you say around people, asshole," said George. I hadn't felt the van settle when she sat down, because she wasn't really there. I couldn't keep myself from feeling vaguely disappointed all the same. "Look at me when I'm talking to you."

"Sorry." I turned to face my dead sister, offering her a small smile. "Hi, George. How're you tonight?"

"Worried," she said. "You need to be careful. Everyone's already on edge without you going around talking about shooting people."

"I haven't hit anyone since we got here."

"That doesn't mean they're not waiting for you to start." Her expression dared me to argue. I couldn't, and so I just looked at her instead.

Maybe the fact that George sometimes appears to me is a symptom of the fact that I'm sliding farther and farther down the funhouse chute into insanity, but at moments like these, I can't force myself to care. When she died—when I shot her—I thought that was it; I would never see her again, except in pictures, and in my dreams. Only it turns out that's not true, thanks to my slipping grasp on reality. See? There are upsides to going crazy.

She still looked almost exactly like she did on that last day in Sacramento, pale-skinned from her near-pathological avoidance of sunlight, with dark brown hair cut in a short, efficient style she sometimes maintained with a pair of craft scissors. She was frowning. Since that was the expression she wore most often when she was alive, that was right, too. Really, if it hadn't been for the clear brown of her irises, she would have been indistinguishable from herself. If I could just convince my hallucination to put on a pair of sunglasses, the illusion would be perfect.

George frowned. "Shaun. Are you listening to me?"

"I am. I swear, I am." I reached one hand toward her face, stopping just short of the point where my fingertips would have failed to brush her skin. "I always listen to you."

"You just ignore what I have to say about half the time, is that it?" George sighed. I let my hand drop. As long as I didn't try to touch her, I didn't have to think of her as what she was. Dead. "Shaun—"

"It's good to see you."

"It's *bad* that you can see me. You need to talk to Dr. Abbey. Maybe she can put you on antipsychotics or something until this is all over."

"I'll go psychotic if I go on antipsychotics, which sort of defeats the purpose, don't you think?" I was trying to make it sound like a joke. We both knew I wasn't kidding. The one time I'd tried to block her out, I'd nearly committed suicide. "I can't take the silence, George. You know that."

"You asked once if I was going to haunt you forever, remember?"

"That was before Florida." I held up my left hand, showing her the faint scarring on my bicep. "That was before we found out that I'm immune to Kellis-Amberlee. That was before a lot of things."

"You know you're immune because we—"

"I know." I sighed, letting my hand drop. "Things are all fucked up. I was supposed to be the one who died. I'm not equipped to deal with this shit."

"You're wrong." Her voice was firm enough to surprise me. She met my eyes without flinching, and repeated, "You're *wrong*. Dr. Wynne wasn't kidding when he said that whoever's behind this would have been able to get away with everything if you'd been the one who died. You know that, right? I would have believed Tate when he started ranting about how he was behind everything, just him, from the start. I would have been so eager for a black and white solution, for a villain I didn't have to feel any conflict about ... I would have believed him."

"I believed him," I whispered.

"Not all the way. If you'd believed him all the way—if you'd believed him the way I would have believed him—you would have done what we both know I would have done. You would have written your reports, held my funeral, gone home, and killed yourself." She smiled faintly. "Probably by overdosing on everything in our field kit before blowing the top of your head off. You never were one for leaving things to chance."

"What would you have done?"

"Slit my wrists in the bathtub," she said matter-of-factly. "Even if I amplified before I bled out, the bathroom security sensors would never have let me out into the house. I would have been bleached to death. The Masons would have had to pay if they wanted to clear the outbreak off their home owner's insurance, and you and I could have sat in the afterlife and laughed at them until we both cried."

Now it was my turn to smile. "That sounds like something you'd do," I agreed.

"But I didn't get the chance." She leaned over. This time, she was the one to reach for me, and when her fingertips grazed my skin, I felt it. Tactile hallucinations aren't a good sign of mental health, but sometimes I feel like they're the only things letting me keep body and soul together. "You got it. And you were stronger than I would have been. You're stronger than you think you are. All you've ever needed to do was let yourself see it."

"I don't know how much longer I can keep this up."

"Not too much longer, I'd wager," said Mahir, from behind me. His normally crisp accent was blurred around the edges, like he was too tired to worry about being understood by the Americans. "How's it coming?"

"About as well as can be expected," I said, stealing one last look at Georgia before I turned, casting an easy smile in his direction. I didn't need to look back to know that George was gone. She generally disappeared as soon as I took my eyes off her. I was seeing her more often with every day that passed, and that was wonderful, because I missed her so much, and it was terrible, because it meant I was running out of time.

We can cure cancer. We can cure the common cold. But no one, anywhere, ever, has found a reliable cure for crazy.

"Maggie spoke with you?"

I nodded. "She wanted to make sure I knew she wouldn't be coming back from Seattle."

"And you were all right with that?" Mahir walked toward me, stopping when he was still a few feet clear of the van. Maggie was a much more touchy-feely kind of person than he was. I appreciated that. One hug per day was pretty much my limit.

"No," I admitted. "I don't want her to go. The rest of us . . . You're going to be able to put your own name back on when you get home, but the rest of us, we're done. We'll be lucky if we don't wind up hiding in Canada being chased by zombie moose for the rest of our lives."

"There's always the chance we'll successfully manage to bring down the United States government somehow, and that will negate the need to flee to Canada," said Mahir helpfully.

I gave him a startled look. He smirked, fighting unsuccessfully to keep himself from smiling. Somehow, that was even funnier than what he'd said. I started laughing. So did he. We were both still laughing five minutes later, when Becks came out to the garage with a can of soda in one hand and a perplexed look on her face.

"Did I miss something?" she asked.

"We're going to topple the US government!" I informed her.

Becks appeared to think about that for a moment. Then she shrugged, cracking the tab on her soda at the same time, and replied, "Okay. Works for me."

Mahir and I burst out laughing again. Becks waited patiently for us to stop, taking occasional sips from her soda. Finally, I wiped my eyes with the heel of my hand, and said, still snickering, "Okay. Okay, I think we're done now. Did you see Maggie?"

"I did. She said something about you and me heading to Berkeley to kill your parents?"

"That's not quite what I said, but I guess it's close enough. We're going to Berkeley to ask the Masons if they'll tell us how to find a clear route into the Florida hazard zone."

"And what will you be giving them in return?" asked Mahir.

I sighed. "You know, I really kind of miss the days when I could just e-mail a memo to the team, and everybody would know what was going on, and I wouldn't have to repeat things seventeen times."

Not that you ever remembered to send the memos, said George.

"Because you did that *so* often," said Becks, saving me from the need to respond to someone no one else could hear. Again.

"I *could* have done it, if I'd wanted to," I countered. "That made the endless repetition a choice, and hence way less irritating. I'm going to tell them how to unlock the flat-drop of all our files. The one I had Alaric send while we were running from Memphis."

"And when they post our research far and wide? What happens then?" Mahir didn't sound annoyed, just curious. Even so, I was relieved when Becks crunched her empty soda can in her fist and chucked it into the trash can against the wall, where it landed with a rattling clunk.

"If the Masons post the things we've been withholding, they'll be the target of the firestorm that follows," she said. She sounded utterly calm. Her calm continued as she added, "Which means we can't let them do it."

"Hey!" I frowned at her. "I thought you were supposed to be on my side here."

"I'm on the side that doesn't get us slaughtered, Mason. Think about this for thirty seconds, why don't you? We give them the key to the files. They unlock them, and go all kid in a candy store over the contents, since hey, their stupid son just gave them the scoop of the century. They toss it all online. And people everywhere stop shooting zombies because they think their loved ones might get 'better.'"

I grimaced. "Not good."

"Not good at all. And then the government will lean on the Masons to tell them where to find us, so we can be used to 'prove' that it was all a hoax."

"Lovely," said Mahir.

Becks shrugged. "If you're going to think like a paranoid, you need to really *commit* to thinking like a paranoid."

Mahir looked at her quizzically. "What makes you so good at it?"

"I'm from Connecticut," said Becks. "It's not a *bad* idea—going to the Masons may be the fastest way to get ourselves access to a reasonably safe way through some pretty bad territory, and since I'm not leaving the van without dipping myself in DDT, I'd like it if we could make the trip in reasonable safety. But you're going to need another carrot to dangle in front of your freaky parents. Telling them how to get at our data isn't the way."

Yes, actually, said George, very quietly. *It's exactly the way.*

"What are you—" I began, and froze. "Oh, no. No, you can't be serious."

You know I'm serious. It's the best shot you've got.

"I won't."

You will.

Mahir and Becks had gotten good at knowing when I wasn't actually talking to them. They watched me with varying degrees of impatience, waiting until I stopped protesting before Mahir broke in, asking, "What does Georgia say we should do?"

"You know, addressing my crazy by name doesn't exactly help me stay sane," I said.

"Nothing can help you stay sane at this point, Mason," said Becks. "That ship has sailed. Now what does she say?"

I took a deep breath. "She wants me to sign her unpublished files over to the Masons. The stuff they were willing to take me to court over." I stopped, waiting for them to protest. Neither of them said a word. I scowled. "Well?"

"It's not a bad idea," said Mahir slowly. "I mean, it's true that her unpublished op-ed pieces were reasonably lucrative when we were able to publish regularly, but her news articles have been timing out at a fairly high rate. We've had our exclusive. If what's left can be used to benefit us—"

"You're fucking with me, right?" I stood, glaring at them, barely aware that my hands were balled into fists. I could hear George at the back of my head, telling me sternly to calm down, but I didn't pay any attention. That was nice, in its way. I so rarely felt like I could ignore her anymore. "Those files are her *private thoughts*. They're the last privacy she has left in this world. And you want me to just sign it over to those . . . those . . . those *people*?"

"Yes," said Mahir, sounding utterly calm. "That's exactly what we want. And I'd wager it's what Georgia wants as well, or you'd not be so angry about it. You'd be laughing it off."

"We've been using her private thoughts for our gain since she died," said Becks. "I've been okay with that, because you're okay with it. But, Shaun, you're the one who *really* knows what she would have wanted. You're the one who really knows *her*. If she were alive, would she be saying no, no way, not going to happen? Or would she be suggesting we stop fucking around and get our asses to Berkeley with the transfer papers already?"

George didn't say anything. George didn't need to say anything. I forced my fingers to unclench, waiting until I could feel my palms again before I looked away from Becks and Mahir, and said, "I'll get the transfer papers drawn up before we leave. That way, all we have to do is hand them over and get the hell out of town."

Thank you, murmured George. I felt the shadow of a hand brush my cheek, and shivered. I don't believe in ghosts. Never have, never will. George is a figment of my overactive imagination, nothing more, and nothing less. But moments like that, when she touches me with other people in the room . . .

At moments like that, I genuinely believe that I'm haunted.

"You're doing the right thing," said Mahir. I glanced up, meeting his eyes without meaning to. He smiled. Just a little. Enough for me to see that he meant it. "You're a crazy bastard, Shaun Mason, and I think sometimes you're not going to be happy until you've managed to get every last one of us killed, but you're a good man, all the same."

"Remind me to have that inscribed on my urn," I said, and Becks laughed, and things felt like they might be okay again. We had a direction. I didn't like it; I didn't have to. All I had to do was follow it, and let it lead me to whatever the next step on this increasingly insane journey would prove to be.

"Can I help you finish getting the van ready?" asked Becks. "Since we're going to be sleeping in the thing for God only knows how long, I want to be absolutely sure that there are no old tuna sandwiches moldering under the seats."

"Be my guest," I said, waving toward the open van doors. "Mahir, tell Alaric and Maggie we're rolling out in the morning. Team meeting at five."

Mahir grimaced. "A.M.?"

"Naturally."

"I take back what I said about you being a good man."

"Too late. There are no take-backs in real life."

Becks chuckled darkly. "Ain't that just the truth?"

"Sadly?" I asked. "Yes. It is. Now let's get back to work. We have a lot to get done, and not much time to do it in."

Mahir was opening his mouth to answer when a scream rang out from the other side of the garage door, followed by the sound of gunfire. In the brief pause between the first volley of shots and the second, we could all hear the moaning coming from inside.

"Never a dull moment, is there?" I asked. Grabbing my pistol, I ran for the door. Becks was there just ahead of me. She pushed it open, and we ran together into chaos.

Dr. Abbey gave me a dressing-down this morning for yelling at her staff. "They didn't sign up for this." That's what she said. Like it made all the difference in the world, somehow. "They didn't sign up for this. Don't treat them like they did."

You know what, lady? None of us signed up for this. Not me, not Mahir, not George, not anyone. And I definitely didn't sign up for keeping my mouth shut while a bunch of amateurs treat zombies like lab rats.

Zombies are dangerous. Science doesn't protect you from that reality. If anything, science makes it worse.

I didn't sign up for that, either.

—From *Adaptive Immunities*, the blog of Shaun Mason, July 23, 2041. Unpublished.

Yes. You were right.

We will proceed.

—Taken from a message sent by Dr. Danika Kimberley, July 23, 2041. Recipient unknown.

Seven

Dr. Shaw's tests were actually soothing, despite the partial nudity and the being touched by strangers. She was calm and professional, leading her team with an unwavering precision that gave them a degree of serenity I hadn't previously encountered at the CDC. Everyone else I'd dealt with had been uneasy when forced to come into direct contact with my skin, like being a clone was somehow catching. Dr. Shaw's assistants showed no such discomfort. They affixed their sensors without hesitation, even peeling them loose and sticking them back down in new configurations. It was so matter-of-fact and impersonal that it was almost wonderful.

I didn't realize I was starting to drift off until Dr. Shaw cleared her throat and said, "It would help us measure your waking brain wave patterns if you would do us the favor of remaining awake while they're being recorded."

"Oh." I opened my eyes, offering her a sheepish smile. "I'm sorry."

"It's understandable. You've been through a great deal. Still, the cause of science must take precedence over comfort." She leaned forward to affix a sensor to my forehead. Her lips almost brushed my ear as she murmured, barely audible even at that range, "The locks will be reset tonight at midnight. You can answer many of your questions then, if you're quick about it."

Pulling back before I could react, she pressed the edges of the sensor down and said, "Begin the next phase, James, if you would be so kind." One of her assistants nodded. Dr. Shaw turned away, attention seemingly fixed on the machine in front of her.

Right. Information exchange time was over, at least for the moment. Her words had definitely had one effect, at least—there was no way I was going to start nodding off again.

All the tests I'd been through since I'd woken up had been different. That was unusual, all by itself. Blood tests, muscle memory response tests, even psychological exams performed by people who didn't seem to understand the questions, much less the answers I was giving. The medical teams changed constantly, and each was directed by a different administrator. So what did that mean, exactly? What were they looking for that didn't require a single supervising doctor to find?

Dr. Shaw was the first to outright admit to measuring my brain waves. I was reasonably sure she wasn't the first one to do it. The chance to study a cloned brain that was actually functional and responsive had to be irresistible to them—and despite my fervent wish to believe otherwise, I knew my brain was as cloned as the rest of me. Nothing else made *sense*. When the virus went live in my original bloodstream, it attacked the brain with a ferocity unequaled by any naturally occurring pathogen. I'd been able to *feel* my memories eroding as I typed up the final entry on my blog. If they'd placed my infected old brain in my clean new clone body, I would have gone straight into amplification, and all their hard work would have been for nothing.

I watched the colored lines representing my brain's activity spike and tangle on the monitor across from me. None of them made a damn bit of sense. I never studied medicine, beyond the first aid required for field certification. Mahir might have been able to decode the peaks and valleys, turning them into comprehensible data. Mahir wasn't with me.

One of Dr. Shaw's assistants was trying to peel the sensor from my left bicep. I lifted my arm, tightening the muscle to give him more traction. He shot me a relieved look. "Thanks," he said. "This bio-adhesive can be tricky."

"What is it?" I asked, half from sincere curiosity, and half to keep him talking to me. It's easier to get information from people who think you're interested in the same things they are.

"Slime mold," said the assistant. He sounded happy about it, too.

"Oh," I said, unable to quite mask my dismay. Then again, I *was* the one who had living goo smeared on something like fifteen percent of her skin. I think I was allowed a little dismay. "That's . . . special. What happens to it when you're done with me?"

"We'll dust it with a powder that makes it go dormant, and then just roll it off your skin," he said. "Can you relax your arm for me?"

"Sure." I let my arm drop back to its original position. He attached the sensor to the inside of my elbow. "I guess that makes sense. No residue, no medical waste . . . "

"It's self-cleaning, so even if it gets bloody, it's safe to use again after eight hours. It also reacts to the presence of live virus."

"Really?" I asked, blinking. "How?"

"It tries to ooze away."

This time, I couldn't suppress my shudder. Several alarms went off on the machines connected to the various sensors, earning me dirty looks from a few of the assistants. "Sorry!" I said.

"George, please refrain from making the subject wiggle," said Dr. Shaw, not looking away from the monitor she was studying.

The assistant—George—reddened. "Sorry, Dr. Shaw."

I waited for him to get the sensor on my elbow firmly seated, then asked, "So you're another George, huh? The original form?"

"George R. Stewart," he replied. "And yes, the 'R' stands for 'Romero.' My parents were grateful, not creative."

"Georgia, here," I said. "One of my best friends was a Georgette."

"Georgette Meissonier, right?" George caught my startled expression and reddened again. "I, um. I'm a big fan of your work. Your last post was . . . it was amazing. I've never read anything like it."

I wasn't sure whether I should feel flattered or embarrassed. I wound up mixing both reactions as I said awkwardly, "Oh. So you know the part where I'm dead."

"The dead have been walking for a quarter century." He moved to my other side, adjusting another sensor. Dr. Shaw's other assistants all seemed to have machines to tend, leaving George with the dubious honor of working with the living equipment. Me, and the slime mold. "I'm glad you're back. If anyone deserves to be back . . ."

"Let's hope the rest of the world feels the same way when I start doing the celebrity blog circuit," I said, putting a lilt in my tone to show that I was joking. I wasn't joking.

"They're waiting for you," he said, cheeks getting redder still. He stopped talking after that, focusing all the more intently on the sensors he was shifting. I blinked a little, watching him. I'd expected a lot of reactions. That wasn't one of them. My last post . . . it made me another name on The Wall, but that was all, wasn't it?

Wasn't it?

The idea that I'd become some sort of symbol worried me. I'm a realist. I've been a realist since the day I looked at the Masons—who'd been Mommy and Daddy until that moment—and realized that Shaun was right, and they didn't love us.

I'd already known the CDC was never going to let me go. Whatever they brought me back for—blackmail or science project or just because I was the most convenient corpse when they decided to prove they could do it for real—it wasn't going to include opening the doors and telling me to go on my merry way. I was a prisoner. I was a test subject. I was, in a very real way, as much a piece of lab equipment as the machines that I was connected to. The only difference was that the machines couldn't resent the fact that they had no choice in their own existence.

And if I was a symbol, I was also a weapon, whether I wanted to be one or not.

"Are any of them pinching you?" asked George.

"No," I said, resisting the urge to shake my head. I didn't want to trigger any more alarms if I didn't have to. "I think we're good to continue."

"We're almost done," he said, and offered one more awkward, almost worshipful smile before moving away.

The remainder of the tests passed without incident. More living slime was applied to my limbs and torso, sometimes by George, sometimes by one of the other assistants; more sensors were attached or moved, allowing Dr. Shaw's equipment to record a detailed image of everything going on inside me. I resisted the urge to spend the whole time staring at the monitors. I didn't understand them. All I could do was upset myself more by watching them.

I'd almost managed to drift off again when the assistants began pulling the sensor pads off, letting George sprinkle what looked—and smelled—like baby powder on the sticky green residue the sensors left behind. True to his word, the green stuff rolled into tight little balls, which he scraped off me with the edge of his hand, gathering it all into one gooey-looking mass.

"Please don't forget to feed the slime mold," said Dr. Shaw, moving to disconnect the sensors at my temples. "I have no desire to listen to a week of complaints because we have to culture ourselves a new colony."

"Yes, Dr. Shaw," said George, and hurried off with his handful of inert green goop. Most of the other assistants followed him, leaving me alone with Dr. Shaw and Kathleen, the assistant who had initially brought me my currently discarded robe. She was holding it again, face a mask of patience as she waited for Dr. Shaw to finish freeing me from their equipment.

"Kathleen, what is our time situation?" asked Dr. Shaw, working a thumbnail under one of the sensors on my forehead. Either these had been pressed down harder, or they'd used a particularly robust batch of slime mold to glue them to my head and neck; it felt like she was trying to chip her way through concrete.

"We have fifteen minutes remaining in your original research appointment," said Kathleen serenely. "We have ninety-three seconds of previously untransmitted sensor data, which James is now feeding through the main uplink. It will remain unquestioned for approximately fifty-four more seconds."

I was still blinking at her in confusion when Dr. Shaw nodded, said, "Good," and ripped the recalcitrant sensor from my forehead. I yelped, clapping a hand over the stinging patch it left behind. Dr. Shaw watched me, calm appraisal in her eyes. "Are you paying attention?"

"Yes!" I gasped, half glaring at her. "I was paying attention *before* you tried to scalp me!"

"There will be an accident with the building's EMP shield tonight, at six minutes past midnight. The shift change will have occurred an hour previous, and you will have a thirty-minute window before anyone realizes they've lost the visual feed to your quarters." The certainty in her voice told me this wasn't the first time she'd had to give this little spiel. "Your contact will come to collect you. There's something we feel you need to see."

"Eleven seconds," said Kathleen.

"Do you understand?" asked Dr. Shaw.

I understood that they'd obviously timed this little window of stolen security so as to leave me no room for asking questions. "Yes," I said. "I understand."

"Good."

"Four seconds."

Dr. Shaw bent to remove the last sensor from the underside of my jaw. This time, her fingers were gentle, and the slime mold let go without resistance. The professional chill was back in her eyes as she stepped back, saying, "You may get dressed now. We appreciate your cooperation."

"Yeah, well, you're welcome," I said, standing. My legs were surprisingly shaky; I'd either been sitting still for longer than I thought, or there was some form of muscle relaxant engineered into their adhesive slime. Possibly both. Kathleen passed me the robe, and I leaned against the side of the chair to shrug it back on. Being clothed didn't make me feel any better. As the tests Dr. Shaw and her team had been running proved, I was always naked here. What difference did fabric make when these people could look inside my body, and understand it in ways that I didn't?

Kathleen and Dr. Shaw waited as I got my balance back. "Better?" asked Dr. Shaw.

"I think so."

"Good. Make yourself decent; I'll go unseal the door before Dr. Thomas decides to knock it down." She almost smiled as she turned and walked away from us, her heels clacking against the floor.

"This way," said Kathleen, motioning for me to follow her—in case, I supposed, I had somehow managed to forget where I left the screen that was protecting my flimsy CDC-issue pajamas . . . and the gun Gregory had somehow managed to smuggle to me. That was the last thing I was going to forget.

Becoming a licensed journalist requires passing basic gun safety and marksmanship exams; even if you're planning to do nothing but sit at home typing to an anonymous audience, having the phrase "accredited journalist" after your name means having a carry permit. Becoming a licensed field journalist, like I am—like I *was*—means taking a lot more exams, and learning how to handle a lot more varieties of weapon. I never shared Shaun's interest in the more esoteric firearms. The basics suited me just fine, and I'd been carrying at least one gun at pretty much all times since I got my first permit. I was twelve that summer. Knowing that I had a gun again, that I had a means of protecting myself if I needed it . . . that made a lot of difference. The robe didn't make me feel any less naked. The gun would.

Kathleen waited outside the screen while I went behind it and put my pajamas back on. The small plastic gun tucked easily into the top of my right sock, not even creating a noticeable bulge once my pants were on. As long as I could act natural, Dr. Thomas would never know that it was there. That was probably what Gregory was counting on.

Gregory, and the EIS. There was no way Dr. Shaw wasn't working for them, and if she was one of theirs, her assistants probably were, too. Definitely Kathleen; no one who was loyal to the CDC would have stood there calmly counting down our privacy window. Not unless she was a double agent hidden in the EIS, and that idea was too James Bond for me to worry about, since there was nothing I could do if it was true. The CDC had been infiltrated. The EIS might not be the good guys by any objective measure, but given the choices I had in front of me, I was going to go with the team that gave me firearms and told me Shaun wasn't dead.

Dr. Thomas and the guards were standing just inside the lab when I emerged. His eyes widened at the sight of me, and then narrowed. "What have you done to her hair?" he demanded, attention swinging back toward Dr. Shaw.

She watched him with cool, if evident, amusement, and said, "It was interfering with the placement of my sensors. As none of the tests scheduled for the remainder of the month required uncut hair, I thought it best to eliminate the issue in the most efficient manner possible. Is there a problem?"

"No, but . . ." Dr. Thomas stopped, obviously torn as to how to complete that sentence. Finally, looking almost sullen, he said, "You should have consulted with me before cutting her hair. Sudden changes to her environment can be stressful at this stage in her recovery."

Dr. Shaw's laugh was surprisingly light and delicate, like it belonged to someone much younger and less put together. "Oh, come now, Matthew. You can't really expect me to believe that you consider a *haircut* a sudden change in her environment. I understand the necessity of controlling all variable factors while she gets her strength back, but no sensible young woman would take something this simple and medically necessary as a new source of stress."

"I like it," I contributed, before Dr. Thomas could say anything else. He turned to frown at me as I made my way across the lab to where he was waiting for me. "It's going to be a lot easier to brush. I've never tried to deal with long hair before."

"I suppose the convenience will make up for the aesthetic failings," he said stiffly.

I frowned. I couldn't stop myself, and quite frankly, I didn't want to. "This is the length I prefer my hair to be," I said. "The only 'aesthetic failing' is that I keep taking bleach showers without access to hair dye. I'm going to wind up blonde if this keeps up much longer, and that's not a good look for me."

"We all have our trials in this life," said Dr. Shaw. "Georgia, thank you for your cooperation today. You were very easy for us to work with, and I appreciate it."

"No problem, Dr. Shaw," I said. "It was my pleasure."

"It's time for us to go, Georgia," said Dr. Thomas. There was an edge to his voice that I normally heard only when I was pushing for privileges he didn't want to give. My curious look just seemed to fluster him. He scowled, cheeks reddening. "It's time to *go*," he repeated.

"Okay," I said, trying to look unconcerned as I followed him out the door. He hadn't put the handcuffs back on me, and with every step, it became a little harder not to panic. I'd been so sure I could get the gun back to my room without getting caught, but now . . . now . . .

I made it to the hall without either of the guards so much as batting an eye. I'd done it. Maybe not forever—maybe not even until the next day—but I'd done it. I had a weapon, and I was loose in the halls of the CDC. For one brief, drunken moment, I fantasized about opening fire and running like hell, heading for the nearest exit and never looking back. It would never have worked. It would have been a poor way to repay Dr. Shaw and Gregory for arming me. But God, I wanted to do it.

The only thing that stopped me was knowing that Shaun really was alive, somewhere. If I ran, they'd shoot me. I was smart enough to know that. And then Shaun would be alone again, in a world where people would do this sort of thing to a girl who'd been innocently going about the business of being dead. He needed to be warned. I needed to survive long enough to be the one who warned him. They could make another Georgia Mason if I didn't survive . . . but I wanted it to be me. Not some other girl who shared my memories. *Me.*

Dr. Thomas scowled all the way back to my room. He didn't say a word, and neither did the guards. Once we were there, he slapped his palm against the exterior sensor to open my door, and spoke his first words since we left the lab: "Do you need to use the lavatory?"

"Not right now," I said. "I am hungry, though."

"Your diet is still restricted, but I'll see about having some soup sent." His eyes flicked to my hair, expression hardening. "You may have to wait. I recognize that you have little experience with waiting."

"I didn't ask her to cut my hair," I said, too annoyed by the way he was looking at me to watch what I was saying. "She did it so she could get the sensors to stay on. Sensors she glued down with *slime mold*, mind you. I think I've paid for this haircut."

"I'm sure you didn't argue with her either, Georgia. If you don't need to use the facilities, you can enter your room now."

"Thank you," I said sourly, and kept my head up as I walked inside. The door slid shut behind me, leaving me with the appearance of solitude. It was a lie—it was always a lie. I was being watched, possibly even by Dr. Thomas, who could be standing on the other side of that stupid mirror for all that I knew. I never thought I'd miss my fucked-up eyes. Then I died, and I learned that there are things a lot worse than needing to wear sunglasses all the time. Things like being spied on, knowing you're being spied on, and not being able to do a damn thing about it.

Lacking anything else to do to distract myself, I climbed into bed. Eventually, the lights were dimmed. I closed my eyes, feigning sleep, and waited.

False sleep turned into the real thing at some point. I awoke to the sound of the door sliding open. Sitting bolt upright, I squinted into the glare from the hall, trying to make out the figure standing there. Even shading my eyes with my hand couldn't turn him into anything more than an outline.

"It's all right, Georgia," said a familiar voice—Gregory. He motioned for me to get up, the gesture clear even without fine details. "Come on. If you want to understand what's really going on here, you need to come with me."

"I'm coming," I said. Taking a breath to steady my nerves, I slid out of the bed and walked to the door, where the chance to get my answers was waiting.

Book II

Lost Souls

Fuck survivor's guilt. I'm not supposed to be the guilty one here. The people who made me the last man standing . . . they're the guilty ones. And they're the ones who should be afraid.

—Shaun Mason

There are three things in this world that I truly believe in. That the truth will set us free; that lies are the prisons we build for ourselves; and that Shaun loves me. Everything else is just details.

—Georgia Mason

Tomorrow morning, my boss and Becks will be heading to Berkeley to deal with his crazy parents. Why? So they can get a map to lead them past the government barricades between here and Florida. Maybe. If my boss's crazy parents don't sell them out for the ratings boost. And once they get there, they'll have to deal with government patrols, rampaging zombies, killer mosquitoes, and God knows what else, all of which are going to try to kill them. Why are they doing all this?

To get my sister safely back to me. I don't know whether to be grateful to them for going, or ashamed of the fact that I'm genuinely glad it's not going to be me out there. I'm even glad I'm not going to Seattle with Maggie, and I think I'm about halfway in love with her.

I guess I'm a coward after all.

—From *The Kwong Way of Things*, the blog of Alaric Kwong, July 23, 2041. Unpublished.

Let us, who are the lost ones, go and kneel
  before the dead;
Let us beg them for their mercy over all we
  left unsaid,
And as the sun sinks slowly, the horizon
  bleeding red,
Perhaps they'll show us kindness,
Grant forgiveness for our blindness,
Perhaps they'll show us how to find the
  roads we need to tread.

Let us, who are the lost ones, ask the
    fallen where to turn,
When it seems that all the world is lost,
    and we can only burn,
For in dying they have learned the things
    that we have yet to learn.
Perhaps they'll see our yearning,
And may help us in returning
To the lands where we were innocent, that
    we have yet to earn . . .

—From *The Lost Ones*, originally posted in *Dandelion Mine*, the blog of Magdalene Grace Garcia, July 23, 2041. Unpublished.

Eight

Becks slammed her back against the open door, keeping it pinned against the wall. That gave her a good vantage position on the rest of the room, while defending her against rear attacks. She held her pistol in front of her in a classic shooting stance that would have sold a thousand promotional posters for her blog if she'd been wearing something other than jeans and a bleach-spotted gray tank top.

I couldn't admire the precision of her pose; I had issues of my own to worry about, like the screaming lab technicians running for the doors. Half a dozen of our previously captured zombies were shambling after the fleeing technicians. Three former technicians were shambling with them, only their increased speed and bloody lab coats distinguishing them from the rest of the mob. All the zombies were moaning in a pitch that made my bones itch. No one knows why zombies moan. They just do, and it's enough to drive you crazy if you listen to it too long.

Mahir stopped behind me, managing only a startled "Oh dear Lord . . ." before I whirled and shoved him back.

"Get in the van," I snapped. "Lock the doors, engage the security. If we don't come back for you, drive. Drive until you get back to England, if you have to."

"Shaun—"

"You're not made for fieldwork! Now get back in there!"

"Don't argue, Mahir," said Becks. Her tone was calm, like she was asking us not to raise our voices during a business meeting. "I need his gun, and you're not equipped for this."

Mahir's mouth set in a thin line, and for a moment, he looked like he was seriously pissed. Someone else screamed in the main room, the sound cutting off with a gurgle that told me the infected had stopped trying to spread the virus, and started trying to feed.

"Get the others on the com," I said, more gently. "Make sure they're safe, and that they've managed to get themselves under cover. I don't want to lose anyone today."

The line of Mahir's mouth softened slightly as he nodded. "Be careful," he said, and turned to walk toward the van. I watched him just long enough to be sure he was actually going to get inside.

"Any time now, Mason," said Becks. The moaning was getting louder. So were the screams. The fact that we hadn't been attacked yet was nothing short of a miracle—one we could probably attribute to the fact that we were standing relatively still in a room full of much more active targets. Faced with a choice between someone who isn't moving and someone who is, a zombie almost always goes for the runner. It's something in their psychology, or in what passes for psychology inside the virus-riddled sack of goo that used to be a human brain.

"On it," I said, and turned to face the main room, bracing myself in the doorway. As long as we held our positions, we knew we had a clear line of retreat.

"About fucking time," said Becks, tracking the progress of one of the infected with her gun. As soon as one of us fired a shot, they'd stop looking at us like furniture and start looking at us as potential meals. That would be bad. Even if I was immune, Becks wasn't, and immunity wouldn't stop them from tearing me apart. "Got any bright ideas?"

"Prayer would be good, if either of us believed in a higher power."

Becks's eyes widened, disrupting her carefully schooled expression. "I don't say this often, but you're a genius."

"Because I don't believe in God?" I trained my gun on another of the infected, one that was drawing a bit too close to our position for me to be comfortable. The screams seemed to be getting quieter. I had to hope that was because most of the technicians were out of danger, and not because most of them were dead.

"No. Because there *is* a higher power at work here." Becks removed one hand from her gun long enough to tap her ear cuff, saying in a calm, clear voice, "Open general connection, main lab." There was a single loud beep.

Too loud. The nearest of the infected looked up from her meal—the torso of a technician whose name had either been Jimmy or Johnny; I wasn't sure, and it didn't matter now. Her eyes searched the area, looking for new prey, and settled on Becks. With a low moan, she stood.

"Becks, whatever you're doing, do it fast," I muttered, adjusting my stance so that I was aiming directly at the standing infected. "Once the shooting starts, this is going to turn into one hell of a duck hunt."

"I can handle myself," she said. More of the infected were turning to face us, their attention attracted by the strange silence of the one nearest our position.

Steady, cautioned George. I thought I felt her fingers ghost across the back of my neck, and that was more frightening than anything else about our situation. If I started hallucinating during combat, there was no telling who I'd shoot, or what I'd let get past me.

"Not now," I whispered. "Please, not now."

Becks's ear cuff beeped again, and Dr. Abbey's voice said loudly, "A little busy right now, children! Maybe you could do something to help with that?" Joe—her English mastiff—was barking in the background, almost drowning out the sound of moaning.

"Working on it," said Becks. She must have realized there was no way we could fade back out of sight. The sound of Joe barking would have guaranteed that, even if nothing else could. "Mahir's secure, but the lab's in chaos. What's your twenty?"

Dr. Abbey's answer was drowned out by the local infected, all of whom started moaning at the top of their lungs as they lunged, shambled, and even ran toward us. "Less talky more shooty!" I snapped, and started firing.

"We'll be there," said Becks. She tilted her head, studying our onrushing attackers, and chose her first two shots with an almost languid care. Two of the infected went down, each with a hole in the middle of its forehead.

"Show-off," I muttered, and kept firing, trying to assess the tactical options presented by the room. I counted eight active infected in closing range; five of those were old, probably from the most recent batch of catches, while the other three wore lab coats and scrubs that identified them as former members of Dr. Abbey's staff. I recognized one of them as the tech I'd yelled at the day before for being careless around the infected.

Guess he'd learned his lesson, even if it hadn't done him any good. Anyway, those three would be the fastest movers, and the slowest to react. The virus that drove their bodies was still adjusting to being in control. Even the smartest zombie is pretty damn stupid, but new zombies are the dumbest, nastiest of them all.

I don't think they've got the density to start reasoning, said George.

I nodded, acknowledging her words, and stepped forward as I kept firing. "Becks! Fall in, and tell me where we're going!"

"On it, Boss!" She moved to flank me, our shoulders almost touching as we began to make our way forward. The door, freed from her weight, swung shut, slamming with an ominous bang. "Dr. Abbey's in her office on the second floor! They're holding the line, but they can't do it forever!"

"Got it!" I took aim and fired again, silently counting my bullets.

There were two of us; that was good. That meant we might have time to reload, assuming we didn't both run out at the same time. I had a second pistol on my belt, for emergencies—and this qualified—but I didn't have my cattle prod, or anything as convenient as, say, a brace of grenades. That would teach me not to stay fully armed at all times.

"Look at it this way." Becks shot a former technician in the throat, sending the man backward. We continued to advance, moving in smooth, long-practiced tandem. "If we run out of bullets, we can just let them chew on you for a little while."

"I feel much better." I fired again. One of the older infected went down. "Any idea how many of these things we're dealing with?"

"Not a fucking clue!"

"My favorite kind of duck hunt." My breathing was starting to settle, the adrenaline in my bloodstream slipping away. The endorphins that replaced it were soothing, my old, familiar drug of choice. This was the feeling that used to drive me into the field with a baseball bat and a cocky grin, this floating, flying, nothing-can-hurt-me feeling. Georgia's death clipped my wings. In moments like this, I could almost forget that. There were no voices in my head that shouldn't be there, but they were replaced by contentment, and not the yawning void that usually opened when George stopped talking. This used to be what I lived for. I couldn't live for it anymore. But oh, God, I missed it.

Fire. Step forward. Fire. Becks ducked behind me, letting me cover her while she reloaded her gun. I pulled my second pistol, buying us a few more steps before she needed to repeat the favor.

"This is not cool," I muttered. "Becks? You got another reload on you?"

"No," she said grimly.

"Didn't think so. On my signal, we're going to run."

I didn't need to see her face to know what her expression looked like. "That's a *terrible* idea."

"So is staying here! Either Dr. Abbey's been doing independent collections, or the locals called for friends. Either way," I aimed, fired, and took down another zombie, "we're going to run out of bullets before we run out of walking corpses. We run or we die. Got a preference?"

"I like running."

"Good. One . . ." I took another shot. This one went wild, barely grazing the zombie I was aiming for.

"Two . . ."

"Three!" I shoved Becks in the direction of the stairs, firing rapidly to cover her. She'd been right about one thing; if one of us was going to get chewed on, it needed to be me. One bite and it was game over for her. I'd consider a few more scars to be a fair trade for getting Becks out of this alive.

They can still kill you, hissed George.

"Maybe I deserve it," I replied, and ran after Becks.

One nice thing about stairs: Zombies can navigate them, but they can't do it fast. There's a certain comedy to watching them try, as long as you're not in a position to get knocked over by an infected body tumbling back down to the ground floor after it manages to misjudge the positioning of its feet. A few zombies had already fallen by the time we reached the bottom step.

Becks shot the first of them and ran on, leaving me to take out the other two. Both of them were wearing lab coats. They moaned, reaching for me. I grimaced as I jumped over them, and paused long enough to turn back and shoot them in the head. It took a few seconds to be absolutely sure they were dead, not just incapacitated. I spent the time. I knew these people. I might not know their names, but I knew them, and this was at least partially my fault. I could have forced Dr. Abbey to up her security. I could have helped more. I could have stopped this from happening.

You need to stop taking responsibility for things that aren't your fault, said George, sounding cranky enough that I could almost see her frown.

"You need to stop telling me that things aren't my fault," I countered, turning to shoot a zombie that had been lurching up behind me. It went down hard. I kept my gun raised and began backing up the stairs, scanning the lab below me. The occasional gunshot from above told me that Becks was doing her part to clear the landing.

My ear cuff beeped. I jerked my chin upward, answering the call. "Kinda busy, so this better be good."

"Maggie's upstairs, locked in one of the cold storage rooms. She's not injured, but she's bloody pissed at whoever it was that shoved her in there," said Mahir. "Dr. Abbey says she made contact with Becks?"

"We're en route now." I took another shot. That left three. Four if I decided to use all my bullets, rather than going with the traditional approach to zombie-killing, and saving the last one for myself. The thought made me crack a smile. Saving bullets for myself was something I didn't have to worry about anymore.

You are so fucking morbid, muttered George.

"Learned from the best," I replied. There were only two visible zombies left on the floor, and both of them had been infected for long enough that they were moving slowly, in that classic Romero shuffle. Better yet, killing so many of their pack mates meant the viral intelligence driving them all had been reduced from mob level smarts back to individual stupidity.

No one knows why zombies get smarter when you have a bunch of them in one place, but they do, and it's a problem. Tactics that work against one or two lone undead will get you killed when you go up against a mob. I've seen them demonstrate complicated hunting techniques, like actual ambush preparation, and it's scary as hell. If nothing else, it forces you to remember that the things inside those rotting shells used to be human, and on some level, still might be. They just got sick. It could happen to anybody.

Anybody but me.

"Shaun? Shaun, are you there? Shaun?" Mahir's voice in my ear dragged me out of my thoughts and back into the situation.

"Sorry, just assessing." I turned, running up the stairs. Becks was waiting on the landing. She had her gun up, and was braced against the banister; two infected were shambling toward her, neither moving fast enough to be a major threat at their current distance. She was letting them set up the shot. It's a classic field tactic, and a good way to save your ammunition. There was just one problem with it.

If there were only two zombies out here, where was all that moaning coming from?

"What's your assessment?" asked Becks.

"We're fucked. Where's Alaric? I'm pissed off, I'm almost out of bullets, and I'm not having any *fun*." And that, right there, was the reason I stopped doing active fieldwork, even before we stopped really being a news site. You can't be a professional Irwin when you can't at least pretend to enjoy what you're doing. It doesn't work. The center does not hold.

"He's with Dr. Abbey."

"Good."

Becks took the first of her shots as I reached her. The zombie went down. She didn't even glance in my direction. "We clear below, Mason?"

"Two zombies, both too uncoordinated to handle the stairs. I made an executive decision. We need to conserve bullets more than we need to perfectly secure the area."

"Well, just don't forget that they're down there and sound the all-clear without going back to mop up your mess." She squeezed off her second shot. This wasn't a clean hit; her bullet took the infected in the throat, reducing it to a mass of torn flesh and visible bone. It kept shuffling forward.

"Uh, Becks—"

"One," she said. "Two. Three . . ."

The zombie went down, the virally enhanced clotting factors in its blood finally giving up the task of repairing the arteries shredded by her bullet.

"Three," she said, and flashed me a self-satisfied smile. "Just like getting to the center of a Tootsie Pop."

"Did you know they made that commercial in the 1970s?" I asked. There were no more infected in sight. The moaning in the distance continued. "How are you for bullets?"

"I did know that, yes. Three bullets left. You?"

"Four."

"Great. Let's hope this party isn't strictly BYOB." She turned and ran in the direction of the dead.

"We're on our way, Mahir," I said, and ran after her.

"Do they train you people to say stupid things when in mortal danger? I'm just curious, you understand, I'm not judging you."

"Yes, you are."

"Yes, I am."

"There are classes." I followed Becks around a corner, skidding to a halt. "Uh, Mahir? I'm going to need to call you back."

"What are you—"

I reached up to tap my ear cuff, breaking the connection. Becks raised her hand, signaling for silence. I nodded understanding. And then we both just stood there, staring at the five-deep wall of zombies that was trying to claw its way through the door into Dr. Abbey's office. They weren't paying any attention to us yet. That was the good part. The bad part was that they would inevitably either break down that door or lose interest in what was behind it, and either way, we'd eventually wind up on the menu.

"Here," I mouthed, pressing my gun into Becks's hand. I shook my head at her questioning expression, nodding back the way we'd come. Slow understanding bloomed in her face, and she nodded, pressing herself against the wall as I turned and crept quietly away. Once I was back in the main hall, out of sight of the infected, I broke into a run.

This floor's armory was located at the far end of the building, in what used to be a bathroom. Dr. Abbey's technicians couldn't get the water working in the corroded old second-story pipes, and so the room had been converted to hold all the weapons of mass destruction that a bunch of geeks who insisted on playing with dead things could possibly need. I don't know what science geeks were like before the Rising, but these days? After seeing the kind of armaments they pack, you couldn't pay me to get on their bad side.

It was just too bad they hadn't been carrying more of those armaments while they were "at home" in the lab. Maybe I wouldn't have needed to shoot so many of them.

I passed the bodies of three dead technicians as I ran. Really dead—they'd been torn apart, practically shredded by the hungry infected. Their screams probably saved the lives of everyone who was now huddling behind a locked door. The people who ran toward the trouble—or toward the armory, wanting to get ready to face the trouble head-on—had been the second wave of victims. That was how it almost always went in an outbreak. The first wave dies. The second wave rises.

The last of the bodies was right in front of the armory door, fallen like he had almost reached it when they finally managed to run him down. I grimaced as I stepped over him, leaning into the armory to turn on the light.

The zombie that had been lurking there lunged, the moan escaping from its lipless mouth bare seconds before the startled shout of "Whoa!" escaped from mine. I managed to jerk my arm back before it could get its teeth into me, and they clacked shut on empty air. The zombie lunged again.

"Back off, ugly!" I grabbed it by the hair, using its own momentum as I shoved it past me, into the hallway. If Dr. Abbey was wrong about my being immune, I was going to regret that in a minute. I would have regretted it a hell of a lot more if the thing had managed to get its teeth into me.

The zombie stumbled as I released it, taking several steps forward before it could get its balance back and remember how to turn itself around. I took advantage of those precious seconds, darting into the armory and looking frantically around me. I didn't use this room very often. We had our own equipment, and while Dr. Abbey was perfectly willing to be generous with the ammo, she usually didn't want us fetching it ourselves. The grenades were—were—

"Over here, Shaun," said George. I turned. She was standing in the far corner of the room, next to a stack of beautifully familiar olive-green boxes. "This what you were looking for?"

"Yeah. Thanks, George."

"Not a problem. Now kill your friend." She was abruptly gone, blinking out like she had never been there at all. That was reasonable. She *hadn't* been there.

I grabbed the nearest pistol that looked like it might be loaded—bad gun safety, good zombie safety, it balances—and whirled, taking aim right at the place I estimated my dead friend's head would be. "Bang, ugly," I said, and pulled the trigger.

Thank God for paranoia and overpreparedness. The gun barked and a large chunk of the zombie's skull vanished, transformed into red mist and a hail of bone fragments. I shoved the pistol into my belt and tapped my ear cuff, heading for the back of the room.

"Shaun?"

"Mahir, listen. If you can get a connection to Becks, tell her she needs to back up. I'm coming in with grenades." I grabbed guns as I walked, dropping anything too light to be loaded and cramming the rest into my belt. If I was making a last stand, I was doing it so ridiculously overprepared that I'd rattle when I walked.

Mahir sighed deeply. "Of course you are. Couldn't you try something a little less, I don't know, insanely idiotic?"

"I could, but they don't have a flamethrower here. Now let her know."

"I'm on it." The connection died.

Grabbing the top box of grenades, I paused only long enough to check that its contents were both intact and well secured. Then I ran.

Becks met me halfway down the hall, somehow managing to run silently in her combat boots. There was one more skill I'd never mastered. "What are you *doing*?" she demanded, tone barely above a whisper. "Mahir called me! He said you told him to do it! I could've been killed! Are you really planning to use *grenades*?"

"You got a better idea?"

"No, but the risk of structural damage—"

"Is minimal. Are the zombies where you left them?"

"What? Yes."

"Then you *would* have been killed if you'd still been in that hallway." I kept moving, holding the box up just enough for her to see the shape of it. "I'm going to aerosolize me some dead guys."

"You're insane."

"Yeah, probably." I pulled the first pistol I'd snagged out of my waistband, passing it to her. "Stay out here and guard my back. Oh, and if you could call Dr. Abbey and tell her to turn off the lab ventilation system until the spray settles, that would probably be good. I don't want to zombie-out the whole room trying to save them."

"You're *dangerously* insane," Becks amended—but she took the pistol, and added a quick, "Good luck," before retreating farther down the hall.

I felt better knowing she was out there. One close call per day is pretty much my limit. I walked until I reached the end of the short hall leading to Dr. Abbey's lab. The zombies were still trying to claw their way inside, their moaning echoing through the confined space until it seemed loud enough to drive a man insane. They were still focused on the prey in front of them, and not on things moving around behind them. That was good. I'd be changing that in a moment, but for now, distracted zombies were in my best interests.

Putting the box of concussion grenades on the floor, I opened the lid and pulled out the top two. They were designed for use in situations like this one, and would do maximal damage to soft tissue—such as zombies—while doing minimal structural damage to the building surrounding the zombies. They were usually used for large government extermination runs. A series of helpful cartoon thumbnails on the inside lid of the box used stick figures and the universal sign for NO to remind me that I shouldn't use concussion grenades without putting on a gas mask first, since aerosolized zombie isn't good for anybody.

"Too bad I have no respect for safety precautions," I muttered, and pulled the pin on the first grenade.

I might be willing to stand in the open air while I created a fine red mist of viral particulates, but that didn't make me stupid. I chucked the first grenade into the middle of the mob, causing about half of them to turn in my direction. I threw the second grenade about three feet in front of the mob. Then I ran, pausing only to grab two more grenades out of the top of the box. I pulled the pins and threw them behind me, into the path of the onrushing mob.

One, said George. *Two, three . . .*

"Four, five," I added, and kept running.

The first grenade went off with a low crumping sound, muffled enough to tell me that it had been buried by a substantial number of bodies when it exploded. The other three went off in rapid succession, each of them a little louder and less cushioned by the weight of the bodies on top of it. I kept running. When Becks came into sight ahead of me, I stepped to the side, giving her a clear line of fire, and pulled two of the guns from my waistband.

"God, I wish we had cameras on this," I said . . . and then the infected who'd managed to survive my little party tricks came shambling and running down the hall, and I forgot about cameras in favor of keeping us both alive.

They were a sorry-looking bunch, even for zombies. It's true that you can kill a zombie with trauma to the body; once they lose enough blood, or a sufficient number of major internal organs, they'll die like everybody else. The trouble is that they don't feel pain like uninfected humans do, and they can keep going long after their injuries would have incapacitated a normal person. Some of the zombies making their way down the hall were missing arms, hands, even feet—those stomped along on the shattered remains of their ankles, shins, or knees, giving them a drunken gait that was somehow more horrifying than the normal zombie shuffle. One had a piece of grenade shrapnel stuck all the way through his cheek, wedged at an angle that would make it impossible for him to bite even if he managed to grab us. That wasn't going to stop him from trying.

"Becks? You clear?"

"Clear!" came the shout from behind me.

"Great," I said, and opened fire.

The bad thing about setting up a kill chute like the one we were in is that it can just as easily turn into a "die" chute. The good thing about setting up a kill chute—the reason that people keep using them, and have been using them since the Rising—is that as long as your ammo holds out and you don't lose your head, you can do a hell of a lot of damage without letting the dead get within more than about ten feet of you.

The injuries to our mob were extensive enough that most of them weren't moving very quickly, and the ones who'd been shielded from the worst of the blast by the bodies of their companions were hampered in their efforts to move forward by those same bodies. The fast zombies got mired in the slow zombies, and their efforts to break free of the mob just slowed everything down a little more. Becks and I didn't bother aiming for the fast ones. We just went for the head and throat shots, and kept on knocking them down.

"Shaun!" called Becks. "Dr. Abbey just called! They're opening the lab door!"

"Awesome!" I shouted back, barely a second before gunfire started from the direction of the lab. I fell back several yards, pulling another gun from my waistband and holding it out behind me. "Reload?"

"Thanks." Becks snatched the pistol from my hand, taking aim on another of the infected. "So this is fun. This is a fun time."

"Sure." I fired twice, taking down two more zombies. I was about to shoot a third one when Joe came bounding into my line of fire. He grabbed a zombie by the leg, shaking so hard that the entire leg came off. The gunfire continued behind him, but for Joe, the party was all out here in the hall.

It probably says something about Dr. Abbey that she named her massive black English mastiff after her dead husband and used him for illegal medical experiments. I'm not sure *what* it says, exactly. I just know that Joe is now functionally immune to Kellis-Amberlee—he can get sick, but he can't go into conversion—and that meant that the enormous, angry carnivore now spreading zombie guts around the hall was on our side. Thank God for that.

"That's disgusting," said Becks, and shot a zombie who was continuing to advance on our position, ignoring the chaos behind him. "Oh, jeez. Is that a spleen?"

"I think that's a spleen, yes." I fired one more time, taking down a zombie that had gotten a little too close for comfort. Joe looked toward the sound of the shot, ears perked up questioningly, and barked once. "It's cool, Joe. We're not hurt."

"How cute. The giant dog is concerned."

"Someone's got to be." I leaned against the rail, watching Joe work. The gunshots from behind him were starting to taper off. Only three zombies that I could see were still making any real progress, and all of them were badly wounded. Becks raised her gun to fire. I pushed her arm gently down again. "Let him have his fun. He's had a long day, and he deserves the chance to kill some things."

"If you say so." Becks looked at me, seeming to tune out the sounds of slaughter coming from the hall in front of us. She frowned. "You have blood in your hair. And on your face."

"Great. I've been exposed. Dr. Abbey will be thrilled."

The gunshots from the hall had stopped. Becks and I exchanged a look, nodded, and waited where we were for a few more minutes before starting to make our way in that direction. Joe barked again as we approached him, the sound only slightly garbled by the fact that he had most of a human throat in his mouth.

"Don't talk with your mouth full," I told him. He dropped the throat, chuffing happily, and fell into step beside us. I patted his blood-tacky head with one hand. "Good dog." There was no possible way of minimizing my exposure at this point. I might as well just go with it.

Dr. Abbey, Alaric, and four of her technicians were in the hall, their faces covered by ventilator masks and eye protectors. "You made it," she said, sounding unsurprised. "Are we secure?"

"Not quite. There are at least three shamblers on the ground floor, Mahir's in the van, and Maggie's locked in a storage room," I replied. "Alaric? You okay, buddy?"

"Shaken, but intact," he said.

"Good." I looked to Dr. Abbey. "I've been exposed."

"There's a shocker." She shook her head, shoulders slumping. She looked tired. That wasn't normal. Not for Dr. Abbey. "Help with the cleanup, and I'll get blood test kits for both of you. Shaun—"

"I know, I know," I said. "I'll be donating a few more vials to the cause of science."

"We're still leaving in the morning," said Becks. I turned to blink at her. She shrugged. "There's always something, isn't there? We have to go. It's never going to stop long enough for there to be a good time."

"She's right," said Alaric. "Alisa can't wait."

"Well, then, I guess we're leaving in the morning," I said. "Let's get this place cleaned up, and figure out what happened with the security. Oh, and can someone go let Maggie out before she kills us all?" I looked at the mess surrounding us, and sighed inwardly.

It was going to be a long night.

We lost over a dozen techs, Joey—people who've been working with me for years, people who trusted me to keep them safe. And for what? So I could learn some more things we already knew? This was my fault. Half the people who were bitten knew better than to engage the infected the way they did, but they believed the treatment I've been working on could protect them, and they weren't careful enough. Looking into Laurie's post-conversion eyes . . . it was enough to break my heart. Shaun Mason may hold the answer to this pandemic, but if he does, I haven't found it yet.

I know you don't think I should send them to Florida. I have to. We need to know what they used when they built those mosquitoes—and I need to know who built them. If I can pick apart their genetic structure, we may stand a chance in hell.

—Taken from an e-mail sent by Dr. Shannon Abbey to Dr. Joseph Shoji at the Kauai Institute of Virology, July 24, 2041.

I don't know how much longer I can do this. I don't know how much longer I can keep convincing my team that I can do this. I don't know how much longer I can trust myself to keep them alive.

And I don't know if I could live with myself if I didn't keep trying.

We've been frozen here, just like we were frozen in Weed, back when the world seemed a lot less fucked up. It's time to start moving again, and I'm terrified, and I'm so damn relieved. I don't think I'll be coming out of this alive. I'm going to go out there, find out what really happened to George, make sure the whole damn world knows what she died for, and then I'm going to come home, and I'm going to go to where she is. I don't know how much longer I can do this, but that's okay, because I'm not going to be doing it for much longer.

—From *Adaptive Immunities*, the blog of Shaun Mason, July 24, 2041. Unpublished.

Nine

Gregory motioned for silence as we left my room. I nodded, for once grateful for my lack of shoes. My socks didn't squeak against the tile. Somehow, he managed to walk so that his shoes didn't make any noise, and we passed through the darkened CDC building like ghosts.

The door at the end of the hall was open, the light above it glowing a steady amber. Alarm lanced through me. Green lights mean there's no danger; red lights mean the danger is near. Amber lights mean something has gone wrong.

Gregory's hand landed on my shoulder, stopping me before I could do more than stiffen. "It's part of our window," he said, keeping his voice low. "Come on. We're almost there."

"Where are we going?" I asked, taking his words as license to break my own silence. He led me through the door and into another hall, one I'd seen only in passing, when they were taking me from one lab to another.

"Someplace they'd rather you didn't see," he said. He didn't need to tell me who "they" were. "They" were the people who'd brought me back from the dead, and who gave Dr. Thomas his orders. "They" were the people behind all of this.

"So it's something that's going to cause me some of that stress they're so interested in minimizing," I guessed, more for the comfort of speaking than out of any serious desire to have my thoughts validated.

"You could say that," Gregory said. We reached a corner. He raised a hand, signaling me to stop, and stepped around it alone. "We're clear. Come on."

I came.

We walked to another door with an amber light above it. This one led to a hall I hadn't seen before. It was less pristine than the others. There were whiteboards on the walls, scribbled with notes about cafeteria menus and security sweeps. There were even a few flyers taped up, advertising cars for sale or asking if anyone knew a good tutoring service for high school biochemistry. It looked so much more real than the place I'd been since I woke up, so much more *human*, that it almost made my chest hurt. The world still existed. I'd died and come back, and the whole time I was gone, the world continued.

Gregory started walking faster, saying, "We're almost there. We allowed six minutes transit each way, which gives us fifteen minutes at our destination. I'm going to need you calm at the end of that time. I can't drag you down these halls if you're not working with me."

"Meaning what?" I asked, trying to sound like my stomach wasn't balling itself into a small, hard knot of fear.

"Meaning that if you lose it, I'll leave you." The words were kindly spoken—he wasn't trying to be cruel, just stating a fact. If I couldn't control myself, he'd leave me. The other half of that statement didn't need to be spoken: The EIS couldn't afford to have his cover blown because I couldn't keep myself calm. If he left me, he probably wouldn't be leaving me alive.

"I understand."

"Good," he said. He stopped at a door marked Authorized Personnel Only, producing a thumb drive from his pocket. He plugged it into the side of the blood testing unit. The unit beeped twice, and the light above the door went out. Gregory put his hand on the doorknob, but didn't turn it. Instead, he looked at me gravely and asked, "Are you ready?"

"No," I said. "I'm pretty sure I've never been ready for anything that had to be prefaced with that question. Now open the door."

A small smile crossed his lips. "That's the answer I wanted to hear," he said, and opened the door, revealing a darkened lab. A dim blue glow filled the back third of the room. I looked back at Gregory, raising my eyebrows. "It's okay," he said. "Go on."

"There's an invitation to die for," I said, and stepped across the threshold. The overhead lights clicked on immediately, starting low and climbing to a normal level of illumination. I appreciated that small courtesy. I may not be as photosensitive as I used to be, but that doesn't mean I enjoy being blinded.

Gregory stepped in behind me, closing the door. "Here we are," he said.

"Where is 'here,' exactly?" I asked, squinting as I looked around the room. It looked like it had been cast from the same mold as all the other CDC labs I'd visited, with undecorated walls, stain-proof linoleum floors, and lots of equipment I didn't recognize. My heart leapt a little at the one thing I *did* recognize: a computer terminal.

Gregory followed my gaze and grimaced, looking genuinely sorry as he said, "I can't let you get on the Internet from here, Georgia. It's not safe."

"But—"

"That's not why we're here." He nodded toward the back of the room. The blue glow was less evident now that the lights were on, but it was still there.

"Right," I muttered, and turned to look in that direction. From where I was, it looked like a fish tank filled with luminescent blue liquid. I frowned and started toward it, trying to figure out what it was, and why it was important enough for Gregory to risk both our lives by bringing me here.

I think, on some level, that I knew what it was even before I saw it; I just had to put off understanding for as long as possible if I wanted to be able to handle what I was about to see. But maybe that's hindsight, me trying to justify things to myself. I don't really know. What I do know is this:

The blue liquid wasn't fully opaque; it just looked that way from a distance. It cleared as I approached, and by the time I reached the tank, I could see the outline of a human figure through the blue. I squinted, but couldn't make out any real details beyond the fact that it was female, and surrounded by a forest of tangled cords.

Gregory stepped up behind me and leaned to my left, pressing a button at the top of a control panel I hadn't noticed until then. The glow brightened, and the liquid began turning transparent, small lines of bubbles marking the spots where filters were cleansing some element out of the mix. In only a few seconds, I could see the figure floating in the tank.

She was naked, in her mid-twenties, and curled in a loose fetal position, like she had never needed to support her own limbs or head. Her hair was dark brown and badly needed to be cut. It was long enough that the movement of the liquid around her made it eddy slowly, wrapping around her neck and arms. Sensors were connected to her arms and legs, running up to join with the main cable. Her mouth and nose were exposed—she was breathing the liquid; I could see her chest rise and fall—and a thicker tube was connected at her belly button, presumably providing her with oxygen and nutrients. I stared at her, watching the way her fingers twitched and her eyes moved behind the thin shields of her eyelids.

Gregory waited, watching me watch her. The room seemed to be holding its breath, both of us waiting to see what I would do, whether I would be able to look at what was in front of me without snapping. For a moment, I didn't know the answer.

The moment passed. I took a shaky breath, followed it with another, and asked, "How many of us are there?"

"At the moment, three." Gregory turned his attention to the tank where another Georgia Mason floated. Her hair had never been bleached, and was still the dark brown that mine was supposed to be. I felt a brief flare of jealousy. She looked more like me than I did. "This is subject number 8c. It's the last member of the subject group following yours."

"Wait—subject group?" I turned my back on the tank, unsure of my ability to keep my cool while I watched my own silent doppelganger floating in the blue. "What does *that* mean?"

"Your designation is 'subject 7c.' Subject 7a didn't mature properly; 7b went into spontaneous amplification during the revivification process." He gestured at the tank. "Subject 8a was shut down due to issues with spinal maturation at about this stage."

"And 8b?" He wasn't using names for any of the other subjects, I noticed—he wasn't even giving them genders. They were just things to him, at least until the moment they woke up and turned into people. That was actually reassuring, because he treated *me* like a person. I wasn't the same as them.

I wasn't.

"Subject 8b is part of why we're here. Subject 8c is just the backup, in case something goes wrong." Gregory looked at me carefully. "Are you ready to proceed?"

"You mean, do I want to scream and throw things and maybe vomit, but can I keep myself together a little longer? Yes, and yes." I shook my head, taking comfort in the fact that I could feel the air against my ears. I might have started out like that girl in the tank, but I wasn't her anymore. I was awake, and alive, and my hair had been cut. We have to take our comforts where we can find them.

"All right," said Gregory. "Follow me."

He led me to a large metal rectangle on the far wall. He tapped a button on a control panel next to it, and stepped back as a whirring sound began to emanate from the wall itself. The metal rectangle slid slowly upward, revealing the room on the other side of the thick, industrial-grade glass. He tapped the control panel again, and the lights came on.

The walls of the room were featureless and white. The only thing that even resembled furniture was a narrow hospital bed with white sheets, surrounded by IV drips and beeping monitors. Thick black straps secured the room's single occupant to her bed, holding her in place. Unlike the girl in the tank—unlike me, when I first woke up—her hair was cut short, in a precise replica of the haircut I'd worn since I was twelve. I touched the close-shorn hair at the back of my neck without realizing I was going to do it, feeling how uneven the strands were. Dr. Shaw had done her best, but she was no hairdresser.

"This is 8b?" I asked. My voice was weaker than I wanted it to be. I swallowed hard, trying to clear away the dryness that was growing there. "What are they doing with her?"

"They're stabilizing her." Gregory touched another button. A video projection appeared on one side of the window, obscuring that half of the room. It showed subject 8b being removed from her tank and shifted onto a gurney. Her hair was long in the recording, and it stuck to her face and shoulders like seaweed. "This was taken a week ago."

"A week—but that was after they knew that I wasn't going to amplify. They knew I was viable." Panic tried to rise inside me like a small, biting animal. I forced it down again as hard as I could, breathing in and out through my nose several times before I asked, "Why are they stabilizing her? What are they planning to *do* with her?"

Gregory touched another button. The recording skipped, the image of the extraction being replaced by an image of the clone, now clean, clothed, and dry, with her head held up by a wedge-shaped foam pillow. Voices were speaking softly, just offscreen. I almost jumped when Dr. Thomas said, in a loud, clear tone, "Georgia, open your eyes."

And the recording of subject 8b opened her eyes.

A squeaky moaning sound escaped my lips before I could hold it in. Gregory put a hand on my shoulder, but he didn't say anything. There was nothing for him to say.

Her eyes were black, her pupils so enlarged that there was no band of color between them and the surrounding sclera. Shark's eyes, zombie eyes . . . or the eyes of a person with retinal Kellis-Amberlee, the reservoir condition I'd lived with for most of my life. With those eyes, she looked more like me than I ever could. Someone who was shown a picture of me would probably allow that I looked a lot like a reporter who died during the Ryman campaign. Someone who was shown a picture of *her* . . .

"How?" I managed to rasp.

"Surgical alteration," said Gregory. He took his hand off my shoulder. "They couldn't induce a specific reservoir condition—when they tried, it either caused immediate amplification, or it triggered a reservoir condition in a different part of the body. Getting one with stable retinal Kellis-Amberlee in both eyes could have taken years."

I didn't say anything.

"They've had to do more procedures than originally planned. It turns out we don't really understand the changes retinal Kellis-Amberlee makes to the structure of the eye as well as we thought we did. As soon as they removed the irises, the retinas began to detach. They've been replaced with artificial lenses, and the eyes have been stabilized."

And since I was known to have retinal Kellis-Amberlee, no one would raise any red flags over anomalies in her retinal scans, and the surgical tampering would never be caught. "Slick," I said. My voice sounded flat, like all the emotion had been somehow pressed out of it. That was a reasonably accurate assessment of how I was feeling. I swallowed again, and asked, "How much time do I have?"

Gregory shot me a sharp look. "What do you mean?"

"They didn't fix my eyes. They wouldn't have fixed . . . her . . . eyes if they didn't expect people to see her. Logically, that means they didn't expect people to see *me*. If I was the finished product, they would have stopped once I was stable." My voice was starting to rise at the end of my sentences. I forced it back down, and repeated, "How much time do I have?"

"We think it'll take about two weeks for them to finish all the tests they have scheduled, and for them to get subject 8b all the way functional. Again, they expected everything to be ready sooner, but they don't want any lingering pain from the operations to distract from the recovery process."

I wouldn't have paid any special attention to my eyes hurting when I woke up. I'd been too busy freaking out over not being dead. I decided to let that go for the moment. "After that?"

"Another two weeks, to be sure the subject won't spontaneously amplify or suffer organ failure."

So that had been a genuine risk, not just another way to scare me. Funny thing; even knowing that, I was still scared plenty. "What's going to happen to me?"

"They're going to keep you as long as you stay useful, and then . . . " Gregory's voice trailed off. "I'm sorry."

I sighed. "Right. That was a bad question. Why are they doing this? Why waste all this time with me if they're just going to bring her out of her chemical coma and drop me down the incinerator chute? What are they *gaining* from keeping me around?"

"You're the display model. Why do you think Dr. Thomas was so upset when you went and got your hair cut? They want you to be as pretty as possible, to show the investors that this process is safe and painless and yields the best possible results." Gregory touched the control panel. The image of subject 8b's eyes vanished, replaced by a four-way split-screen of me being . . . me. Me, sitting on the bed, one leg tucked under my body, the other rhythmically kicking the mattress. Me, pacing around the edges of the room, my fingers snarled in the short hair above my ears. Me, eating. Me, walking down the hall. The views flickered from perspective to perspective, making it clear both that I had been recorded from multiple angles, and that someone had taken the time to edit it all together into a single continuous feed.

"What?" I asked, staring at the screen. My face stared back at me from a dozen different angles, and every angle showed the eyes that didn't look as much like my own as the eyes on the clone intended to replace me.

"Everyone knows who Georgia Mason is. The girl who broadcast her own death and turned the tide of a political election. The one who told us to rise. You were the perfect candidate to prove that a person—a real, recognizable person—can return from the grave as *themselves*, rather than as a pretty, mindless toy." Gregory glanced at me as he spoke. "They made you as accurate as possible, so that you could be the showroom model. You didn't think the CDC bankrolled you on their own, did you?"

"I didn't really think about it," I said. "So what's . . . the other one . . . supposed to be?"

"The street model. They spent a lot of money getting you right, and while you have a certain 'unwitting celebrity spokesperson' cachet, there's no reason to waste good research. Building an accurate Georgia Mason taught them how to make an inaccurate one."

For a moment, I just froze. It was like everything in me shut down, my brain refusing to cope with the enormity of what it was being asked to process. Then, slowly, I took a breath, nodded, and said, "How inaccurate are we talking? If I'm Georgia Mason, who's she?"

"Not quite Georgia Mason." He tapped the control panel again. There was a single muted beep before the servos engaged, followed by the deeply comforting whir of the metal shutter descending. I wouldn't have to look at her anymore. Thank God.

"But I'm not quite Georgia Mason either, am I?" I looked up at him. "I *can't* be. I'm willing to believe that the CDC can clone people. Hell, I've known for years that the CDC could clone people.

But there was no convenient backup of my—of her—memories. So who am I?"

"You're Georgia Mason." Gregory stepped away from the wall, moving back into my field of view. "The point of all this was proving that the CDC *can* conquer death. I don't understand all the science. My field is virology and corporate espionage, not human cloning and memory transfer. But I've seen your charts, and while you're not a perfect replica of yourself, you have a ninety-seven percent accuracy rating. You're as close as science can get to bringing a person back from the dead."

"But *how*?"

"Neural snapshotting."

I had to allow that it made sense, as much as I understood it, which wasn't all that well. Thought, memory, everything that makes a person who they are, it's all electricity, little sparks and flashes encoded in the gray matter of our minds. The Kellis-Amberlee virus takes us over, but it also preserves the brain long after the point of what should be death. It turns those electrical impulses back on, over and over again. If the CDC had a way of taking a picture of those electrical patterns, and then somehow imprinting them on a blank mind . . . it could work.

I shook my head, frowning at Gregory. "How can you be so calm?"

"How can you?" he shot back. "You're not the first Georgia I've brought here, although you're the most accurate. The highest transfer score before yours was seventy-five. She started screaming as soon as she saw the clone, and she didn't stop. You're the only one who hasn't cried."

"I'll cry later, I promise," I said, and I meant it. This was the sort of thing that needed to be processed before I could really let myself get upset. "How close is she? If I'm the ninety-seven percent girl, what's she?"

"Subject 8b has been prepared through a modified conditioning process, which should, if fully successful, result in a forty-four percent accuracy rating when compared to the original, but with some behavioral adjustments," said Gregory. "She'll look like you. She'll act like you . . ."

"She won't *be* me," I finished. "So what's she for?"

For the first time since we'd arrived in the lab, Gregory looked at me like I'd said something wrong. "You mean you don't know?" he asked.

"No. How would I—" I stopped mid-sentence, a sudden horrible certainty flooding over me. "They wouldn't."

"Wouldn't what?"

Somehow, the one word I needed to say was harder to force out than all the others had been. "Shaun?"

Gregory nodded. "That's the plan. You'll stay here as long as you're useful, and she'll be put where he can find her. Mr. Mason is not particularly stable these days, and they're reasonably sure he'll believe whatever he's told if he thinks it's going to get you back. He's not going to ask questions. He's not going to look for double-crosses. He's just going to open the doors and let her in."

My lips thinned into a hard line. Maybe I wasn't really who I thought I was. Maybe I wasn't really anyone at all—if I wasn't Georgia Mason, but I shared her DNA and ninety-seven percent of her personality profile, who else could I be? The one thing I was absolutely sure of was that none of that mattered, because these bastards were *not* going to use my genetic code to honey-trap the only human being in this world that I had ever been willing to die for.

"Then that's just not going to happen," I said. "What do we need to do?"

Gregory glanced at his watch. "Right now, we need to get you back to your room before our window closes. I should be able to get another message to you tomorrow night. You need to keep your eyes open. Keep behaving normally. They're not going to take you off display unless you do something that makes it look like you're beginning to destabilize."

"By 'take me off display,' you mean kill me, right?"

He nodded.

"Got it," I said. "And after that?"

"After that?" said Gregory. He smiled a little, clearly trying to look encouraging. I didn't have the heart to tell him that all he was really managing to do was look scared. "I think it's about time that we got you out of here, don't you?"

"My thoughts exactly," I said. "Let's go."

I don't know why I bother writing these entries. It feels less like a blog and more like a diary every day, like I should be drawing hearts in the margins and writing stupid shit like "OMG I wonder if he'll ever get over his stupid dead sister and love me" or "wish I could go shopping, I've had to burn half my favorite shirts due to contamination." But it's routine, and it's a form of saying "fuck you" to the people who've driven us to this. Fuck you, government conspiracy. Fuck you, CDC. We'll keep writing, and someday, we'll be able to post again, and when that happens, you'd better pray we have something better to talk about than you.

But I don't think we will.

Shaun is starting to crack. He's covering it well, but I can see the fractures. During the outbreak yesterday, there were points where he just *froze*. It was like he wasn't even a part of the situation anymore. I don't know if he knows he's doing it, and I'm scared. I'm scared he's going to get one of us killed, and he's never going to forgive himself. I'm scared he's going to get even worse, and we're going to let him, because we love him, and because we loved Georgia.

And I'm still going to follow him to Florida. God. My mother was right. I really am an idiot.

—From *Charming Not Sincere*, the blog of Rebecca Atherton, July 25, 2041. Unpublished.

She remained calm and reasonable throughout the encounter. She was able to ask coherent questions and give coherent answers.

She remained controlled during the walk back to her room, and was able to return to her bed and feign normal sleep successfully enough to convince the orderly who came to relieve me. Stress fractures are still possible, but I believe we should continue as planned. I think this one is stable.

—Taken from a message sent by Dr. Gregory Lake, July 25, 2041. Recipient unknown.

Ten

The morning dawned bright and clean, with a clear blue sky that afforded absolutely no cloud cover. Any spy satellites that happened to pick up on our anomalous route—not many people take the back roads anymore, and fewer still do it in a way that allows them to skip all security checkpoints—would have a perfect line of sight.

"If we get picked up by the DEA on suspicion of being Canadian marijuana smugglers, I'm going to be pissed," I muttered.

Becks looked up from her tablet, fingers still tracing an intricate dance across the screen. It was sort of unnerving that she could do that by nothing but the memory of where her apps were installed. I need a keyboard, or I lose my place in seconds. "What's that?"

"Nothing." I kept my eyes on the road.

Liar.

I didn't answer. We'd get into a fight if I did, and then Becks would have to pretend she didn't mind sitting there listening while I argued with myself. Back at the lab, she'd been able to leave the room when that started. Now that we were on the road again, she had nowhere to run. And neither did I.

The reality of what we were doing was starting to sink in. Dr. Abbey had insisted we get some sleep after the lab cleanup was finished—although not before she'd drawn enough blood from me to keep her surviving lab monkeys busy for a couple of weeks. "Some of us have to work while you take your little road trip," she'd said, like this was some sort of exciting pleasure cruise. Just me and Becks and the ghost of George, sailing gaily down the highway to meet our certain doom.

Not that we were actually *on* the highway unless we absolutely had to be. Dr. Abbey had installed a new module on our GPS, one programmed with all the underground and questionably secure stops between Shady Cove and Berkeley. Once that was done, Alaric and Mahir worked together to reprogram our mapping software, convincing it the roads we should take were the ones the system flagged as "least desirable." So we left Shady Cove not via the convenient and well-maintained Highway 62, but on a narrow pre-Rising street called Rogue River Drive.

We'd been on the road for almost four hours, playing chicken with major highways the entire time. Alaric and Mahir's mapping software sent us down a motley collection of frontage roads, residential streets, and half-forgotten rural back roads, all of them combining to trace roughly the same directional footprints as first Highway 62, and then Highway 5, the big backbone of the West Coast. As long as we stuck to the directions and didn't get cocky, we'd be able to stay mostly off the radar. As for the rest of the time . . .

"We're going to need to stop for gas in fifty miles or so," said Becks, attention focusing on her tablet. She tapped the screen twice; out of the corner of my eye, I saw the graphics flash and divide, changing to some new configuration. "Do we have any viable gas stations?"

"Let me check the map." I took one hand off the wheel and pushed a button at the front of our clip-on GPS device, saying, "Secure gas."

"Recalculating route," replied the GPS. The module had the same pleasant Canadian voice as Dr. Abbey's main computer. "Please state security requirements."

"Uh, we'd like to not die, if that's okay with you," I said.

"Recalculating route."

"Notice how she says that no matter what we ask for?" I slanted a glance at Becks. "Half the time she doesn't even change her mind about where we're going."

"Maybe she's just fucking with you."

"The thought had crossed my mind."

"The nearest secure gas station is approximately twenty-seven miles from your current location," announced the GPS. "Do you wish to continue?"

Becks looked up. "Define 'secure.'"

"The station is located in a designated hazard zone, and has been officially abandoned for the past eighteen years. Security systems are running at acceptable levels. The last known transmission was received three days ago, and indicated the availability of fuel, food, and ammunition."

"Works for me," I said. "Let's go."

"Recalculating route," said the GPS, and went silent, a new set of street names flashing on the tiny screen.

"I so wish we could do an exposé on all of this," said Becks wistfully. "I mean, the actual smuggler's railroad? Think about the *ratings*!"

"Too bad we're not purely in the ratings business these days, isn't it?"

"Yeah. But still . . ."

"Think about it this way, Becks. If these people had been exposed a year ago, they wouldn't be here to help us now. Everything's a tradeoff." I turned off the frontage road we'd been traveling down, onto a smaller, even less well-maintained frontage road.

Becks sighed. "I guess that's true."

I grew up in California, and if you'd asked me two years ago whether it was possible to drive from Oregon to my hometown without taking I-5, I would have said no. The longer I drove the route assembled by our modified GPS, the more I realized how wrong I'd been—and how much of the country we actually lost during the Rising. Most of the roads we were following didn't appear in normal mapping software anymore, because they'd been abandoned to the dead, or were located in places that were considered impossible to secure. Deer and coyotes peeked out of the woods at us as we drove past, showing absolutely no fear. I couldn't tell whether that was because they'd been infected, or because they had forgotten what humans were. As long as we stayed in the van, it didn't really matter.

"There used to be bears out here, you know," I said.

"Really?" Becks glanced up, frowning suspiciously in my direction. "Is there a reason you're telling me this? Should I be going for the biggest gun I can get my hands on?"

"No. I'm just wondering if there might not be bears out here again. I mean, California used to have a grizzly bear on the state flag, even."

Becks shuddered. "I do *not* understand how anyone ever thought that was appropriate. I like the current flag a lot better."

"You don't think it's a little, well . . . sanitized?" The old bear flag might not have been politically correct in a post-Rising world, but it felt like there was passion behind it, like once upon a time, someone really *cared* about that symbol and the things it represented. Its replacement—a crossed redwood branch and California poppy—always struck me as something cooked up by a frantic marketing department for a governor who just needed something to hang over the state capitol.

"There's a reason the word 'sanitized' contains the word 'sanity.' Using a giant carnivore as your state symbol is insane, zombies or no zombies."

"What's the Connecticut state flag?"

"A shield with three grapevines on it."

What? George sounded confused.

"My sentiments exactly," I muttered. Louder, I asked, "What's that supposed to mean? 'Welcome to Connecticut; we'll get you nice and drunk before the dead start walking'?"

"I have no idea what it means. It's just the stupid flag. What did the bear mean? 'Come to California; you won't have to wait for the zombies if you're looking to get eaten'?" Becks shot me a glare, expression challenging.

I couldn't help it. I started to laugh.

"What? What's so funny?"

"We're on the run from the Centers for Disease Control, heading for a gas station that caters to drug-runners and mad scientists, and we're fighting about the meaning of state flags."

Becks blinked at me. Then she put her tablet down on her knees, bent forward to rest her forehead on the dashboard, and began to laugh. Grinning, I hit the gas a little harder. If we were laughing, we weren't thinking too hard about what was waiting for us down the road.

Years before I was born, President Richard Nixon declared a "war on drugs," like drugs might somehow realize they were under siege and decide they'd be better off going somewhere else. That war went on for decades even before the Kellis-Amberlee virus gave us something more concrete to fight against. A sane person might think the dead rising would be a good reason to stop stressing out over a few recreational pharmaceuticals. It turns out the lobbyists and corporations who stood to benefit from keeping those nasty drugs illegal didn't agree, and the war on drugs continued, even up to the present day.

Smuggling is a time-honored human tradition. Make something illegal, create scarcity, and people will find a way to get it. Better, they'll find a way to make it turn a profit. In some ways, the Rising was the best thing that could have happened to the world's drug smugglers, because suddenly, there were all these roads and highways and even entire towns with no population, no police force, and best of all, no one to ask what those funny smells coming out of your basement windows were. They had to be constantly vigilant, both against the threat of the infected and the threat of the DEA, but they had more space than they'd ever had before.

The question remained: How were they supposed to move their product into more civilized areas? If drugs had been the only things in need of smuggling, maybe the answer would have involved tanks, or strapping backpacks to zombies before releasing them back into the wild. But drugs weren't the only things people needed to move. Weapons. Ammunition. Livestock—the illegal breeding farms on the other side of the Canadian Hazard Line were constantly looking for fresh genetic lines, and would go to incredible lengths to get them. George and I once followed a woman all the way to the California state border as she tried to get her Great Dane to safety without being stopped by the authorities.

I don't know whether she made it or not. We lost track of her shortly after she crossed into Oregon. But Buffy convinced George to let her scrub the identifying marks from our reports. These days, after spending some time on the wrong side of the rules, I sort of hope that woman and her dog made it over the border, into a place where they could live together the way she wanted them to.

That's because you're a sentimental idiot, said George.

"Probably," I said, getting my laughter under control. "But isn't that why you love me?"

Becks lifted her head from the dashboard, still chuckling, and went back to tapping on her tablet. "How much farther?"

"About ten miles," I said. "Get the trade goods."

"On it."

The smuggler's supply stations were largely maintained by people in the business of stealing the most forbidden commodity of all: freedom. They were the ones who chose to live in the places we'd abandoned, not because they were breeding large dogs or making meth, but because they wanted to live the way they always had. They wanted to open their doors on green trees and blue skies, not fences and security guards. I couldn't blame them. Oh, I was pretty sure they were insane, but I couldn't blame them.

Living off the grid came with its own set of problems, including limited access to medical care. So while the people we were on our way to buy gas from *might* take cash, they were likely to be a lot more interested in fresh blood test units, antibiotics, and birth control. More than half the "trade goods" we'd received from Dr. Abbey were contraceptives of one type or another.

"They choose their lives, and they love their lives, but bringing children into that environment isn't something you want to do by mistake," was her comment, as she showed Becks how to load the contraceptive implant gun. "This stuff is worth more than anything else you could possibly carry, and it'll keep them from trying to barter for your ammunition. Just make sure they see that you're armed, or you're likely to find yourselves at the center of a good old-fashioned robbery."

Becks unbuckled her seat belt and climbed over her seat into the rear of the van. I could hear her banging around back there as she got our kits ready. Glancing into the rearview mirror, I could see the back of her head. Her medium-brown hair was pulled into a no-nonsense braid, the streaks of white-blond from Dr. Abbey's chemical showers striping it like a barber pole.

"We need gas, and maybe some munchies," I called. "I think we can make it another eight or nine hours before we need to stop for the night."

"Got it," she called back. "Should I pack any of the antibiotics?"

"No, but grab the poison oak cream. That probably has some local demand." I turned my attention back to the road. The counter on the GPS indicated that our turn was somewhere just up ahead. "How we wound up here is a mystery to me," I said, almost under my breath.

The part where we're about to bribe criminals for gas, or the whole situation? asked George.

"A little bit of both."

"I wish I'd known about this while I was alive." It wasn't that surprising when I heard her voice coming from the seat Becks had vacated. I glanced over to see George with her feet braced on the dashboard and her knees tucked up almost against her chest. "I mean, Becks is right. This would have made a fantastic exposé."

"And destroyed these peoples' way of life. They've never done anything to earn that."

"How many of the people we exposed did? I mean, we were never tabloid journalists—"

"And thank God for that," I muttered.

"—but we weren't saints, either. If a story caught our eye, we chased it down, and sometimes people got hurt. Like that woman with the dog that you were just thinking about."

"Can you not remind me that you can read my mind? That's where I keep all my private thoughts."

"Please. Like there's anything in your head that could shock *me*?" George leaned forward, resting her cheek on her knee as she smiled at me. "The woman with the dog, Shaun. Even if she got out, how many of the routes we documented her taking were closed by Homeland Security immediately afterward? How many people like her tried to run when they saw our report, and got driven straight into a trap we'd created?"

"That's not our fault."

"Was it Dr. Kellis's fault when Robert Stalnaker decided to write a sensationalistic article about his cure for the common cold, and kicked off the whole stupid Rising? We're supposed to be responsible journalists. How do we cope when the stories we report get people hurt?" She sighed. "Do you honestly think Buffy and I were the first casualties?"

"Right now, I just think I'm lucky Buffy isn't haunting me, too," I said sourly.

"Shaun?"

I twisted in my seat to see Becks standing behind me. She looked concerned. I couldn't blame her. I'd have looked concerned, too, if I were the one in her place.

"Hey, Becks," I said, glancing to the empty passenger seat as I turned my eyes back to the road. George was gone. She'd be back. "Everything okay back there?"

"Yeah, everything's fine—is everything okay up front?"

"Just arguing with myself again. Nothing new."

"Please turn left," said the GPS, cutting off any reply from Becks. That was probably for the best. Ignoring my crazy might seem okay when we were in a nice, relatively safe lab environment, but that didn't mean her tolerance was going to extend to the field. I really didn't feel like arguing about whether or not I could decide to be sane again.

The road the GPS directed us down was barely more than a dirt path winding into the trees. Tires had worn deep ruts into the earth, and the van shuddered and jumped as we jounced along. Becks dropped into her seat, grabbing hold of the oh-shit handle with one hand and bracing the other against the dashboard.

"Are you sure this is the right way?" she demanded.

"Destination in one hundred yards," said the GPS.

"According to the creepy computer lady, yeah, it's the right way." I eased off on the gas. No sense in killing our shocks over a road that didn't even come with any zombies.

"I hate this road."

"It clearly hates us, too."

"Destination in twenty yards," said the GPS.

I frowned. All I could see ahead of us was more dirt road . . . at least until a pair of men stepped out of the trees, each holding a shotgun large and impractical enough to be essentially useless. Sure, you could shoot a zombie with one of those things, and sure, it would go down, but the kick from a shotgun that size would probably knock you down at the same time. Not to mention the weight of the ammunition. If you wanted to carry something like that *and* have the option to run for your life when the need inevitably arose, you'd be carrying less than two dozen rounds.

"Shaun . . ."

"It's cool, Becks," I said, turning off the engine. The men with the shotguns trained them on our windshield. I responded by blowing them a kiss and waving cheerfully. "They're not planning to shoot us. Those guns wouldn't make sense if they were planning to shoot us."

"So what *are* they planning to do? Please, enlighten me." Becks scowled.

I undid my seat belt. "They're trying to scare us," I said, and opened the van door. I kept my hands in view as I slid out of the driver's seat. The men with the guns shifted to train them squarely on me. I smiled ingratiatingly at them, stepping far enough from the van that they could see for themselves that I wasn't hiding anything. "We come in peace," I called. More quietly, I added, for Becks's benefit, "I have *always* wanted to say that."

Sometimes you are an enormous dork, said George.

"True," I agreed. The men were still pointing their guns in my direction. I sighed and raised my voice, trying another approach: "Dr. Abbey sent us. We just need gas, and then we'll be on our way."

The man to my left lowered his gun. The one to my right did not. Eyes narrowed with suspicion, he asked, "How do we know you're telling the truth?"

"You don't, although I suppose you could make us stand out here while you try to find someone who has the current number for Dr. Abbey's lab and get her to give us her okay. But I really am telling the truth. I'm Shaun Mason. The lady in the car is Rebecca Atherton. We're from After the End Times, we're hiding from the CDC, and Dr. Abbey sent us."

Most of that would qualify as "too much information" if I were talking to anyone else. But these were men who had chosen, for whatever reason, to remove themselves from the grid of modern existence—no small task, with government surveillance and public health tracking becoming more invasive with every year that passed. Telling them we were hiding wouldn't give them a lever to use against us; it would give *us* a point of commonality with *them*. We were all hiding from the world together.

The second man lowered his gun. "How's that damn dog of hers doing?" he asked. I could barely see his mouth through the bushy red thicket of his beard. He was wearing denim overalls and a plaid lumberjack shirt with the cuffs pegged up around his elbows. It was like being questioned by Paul Bunyan's much, much shorter brother.

"Still the size of a small tank," I said.

"She tell you we don't take plastic?" asked the first man, apparently unwilling to let his companion do all the talking. If the second man was Paul Bunyan's midget cousin, the first man would have made a decent stand-in for Ichabod Crane, even down to the prominent Adam's apple and impressively oversized nose.

I wish we were filming this, said George.

I swallowed my automatic "Me, too," focusing instead on looking as harmless and sincere as possible. It wasn't easy. Most of my training had focused on looking daring and oblivious, which probably wasn't going to fly here. "She told us our money wouldn't be any good," I said, still smiling. "She also said you might be willing to consider blood test units that wouldn't give you tetanus as a fair trade for some gas and a couple of sandwiches."

Paul Bunyan frowned for a moment—long enough that I was starting to wonder whether Becks would be able to move into the driver's seat and hit the gas before we *both* got shot. Then he grinned, showing the gaps where his front teeth had presumably been, once upon a time. "Well, hell, boy, why didn't you open with that?"

"We're still new at this," I replied. "Does that mean we can come in?"

"Sure does," said Ichabod. He and Paul started toward the van, leaning their guns against their shoulders in an almost synchronized motion. "Hope you're not averse to giving us a lift."

This had all the hallmarks of a test. "Sure," I said, motioning for them to follow me as I moved to climb back into the van. As expected, Becks had her pistol out, and was holding it just out of view behind the dashboard. I gestured for her to put it away before one of our new "friends" saw it.

"Are you *sure* this is a good idea?" she hissed, voice barely above a whisper.

"Nope," I said. I would have said more, but Paul and Ichabod had reached the van. "It's open!" I called.

"Much obliged," said Ichabod. He opened the van's rear door and climbed inside, with Paul close behind him. "I'm Nathan. This is Paul."

"Nice to meet you folks," said Paul.

"Charmed," said Becks, with a professional smile. Anyone who didn't know her would have trouble telling it from an expression of actual pleasure. Anyone who did know her would recognize it as a cue to grab a weapon and run.

"You look like a Paul," I said, ignoring the danger inherent in Becks's expression. She might not be happy about having strangers in our van, but she could cope. In the back of my head, Georgia laughed. "Go ahead and close the door. I assume you know where we're going?"

Paul slammed the van door and replied, "Just keep heading up the road. You'll see the turnoff in about another twenty yards."

"Awesome." I started the van's engine and began driving slowly down the uneven dirt road. Much to my surprise, the surface leveled out dramatically before we'd gone very much farther. The van stopped jarring and jouncing, settling into a more normal, smooth ride. The look on my face must have been good, because Nathan and Paul both burst out laughing.

"Oh, man, that gets you newbies every time!" said Paul, slapping his knee with one meaty lumberjack hand. "We maintain the road once you get far enough off the surface streets. Never know when you're going to need to burn rubber without blowing an axle."

"Yeah, that was high comedy," I said, barely managing to keep the annoyance out of my voice. I couldn't *afford* to get annoyed. Becks was already halfway there, and one of us needed to be the reasonable one.

I could do it, offered George.

One of us who actually had a *body* needed to be the reasonable one, I inwardly amended. "Where to next?" I asked.

"Keep going," said Nathan. "You'll know the turnoff when you see it."

"Sure," I said, and hit the gas a little harder, accelerating from two miles an hour to a more respectable five. The turnoff came into view a few seconds later, leading to a broad gravel road. Trees shaded it almost completely; I could tell just by looking at the branches that it would grant almost total protection from aerial surveillance.

Even Becks abandoned her suspicious observation of our passengers as she leaned forward to study the road, and pronounced her verdict: "Cool."

"Very cool," I agreed, and made the turn.

The trees that sheltered the road also cut off most visibility as we drove. That, too, was almost certainly intentional. We had been following the gravel road for about five minutes when it curved gently to the side, a last veil of foliage fell away, and we found ourselves facing a pre-Rising building that looked almost unchanged from those careless, bygone days. Unchanged except for the electrified fence with the barbed wire around the top, that is. The fence didn't fit with any of the pictures I'd seen of pre-Rising architecture. The rest of the structure, however, was almost certainly older than I was, built when this area was a thriving tourist corridor, and not the blasted back end of nowhere. Two men were pulling the gate open.

A row of fuel pumps sat off to one side, inside the fence but distanced from the main building, as if they had been an afterthought. There was also a row of portable toilets, and what looked like a portable decontamination shower. These people had thought of everything, and then they'd jury-rigged it all with plastic sheets and duct tape.

"Welcome to Denny's," said Nathan.

I glanced over my shoulder at him as I pulled the van through the open gate and steered to a stop just outside a second, shorter fence. This one only encircled the main building. "I thought that was a diner chain."

"It was. So was this." He grinned. "We're handy out here."

"Really?" I turned back to the building, blinking. "I've never seen one with the windows intact."

"We got lucky out here," said Paul. "The Denny's was already closed down when the Rising hit. They said it was an 'economic downturn,' and then the zombies came before anybody had to admit that we were having a depression. Good timing for everybody."

"Except the people who got eaten," said Becks.

"Well, true; probably not for them," allowed Paul. He opened the van door, sliding out. His boots crunched when they hit the gravel. "Come on. Let's see what we can work out in terms of trade."

Nathan followed him out of the van. The two of them seemed to be perfectly at ease as they ambled toward the refitted diner. I stayed where I was for a moment, squinting at the trees.

Becks paused in the process of unbuckling her seat belt. "What?"

"We're in the woods. Even if there aren't any bears out here, there should be deer. So why are our friends so calm?" A glint of light high in a tree—in a spot where light had no business glinting—caught my eye. I jabbed a finger toward it, not caring if anyone saw me. "There. They have cameras in the trees. Possibly snipers, too. They were stalling us on the road while their people got into position."

"Did anyone ever tell you that you really know how to make a girl feel all warm and fuzzy inside, Mason?"

"It's one of my best qualities," I said. I climbed out of my seat to exit through the van's rear door, grabbing the first of the boxes of trading supplies as I passed it. Becks followed me, muttering something under her breath. Not for the first time, I was glad that George was the only woman who had a direct line to the inside of my head.

You'd go crazy if there was more than one of us in here, said George.

I smothered a snort of laughter and didn't say anything at all.

Nathan and Paul were waiting by the second fence when Becks and I came walking up to them. This gate was standing open, with no blood test in evidence. Nathan must have seen the surprise in our faces. He shrugged, scarecrow shoulders jerking up and down in a sharp, birdlike motion as he said, "We can't afford the kind of paranoia you get out there in civilization. Unless we've got reason to think you've been exposed, we handle our outbreaks the old-fashioned way."

"With bullets," added Paul, just in case we were too dumb to get the point.

"Yeah, thanks for that," I said. Hoisting my box of trade goods, I asked, "Is this where we get down to business, or can we go inside first?"

"Sure thing," said Nathan. "Indy's got coffee on." He beckoned for us to follow as he stepped into the circle of ground protected by the fence. Paul stayed where he was. They weren't going to let us get behind them both once we were past the gate. Smart. I like people who can manage to be paranoid and smart at the same time. They're usually the ones who make it out of any given situation still breathing.

"Any chance I could get a Coke?" I asked. Becks glared at me as we followed him past the fence. Unsurprisingly, Paul swung the gate shut behind us, leaving himself on the other side.

"I'm not comfortable leaving the van unattended," said Becks.

"If you're worried we'll loot it, don't be," said Nathan. "If you pass the last checkpoint, we'll give you gas and supplies and whatever else you need, and no one will touch anything you don't trade freely. We're civilized here. That's probably why the Doc told you to come see us."

I winced a little. One of our former team members, Kelly Connolly, went by "Doc" most of the time. My choice, not hers. She's dead now, like so many others. "And if we fail the last checkpoint?" I asked.

"It's not looting to take from the dead," said Nathan implacably. He opened the diner door and stepped inside.

"And on that cheery note . . ." muttered Becks.

Durno v. Wisconsin was the case that decided the dead had no rights regarding property on or around their immediate persons at the time of death, making it perfectly legal to take a zombie's car and claim it as your own. It's been abused a few times over the years. It's still seen, and rightly, as one of the best legal decisions to come out of the Rising. I mean, who has the time to transfer a pink slip in the middle of a zombie uprising?

"At least there's coffee." I caught the diner door as it was in the process of swinging closed, indicating the doorway with a grandiose sweep of my free arm. "Ladies first."

"What, assholes second?" asked Becks—but she smiled as she stepped inside, and that was what I'd been shooting for. I followed her into the surprisingly bright interior. The windows must have been tinted to make it harder to tell that people still used the place. That made a lot of sense. The infected don't seem to recognize light as a sign of possible human habitation. The police do.

The last Denny's in California closed years ago, when the new food service and hygiene laws were still shaking out. I was pretty sure this one had been heavily modified from the original floor plan, since I can't imagine many "family diners" would have ammo racks or hospital beds in the middle of their dining areas. A few booths were intact, cherry-red vinyl upholstery patched with strips of duct tape. Most had been ripped out, replaced with wire convenience store shelving. About half the shelves were empty. The rest were filled with packaged snack foods, first aid supplies, and the necessities of life: toilet paper, tampons, and cheap alcohol.

The diner's original counter was also intact. Standing behind it was a tall African-American woman with strips of bright purple fabric wound around her dreadlocks and a suspicious expression on her face. She had a pistol in either hand. I was relieved to see that they were pointing downward, rather than aimed at us. Somehow, I didn't think she'd hesitate for a second before shooting us both.

"Indy, these are the folks that our cameras caught coming down the old post road," said Nathan. "They say the Doc sent 'em. They need to gas up."

"Hi," I said. "Nice place you've got here."

"Hello," said Becks.

Indy frowned, eyes narrowing. "What's the password?" she asked.

Becks blinked. "There isn't one." Then she froze, tensing. I did the same. If these people had been looking for an excuse to shoot us, our not knowing the password would probably count.

Hold on, cautioned George. *Look at her face.*

Indy was smiling. She looked a lot less menacing that way. "See, if you hadn't been from the Doc, you would have tried to make something up. Welcome to Shantytown."

"Is that the name of this place?" asked Becks.

"Hell, no. They're all Shantytown. That way, no one can ever really give away a location. Nathan says you've come looking for fuel?"

"Snacks would be good, but gas is the primary objective," I said. Holding up my box again, I said, "We brought contraceptives."

"And poison oak ointment."

Indy laughed. "Those are two things that go together more often than not out here. Come on over, kids. Let's look at your toys, and see if we can't come to some sort of an agreement about what they'll buy you."

Becks and I exchanged a relieved glance as we walked over to the counter. Indy held out her hands for the box. I briefly considered refusing to hand it over, since that would reduce our bargaining power. Stupid idea. Bargaining power wouldn't do us any good if we didn't get out alive. I gave her the box.

"Where you kids heading?" Indy asked, as she put the box down and began picking through its contents.

"Berkeley," said Becks.

"Florida," I said at the same time.

Indy glanced up, a glint of amusement in her eyes. "Long-term and short-term goals, I see. The Doc put you up to this?"

"She wants mosquitoes," I said with a shrug. "There are some people in Berkeley who may be able to help us get to Florida and back out again without getting arrested for suspected bioterrorism. I'm pretty sure the people maintaining the blockades out there won't like the idea of us just popping in."

"The Masons can probably help you," agreed Indy, pulling three packs of contraceptive implants out of the box and setting them on the counter. "Don't look so surprised. I looked you up as soon as you told my boys who you were."

"We know what the Internet is," contributed Nathan.

"Not all the old networks have been shut down," said Indy, and straightened, pushing the box toward me. "The implants—we have our own injection gun—two boxes of condoms, four test kits, and some antibiotics. We'll give you a full tank of gas, feed you lunch, and let you leave here alive. We'll even throw in a shower, if you want one."

"I'll pass on the shower for now, but the rest works," I said.

"It's amazing that you can live out here like this," said Becks.

"Well, honey, if you grew up before the whole world was behind walls, this can seem like the only way to live." Indy smiled a little wistfully. Then she caught herself. Wiping her hands briskly against her jeans, she straightened. "Come on. Let's get you fueled up."

Paul was still standing at the gate when we emerged. He and Indy exchanged a nod, and he watched silently as I got back into the van and pulled it up to the fuel pumps. Becks went back inside while I pumped the gas, emerging a few minutes later with a brown paper sack of something that smelled spicy and delicious.

Indy followed her, watching with folded arms as I finished pumping. "You want some free advice?" she asked. "It's worth what you'll pay for it."

"I'm listening," I said, hanging the fuel pump back on its hook.

"Trust the Doc as long as you're not between her and whatever crazy-ass thing she's working on right now. Trust the Masons as far as you can throw them."

"I learned that second part a long time ago," I said, with what I hoped was a wry smile. "Thanks for your hospitality." I wanted to ask what she knew about the Masons. I didn't think it would be a good idea, and so I kept my mouth shut.

"Any time." Indy turned to smile at Becks, who was staring at her like she'd just seen a ghost. "Drive safely, kids." She walked back inside before either of us could answer.

Becks followed me back to the van in stunned silence, climbing into the passenger seat without saying a word. I waved to Paul and Nathan as I started the engine, and navigated the van carefully around the closing gate, back onto the gravel road.

It wasn't until we reached the end of the gravel and started down the uneven dirt road that she spoke. "That was Indigo Blue," she said.

"What?" I asked, only half listening as I fought to keep from losing control of the van. "I hate this road."

"I said, that was Indigo Blue. The Newsie? The one who disappeared after she collaborated with your father?"

"Adoptive father," I said automatically. Then I blinked. "Wait, really? Are you sure?"

"We covered her in my History of Journalism class. I didn't recognize her immediately, but yes, I'm sure."

"Huh. I wonder what she's doing out here?"

"I wonder why she isn't *dead*! Everyone thought she was."

"Want to go back and ask her?"

"No!" Becks's answer was fast enough to make me take my eyes off the road and frown at her. She sighed. "If she's out here, she's got a reason. I want to know what it is, but I'll respect it. We're not here for that."

"I guess not." I turned my eyes back to the road. "I wonder if Dr. Abbey knew."

"I wonder if Dr. Abbey cared."

"There's always that. I—" My sentence went unfinished as I hit the brakes, causing my seat belt to cut painfully into my shoulder. Becks yelped as she was flung forward.

"Shaun! What the *fuck*?"

I didn't answer her aloud. I just raised my hand, pointing at the shaggy hulk that was standing at the end of the dirt road. Becks turned to follow my finger, her eyes going wide.

"Shaun. Is that . . . is that a bear?"

"Yeah," I said, not quite managing to keep the glee out of my voice. "You ever killed a zombie bear before?"

"Can't say as I have."

"Maybe we'll be going back to use their showers after all." I unbuckled my seat belt, moving slowly. "First one to get the headshot gets first shower."

"Deal," said Becks, and grabbed her gun.

Please make it back alive. Please make it back alive. Please make it back alive. Please make it back alive. Please make it back . . .

—From *Dandelion Mine*, the blog of Magdalene Grace Garcia, July 26, 2041. Unpublished.

My dearest Nandini;

You will only see this letter if I die during the fool's errand I am about to undertake—one more foolish quest in a life that has been defined by them. Do you ever regret that you chose a husband who would forever be leaving you to chase some elusive platonic ideal of the truth? I wouldn't blame you if you did. Please, consider this letter my blessing, and remarry when you're ready. Find an accountant or a computer programmer—a nice, stable profession that won't lend itself to this breed of madness.

Oh, but I loved you. Maybe not at first, when our parents brought us together and said we should marry, but it didn't take me as long as some thought it would. I am truly sorry I have not been the husband you deserved. You were always more wife than I was worthy of. I love you, my Nan. Believe me, even if you believe nothing else I have ever said. I love you, and I am blessed beyond all words that you were willing to take a risk, and marry me.

—Taken from an e-mail composed by Mahir Gowda, July 26, 2041. Unsent.

Eleven

Dr. Thomas smiled indulgently across the table separating us. "Now, Georgia, I know things have been very stressful for you these past few weeks—"

"Boredom and stress aren't the same thing," I said. "You can check the dictionary if you want. I'll wait."

He made a note on his tablet. "Inappropriate humor is a defense mechanism, isn't it?"

"No, Shaun was a defense mechanism. Since he's not here, I have to fill in." I took a breath, trying to look miserable. It wasn't easy. I've never had to worry about what my eyes were doing. People say the eyes are windows to the soul, and I was accustomed to having black-out curtains over mine. Without my retinal KA, they might be giving me away without my even knowing it. "Are you ever going to tell me what happened?"

"When your system is ready to stand the stress," said Dr. Thomas, making another note on his tablet. "Dr. Shaw says you were very cooperative with her tests, and confirms your story about the haircut. I'm sorry to have doubted you."

"Yeah, well." I shrugged, trying to look frustrated and innocent at the same time. The frustration was easy. The innocence wasn't. "I've never been much of a liar."

That little dig hit home; Dr. Thomas winced. I made my reputation as a Newsie based on my refusal to lie—a refusal that got me fined several times early in my career, when I was found in places I wasn't supposed to be and couldn't come up with an even half-decent excuse for what I was doing there. I never got better at making excuses. I just got better at refusing to let Shaun talk me into climbing over fences marked NO TRESPASSING.

My memories of those early escapades were fuzzy, like I'd reviewed them so many times that the edges had begun to blur. A lot of my earlier memories were like that, and had been since I'd woken up. I'd been trying to figure out what that meant. Given what Gregory had shown me the night before, I was pretty sure I finally knew.

The memories weren't fuzzy because the things I remembered happened a long time ago, or because there was a glitch in the process that transferred my consciousness into a freshly cloned body. The memories were fuzzy because the things I remembered never happened at all—not to me, anyway. I was "remembering" an implanted incident extracted from the mind of a dead woman. A certain loss of fidelity was only to be expected.

Somehow, knowing that I wasn't *really* who I thought I was—knowing that Georgia Mason was dead and gone and never coming back—made dealing with Dr. Thomas easier. I don't like lying. I've never liked lying. And when I was myself, I wasn't any good at it. Now that I was someone else who just thought she was me, it seemed like a skill worth developing. I wasn't compromising my values. I was creating my values, and compromising the values of a dead woman.

And maybe if I told myself that enough times, I'd convince myself to believe it.

Finally, Dr. Thomas cleared his throat, and said, "Your test results have been good so far. I believe you may be stabilizing."

"Bully for me."

"The people who have been monitoring your case remotely are very encouraged. You're getting high marks."

After Gregory's revelation that I was being used as a display model, that announcement made me want to start smashing things. I forced the urge back down, asking coldly, "Will any of these people be coming to see me in person?"

Dr. Thomas smiled, chuckling in practiced amusement. It was so at odds with his generally nervous demeanor that it made me want to slap him and send him to acting classes at the same time. "Vice President Cousins is too busy to come to the CDC for social calls, even when he's calling on an old friend."

I sat up a little straighter, old journalistic instincts locking my shoulders tight as his words sunk in. "*Vice President*? Rick? *My* Rick? From After the End Times?"

"Ah . . ." Dr. Thomas looked suddenly uncomfortable, realizing he'd said more than he should have. "Yes. Governor Tate was another unfortunate casualty of the incident which claimed your . . . I mean to say, the incident that resulted in your untimely . . ." He stopped, looking even more uncomfortable.

"Death?" I suggested. "Murder? Martyrdom? I always wanted to be a martyr." That was my second lie for the day. I *never* wanted to be a martyr. I wanted to live long enough to bury Shaun, however long that happened to be, and I wanted to die in my time, and on my own terms.

"Yes." Dr. Thomas nodded, looking relieved. "After the governor's death, President Ryman selected your colleague to stand with him. He said it was the least he could do to honor your memory, and to show the blogging community that it would still have a voice."

My shoulders tightened. He said "blogging community" the way most people would say "dead rat." Choosing my words carefully, I asked, "So Ryman won the election?"

"By a good margin. The events in Sacramento, unfortunate as they were, only provided his campaign with additional exposure."

"Yeah, I'm sure they did." What happened in Sacramento would have given Ryman's campaign virtual domination over the news cycles, regardless of what his opposition did to try to force themselves back into the picture. As long as Ryman himself made it out alive, he'd been all but guaranteed the White House. "Can you let Rick know I'd like to see him?"

"I'll pass the word, but the vice president is a very busy man."

I'm sure you will, I thought. Aloud, I said, "Thank you. It would be nice to have someone to talk to. I'm going a little stir-crazy in here."

"I understand, but, Georgia, things have changed since your death. Your face is very well known in the outside world, and even some of our personnel are . . . uncomfortable . . . about the implications of your presence. I'm sure you can see where it would be bad for everyone if someone assumed you had amplified because they were aware of your current legal status."

"Right." I forced a smile. From the look on Dr. Thomas's face, I could tell that it didn't look any more genuine than it felt. Given the circumstances, that was probably okay. There was no way the comment about "current legal status" was intended as anything but a warning: He was telling me I was still listed as deceased in all the government databases that mattered, and that if someone shot me, they wouldn't be guilty of murder. They'd be acting within the law.

Life was easier when I was dead.

Dr. Thomas stood. "Now, if you'd come with me, we've prepared a little treat for you."

"A treat?" The gun in my sock pressed reassuringly against my calf as I stood, reminding me that whatever else I might be, I was no longer defenseless. Sure, I'd be lucky if I could take out more than one of them before they were on top of me, and that assumed that my memory of knowing how to fire a gun could overcome the fact that my new body had no muscle memory, but there was a *chance*. That was more than I'd had before. I was going to hang on to it with everything I had.

"Come with me." Dr. Thomas turned and walked toward the

door, confident that it would open at his approach. It did, of course, sliding smoothly aside to reveal the hallway. Envy burned my throat as I walked after him. The doors wouldn't respond to me. I walked toward them and they stayed stubbornly closed, like I was infected.

Like I was still dead.

The ever-present guards were waiting outside the lab. They fell into position ahead and behind us. We walked the length of the familiar hall, passing the doors I was accustomed to stepping through. I was starting to get worried—maybe this whole thing had been a test; maybe Gregory was working for the CDC after all, and I'd failed by going along with his grand conspiracy theory—when Dr. Thomas finally stopped. The lead guard did the same.

"Here we are," said Dr. Thomas. He touched the apparently featureless wall. A piece of paneling slid aside to reveal a blood test unit. "Georgia. You understand that this is a privilege, and that any inappropriate behavior on your part will result in your being sternly reprimanded."

I didn't want to think about what a reprimand might constitute, given that I already lived in a small, isolated box with no privacy. "I understand," I said.

"Good. I told them we could trust you to be cooperative." Dr. Thomas slapped his hand down on the blood testing unit. The light above the door clicked on, going from red to green, and the door swung open. Swung—not slid.

Light lanced into the hall, so bright it seemed almost like a physical attack. I automatically moved to shield my eyes, the part of my brain that handled reflexes kicking in before my conscious mind realized my retinas weren't burning. I slowly forced my arm down, raising my head and squinting into the brightness.

Sunlight. It was sunlight. I could smell green things, the sharp bitterness of tomato plants, the sweet bland scent of grass. I started hesitantly forward, my feet carrying me almost without consulting the rest of my body. The guards followed me, but at a distance, giving me a few meters of space as I moved out of the antiseptic CDC hall, and into the green.

I've never been an outdoorsy person. Shaun used to say the only reason I ever left my room was to yell at him for doing dangerous shit. He wasn't entirely right, but he wasn't entirely wrong, either. And stepping through that door was still just shy of stepping into Heaven.

It wasn't the actual outdoors; a quick glance upward was enough to confirm that I was actually in a moderately sized biodome, with a ceiling of steel and clear, bulletproof glass protecting me from any chance of feeling an actual breeze. I was standing in a lie. A big green lie, filled with flower beds and vegetable gardens and an expanse of grass even bigger than our yard in Berkeley. I didn't care. In that moment, the lie was as good as the truth would have been, because I was standing in the green, and there were butterflies—*butterflies*—fluttering past like it was no big deal. Like there were green things and butterflies everywhere in the world.

"What is this?" I asked, turning back to Dr. Thomas. My eyes were burning; that weird tingling burn that I was learning to recognize as a sign of tears. I fought the urge to swipe my hand across them. I'd been capable of crying for a little under a month, and I already hated it.

"Those of us involved with your care thought you might benefit from a little fresh air." Dr. Thomas was smiling that paternal smile again. I stopped fighting the urge to wipe my eyes, and started fighting the urge to punch him in the nose. "Welcome to Biodome six-eighteen."

Something croaked in one of the apple trees to my left. I glanced over just in time to catch a flash of black wings as what could only have been a crow took off, presumably to find a tree that wasn't next to unwanted humans. The distraction gave me the time I needed to get my breathing—and threatened tears—under control.

My expression was one of wide-eyed amazement as I turned back to Dr. Thomas.

"You mean this has been here all along?" I asked.

His smile widened. Asshole. "This is one of the larger CDC establishments. This habitat allows us to grow some of our own food, and studies have shown that access to outdoor environments can assist in psychological recovery."

"Wow. I had no idea." I might have been laying it on a little thick with that last one, but I was too distracted to care. I was busy reviewing everything my damaged memory contained about the North American CDC facilities.

"I thought it would make a nice treat for you."

Nice how he was willing to take credit for it, now that I'd stepped "outside" without losing my shit. "It's amazing," I said, trying to infuse my words with an air of wonder.

It must have worked, because Dr. Thomas didn't say anything. He just kept smiling, watching as I apparently soaked in the wonders the CDC had prepared to impress me. I was impressed, all right; impressed by how much of Mahir's series on the various CDC installations had managed to survive the transfer of my memories. He'd broken them down by region, listing their major features, like helipads, private airstrips . . . and biodomes.

There were eight CDC facilities equipped with biodome simulators. Only four used them for agricultural purposes. Assuming this was one of the facilities that had existed when Mahir wrote his report, I was in one of those four.

None of the staff I'd spoken to had Southern accents. Dr. Thomas sounded like he was from the Midwest, but his accent was blurry, like he hadn't been home in a long time. Dr. Shaw sounded sort of like Becks, which meant she was probably from somewhere in New England. Everyone else had the Hollywood non-accent that meant West Coast, and I doubted the CDC was bussing in guards and orderlies just to confuse my sense of place.

So we weren't in the South—that took Huntsville off the list—and while we might be in the St. Paul facility, I didn't think so. The accents were wrong. That left either Seattle or Phoenix.

My smile was genuine as I turned back to Dr. Thomas. "Thank you so much for letting me see this," I said. "I think you're right. I feel better just being here."

Being in either of those two cities meant we were near a dozen bloggers who knew me. More importantly, we were near a dozen bloggers whose hunger to be the first at the scene would mean they listened first and shot second if I managed to show up on their doorsteps. All I had to do was find a way out of the building, and while I wouldn't be exactly in the clear, I would be in a much better situation than I could have been. I would have a chance.

"Well, as long as your recovery continues without any setbacks, and as long as you continue to cooperate, I believe I can see clear to letting you out for a constitutional every other day. How does that sound?"

My smile froze again. *It sounds like you think I'm some sort of house pet, you patronizing bastard,* I thought, but said only, "That sounds great."

"We have half an hour before your next tests. Would you like to explore the dome?"

"Can I?" I didn't have to feign my interest. The biodome was a new environment. After weeks in the sterile CDC halls, I needed that more than I could have guessed.

"I wouldn't have brought you here if I wasn't going to let you have a little time to roam," said Dr. Thomas. That damn paternal smile was back on his face. "Go ahead. Look around. You're completely secure here. No one will come in and trouble you." His smile slipped a bit, turning stern as he added, "But, Georgia, if you were to attempt to open any of the doors—"

"You wouldn't blame a girl for trying?" I asked.

Dr. Thomas's eyes narrowed, all pretense of a smile fading. "I most certainly would."

"Understood." I offered a cool nod to the two guards who were still standing next to Dr. Thomas, and turned to walk deeper into the biodome.

I found the first wall less than twenty yards from where I'd started, mostly hidden behind a tall patch of something I assumed was probably immature corn. It looked like corn, anyway. I never spent that much time studying agriculture. The wall was white, and should have stuck out like a sore thumb in the primarily green biodome, but it didn't. Like the door we'd entered through, it was somehow part of its surroundings.

The dome wasn't a perfect circle, although it wasn't a square, either; after following the wall long enough to map the angles of two corners with my hands, I decided that it was most likely an octagon. This campus was even bigger than I'd initially assumed. I kept walking, enjoying the springy feel of the grass beneath my feet, and tried to figure out what else I might learn from the structure of the dome.

I crested a low hill and found myself facing a pine forest. It was small, no more than fifteen trees forming the edge, but it was enough of a surprise to stop me in my tracks for a moment. The shock was probably a good thing; it kept me from punching the air in sheer delight. We were in Seattle. The Seattle CDC was the only campus with an evergreen forest inside their biodome. I'd seen pictures.

As I stood contemplating the pines, I realized that my feet were cold. I looked down. My thick white socks—so perfect for roving the halls of the CDC—were less perfect for wandering around a grassy meadow. They were soaked to the ankles, with grass stains around the toes. There was no way Dr. Thomas would let me wear them back into the main building.

"Georgia?"

I stiffened, glancing back toward the sound of his voice. He wasn't in view; if he was coming after me, or sending his guards, he was still a little ways away. With only a few seconds to move, I didn't stop to think about what I was doing. I just bolted for the trees.

Shaun was always the one who put himself in mortal danger for kicks, but I still tried to stay in decent physical condition. It was the smart thing to do if I was going to keep following him into hazard zones, looking for the "perfect story" to slap up on his side of the site. I'd never been an athlete, but I'd been running ten-minute miles since I was fourteen, and that was enough to outrun any zombie that ever shambled into my path. I felt weirdly betrayed when I found myself gasping for breath, my heart hammering hard against my ribs as I slumped against a tree. All those hours of work, undone by one little death.

I yanked my socks off. The little gun fell to the grass. I scooped it up, lifting my top long enough to tuck the gun into my waistband, the muzzle digging painfully into my stomach. I pulled the drawstring on my pants a little tighter. The pajama top was loose enough that when I let it go, it fell to cover the weapon without a trace.

"Georgia?" Dr. Thomas's voice was closer this time; he was coming for me himself, rather than sending his flunkies to fish me out of the biodome. That was good. He'd be less attuned to the little details than a professional guard would have been—they would have noticed the high color in my cheeks and the slight unsteadiness of my legs as I stepped out of the cover of the tree line.

"Here," I said, proud of the way that I was barely gasping at all. My bare toes dug into the grass, tangling deep. I was going to need a serious shower when all this was over. "I'm sorry. Were you calling me?"

Dr. Thomas fixed me with a stern eye. "What did I say about no funny business?" he asked.

Cold arced down my spine. Someone must have seen me pull the gun out of my sock. *He knows,* I thought, desperately wondering if I could draw before he had a chance to call for his guards, and whether it would do me any good if I did. Even if I didn't shoot myself, they'd just decommission me, or whatever it is you call getting rid of a clone that you don't need anymore. They'd throw me out like yesterday's garbage—and all because of a pair of goddamn *socks*—

"That means you *come* when I call," said Dr. Thomas. "I'm willing to forgive it this time—we can call it youthful exuberance, and it doesn't need to go into my report of the day's activities. But that assumes you'll behave from now on. Can I trust you to behave, Georgia?"

"What?" Relief flooded over me, washing away the cold. I nodded so hard it felt like I was going to sprain something. "Yes, absolutely. I'm sorry, I didn't mean to ignore you, I was just . . . the grass, and then the *trees*, and . . . " I paused, making my voice very small before I said, "It reminded me of home, that's all."

If the CDC did their research on Berkeley, they knew we had more green space per capita than any other densely populated city in the state of California. Chalk it up to general perversity and being built around a university that resisted all attempts to render it fully secure. The idea of trees being something I would miss was believable if you didn't know me well enough to know that I'd been avoiding unnecessary exposure to the outside world for my entire life.

Dr. Thomas's expression softened. "I can understand that." His frown returned as he glanced down at my feet. "Georgia, what in the world happened to your socks?"

"They got wet, so I took them off." I held up my grass-stained socks. "At least we have plenty of bleach, right?"

To my surprise, Dr. Thomas actually chuckled. He seemed more human in that moment than he had since the first uneasy hours after I woke up in an unfamiliar bed. Too bad that wasn't going to make me change my mind about getting the hell out of here before they had me "decommissioned" and replaced me with something more tractable.

"We can get you new socks. Come on, now. We'll have just enough time to get you cleaned up before they expect you at the lab."

"All right, Dr. Thomas." I walked toward him, the grass damp beneath my feet. I was getting better at deceit. I didn't like it—I didn't think I would ever like it, and that was good, because the day I loved a lie was the day I stopped being even remotely Georgia Mason—but I was getting better. I was going to need those skills if I wanted to get out of the CDC still breathing, rather than going out in a biohazard container bound for the incinerator.

I took the deepest breaths I could as we left the biodome, trying to capture the smell of the green in my lungs. That was what freedom would smell like. And I was *going* to be free.

Things I have done today that were *awesome*, whether or not I am currently a practicing Irwin: I shot a zombie bear in the head. Six times. Becks shot it four times, which I would gloat about, except she's the one who managed to shoot the damn thing straight through the eye, taking it down before it could, you know, maul and devour us. The denizens of the gas station came out when they heard the shooting, loaded, as the old colloquialism goes, for bear; I don't think they expected to actually *find* one.

Indy—the lady who runs the supply depot where we encountered the bear—said it was a grizzly. So hell, maybe we just killed the last grizzly in the world. I'd feel bad about that if it hadn't been *an infected zombie bear* that wanted to *eat my delicious flesh.*

Damn, that was fun.

—From *Adaptive Immunities*, the blog of Shaun Mason, July 26, 2041. Unpublished.

Please tell me you know where they're going, and you didn't just lose track of our only known living human with a full immunity to Kellis-Amberlee amplification. *Please.* I don't want to be the one who has to come out there and kick your ass.

Seriously, Shannon, be careful. You're starting to get a little hard to follow, and that scares me. We both know who *didn't* build those bugs, but if you make yourself too big of a target, when the time comes, you're the one they're going to come for.

—Taken from an e-mail sent by Dr. Joseph Shoji to Dr. Shannon Abbey, July 26, 2041.

Twelve

Berkeley was asleep. We pulled off Highway 13 onto the surface streets, using my still mostly accurate mental map of the area to guide us to the intersections and off-ramps that hadn't been outfitted with blood test units. I was only wrong once, and that one time, the line for the testing station was long enough for me to get into the back and climb under a counter, where I would be safely out of view. Our van's occupancy beacon was "broken," courtesy of Alaric and a socket wrench, and they're not yet legally required for a vehicle to be considered road safe. "Yet" is the operative word—I expect tricks like the one we pulled to be illegal within the next five years. God bless "yet."

Becks pulled up to the manned booth monitoring traffic as it moved from the highway onto surface streets. I heard the slap of her hand hitting the metal testing panel, and the disinterested voice of the nightshift security officer as he asked where she was heading. As a university town, Berkeley has never been in a position to crack down on traffic as much as, say, Orinda, where the city limits basically seal themselves as soon as the sun sets. In Berkeley, only the individual neighborhoods can go for that kind of expensive paranoia.

Becks's answer was muffled by the seat and the sounds of traffic coming in through her open window. Whatever she said must have passed muster, because she put the van back into drive and went rolling on after only about a minute and a half.

Don't even think about going up there until she says it's safe, said George. *This would be a stupid way to die.*

I couldn't answer without the all clear, and so I just glared into the darkness at the back of the van, trusting her to get the point. She did; her laughter filled my head, amusement tinged with a grim understanding of just how bleak our situation could easily become.

Finally, after what felt like an eternity, Becks called, "We should be out of range of the cameras. You can come out now."

"It's about time." I crawled out from under the counter and back into the front seat, not bothering with my seat belt. "I was starting to get a cramp back there."

"You would have gotten more than a cramp if one of those guards had seen you."

"I'm clean."

Becks slanted a disbelieving look at me. "Do you *honestly* think no one's going to be looking for you? After everything that's happened?"

"No." I shook my head. "I mean, we haven't committed any crimes—well, technically, we could probably be charged with breaking and entering at the Memphis CDC, since the Doc was legally dead when she let us in—but I know there are people watching for us."

"Watching for *you*," said Becks, almost gently. "You're the only remaining blogger from the Ryman campaign. You've got a level of credibility with people who aren't blog readers that the rest of us can only dream about—and here, you'll be recognized by just about anyone. Hometown boy makes good and then goes bad? You're the target, Shaun. Not me, not Alaric, and not even Mahir."

"You're a ray of sunshine, aren't you? Take the left on Derby."

"Forgive me if I'm not that excited about the idea of going to visit your parents."

"Adoptive parents," I said automatically.

Becks wasn't listening. That was probably a good thing. "I used to look up to them, you know? They were heroes. What your father did for his students—he should have received a medal for that."

"He agrees with you." I couldn't keep the sourness out of my voice. I wasn't trying very hard. Becks grew up with the Masons as celebrity faces for the news, but I grew up with them exploiting me—exploiting *George*—for the sake of ratings, and a kind of public approval so damn fickle it was almost unreal. And now here I was, creeping back to them under the cover of darkness, ready to beg for their help. Home sweet self-destructive emotionally abusive home.

"I didn't find out what they were like until I started working for Georgia. She talked about them more than you do. Which is sort of funny, since you talk about almost everything else so much more than she ever did."

"She loved them," I said defensively. I didn't know why I felt the need to defend George's love of the Masons, but I did. Maybe it was because I stopped loving them so long ago. Maybe it was because, awful as they were, she could never quite bring herself to do the same. "She didn't want them to be the people that they were."

"And you did?"

"What? No! No. I just . . . " I let the sentence drift off, watching Berkeley slide by outside the van window. I'd made this trip in the passenger seat so damn many times; any time we had to go out on location when the weather conditions made it unsafe for George to take the bike, or when parking was going to be at a premium. She insisted on driving after the sun was down, saying her retinal KA gave her an advantage over my puny, uninfected eyes. So I would sit in the passenger seat and watch Berkeley going by, tired, cranky, and utterly content with the world. Maybe it was nostalgia speaking, but I couldn't remember a single night trip home where I hadn't been happy to be where I was, riding in the van with Georgia, and both of us alive, and both of us together.

Finally, slowly, I said, "George knew who the Masons were—*what* the Masons were—as well as I did. But she wished they were different. I think she thought that if she could just bring home a big enough story, find a big enough truth, that maybe they'd get past Phillip—their son, the one who died—and finally start loving us."

"And you didn't think that?"

"They were never going to start loving us. That's why we had to love each other as much as we did."

"Oh."

Becks was quiet after that, and I was glad. I wanted to make this last little part of the trip in silence.

The GPS didn't take us down the streets I would have chosen—it was going by distance, not by a local's knowledge of road conditions and traffic lights—but that was good, too, in its way. I needed this trip to be a little different. I spent too much time living in the past, and I didn't need to encourage the part of me that would be happy to stay there forever. The businesses clustered around Shattuck and Ashby gave way to the outlying buildings of the U.C. Berkeley campus, and finally to the low, tight-packed shapes of the residential neighborhoods. Becks pulled up in front of a familiar house, the windows shuttered, the porch light dark.

"Now what?" she asked.

"This." I dug a hand into my pocket, pulling out the sensor disk I'd been carrying since we left Dr. Abbey's lab. It wasn't mine, ironically; my identity key to the Masons' house was lost when Oakland burned. This one had been Georgia's, and had been a part of her little black box—the only thing I'd taken the time to save before the bombs came down. I slipped the chain on over my neck, pressing the disk to my skin and flipping it into the "on" position. It beeped, twice, acknowledging that it had managed to locate a matching signal in the immediate vicinity.

A light above the Masons' garage door flashed on, blinking twice in response to the disk's location pulse. Without any further fanfare, the door began spooling smoothly upward.

"Go on in," I said, in response to Becks's surprised expression. "The house was programmed years ago to let this van inside with multiple passengers. It was an expensive enough upgrade that there's no way they've taken the time to have it pulled out of the security programming."

Unless they were really, really angry with you when you refused to give them my files, said George. *They could have done it out of spite.*

"'Could' doesn't mean 'would,'" I said.

Becks shot another glance my way, frowning, and started the engine again. "Please try not to talk to dead people while we're here? I don't want you getting shot because you look like you're getting the amplification crazies."

"Amplification doesn't make you talk to yourself."

"And you don't get better once you're infected. There's a first time for everything."

"Fair enough." The garage door slid closed again once we were inside. "Come on. We'll need to pass security if we want to get into the house."

"I figured."

I hadn't expected the Masons to make any updates to the security system, and I hadn't been wrong: The two testing stations were still in place, each of them equipped with the standard wall plate for blood sampling and the more expensive display screens for verbal confirmation. Becks and I stepped into position. A red light clicked on above the door leading into the house.

"Please identify yourself," said the bland, computerized voice of the house system.

"Shaun Phillip Mason and guest," I said.

"Rebecca Atherton, guest," said Becks. Her words were almost precisely overlaid by Georgia's, as she said, *Georgia Carolyn Mason.*

The light above the door blinked several times as the house

checked my voice against its records. I was allowed to bring guests home—had been since I was sixteen—but I hadn't done it very often. Part of me was even ludicrously afraid the house would somehow pick up on George's phantom voice and refuse to let us in until it had figured out how to test her for viral amplification.

The light blinked just long enough for me to get nervous before the house said, "Voice print and guest authorization confirmed. Please read the phrase on your display screen."

Words appeared on my screen. "Ride a cock horse to Banbury Cross to see a fine lady upon a white horse," I read. The words blinked out.

On the other side of the door, Becks recited, "Jack be nimble, Jack be quick, Jack jump over the candlestick." The light above the door began blinking again. She cast me a nervous glance, which I answered with an equally nervous smile. The feel of George's phantom fingers wrapping around my own didn't help as much as I might have hoped. Every time she touched me, it was just a reminder of how little time I had left before I wound up going utterly insane.

The light over the door changed from red to yellow.

"Please place your right hands on the testing pads," requested the house. I did as I was told, slapping my palm flat against the cool metal. It chilled half a second later, and something bit into my index finger, a brief sting followed almost instantly by the cool hiss of soothing foam. The light above the door began to flash, alternating red and yellow.

"Isn't this fun?" I asked, with forced levity.

Becks glared. She was still glaring when the light stopped flashing.

The door hissed open. "Welcome home, Shaun," said the house. "We hope you'll have a pleasant visit, Rebecca."

"Um, thanks," said Becks, looking to me for what she should do next. I shrugged, smiled, and stepped through the open door.

The kitchen hadn't changed since Georgia and I lived with the Masons. The floor was still covered in the same off-brown linoleum, and the walls were still papered in the same cheerful yellow floral print. Papers and clippings from the U.C. Berkeley student newspaper—printed on actual paper, although it was hemp, not wood pulp—covered the refrigerator. The urge to open it, grab a snack, and go up to my room was as strong as it was unexpected. Walking into that kitchen was like walking backward through time, into a part of my life where the biggest thing I had to worry about was whether the new T-shirt designs in my shop would sell well enough to justify their printing cost.

A part of my life where Georgia was alive, and not just a voice in my head and a ghostly hand on my arm.

"Shaun?" said Becks, voice barely louder than a whisper. "Are you okay?"

"I'm fine." I shook off the past, shoving it away from me as hard as I could. "Come on." I gestured for her to follow as I stepped out of the kitchen and into the front hallway, intending to wait in the living room until the Masons woke up and came downstairs for breakfast. It was a good plan. It was a plan intended to leave them off balance and catch them during the one time of day when they were as close to unarmed as possible.

It was a plan that died as soon as we turned the hall corner and found ourselves facing my adoptive mother, Stacy Mason. She was wearing a robe over sensible cotton pajamas, and holding a revolver. It was aimed straight at my chest. I stopped. Becks stopped. None of us said a word.

Correction: None of us said a word that anyone but me could hear. *Hi, Mom,* said George, her voice falling into the silence like a stone. I managed somehow not to flinch.

Finally, Mom lowered her pistol, saying calmly, "You must be hungry. Why don't you kids go back into the kitchen, and I'll see if I can't whip us up some pancakes or something?"

"That's okay, Mom," I said. "We didn't come here for breakfast."

"I know," she said, voice utterly calm—the voice that used to greet me when I came home late from school, or got another detention for fighting with the kids who picked on George because of her eyes. "I raised you better than that. At the same time, whatever you *did* come for can wait until we've all had a chance to sit down and eat like civilized people. All right?"

I know when I'm beat. "Okay, Mom." I hesitated before adding, "You know you can't upload any footage of us being here, right?"

"I invented the rules to this game, Shaun," said Mom. "Now go wash your hands."

"Yes, Mom," I said. Georgia echoed the words inaudibly, her voice half a beat out of synch with mine. "Come on, Becks."

Looking uncertain, Becks turned to follow me back to the kitchen. We had barely crossed the threshold when Mom called, "Oh, and Shaun?"

I tensed, not turning. "Yeah?"

"Welcome home."

Somehow, that didn't reduce the tension. "Thanks, Mom," I said, and kept walking.

Now that we were back in the kitchen, I could really look at it, rather than letting the overwhelming impression of coming home wash over me. Everything was old-fashioned to the point of parody, with frilled gingham curtains hiding the security mesh worked into the windows and fixtures originally installed sometime in the 1940s. It was all part of the homey atmosphere the Masons worked so hard to project—the homey atmosphere that had required, once upon a time, that they go shopping for adorable orphans to complement the rest of their décor. The worst part was the way I could see Becks buying into it, the tightness slipping from her shoulders and the lines around her mouth relaxing. Stacy and Michael Mason were heroes of the Rising. They were two of the best-loved faces of the media movements that came after it; between them, they *defined* what it was to be an Irwin, what it was to be a Newsie . . . what it was to be a blogger.

Maybe it's insane that a news movement that started as the chosen medium of politicos and techno-nerds and geeks of all stripes wound up with a college professor and a former dental hygienist as its primary poster children, but that's the thing about reality. It doesn't need to make sense. They were in the right places at the right times, they had the right level of heroic dedication and personal tragedy, and maybe most important, when their backs were against the wall—when their son was dead and the world was changed forever, and the things they'd been doing during the Rising to keep themselves from thinking about those two unchangeable facts weren't an option anymore—they decided to become stars in the highest-rated reality show anyone had ever seen. The news.

I dried my hands on the blue towel next to the kitchen sink before stepping aside to let Becks at the faucet. "Remember why we're here," I said, voice a little sharper than it needed to be. "This isn't a social call."

"I'm sorry. It's just . . . " Becks stuck her hands under the running water, using that small domestic activity to buy herself a few seconds. Finally, she said, "I thought she'd be taller. It's a cliché, I know, but I really did. I should know better—I've seen pictures of her next to you—but somehow, I still thought she'd be . . . " She stopped, and then finished, lamely, "Taller."

"I get that a lot." Along with requests for autographs, and occasional offers of money if I could somehow get my hands on naked pictures. My college journalism courses were hell. George had it a little better—I guess Irwins feel more entitled to demand the gory details, while Newsies just look for something they can hang you with.

"I wanted to be your mother when I grew up." Becks said it like it was somehow shameful, the sort of admission that could only be dragged out of her by a kitchen with yellow wallpaper and stupid curtains. Mom would have been proud of her environmental design. Hell, for all I knew, she already was. For all I knew, she was watching us from upstairs; they'd had this place bugged since before I could walk. "She was so . . . brave, and strong, and she always knew what she was doing. Not like me. I was just sleepwalking through the things my parents wanted me to do, until the day I finally got up the nerve to run."

We never did that, said George. Her voice echoed oddly, coming half from right beside me, half from the inside of my head. It was the house. I'd spent too much of my life in this house with her; she was haunting it as much as she was haunting me.

God, was that what it was like for the Masons after Phillip died? Did they see him every time they turned around, a bright-eyed little ghost that never refused to take a nap, never drew on the walls with his crayons, never screamed because he couldn't have another cookie? No wonder they adopted us. We weren't just another way of bringing in the ratings. We were a living attempt at exorcism.

"We never ran," I said softly.

Becks shot me a startled look that softened into understanding. We were raised by journalists; we grew up to be journalists. That wasn't the whole story, but it was enough to make a nice headline. We were raised by people who hurt everyone around them in their single-minded pursuit of the story. No one could look at the number of bodies in our wake and not believe that Georgia and I were two apples that didn't fall far from the transplanted tree.

"Shaun?" The voice was jovial and dry at the same time, the voice of every college professor who ever told a slightly off-color joke and laughed with his undergrads, proving he was "part of the gang" without giving up an inch of his authority. It was the voice of my childhood, the man I watched George beat herself to death trying to become.

Sometimes you *can* go home again. That's what hurts most of all.

"Hi, Dad," I said, turning to face him.

Dad smiled as he studied my face, his calculating expression making him look so much like George that it hurt, even though the two of them weren't biologically related. "The prodigal son comes rolling home. And who is this charming young lady?" His smile turned more sincere as he aimed it at Becks, the consummate showman finding an audience he could charm. "Please tell me our son didn't bring you here thinking you were going someplace pleasant."

"Hi," said Becks, smiling glossily. I resisted the urge to groan. "I'm Rebecca Atherton. It's a pleasure to meet you, sir. I'm a real fan of your work."

"Rebecca Atherton, from After the End Times?" Dad glanced my way for a split second, like he was making sure I saw how intimately he knew our site. "The pleasure is mine. Your report on the events of Eakly, Oklahoma, during the Ryman campaign was positively chilling. You have an eye for the news, Miss Atherton."

"Okay, you're laying it on a little thick," I said, unable to contain myself any longer. "Can you stop trying to spin Becks for thirty seconds and let us tell you why we're here?"

"Now, Shaun. Your mother was looking forward to having a nice family breakfast, just the four of us." Dad's smile faded. "I'm sure you wouldn't want to disappoint her."

"I gave up on trying not to disappoint her a *long* time ago." I glared at him.

He glared back. Something about that expression made him look as out-of-date as the kitchen, and somehow, between one second and the next, I started to *see* him, not just the man I remembered from my childhood. He was wearing pajama pants and a belted gray cotton robe, preserving the illusion of collegial dignity, but his already-thinning red Irish hair was almost gone, leaving an expanse of gleaming forehead in its wake. His eyes were tired behind the lenses of his glasses. I'd never really thought of him as tired before.

"Be that as it may, I'm assuming you wouldn't have come out of whatever hidey-hole you've been tucked away in without something you considered a very good reason, and that means you need us." Dad kept glaring as he spoke, choosing each word with exquisite care. That was something else he had in common with George. Both of them knew how to use words to wound. "If you want us to cooperate with whatever mad scheme has brought you back here, you will sit down, and you will eat breakfast with your parents like a civilized human being."

"Right." I shook my head. "And if you get some ratings out of the deal, well, that won't suck for you, will it?"

"Perhaps not," he allowed.

"Oh, good, we're all together." Mom appeared behind him, hair brushed, and a light layer of foundation on her cheeks. Not enough to show on camera—oh, no, never that—but enough to take fifteen years off her age. Her hair was the same silvery ash blonde it had always been.

How many times have you had to dye your hair in the last year? I wondered, and felt immediately bad about even harboring the thought. I didn't like the Masons. I didn't trust them. But at the end of the day, they were the only family I had left—and I *needed* them.

"Hands are clean," I said, holding them up for inspection. Becks mirrored the motion, letting me take the lead. I was so grateful I could have kissed her.

"Good. Now go set the table." Mom kissed Dad on the cheek—a glancing peck she normally reserved for public photo ops—and pushed past us into the kitchen. "Eggs and soy ham will be ready in ten minutes."

"Thanks, Mom," I said. I opened the nearest cabinet and took down four plates, passing them to Becks. Getting the glasses and silverware out of their respective places only took a few seconds more. "Come on, Becks."

"Coming," she said, and followed me out of the kitchen. Unsurprisingly, Dad tagged along behind her, looking studiously casual, but almost certainly making sure we didn't make a break for it before he'd had a chance to grill us on what, exactly, we had come for.

The lights were on in the empty dining room. I stopped in the doorway, a lump forming in my throat. The dining room table was clear. The dining room table was *never* clear, not even when someone was coming to interview one or more of us; it was a constant bone of contention between the two generations in the household, with Mom and Dad insisting the dining room was meant for eating, and George and I insisting it was a crime to let a perfectly good table go to waste for twenty hours of any given day. We fought over it at least once a month. We . . .

But that was the past. I shook it off, blinking away the tears that threatened to blur my vision, and felt Georgia's hand on my shoulder, steadying me.

The house is haunted, she said softly, *but so are you, and your haunting is stronger than theirs. You can do this.*

"Shaun?" asked Becks. "Are you okay?"

"Yeah," I said, answering them both with a single word. I stepped into the dining room and started putting glasses down on the table. "Sorry. Just memories."

"We have a lot of memories invested in this house—in this family," said Dad, moving around the table to keep us in view. "It's good to see you, son."

"Can we not?" This time, the tears were too close to blink away. I swiped my arm across my eyes in a quick, jerky motion. "Don't bullshit me, okay? Please. The last time we saw each other, you were threatening to take me to court over Georgia's will, and I'm pretty sure I told you to go fuck yourselves. So can we not play happy families for Becks's benefit? She knows better."

Dad's smile faded slowly. Finally, he said, "Maybe it's not only for her benefit. Did you consider that? Maybe we missed you."

"And maybe you're trying to get the best footage you can before I run out of here again," I said. Suddenly weary, I pulled out one of the dining room chairs and collapsed into it. "You missed me. Fine. I missed you, too. That doesn't change who we are."

"No, I suppose it doesn't." Dad turned to Becks, a seemingly genuine expression of apology on his face. "Would you like to wait in the kitchen while we have this conversation? I'm sure it's not very comfortable for you."

"I've come this far with your son. I think I'll stick with him a little longer." Becks took the seat next to mine, folding her hands in her lap as she directed a calm, level stare at my adoptive father.

He blinked, glancing between the two of us before clearly coming to the wrong conclusion. A smile crept back onto his face. "Ah. I see."

No, you don't, I wanted to scream. I didn't. Instead, I said, "We're here because we need your help. We didn't have any place else to go."

"That's the sort of thing a mother always loves to hear from her only living child," said Mom, stepping into the dining room. She was carrying a tray loaded down with quiche, slices of steaming artificial ham, and even a pile of waffles. It would have been more impressive if I hadn't known she'd pulled every bit of it out of the freezer. But it was food, and it was hot, and it smelled like my childhood—the parts of it that happened before I knew just what the score in our happy little family really was.

"At least I'm honest." I leaned over as soon as she put the tray on the table, driving my fork into the top waffle on the stack. She smiled indulgently, picking up the serving spoon and using it to deposit a slice of quiche on my plate. "Isn't that a virtue around here?"

"Sometimes. Rebecca? What can I get you?"

"It all looks fantastic, Ms. Mason. I'd like some of everything, if that isn't too much trouble."

"Nonsense. Why would I have cooked if I didn't want you to eat?" Mom made a flapping gesture with her free hand, indicating one of the empty seats. "Michael, sit down. Shaun's big pronouncement can wait until you have something in you."

"Yes, dear," he said, and sat. He winked at me, clearly trying to look conspiratorial, like we were the same because Mom was making us both eat. I ignored it, spearing a slice of "ham" with my fork rather than trying to come up with a less violent response. Anything I said would have ended with my screaming at someone—or maybe just screaming. The room, the hour, the false domesticity, it was rubbing at my nerves even more than I'd been afraid it would.

I may be a haunted house, but that doesn't mean I was emotionally equipped to sit in someone else's haunting, eating breakfast and pretending everything was normal.

It took about ten minutes to eat our breakfasts. While we ate, silence reigned, broken only by the clank of silverware against ceramic and the occasional sound of someone chewing a bit too loud. I kept catching glimpses of George. She was sitting in one of the otherwise empty seats, no plate in front of her, watching mournfully as the rest of us ate. She disappeared if I looked at her directly, and I was glad. If I'd been forced to sit in this house, with these people, looking at her ghost, I think I would have finally gone all the way insane.

At last, Dad pushed his plate away, patting his lips with his napkin, and turned a calm gaze on me. Becks was all but ignored; she'd had her opportunity to be a part of this little drama, to either side with the Masons or establish herself as a third party, and she'd chosen to stick with me. That meant she was basically a nonentity as far as he was concerned.

"Well, Shaun?" he asked. "To what do we owe the pleasure?"

"We need your help," I said again, not sure where else to start.

"With what, dear?" asked Mom, tilting her head inquisitively to the side. Light glinted off her diamond earring. My mother never slept in diamond earrings. That was a miniaturized camera. It had to be. She was recording us.

That wasn't unexpected. "Becks and I need to get to Florida without being stopped by the border patrols," I said, not bothering to sugarcoat the words. "I know you know people who can get you past the hazard lines. I need to know them, too."

"Why don't you go looking for your own contacts?" asked Dad. "You've never asked us to do your research for you before."

"Because there isn't time, and because any contacts I could find that easily wouldn't be as good as the ones you've been working on for years." I shrugged. "I'm smart enough to know a plan is only as good as the tools you use to carry it out."

"How were you planning to deal with the mosquitoes?" asked Mom. "Florida's a death sentence right now."

"Bug spray," said Becks. "Mosquito netting. The things they've been using to stay alive in regions with malaria problems for generations."

"Kellis-Amberlee is a bit nastier than malaria, young lady," said Dad.

"Guess that 'Miss Atherton' routine couldn't last, huh?" I took another slice of fake ham. "We have a plan for handling the bugs. What we don't have is a way to get to Florida without getting arrested."

"What you're asking for, Shaun . . . this isn't some little trinket. This is the name of a trusted ally, one who might never work with us again after we sell you his or her identity." Mom's eyes narrowed, that familiar calculating gleam lighting them from within. "What are you prepared to give us in exchange?"

"Georgia's files."

A momentary silence fell over the room, the Masons staring at me in startled surprise, Becks sitting by my side, and all of us waiting to see what would happen next. Then, finally, Dad began to smile. For the first time since we'd arrived, it actually looked sincere.

"Well, why didn't you say so? Let's go upstairs. You kids are going to need a map."

Dr. Abbey is edgy, which is making everyone in the lab edgy, which is making *me* edgy. I never realized how much space my coworkers occupied until they were gone. I keep expecting to find Mahir at one of the terminals, or have Maggie chase me out of the bathroom, or run into Shaun arguing with the air like he doesn't give a fuck who sees him being bat-shit crazy. It doesn't help that Dr. Abbey lost almost a third of her people in the security failure—and it doesn't make sense that the security failed. It's like the protocols all reset at the same time, and that sort of thing doesn't happen by mistake.

If someone here is letting the dead things out to play, then someone is feeding information back to whoever's driving this crazy train to hell. If someone here is against us, then the people responsible for all this know exactly where we are and what we're doing.

God, I'm scared.

—From *The Kwong Way of Things*, the blog of Alaric Kwong, July 27, 2041. Unpublished.

Michael's gone to pick up Phillip from his school. My office has been shut down for the day, and I managed to get to the Andronico's before they closed the doors. We should have enough canned food to see us through the next week—maybe more than that, if it's necessary. We have a high fence. We have good doors. We're going to be fine.

Paul, Susan, Debbie: If any of you see this, please, leave me a comment; let me know that you're okay. I have my minivan, and I can come get you if I have to, but I need to know exactly where you are. Come on, guys. Just keep me posted.

It's not like this is the end of the world, right? :)

—From *Daily Thoughts*, the blog of Stacy Mason, July 18, 2014. Taken from the archives of The Wall.

Thirteen

The sound of alarms screaming in the hall outside my room slammed me from a sound sleep straight into adrenaline-laced consciousness. I was on my feet with my hands over my ears before I was aware I was awake, every muscle tight with the need to move, move, *move.* I didn't know whether I wanted to run away from the danger or toward it. In a more lucid moment, I would have embraced that confusion, because it was what my journalistic training told me I should be feeling—the need to get the story warring with the need to not die in the process.

Funny thing about dying, coming back from the dead, and finding out you're not actually the woman you think you are: Anything that goes the way it's supposed to becomes reassuring as hell.

The alarms were still going, making it hard to hold any single thought for more than a second. Curiosity and years of working the front-page news beat won out over the shreds of my common sense. I ran to the one-way mirror, uncovering my ears and cupping my hands around my eyes as I tried to squint through the opaque glass. All I could see were blurry outlines of people rushing past, none holding still long enough for me to get an idea of who they were.

None of them were turning toward my door. And the alarm was still going.

"Hey!" I shouted, stepping back from the mirror. "Monitor people! What's going on?" There was no response. A thin worm of fear began working its way through my guts, twisting and biting as it gnawed toward my center. I was alone in here. I had a little gun, but that wasn't going to be enough if things were going really wrong. If they didn't let me out . . . "Hey!"

A group ran by in the hall, making so much noise that I could actually *hear* them through the window and over the alarm, even if I couldn't quite make sense of what they were *doing*. Were they screaming? Singing? Laughing? Or—worst of all, and looking increasingly possible as the seconds slipped by with the alarm still screaming—were they moaning?

I shrank back from the mirror, putting another useless foot between me and the glass. If we were in an outbreak situation, a few feet weren't going to make a difference one way or the other. Either the infected would realize I was there, or they wouldn't. Either the people outside the building would decide it needed to be sterilized, or they wouldn't. Where I was standing wasn't going to do a damn thing to change the outcome.

I wonder if the clone lab is zombie-proof, I thought, almost nonsensically. A titter of laughter escaped from my lips, the sound bright and ice-pick sharp under the shriek of the alarm.

Somehow, that little sound was what I needed to snap me out of my nascent panic and back into the problem at hand. There was something going on outside the room; whatever it was, it wasn't a good thing. I wasn't unarmed, but I might as well have been, for all the good my little gun would do me if this *was* an outbreak. I was, however, observing Michael Mason's first rule of dealing with the living dead: I had enough bullets that they wouldn't take me alive.

Feeling suddenly calmer, I looked up toward the speaker and said, "This is Georgia Mason. I don't know what's going on outside my room, but I am uninfected. I repeat, I am uninfected. Please advise if there's anything I should be doing. In the meanwhile, I'm going to assume none of you people have time for me, and I'm going to go sit down."

I walked back to the bed, keeping my shoulders squared and my chin up. It would have been a lot easier without the alarm wailing in my ears. I was going to have one hell of a headache later, assuming we lived that long. Putting my hands back over my ears, I waited.

All sense of time dropped away, blurred into nothingness by the steady blare of the alarm. Occasional sounds drifted through the mirror—once there was a burst of machine-gun fire that lasted long enough to make the hairs on the back of my neck stand on end; shortly after that there was a piercing scream that rose, buzz saw-sharp, before tapering off and vanishing back into the din—but for the most part, it was just me and the alarm. Not the best company I'd ever kept.

The sudden cessation of the noise was almost shocking. I jerked upright, suddenly aware that I had managed to sink so deep into semi-meditation that I was almost dozing. Wide-eyed, I unfolded my legs and slid into a standing position, keeping my eyes fixed on the door. It didn't open. I took a cautious step forward. It didn't open.

"Well, isn't *that* just fantastic," I muttered.

The sound of the intercom clicking on sent a wave of relief washing through me, so powerful that my knees felt weak for a few seconds. "Hello, Georgia," said Dr. Thomas, in his customary mild tone. "How are you feeling?"

I stared at the wall for a long moment, mouth falling open. Finally, slowly, I said, "Did you just ask me how I was *feeling*? Seriously? What's going on? Is there an outbreak? Are we alone in the building?" A new thought struck me, horrifying in its reasonableness. "Am *I* alone in the building?" He could be using an outside connection to reach the intercom, giving me the opportunity to say good-bye before the sterilization of the facility began.

Dr. Thomas actually laughed. In that moment, any good feeling I might have held toward him died. "Oh, no, Georgia! I'm sorry, you were reacting so calmly, I thought you'd realized."

"You thought I'd realized? Realized *what*?" I balled my hands into fists, glaring at the intercom. It belatedly occurred to me that this could come off as inappropriately aggressive—by CDC standards, anyway; Shaun would have said I was displaying just the right amount of aggression—and I shoved my still-balled hands behind my back, trying to conceal them.

"This was a test. We wanted to see how you would respond to an extreme stress situation—especially one that was a close mirror to things you would have experienced"—Dr. Thomas paused for just a little too long before finishing the sentence—"before."

I kept staring at the intercom. I didn't say anything.

"Georgia?"

I didn't say anything.

More sharply this time: "Georgia?"

I didn't say anything.

Annoyed now, but with a thin ribbon of anxiety running under the words, like my silence was a sign that some unknowable bearing strain had finally been reached: "Georgia, please. Don't be childish."

"Don't be *childish*?" I echoed, my eyes growing even wider for half a heartbeat before narrowing, reducing my vision to a thin line. "Did you seriously just tell me not to be *childish*?"

"Now, Georgia—"

"You faked an outbreak to see how I would respond to stress, and now you're basically saying 'gotcha,' like that makes it all better! I *died* in an outbreak, you bastard! The fact that I'm not crying in a corner should be all it takes to prove that I'm not being *childish*. If anyone's being childish, it's *you*. You're the one playing asshole pranks and getting offended when your target doesn't find them funny."

The silence lasted several seconds before Dr. Thomas said, "I think you're being unreasonable."

"And I think you're being a dick. In fact, four out of five cloned journalists agree that you're behaving badly." I crossed my arms. "So did I pass?"

"What?"

"Did. I. Pass?" I repeated, enunciating each word until it was almost a sentence all by itself. "You said this was a test of how I would react under stress. Well? Did I pass? Am I a fully functional individual?"

Again, silence. Finally, sounding almost subdued, Dr. Thomas said, "We'll go over your test results tomorrow. One of the orderlies will be along shortly with your dinner, and to take you to use the facilities. Thank you for your cooperation."

"What cooperation? You blasted my ears out with your damn special effects and watched me like a bunch of sick voyeurs!" I realized I was yelling and took a deep breath, forcing myself to ramp it back. It wasn't easy. Very little seemed to be, these days.

There was no response. The intercom was already off.

I walked back to my bed, feeling the headache the alarm had summoned starting to construct itself, bit by bit, in the space between my ears. Dropping to the mattress, I let gravity pull me into a slump, catching my forehead on my hands before it could hit my knees. I stayed like that for I don't know how long—long enough for my wrists to start going numb—before I heard the door slide open. I lifted my head.

One of the familiar rotating guards was standing there with an orderly. George, from Dr. Shaw's team. I blinked.

"We're here to take you to the restroom," he said, giving no sign that we'd met before. "Your dinner will be waiting when we bring you back, along with painkillers for your head."

I frowned a little. "Do you have medical sensors in my mattress?"

He risked a smile. "No. We just have cameras that show us the way you're clutching your temples. If you would come with us . . . ?"

Whatever game he was playing, he was probably playing it on Dr. Shaw's behalf, and while I still wasn't sure I trusted her, I trusted Gregory, and *he* trusted her. My relationships with the people around me were becoming increasingly conditional. Trust George because Dr. Shaw trusted him. Trust Dr. Shaw because Gregory trusted her.

Trust Gregory because he was the one who stood the best chance of getting me out of here without getting me killed. Again.

"Sure," I said, and stood.

There was another guard outside. He fell into step behind me, while the first guard took point, and George stayed to my right. We walked to the bathroom, stopping outside the door.

"How's your head?" asked George.

"It hurts," I replied. "How long was I in there?"

"About six hours."

That explained the way reality had seemed to stretch and blur into nothing but alarm bells and waiting. I scowled. "I'd better be getting a *lot* of painkillers," I said, even though there was no way I'd be taking them. The people who prepared my food could drug me at any time, and there was nothing I could do to stop them. That didn't mean I needed to make it easy.

"You'll be getting a medically safe dosage," said George, in what sounded like it was supposed to be a reassuring tone. "Now please, you have about twelve minutes before your dinner is ready. You don't need to rush, but you wouldn't want your soup getting cold."

The last time Gregory had come to remove me from my quarters, he'd done it at midnight. I nodded slightly, indicating that the message had been received—assuming it was a message at all, and wasn't just me fumbling for meaning where there wasn't any. "I'll be quick."

"We appreciate it."

The guards didn't accompany me into the bathroom. I still moved like they were there, watching me; it was the only way I knew to keep from getting annoyed by the knowledge that I was being watched by half a dozen hidden cameras. If Buffy had been here, she could have spotted them all by measuring minute inaccuracies in the grout, and disabled them with soap suds and mock-clumsiness. If one of us was going to come back from the dead, it should have been her. She could have treated it like just another story. She would have handled it better.

Then again, maybe not. The truth is allowed to be stranger than fiction, and the parts of this that weren't making sense yet might have been enough to send her over the edge. The only reason they weren't making me crazy was the fact that I had something to hold on to. Shaun was alive. Shaun was out there somewhere. And wherever he was, he needed me.

I undressed the way I always did, shoving my pants down my legs and peeling my socks off in the same gesture, concealing my little gun. It meant putting the same clothes back on when I was finished, carrying the clean pajamas they'd provided back to the room, and changing under the covers of my bed, but I'd been able to pass it off as a strange form of modesty . . . at least so far. I soaped up and rinsed down in record time, assisted by the fact that my bleach rinse only lasted for about fifteen seconds—a perfunctory nod to regulations, while acknowledging that I hadn't been near anything infectious since I was Frankensteined to life.

George and the guards were still waiting outside the bathroom when I emerged. "All clean," I announced, wiping my damp bangs back from my forehead. "Now, about those painkillers."

George nodded, motioning for the lead guard to take us back to my room. True to his word, my dinner tray was waiting when we arrived, tomato soup the color of watered-down blood and what looked like grilled cheese sandwiches. High-end hospital food. Tomato soup and cheese sandwiches seemed to surface at every other meal. I didn't mind as much as I might have. At least they were well prepared, which was more than I could say for many of the more ambitious things to come out of the kitchen.

Four small white pills were sitting on the tray, next to my glass of milk. "Thanks," I said, stepping through the doorway, into the room.

"Have a nice night, Miss Mason," said George. The door closed, cutting him from view.

I sat down at the table, palming the pills and dropping them into my lap as I mimed swallowing them. The room's white-on-white decorating scheme helped with that. Whoever was monitoring the security monitors currently airing *The Georgia Mason Show* would have to be paying extremely close attention to catch white pills being dropped onto the white legs of my pajamas, where I covered them with my white napkin.

My soup was hot, and had obviously been put on the table seconds before we returned to the room. That didn't fit George's twelve-minute estimate, so either he was wrong, or he really had been telling me to wait for midnight. That was fine. It wasn't like I had anything else to do.

An orderly came and took my empty dishes after I finished eating. The pills I'd managed not to take were safely tucked into the seam of my pillowcase by then. I smiled. He flinched. I smiled wider. If these people couldn't handle the results of their crazy science, they shouldn't be bringing back the dead. The orderly all but scurried from the room, and I started to feel a little bad. It wasn't his fault. None of this was. The orders that controlled my life came from way above his pay grade.

I paced around the room a few times, feigning my normal restlessness, before climbing back into bed. I'd been sleeping more and more, and all sense of time was going rapidly out the window. If the alarms were going off for six hours, and they'd been off for about an hour and half, that meant I'd been awake for less than eight hours. It felt like forever. I was exhausted.

Maybe they were putting something in my food after all.

The throbbing in my head kept me from falling into anything

deeper than a light doze. It shattered when the door opened. I sat up, squinting.

"Hello?"

"We have sixteen minutes," said Gregory. He didn't leave the doorway. Maybe there was too much risk of him getting stuck in the room when the sixteen-minute security window closed. "I'm sorry. It was the best I could arrange on such short notice."

"Don't worry about it." I swung my feet around to the floor, wincing a little. "Did you bring any painkillers I can actually trust?"

"As a matter of fact, yes." Gregory dipped a hand into his pocket. "I even brought water."

"Thanks," I said. The word seemed to stick in my throat. Shaun was always the one who brought me painkillers when the light got to be too much and one of my migraines decided to start making its presence known. I missed him so much.

"We don't have long."

I paused in the process of getting up. Then I stood and walked toward him, holding out my hand for the pills. "What do you mean? Sixteen minutes, right?"

"We arranged the window when today's testing schedule went up on the intranet." Gregory sounded grimmer than I'd ever heard him. "Someone's going to get caught over this one. It won't be me, but whoever it is, they're going to be lucky if all they lose is their job."

A chill started in the pit of my stomach. "What are you saying?"

"They've started stress-testing you. That isn't good." He dropped two pills into my hand, producing a bottle of water from his other pocket. "Four subjects have made it this far. None of them got through the alarm sequence without permanent psychological damage. Georgia, I'm sorry. We didn't realize they were going to speed things up like this, but with your brother—" He stopped dead.

The silence that stretched between us was the loudest I had ever heard. I opened the bottle of water and tossed the pills into my mouth, washing them down without really registering the motion. It was something that had to be done, and so I was doing it; that was all. The silence continued, Gregory waiting to see how I would respond, my mind racing through all the possible ways that sentence could have ended.

None of them were good.

"With Shaun what?" I asked. Gregory didn't answer. "With Shaun *what*?" I repeated.

"Off the grid," said Gregory. He took the empty bottle from my hand. "He and the rest of your old news site dropped off the radar following Tropical Storm Fiona."

He mentioned the storm like it was a big event. I frowned. "Were they in the area? Are they missing?"

"No. There have been a few sightings, all of them on the West Coast. The EIS has been planting sighting reports elsewhere in the country, but it's hard, with as little data as we have."

"So what, they're thinking they can tell me to find him, and I'll know where he's gone to ground?" I scoffed. "That's not going to happen."

"No. They're thinking they can finish running their tests on you, demonstrating to the investors just how stable a clone can be, and then they can decommission you in favor of a Georgia Mason who'll be willing to play the part they ask it to play."

The chill continued to uncurl, spreading to cover my entire body. "What part is that?"

"Bait." I couldn't see Gregory's expression with the light shining so brightly behind him. I didn't need to. His voice told me everything I needed to know. "They're going to put the new Georgia on the air, and they're going to use it to do the one thing they couldn't do on their own."

"They're going to use her to lure Shaun in," I finished, in a whisper.

"They'll use her to do more than that, if they possibly can. I'll be honest, Georgia, because this isn't a time for being anything else. Shaun's psychological profiles since your death have been . . . disturbing, to say the least."

"Disturbing how? Cutting up children and old ladies disturbing, or not showering anymore disturbing?"

"Talking to himself. Refusing to let go of the idea that you'll come back someday. That's part of what let the investors sell the idea that you would have multiple uses."

"But not me in specific."

"No," Gregory admitted.

I took a deep breath. The painkillers hadn't had time to work, but the chill was muffling the pain nicely, making everything seem a little more distant, and hence a little easier to deal with. "Well, all right. I guess that means it's time to get me the hell out of Dodge, doesn't it?"

"Yes, it does," said Gregory—and now he sounded sad, and deeply concerned. "There's just one problem."

I closed my eyes. "You still don't know how you're going to do that, do you?"

"No. We don't."

"Well." I opened my eyes, sighing once. "This is going to be fun."

Book III

Foundations

Given a choice between life and death, choose life. Given a choice between right and wrong, choose what's right. And given a choice between a terrible truth and a beautiful lie, choose the truth every time.

—Georgia Mason

Fuck it. Let's blow some shit up.

—Shaun Mason

Every time I think my life can't get any weirder, it does. Today has included a missing Newsie from the Rising generation who just happens to be running a rest stop on the smuggler's route to Canada, rednecks with guns, listening to Shaun sing along with the radio (badly), and a zombie bear. Who knows what delights tomorrow will bring? And will tomorrow bring a shower with enough hot water to finish washing my hair?

Stay tuned for our next exciting update that I can't post because it might give our location away to some mysterious shadow conspiracy.

Fuck, this sucks.

—From *Charming Not Sincere*, the blog of Rebecca Atherton, July 26, 2041. Unpublished.

IF YOU ARE READING THIS, DO NOT LEAVE YOUR ROOM. If you are already outside your room, find a secure location immediately. The following places on campus are currently secure: The library. The Life Sciences building. The student store. Durant Hall. The Optometry lab. The following places are confirmed compromised: The English and Literature building. The Bear's Den. The administrative offices.

THIS IS NOT A HOAX. THIS IS NOT A PRANK. This is Professor Michael Mason. We are in a state of emergency. If you are reading this, do not leave your room.

Stacy, darling, I'll be home as soon as I can.

—From *Breathing Biology*, the blog of Michael Mason, July 18, 2014. Taken from the archives of The Wall.

Fourteen

Dad's map was just that: a large piece of paper with roads and landmarks drawn on it. He spread it out on the dining room table, smirking a bit when he saw the disbelieving expressions Becks and I were wearing. "What?" he asked. "You've never seen a map before?"

"Not outside of a history book," I said. "Haven't you ever heard of GPS?"

"What isn't on a computer can't be hacked, oh foolish son of mine," said Dad. He was comfortably in professor mode now, that old "I am imparting wisdom to the young" twinkle in his eye. George used to love it when he'd get like this, like it was some secret language the two of them could share—the language of knowledge and the truth. Naturally, that meant I'd always hated it when he'd get like this, because he was lying to her. He was letting her believe he cared.

"Mom, make Dad stop acting like he knows everything," I said, without any real rancor.

"Michael, tell the kids what they need to know," said Mom. "And in exchange, Shaun will tell us what *we* need to know. Isn't that right, Shaun?"

"Yeah, Mom. That's right." *I'll tell you how to steal the last things in the world that belong to your adopted daughter, and you won't even think of yourselves as grave robbers.* The acid in the thought was almost shocking, even to me. I realized I was digging my nails into my palms again. I rested my hands on the edge of the table, forcing my fingers to uncurl. "So what are we looking at here?"

"The trouble is the distance. There's no single safe route from here into the Florida quarantine zone—maybe if you were aiming for something in the contaminated parts of Texas?" Dad glanced up, a canny glint appearing behind the amiable twinkle in his eyes. "You didn't mention exactly what you were trying to accomplish on this little road trip, come to think of it."

"True, and we're not going to mention it, so don't bother fishing," I said. The map covered the Southwestern United States, stopping shortly after it crossed into Texas. "Are you saying this is as far as you can get us?"

"I'm saying this is as far as we can get you before things become complicated," Dad replied. "You don't mind complicated, do you, Shaun?"

"I like to think it's a specialty of mine."

"Good." He beckoned me closer. I motioned for Becks to do the same. He began tapping highways and side roads, rattling off names, security levels, and known geographical quirks with a speed that was almost daunting. I was so busy trying not to lose track of what he was saying that I barely even noticed when Mom slipped out of the room. Dad pulled out another map, this one covering the space from Texas to Mississippi, and kept talking.

Shaun.

"What?" I asked, without thinking about it.

Dad glanced up, eyes narrowed. "What's that?"

"I think I'm confused, too," said Becks smoothly. "What do you mean about fuel shortages in Louisiana?"

Dad smiled at her and began talking again, saying something about fuel pipelines being compromised in the wake of Tropical

Storm Fiona. I couldn't quite make out the details; George was talking too loudly for that. *You need to get Becks and get out of here. Abort the mission. Abort it* now. *There isn't time to argue.*

Maybe there wasn't time to argue, but there was time to scowl at the map, trying to wordlessly express my confusion to the voice inside my head.

It must have worked at least a little, because George groaned and said, *They're hiding something from you. You told them you had the files. They should have tried to make you hand them over before they told you anything, and they didn't. That means they think they can have their cake and eat it, too. You need to get* out *of here.*

I stiffened, hoping Dad was too focused on Becks to notice. George was right. We'd made this plan, which was, admittedly, a stupid, suicidal plan, expecting the Masons to be willing to make a trade. Normally, that would mean they wouldn't expect me to give them the files without proof of cooperation on their part. So where were those negotiations? Where was Dad insisting I give them a single file, just to show that I was serious? Hell, where was Mom? She should have been in the room, keeping an eye on us, making sure Dad didn't get too excited by the process of showing us how clever he was and show us a little bit too much. That was the most damning piece of the admittedly sketchy evidence: Mom should never have left the room.

"Who's paying you?" I asked conversationally, taking my hands away from the table. Becks cast a startled glance in my direction. I smiled reassuringly. "It's cool, Becks. They're just selling us up the river, and I was wondering who they were selling us to. That's all."

Dad paled. "I'm sure I have no idea what you're talking about. You've been on the run too long, son. It's starting to affect your thinking."

"Well, yeah. I know that part. I mean, it's driven me crazy and everything, which I know you know, since you've been looking for an excuse to have me declared mentally unfit and take my stuff since George died—great job mourning for her, by the way, really top-notch—but I don't think this is me being crazy. I think this is an unfortunate moment of me being sane, and when I'm sane, I have to admit that everyone in the world really *is* out to get us." I pulled George's .40 from my belt, bringing it up and aiming it at his head. "I'm only going to ask you one more time. Who's paying you?"

"No one's paying us, darling." Mom's voice came from behind me, calm and even cheerful, with the faintly manic edge that accompanied every mother-son outing we'd ever taken. The click of a safety being disengaged was basically just overkill. "It's simply that we don't think you should be running around besmirching our family name. Not after everything we've done to build the brand."

"Hi, Mom," I said, still aiming the .40 unwaveringly at Dad. He wasn't moving. I always knew he was a smart one. "Is this the part where you tell me to put my gun down?"

"No, this is the part where I save your ass," said Becks. The statement was accompanied by the sound of her revolvers being cocked. "Please believe me when I say that I respect your work greatly, Mrs. Mason, and I will blow your fucking head off if you don't stop aiming that gun at my boss right now."

Mom laughed. It was a joyful, tittering, purely artificial sound. "Oh, how cute. She's willing to step in and *save* you, darling. Such loyalty—and such a pretty girl, too. Is she sweet on you? So many of the pretty girls have been. Not that you ever paid them any attention. Not that your sainted sister, may she rest in peace, ever *let* you. Do you think things would have gone differently if she hadn't been so selfish?"

"Don't talk about George," I said, gritting my teeth to keep my calm from slipping away. "She moves, shoot her, Becks."

"With pleasure, Boss."

"It seems we have a standoff, son," said Dad, raising his hands. It felt almost unfair, letting him be the only one in the room without a gun. Good thing I've never been too hung up on playing fair. "So what now?"

"Now you stay where you are." I took a deep breath before asking, "What did you do, Mom? Who did you call?"

"No one a concerned citizen doesn't have the right to call," she replied, in the same happy, artificial tone. "You shouldn't have come here, Shaun. I'm glad you did—it was nice to see you—but you shouldn't have come." For a moment, I thought I heard genuine regret in her tone. As hard as I'd tried, I'd never quite been able to stop myself from loving the Masons. Maybe, difficult as it was to credit, they had the same problem.

Maybe they hadn't quite been able to keep themselves from loving us.

"The house logged our arrival, didn't it? And you let the information upload. You didn't have to. We're not residents, and no one saw us come. You could have scrubbed it, and no one would have ever known." That's what I'd been counting on when I suggested coming here. I knew what that security system could do. "Why didn't you?"

"Be reasonable, Shaun," said Dad. He shook his head, looking almost contrite. "People are saying you may have had something to do with what's happening right now in the Gulf. We can't even get passes to go into the restricted zones. Other journalists with similar credentials have managed to at least get around the edges, but we're being shut out. Bringing you to justice would counter that. It would show we weren't working with you."

"I'm sure the ratings wouldn't hurt, either," said Becks sourly. I risked a sympathetic glance her way. I'd been disillusioned by the Masons years ago. She was getting her disillusionment in one lump sum . . . and like anything that shows your heroes in an unpleasant light, it had to be bitter. So very bitter.

"No," Mom admitted. "It's been harder to keep the numbers up since we lost that family dynamic. We got a few spikes when things went bad in Oakland, and a few more when your names started coming up in conjunction with the tragedy, but nothing lasting. Nothing that would bring in the numbers remotely like an act of selfless heroism."

"So you're going to sacrifice us for ratings," I said.

"Now, son, it's not like that—" Dad began.

"Isn't it?" I lowered my gun, slowly turning to look at Mom. Feigning curiosity, I asked, "So if you're willing to trade one son for a better market share . . . what *really* happened to Phillip, Mom? Did he just *happen* to get in that dog's way, like the official story says? Or were you afraid your fifteen minutes of fame were already over, and just searching for anything that could make them last a little longer?"

Her eyes widened. There was a moment when I wasn't sure whether she was going to shoot me. Then she was striding across the space between us, Becks forgotten, gun dropping to her side. I could have ducked away from her hand. I didn't, and the sound of her palm hitting my cheek rang through the room like it was the loudest thing in the world. Becks stood frozen, staring. From the silence behind me, Dad was doing much the same.

Mom's eyes were filling with furious tears. "Don't you *ever*, *ever* say something like that to me," she snarled. The anger in her voice may have been the most honest emotion I'd ever seen from her. "You don't get to talk about him."

"Well, then, you don't get to talk about Georgia," I countered. "How is this different, Mom? I'm your son. You didn't give birth to me, but you raised me. You're the only mother I've ever had. And now you're selling my life—my *life*—because you want better ratings. How is this different from what happened to Phillip? Give me one good answer. Please. Just one."

She stared at me, seemingly unable to decide whether she should get furiously angry or break down and start to cry. Becks was still holding her pistols aimed at Mom's head, standing in an easy hip-shot stance that I knew she could hold for hours, if she needed to. I also knew she wasn't going to need to. Someone was going to break this standoff before much longer. I just hoped it would be someone in the room, rather than someone driving an official vehicle and commanding an urban cleanup squad.

"It was an accident," said Dad. I didn't turn. I didn't want to take my eyes off Mom. "Marigold wasn't supposed to be in our yard. Phillip was unlucky. This is different."

"Why? Because it's premeditated? Because you pulled me and George out of some state orphanage somewhere, and that gives you the right to decide how I'm going to die? Don't kid yourselves. If you keep us here, we're *going* to die. Someone's going to be careless, someone else is going to say we moved for a weapon, and we're going to be so much sterilized ash by lunchtime."

"You don't know that," said Mom. She seemed to be getting herself back under control. That probably wasn't good. "They may just take you in for questioning."

"The mosquitoes got loose while we were in the Memphis CDC, Ms. Mason." Becks's voice was as calm as it was unexpected. Mom's head whipped around to stare at her. "If it hadn't been for the storm—if it hadn't been for bad timing—they would have been confined to Cuba. They would never have reached the coast without the wind to help them."

"So?" demanded Mom.

"Stacy." Dad's voice was soft, thoughtful; the same sort of tone that George used to get when something occurred to her in the middle of the night. She'd wake me up and whisper in my ear in that soft, contemplative voice, telling me stories I only half heard, but that would be posted on our site within the week.

"What?" Mom turned back toward him, and consequentially, toward me.

"The weather maps *do* show that the mosquitoes originated in

Cuba. They're on record as a mutation. Some sort of horrible trick of natural selection."

"You don't believe that, do you, Mr. Mason?" asked Becks. "Doesn't it seem a little pat? Twenty years of no insect vectors, and then one comes along at the right time to bury a news cycle no one wants to deal with? If it hadn't been for the storm, we'd be hearing a lot of different stories right now. The Cuban tragedy would be dominating the news for the next year, and no one would ever hear about a break-in at a CDC facility, or about the corruption leading to the death of Dr. Kelly Connolly, granddaughter of the man who broke the news about the Rising."

"But Tropical Storm Fiona had other ideas," I said, taking up her argument. "Whoever let those mosquitoes loose wasn't counting on a big ol' wind sweeping in and carrying their nasty little pets to American soil. So the cycle got buried, and so did a lot of innocent people. It was a mistake. It still did its job. You never heard about any of that, did you?"

"No." Dad stepped up behind me, and stepped around me, moving to stand beside Mom. Becks shifted her position, widening her stance as she adjusted to include him in her line of fire. "We never heard any of those things."

"So either I've gone entirely out of my mind—which isn't out of the question, I guess, since I talk to myself and everything; but if I'm crazy, I've managed to take my team with me—or someone is really out to get us. And whoever it is, they were willing to gamble with the Kellis-Amberlee virus in order to keep us out of the headlines." I took a breath. "Lots of kids died in Florida, Mom. Lots of little kids. And not because they ran into dogs that hadn't been chained up properly. Not because their parents did anything wrong. They got bit by mosquitoes, and it killed them, and it wasn't *fair*. Just like what happened to Phillip wasn't fair."

"I told you not to talk about him," she said. This time, the anger in her voice wasn't there, and the tears were beginning to overflow her lower lids, starting their slow tracks down her cheeks. She looked old, and tired, and like the woman I'd only ever seen in pictures taken before I was even born. She looked like someone who could have loved me.

"Please. We're trying to get to Florida because the family of one of our team members was there when the storm hit. His parents died. His little sister's still alive. We promised him we'd get her out."

Dad shook his head. "That's not going to happen, son."

What? demanded George.

"What?" I asked, half a heartbeat later.

"They've had our house under surveillance for weeks. Even if we'd wanted to hide your presence, we couldn't have done it for long. They'll be here any minute now." He turned to his wife, my adoptive mother, the first of the world's true Irwins. "Stacy. It's up to you."

She hesitated. Then, finally, she nodded. Turning back to me, she said, "It's not like Phillip at all, Shaun, because we couldn't save him." She turned her gun around, offering it to me butt-first. "Make it look realistic, and get the hell out of here."

"Mom . . ."

"You have maybe three minutes. Four, if you're willing to leave the van and take mine instead—but you won't do that, will you?" A smile tugged at the corners of her mouth. "Michael, take Rebecca to the garage and get her set up with one of the portable jammers, will you?"

"Yes, dear," he said. Then he paused, looking back at me, and said, "I'm proud of you, son. We didn't do right by you or by your—by Georgia—but I'm proud of you, all the same. I think I have the right to that much."

"Yeah, Dad. You do."

"Thank you." He motioned for Becks to follow him. "Come along, young lady."

Becks glanced at me, eyes wide. I nodded, hoping the gesture would be reassuring, and not sure what I'd do if it wasn't. "It's okay, Becks," I said. "I'll be right there."

"Shaun . . ."

"Just go. I promise, I'll be *right* there."

Still looking uncertain, she followed him out of the room. Their footsteps drifted back down the hall; then the door connecting the kitchen to the garage slammed, and even that was gone. I returned my attention to my mother.

"You sure?" I asked.

"No." She laughed a little, still holding her gun out to me. "But hell, when have I been sure about anything? I think the last time I was absolutely *sure* of something was in July of 2014. I was sure that was going to be the summer when I finally learned how to swim."

"Mom . . ." I stopped, realizing I had no idea what else I could say to this woman. We were family and we were strangers. She was my mother and my teacher and the one person I had never been able to please, no matter how hard I tried or how much I played the clown. I took the gun from her hand. "What are you going to tell them?"

"That you realized we'd called the authorities, and ran." Her eyes were clear and calm. "Or maybe I won't tell them anything. The choice is yours."

It took me a moment to realize that she was saying I could shoot her: She was unarmed, and I had her gun. They wouldn't be able to use the ballistics to trace me, or to conclusively prove I'd pulled the trigger while she was still alive. I shook my head. "Tell them whatever you have to in order to get them off your back, and then find a way to get to Florida. Alaric's sister is named Alisa Kwong. She's in the Ferry Pass Refugee Center. Get her out."

"Then what?"

I stepped forward, leaning in to kiss her forehead the way she used to kiss mine when there was an appropriate photo opportunity. Until that moment, I hadn't really realized that I was taller than her now. "Do what you couldn't do for us, Mom," I said. "Love her. Until Alaric can come back for her, just love her."

She nodded. "I'll try," she said. "That's all that I can promise."

"That's fine." I smiled at her. She smiled back. She was still smiling when I slammed the gun into her temple. I wasn't trying to knock her out—the human head is thicker than most movies want you to believe, and knocking someone out without killing them is a precise science—just catch her off guard. I managed that. She staggered backward with a shout, the skin split and bleeding above her eye. That was going to be one hell of a shiner.

She didn't grab for the gun. She didn't swear at me. She just clapped a hand over the wound and pointed to the door, saying, "Go. We'll take care of things from here."

I went. As I ran through the kitchen, I threw Mom's gun into the sink. It was still half-full of soapy dishwater. The gun sank into the bubbles. I broke into a run.

Dad and Becks were in the garage with the door standing open. The sky was starting to lighten, hints of sunrise creeping up around the edges. "Come on," I said, gesturing for Becks to follow me. "Dad—"

"The scanner says they're eight blocks out. Miss Atherton has the jammer. Now *go*." He adjusted his glasses with one hand. His shoulder was bleeding copiously. There was no telling what Becks had used to make the wound. Mom's toolbox provided a wealth of possibilities.

He saw me looking and smiled. I smiled back and kept going, heading for the van. Becks ran behind me, a boxy object cradled under one arm that I recognized as one of Mom's highly prized, highly illegal jammers. If we were caught with it, we'd be looking at a nice long stay in prison . . . assuming we lived long enough to get there, which seemed less than likely. But Becks was laughing when we reached the van, adrenaline and exhaustion bubbling over, and I joined in, and we threw ourselves inside just as soon as we could get the locks to disengage.

I didn't even bother to fasten my seat belt before I started the engine and slammed my foot down on the gas. Becks put the jammer on the dashboard, connecting it to the stereo's USB power outlet before turning it on. A soft white-noise whine filled the cab, more psychological than anything else; it was there so we would know the equipment was working.

The sound of sirens was just beginning to split the Berkeley air when we turned the corner, gathering speed all the while, and we were gone.

You really can't go home again.

Sometimes, that's a good thing.

Sometimes, when you try, you find out that home isn't there anymore . . . but that it wasn't only in your head before. Home actually existed. Home wasn't just a dream.

Sometimes, that's the best thing of all.

—From *Adaptive Immunities*, the blog of Shaun Mason, July 28, 2041. Unpublished.

Seattle is gray, damp, and far too proud of being surrounded on all sides by trees which never lose their leaves and hence, never stop providing cover for whatever might be lurking behind them. The natives are as friendly as any Americans, and tend to become extremely helpful when I produce my passport. "I'm an Indian citizen" carries a lot of weight here.

I'm worried about Maggie. We have yet to bribe our way in to see the Monkey, and she's not doing well with all this secrecy and illicit trafficking. I would have said Alaric was the weak link in our particular chain, with his sister as a possible hostage to his good behavior, but I am beginning to fear our dear Magdalene might be just as easily swayed with the promise of a return to her "real life" . . .

—From *Fish and Clips*, the blog of Mahir Gowda, July 28, 2041. Unpublished.

Fifteen

I was left mostly to my own devices after the alarm. That was a good thing; my headache got steadily worse once Gregory's painkillers wore off. I wasn't willing to ask the orderlies for anything else, and I couldn't exactly ring for my buddy the EIS mole. So I spent most of what felt like a day in bed, huddled under the covers and trying to shove my head far enough beneath the pillow to block out the room's ambient light.

Eventually, I managed to go back to sleep. When I woke, my headache was gone. The isolation was another matter. Dr. Thomas didn't appear, and the orderlies who brought my meals were even more perfunctory than usual, like they were performing an unpleasant chore. I considered trying to talk to them, and dismissed it in favor of playing the good little clone, tractable, meek, and willing to be told where to sit, what to eat, and when to go to the bathroom. None of them appeared more than once, and I could see the guards waiting in the hall when the door slid open to allow the orderlies in or out.

That was enough to worry me. Were the guards there because they thought I might be smart enough to get wind of what was coming? Had some other clone of Georgia Mason seen the writing on the wall when her decommissioning approached, and tried to make a break for it? Or had Gregory slipped somehow—was our window not as secure as he thought it was, did he say the wrong thing, did he get *caught*? Were the guards there because the plan to bust me out, sketchy as it was, had been blown?

I realized the fear was irrational almost as soon as I finished figuring out what it was. I still had my gun. If Gregory had been caught, someone would have come to take my gun. As long as I was armed, I had to make myself assume that things were going as planned . . . whatever that plan turned out to actually be.

The next "day" inched by at a glacial pace. By the time dinner came, I was virtually climbing the walls. I forced myself to sit on the bed, holding as still as I could, and tried to focus on what I knew about the layout of the facility. I'd seen plenty of labs, but I didn't have a good idea of where they were relative to one another—the identical halls and rapid walk-throughs had seen to that. If I managed to get out of here, I'd be flying blind unless I had someone to escort me. All of which brought me back to Gregory, and the increasingly pressing question of where he was.

Another unfamiliar orderly brought my lunch, a truly uninspiring combination of cheese slices, soy spread, and sliced bread. "The catering has definitely gone downhill around here," I called after his retreating back. My stomach rumbled, making it clear that no matter how lousy the food looked, I was damn well going to eat it. I needed to keep my strength up.

The cheese was as bland as I'd expected. After the second bite, I started to doubt that it was even cheese, since it tasted more like a blend of soy and artificial flavorings. I wrinkled my nose and kept eating. Cheese meant protein, even if it didn't necessarily mean dairy, and protein was a good thing. That thought was almost enough to motivate me through the rest of the plate before I lost all interest, picked up the bread, and retreated with it to the bed. Who cared if I got a few crumbs in the sheets? It wasn't like there was anyone here to complain about them.

For some reason, that made me wonder if any of the Georgia Masons who came before me tried to seduce an orderly when they hit the last days of their captivity. The image was enough to make me snort with involuntary laughter. It wasn't just that I had no idea how to go about seducing somebody—seduction was never exactly required, given my particular set of circumstances. It was the idea of any of those stiff, buttoned-down orderlies trying to explain that dinner didn't come with a side order of clone sex.

Hell, maybe one of the other Georgias even made a play for Dr. Thomas. That would certainly explain why he was so careful to avoid physical contact, even now that we were well past the point of needing to worry about spontaneous amplification. Maybe he was afraid I'd rip my pajama top open and start trying to buy my freedom.

I was still snickering when the door slid open and a slim blonde woman in a lab coat stepped into my room. "Did I come at a bad time, Georgia?" asked Dr. Shaw. "I can come back later, if you would prefer."

I jumped to my feet, dropping my bread. "Dr. Shaw," I said. "I wasn't expecting you today." Or here. Or ever.

"There are times one must enjoy the privileges of surprise," she said. "Have you finished your lunch? I do apologize for the blandness of the ingredients, but I was unable to come and brief you before your afternoon meal was delivered, and it was important that preparations begin immediately."

My shoulders tensed. I forced them to unlock. *Dr. Shaw is a friend,* I reminded myself. *She gave me the gun. She's not going to do anything to hurt me.* Not unless she had to, anyway. "Preparations?" I asked.

"Yes," she said, and smiled. She was gorgeous when she smiled. Not beautiful; gorgeous, like the cam-girl porn bloggers who make a living on looks and panty shots. Maybe that was the reason she didn't smile much. Save them up, and use them like weapons when she needed them. "I finally got approval for my deep-state sleep study. They would probably have dragged their feet on me longer, but Dr. Thomas has proposed a series of tests that will occupy all your time as of next week, and that gave me the leverage I needed to convince our superiors to let me have you until then." She paused, clearly expecting something from me.

"Um . . . yay?"

"Yes," she said, with an enthusiastic nod. "Very 'yay.' This is going to tell us so *much* about your mental state, Georgia. There are things to be discovered by examining your subconscious that, well . . . I won't bore you with details, but suffice to say that I expect us to both be very pleased with my results. Now, I am afraid you may be slightly inconvenienced by what has to be done . . . " She let the sentence trail off, again waiting for my reply.

This time, I was faster on my cue. "Inconvenienced how, exactly?"

"You'll be sleeping in my lab for the duration. I realize it's an invasion of your privacy, but it can't be avoided if we want to get good results."

I managed not to laugh at the notion of my possessing anything remotely resembling "privacy" in the room I'd been sleeping in. "I think I can handle it."

"Thank you," said Dr. Shaw. Her smile faded, replaced by her more familiar chilly professionalism. "Is there anything you'd like to bring with you?"

I blinked. I hadn't realized she meant we'd be leaving the room *now*. "No," I said, with complete honesty. My gun was tucked into the top of my left sock, and I'd long since finished reading the few books I'd been able to cajole Dr. Thomas into giving me. Nothing else here was mine. They could decant the next girl and put her in this room, and she'd never know I'd existed, just like I woke up not knowing there had been others here before me.

The thought was sobering. One way or another, I was never going to come back here. Either I'd get out, or I'd just be gone, and no one would miss me, or mourn for me, except for maybe Gregory. Maybe not even him. Assuming his cover hadn't been blown, he'd probably be busy trying to find out whether the new Georgia Mason was the one he could finally save.

"Good," said Dr. Shaw, breaking me out of the dark spiral of my own thoughts. "If there's nothing here you'd like to bring, then we're ready to begin."

"I didn't have anything else on my calendar for today," I said. Dr. Shaw started for the door. I followed, resisting the urge to look back at the room that was never mine, not really. It was a stopping point, and yet somehow, walking through the door with her felt very, very final.

Two of the technicians from our first round of tests were waiting for us in the hall, along with two guards I didn't recognize. I was getting used to that. I focused my attention on the technicians, smiling as earnestly as I could. "Kathleen. George. It's good to see you again."

"See?" crowed Kathleen, bouncing in place. The guards looked at her with visible discomfort but didn't move from their positions. "I told you the sleep studies would get approved!"

"I should never have doubted you," I said.

"You're looking . . . well," said George.

"I've had lots of rest," I said.

"Which is excellent for our purposes," said Dr. Shaw. "Now that we're all acquainted again, come along. We have much to do, and little time in which to do it." This said, she turned and strode down the hall, her heels punctuating each step with a gunshot-crisp crack. Kathleen and George fell into step behind her, and I trailed after them, with the guards following after me. Their presence kept me from getting too relaxed. This might be a step toward freedom, but I wasn't in the clear yet.

Dr. Shaw led us down the hall toward the lab where her first round of tests on me had been conducted, stopping at an unmarked door. "You are no longer required," she informed the guards, holding up her ID badge. "I assure you, the automated systems will make sure nothing untoward happens between here and our final destination."

"Our apologies, Dr. Shaw, but we have our orders," said the elder of the two guards, a tall, Hispanic man with a thin mustache covering his upper lip. He looked less nervous than his companion. Maybe that's why he got the unenviable job of telling Dr. Shaw he wasn't going to do what she wanted him to do. "We are to escort the subject to your lab and ensure that she's secured before we leave our posts."

"Bureaucracy will be the death of us all," muttered Dr. Shaw, with what looked like sincere annoyance. "Very well, then, if you must. But if either of you so much as breathes on something you shouldn't, the cost of decontamination will be coming out of your paychecks, and I *will* be speaking to your supervisors. Do I make myself clear?" Kathleen and George stepped up to flank us, presenting a united line. I was the only one not wearing a lab coat. For some reason, that struck me as funny.

The guards looked more uncomfortable than ever, but they stood their ground. I almost had to respect that. "Perfectly, ma'am," said the older guard. "We're just doing our jobs."

"Yes, well, I believe you've established *that*." She swiped her badge down the front of a magnetic scanner in the wall. The scanner beeped once. The door in front of us didn't budge; instead, a door on the other side of the hall swung open. The guards turned. Dr. Shaw looked smug. "Gentlemen, if you're so intent on managing my patient's welfare, you can lead the way."

I frowned at the expression on her face. Then I looked through the open door, and my frown struggled to become a smile.

The door opened in what appeared to be the side of a hall. A sign was posted on the wall visible through the opening—CAUTION: ACTIVE BIOHAZARD LABS BEYOND THIS POINT. CONTAMINATION RISK IS SET AT BIOSAFETY LEVEL 3. DO NOT PROCEED WITHOUT APPROPRIATE CLEARANCE. Beneath that, some joker had taped a printout reading "So come on in, and kiss your ass good-bye."

"Ma'am?" asked the older guard.

"I realize you've been working primarily in Level 1 and 2 areas, but my primary lab is maintained in the Level 3 wing." Dr. Shaw glanced to me as she spoke, giving me a brief but meaningful look that chased away any doubts I may have had about my fate. If I were still Dr. Thomas's pet subject, he would never have let me enter a Level 3 biohazard lab. He approved this. He was done with me.

All CDC properties start at Level 1, including the bathrooms and reception areas. No special training or equipment is needed to enter one. Level 1 biohazard facilities work with agents that don't harm healthy adult humans. Level 2 biohazard facilities work with things that *can* harm healthy adult humans, and will usually have some precautions in place to deal with contamination. It's only once you hit Level 3 that you start needing major protective gear. With the door standing open, I could hear the faint hiss of air being drawn into the hall, caught by the negative pressure filters. Airborne dangers could get in, but they would never make it out.

The guards stared at the sign. Dr. Shaw cleared her throat. "Gentlemen?"

The younger guard actually jumped. "Ma'am?" he asked.

"I realize you're simply trying to do your jobs, but I assure you, no amount of staring at the wall will get us to my lab. Can we proceed?"

"Just a moment." The older guard murmured something to his companion before raising a hand and tapping the skin behind his ear. "I'll be right back with you."

"Subdermal communications implant," I muttered. "Slick." Buffy would have loved to get her hands on one of those. With the way I went through the ear cuffs I used to contact my team, something subdermal would have—would have—

I touched the top edge of my left ear, where my ear cuff should have been. I hadn't even thought about it since waking up, and now that I remembered it, I felt naked without it. Somehow, I found that reassuring. It was one more piece of evidence that I was still me, even if I was someone else at the same time. For the first time, I felt myself feeling sorry for the Georgia Masons who had been cloned, studied, and killed before me. How many of them ever knew they weren't the woman they thought they were? How many of them touched their ears, feeling naked and wondering whether they'd get the chance to be properly clothed ever again?

I hoped none of them. If they hadn't been able to escape—and clearly, they hadn't, because I wouldn't have been here if they had—then there was no reason they should ever have needed to feel like this.

The guard finished his muffled conversation with whoever was on the other side of his connection and turned to face Dr. Shaw, tapping the skin behind his ear one more time as he did. "I apologize for any delays we have caused you," he said, stiffening to ramrod-straight attention. "My superior informs me that you have security of your own beyond this point, and that our services will not be required."

"Thank you for confirming that," said Dr. Shaw, with a smile that could have been used to chill water. "Now, if you gentlemen would please let us pass, I have a series of tests to begin."

"Of course." The older guard stayed where he was. The younger stepped out of Dr. Shaw's way as she advanced toward the door. He mumbled something that could have been "Ma'am," or could have been a short prayer of thanks. I didn't hear it clearly, and I didn't care. We were getting away from the guards. That was what really mattered here.

Kathleen entered first, followed by George, Dr. Shaw, and finally, me. The door slid shut behind us as soon as my heel cleared the doorway. Dr. Shaw reached out and pulled the piece of paper off the bottom of the sign, folding it neatly and tucking it into the pocket of her lab coat.

"Never underestimate the power of a man's fear, Georgia," she said, sounding almost distracted, like part of her was no longer paying attention. "Level 3 labs are no more dangerous to the well prepared than eating at an Indian take-out. Yet somehow, just the name is enough to strike fear into the hearts of man, even though each and every one of us is a walking Level 4 biosafety lab in this brave new world we've created."

"Words have power," I said.

"True." She shook her head. "Well. This way, please." She began to walk briskly down the hall, heels cracking hard against the tile.

Kathleen and George exchanged a look. "Excuse me, Doctor?" called Kathleen.

"Yes? What is it?"

"Do you want us to come with you, or do you want us to initiate cleanup procedures in lab bay two? You're going to need it later tonight."

Dr. Shaw paused, head tilted at what was clearly a contemplative angle, even when viewed from behind. Finally, she nodded. "Yes; that sounds like the correct course of action. Georgia, come with me. We really *do* need to get started." She started walking again, not looking back. I hurried after her.

We passed through three more doors, each of which Dr. Shaw opened with a swipe of her key card. The second door also required a fingerprint check; the third was equipped with a retinal scanner. This was starting to look less like a Level 3 biosafety facility, and more like some sort of maximum security prison for the infected. The distant, steady hiss of the negative pressure filters just made that thought more difficult to shake off.

I was getting distinctly uneasy by the time we reached the fourth door. This one was flanked by blood test units that looked disarmingly like the ones we had in the garage back in the house in Berkeley. "You'll need to provide a sample for analysis," said Dr. Shaw. "It's just a technicality, at this point in the facility, but it came with the security system, and we couldn't disarm it without deactivating several other functions."

"What functions?" I asked, moving toward the testing unit on the left.

"All will be made clear shortly." She slapped her palm flat against the right-hand testing unit, cleared her throat, and said, "Identification, Danika Michelle Kimberley, authorization beta alpha zeta nine four nine two three. Designation, investigative physician. Affiliation, Epidemic Intelligence Service." Her accent was suddenly British, softer than Mahir's, with a rolling edge that I'd heard only from bloggers who lived and broadcast near the Welsh border.

I stared at her. "What—?"

"You are accompanied," said a bland, pleasant male voice from a speaker set somewhere above the door. "Please identify your associate."

"This is Georgia Carolyn Mason, version 7c. Designation, electronic journalist, human clone, presently listed as deceased in the main network. Affiliation, Epidemic Intelligence Service." Dr. Shaw—Dr. Kimberley—sounded calm, and slightly bored, like she was reciting a shopping list. "Georgia, put your hand on the panel, if you would? I'd rather not be standing here when the security system decides we're a threat and floods the hall with formalin."

"Uh. No. That would be bad." I pressed my hand against the flat testing panel, feeling the brief sting as the needles bit into my palm. A cool blast of antiseptic foam was released through a slit in the metal, cooling the small wounds the needles had left behind, and the light above the door began to flash, red to yellow to green and back again. The light stabilized quickly on green, and the door unlocked with a click.

"Ah, good," said Dr. Kimberley. "Come along, Georgia." She pulled her hand away from the test panel and pushed the door open, revealing yet another standard-issue CDC lab.

Well. Standard issue except for the three technicians who were standing just inside with guns in their hands, aiming them at the door. I recognized the one in the middle as James, from Dr. Shaw's—Dr. Kimberley's—other lab. The others were new to me.

Dr. Kimberley sighed. "Oh, yay," she said, deadpan. "This is quite my favorite part. Is it Tuesday? It's Tuesday, isn't it?"

"Yes, Dr. Kimberley," confirmed the technician on the left, a curvy, medium-height girl with a riot of carroty-red curls barely confined by her headband.

"Brilliant. In that case . . . " Dr. Kimberley pointed to the girl. "Matriculate." She turned and pointed to James. "Alabaster." She turned again, pointing to the tall, dark-skinned man on the end. "Polyhedral."

All three technicians lowered their guns. "Glad to have you back, Dr. Kimberley," said James. "Did you encounter any trouble?"

"None that couldn't be handled." Dr. Kimberley turned to me, offering a small, almost apologetic smile. "I was able to depart with what we needed, and that's what matters. In the meanwhile . . . Georgia, I do apologize."

"What?" I blinked at her. Maybe it was everything I'd been through in the past few days, but I was suddenly afraid I'd trusted the wrong people. "What are you talking a—"

And then the syringe bit into the back of my arm, and the world, such as it was, fell away, leaving me in darkness.

Acquisition of the subject has been successful. We will begin analysis immediately. If Gregory is correct, and she is truly close enough to the original to be viable for our purposes, well . . .

I can only hope she'll find it in her heart to forgive us for what we must do. Expect further communication as soon as possible.

—Taken from a message sent by Dr. Danika Kimberley, July 31, 2041. Recipient unknown.

Ms. Hyland is gone. All the chaperones are gone. It's just us kids now, and I don't know how much longer the food will last . . . us kids, and the soldiers outside. They don't let us out of the building, even during the day, even if we promise to wear lots and lots of bug spray. There isn't any hot water. Some of the soldiers are going away. I don't know what's going on. I just know that I'm scared. Hurry, Alaric. Please, hurry.

I don't know how much longer this can last. But I don't think it's going to be long enough, if you don't hurry.

My batteries are dying. I may not be able to write for much longer.

Hurry.

—Taken from an e-mail sent by Alisa Kwong to Alaric Kwong, July 31, 2041.

Sixteen

The drive from Berkeley to Seattle takes fourteen hours if you use major roads and avoid serious traffic. It takes twenty-three hours if you stick to back routes and frontage roads. We split the difference, risking our cover several times in order to eke out a few hundred miles on I-5 before returning to the shadows, and made it from city to city in just under nineteen hours.

We didn't stop in Shady Cove. Tempting as it was, there was too good a chance that we were being followed—and too good a chance that if we stopped there, we'd never leave again. Dr. Abbey tried to send us to the Florida hazard zone, and we failed. Fine. Barring another way to do the same thing, she'd probably insist we stay and start looking for a way to evacuate us all to someplace that was guaranteed to stay mosquito-free.

"I hear Alaska's nice this time of year," I muttered.

"What's that?" George looked up, blinking still-unfamiliar brown eyes at me in honest confusion.

"Just wondering where we could run when this is over. The mosquitoes are going to be pretty damn hard to kill."

"Maybe." She shrugged, returning to her study of the jamming unit. A lock of her hair—it was starting to need a trim—flopped forward, falling in front of one eye. I resisted the urge to lean over and brush it aside. Unless I was having a really crazy day, she'd just vanish if I tried to touch her, and I needed the company too much to have her leave again. Becks had been asleep in the back since we crossed the border into Washington. Without my hallucinatory sister, I would be totally alone, and I wasn't sure how much longer my own wakefulness would last.

"What do you mean, 'maybe'?" I asked.

"Like Dr. Abbey said, an insect vector for Kellis-Amberlee didn't just *happen*. They're probably the product of some lab like hers, full of scientists who think 'I wanted to see what would happen' is a perfectly valid justification for doing anything they want."

"Yeah, and?"

George looked up again, brushing the hair out of her eyes with a quick, economical wave of one hand. This time, she looked almost annoyed. "Shaun. You *know* this. There's nothing I can tell you that you don't already know. Why are you pretending you need me to say it?"

"Because I'm not pretending." I shrugged, trying to keep my attention focused on the road. I didn't want to get so wrapped up in arguing with her that I needed to pull over; not only would that potentially attract attention, but it would annoy the hell out of Becks if she woke up before we started moving again. "Maybe you can't tell me things I don't know, but I *need* you to be the one who says them. That lets me believe in them."

"You are a strange, sick little man, Shaun Mason." George sighed. "The mosquitoes were made. Man's creation, just like Kellis-Amberlee. If you were going to build killer bugs to spread the zombie plague, wouldn't you put in a little planned obsolescence?"

Despite the fact that George could only use words I knew the meaning of, I had to pause while I tried to remember what "obsolescence" meant. Sometimes it's annoying having hallucinations that make me feel dumb. "You mean they'd be built to break down?"

"Now you're thinking. I have to wonder whether the mosquitoes are fertile. If someone built them as a biological weapon, why would they have given them the capacity to breed? All that's going to do is increase the chances of them hurting the people you're trying to protect."

"So how did they wind up in Cuba?"

"Weapons test. Cuba did too well during the Rising. It was almost insulting to certain people. I'm sure they would have loved the opportunity to run a little fear-inducing trial on soil close enough to ours that they could look horrified and appalled when someone implied we might have had something to do with it."

"George . . ."

"I'm not being nihilistic, Shaun. I'm being *right*, and you know it."

"Yeah." I glanced out the window at the high concrete fence dividing the tiny back road we were on from the safe concrete river of I-5. "I just wish I'd stop reminding myself."

George was gone when I looked back. I shook my head, trying to clear the malaise brought on by her last statement, and turned the radio on, scanning channels until I found something with a catchy beat and simplistic lyrics. Then I switched to NPR.

National Public Radio is a dinosaur in the modern age of podcasts and Internet radio stations, but that's part of what makes it useful, because when you turn on NPR, you're getting the thoughts and opinions of the part of the population that has not yet moved into a purely virtual format. Things still move a little slower there. Not predigitally slow—I've read the history books, I know how long a single story used to dominate the cycle—but slow enough that you can learn a thing or two, if you're willing to listen.

Two experts were arguing about ways to save the Everglades. One wanted to send in CDC teams in full-on moon suits to rescue as many noninfected animals as possible, and then dump enough DDT into the water table to sterilize the ecosystem for a hundred years. "We can breed them in preserves and exhibits until we confirm that the Everglades are safe, and then return them to their original environment," was the gist of his argument, wedded to a firm belief that instinct would override generations of zoo-bound living and lead to an immediate, complete return to the wild as soon as the money ran out and somebody in accounting decided it was time to let the animals go.

The other expert claimed this would result not only in the permanent loss of a major piece of America's biological diversity, but render most of Florida uninhabitable whether we got rid of the mosquitoes or not, since pesticide would inevitably get into the human water supply. He was in favor of releasing thousands of insectivores into the impacted areas and letting them take care of things the natural way. And by "insectivores," he meant "bats." He wanted to gather as many bats as possible and dump them on the Everglades, where they could do their batty thing and eat all the mosquitoes. Because the people of Florida would, of course, be totally cool with this.

At no point did either of them mention the idea that the mosquitoes had been *made*, rather than being a natural worst-case scenario. All their solutions started from the premise that the mosquitoes just happened, much like the storm that brought them to our shores. Somehow, that only made me more certain that George was right. Somebody made these mosquitoes, and somebody was going to have a way to deal with them. They were just waiting for the time to be right, just like they'd waited for the time to be right before letting the bugs out of the box in the first place.

Becks climbed back into her seat right about the time the speakers got really involved in yelling at each other. Yawning and rumpling her hair with one hand, she squinted at the radio. "Do I wanna know?"

"I can't get a good wireless signal out here," I said. "So we're listening to the radio."

"Listening to the radio talk about *what?*"

"Bats."

Becks frowned, still clearly half asleep. "Bats?"

"Yeah. You know, flap flap, squeak squeak, works for Dracula? Bats. Because we need a vampire problem to go with our zombie problem." I opened the cooler we had wedged between the seats, pulling out a can of Coke. "Here. You look like you could use the caffeine."

"Oh, thank God. I thought I was going to have to deal with this without chemical assistance." Becks popped the tab before downing half the soda in one long slug. She didn't seem to realize what she was drinking until she lowered the can and blinked at the label. "Shaun . . . this is a Coke."

"I know."

"You gave me one of your Cokes."

"I know."

"Why did you . . . ?"

"Because you needed it." I glanced her way, smiling just a little—just enough to show her I meant it. "If the Masons can let us go and agree to get Alisa out of Florida, I can be selfless enough to give you a can of Coke."

Becks's expression sobered. "Do you really think they'll go after her?"

"I do, yeah." The experts on NPR were still arguing. I leaned forward and turned the radio down. "I don't think they've changed completely. I mean, knowing Mom, she's probably already convinced herself I cheated by bringing up Phillip, and that she and Dad let us go out of the goodness of their hearts, not because it was the right thing to do. But rescuing a little girl from a refugee camp in an interdicted hazard zone? That's the kind of ratings you can't buy. It's just gravy that they have that whole martial law thing going on over there, which gives Dad an excuse to trot out a bunch of old chatter about personal responsibility and freedom of the press."

"So they're going to do it for the ratings." Becks's mouth twisted into a disapproving line. She took another large gulp of Coke, presumably to stop herself from saying anything she'd regret later.

It didn't matter. There was nothing she could say that I hadn't heard before. Some of it I had heard from George. Some of it I had said myself. "There are worse reasons, and the fact that they're always in the public eye means that if they get her back to Berkeley, they can't mistreat her. They can be themselves, which is bad enough, but Alisa's older than George and I were when they took us in. She'll be fine until Alaric can get there and take her away from them."

"You're willing to count on that?"

"I don't think we have much of a choice. We can't head for Florida. We'd never make it past the barricades. We need to get to the rest of the team and regroup."

"How long before we reach Seattle?"

"We're about twenty miles out. I figure I'll try calling Mahir right before we hit the city limits—if he picks up, we can go straight to where he is, and not need to keep the connection open."

"And if he doesn't?" Becks asked, taking a smaller sip of her soda.

"I have no idea. I'm sort of making all this up as I go along, you know."

You're doing an excellent job.

"Thank you," I said automatically, and winced.

Becks politely ignored my slip. "I know you are. I don't envy you the lead on this story."

"Hey, it's worked so far. What are you going to do when we meet the Monkey? You could be anyone. What's your new identity going to be?"

"I think I'll be an Internet journalist." She smiled. "I understand they don't need much in the way of training. Or brains. How about you?"

"I'm going to ask for anything that lets me disappear." I kept my eyes on the road. "This is going to end soon, Becks. It's gone too far to last much longer. Too many people have died. So if I get through this story alive . . . I just want to be left alone."

"You want to be alone with George," said Becks.

"Maybe."

"I don't . . . Shaun, I . . ." Becks paused, taking a breath. "You know I love you, right? As a friend. I may have loved you as something more once, but that's over now. You know that."

"I do."

"So it's as a friend, and as a colleague, that I ask . . . are you sure? You're not holding on that tightly as it is. Going off to be alone with the voices in your head—"

"It's not just voices anymore. I see her sometimes." That stopped her. I continued. "She was sitting in that seat not long before you woke up. We were talking. If I get deep enough into the conversation, if I forget long enough, sometimes I can even feel her. I'm *going* to wind up alone with the voices in my head. The only question is whether or not I get the rest of you hurt in the process. Mahir was Georgia's second. You're mine. You know how badly I could fuck everything up if I refused to let go. So let me plan to let go. It might help me hold on a little longer."

Becks sighed. "You're asking me to help you turn into a crazy hermit living in the mountains somewhere."

"Yeah. I am."

"As long as you realize it." She slumped in her seat, giving the jamming device a light smack with the heel of her hand. "How does this damn thing work, anyway?"

"You want the technical answer, or the honest answer?" I paused. "Actually, those are the same answer."

"Shoot."

"I have no fucking clue. Buffy was always real impressed with it, I know that; she wanted to build one for us, but other stuff kept getting in the way, and then we were working for a presidential hopeful, so it didn't seem like a good political move." And then she was dead, and she wasn't going to be building anything for anybody. Things would have gone so differently if she'd lived. She would have seen what was happening and turned on the conspiracy that had turned her against us, and all this might already be over. George might still be alive. And I might not be looking forward to going all the way insane.

"It was nice of the Masons to give it to us."

"Yeah, it was. I figure we'll kill it with a hammer as soon as it's served its purpose." Becks shot me a scandalized look. I shook my head. "You really think they don't have some sort of a tracking beacon in this thing? Buffy built alarms into the van security system that would have gone off if it were broadcasting—she had to reprogram them not to go off when Maggie got too close, since her parents have her rigged up with 'do not abduct' heiress crap. So I figure they're just waiting until we stop moving long enough that they can assume we're not in the vehicle anymore, and then they're going to start pinging our position."

Becks stared at me. "If they're planning to use the thing to track us, why did you let me take it?"

"Because it was the only thing that would get us out of Berkeley. Even if the Masons just called the local cops on us, they'd be turning on every tracking chip they could think of as soon as we ran. And I somehow doubt they just called the local cops—or called them at all."

"Why?"

"It took too long for them to get there. There's a police station less than eight blocks away. My parents were turning us in for the ratings, remember? They called the CDC. It's the only thing that makes sense." It explained both the delay in their arrival, and why the Masons listened when I said they were making a mistake. The CDC is still the government, and after what happened during the Ryman campaign, trusting them might not have come as easy as it once did.

"Right." Becks sighed and slumped in her seat. Then she leaned forward and turned the radio back up, signaling that she was done talking for the moment. I smiled a little, catching her meaning, and returned my focus to the road.

Things are almost over, murmured George.

"I know," I said, and kept driving.

The outskirts of Seattle loomed up with surprising speed; the relative obscurity of the roads we'd been taking meant that there was minimal traffic. I dug a burner ear cuff out of my pocket, snapping it on. A tap triggered the connection. "This is Shaun Mason activating security profile Pardy. Something's wrong with Brenda, we're out of Mister Pibb, and hunting season's here. Now let's go to Hollywood."

"Your taste in passwords is crap," commented Becks.

I made a shushing motion. Mahir picked up after two rings, asking, "Oh, thank God. Shaun? Is that you?"

"If it weren't, somebody would have just gotten really, really lucky trying to turn this thing on. Where are you guys?"

Mahir's voice turned instantly suspicious. "Why?"

"Because we've just reached Seattle, and we'd like to come join you. Especially if wherever you are has a bathroom. Is there a bathroom? Please tell me there's a bathroom. We've been driving for like, twenty hours, and I need to piss like you wouldn't believe."

"TMI, Shaun," said Becks.

"How did you get out of Berkeley?"

"Wait, what?" Now it was my turn to get suspicious. "What are you talking about?"

"Several local Berkeley bloggers posted yesterday morning about a surprise CDC hazard team drill being run in a residential neighborhood—and their target was your family home. The Masons have even posted about it. They said they were glad to cooperate with anything that might improve safety procedures and response times." He paused before adding, grimly, "We thought they might have turned you in."

I sighed. "They kind of did. They just changed their minds before things could go all the way horribly wrong. How did they look?"

"Your mum had a black eye—"

"Yeah, I gave her that."

"—and a broken arm. Your dad just had some taped-up fingers."

"What?" I demanded. "I didn't do *that*. Neither did Becks. The black eye was so it would be believable when they said we got away."

"Apparently, it wasn't believable enough for the CDC. Snap your transmitter to the GPS, I'll send you the address for our hotel. Wipe it as soon as you get here."

"Done. See you soon, Mahir."

"One hopes," he said.

I removed the cuff from my ear and handed it to Becks. "Here—connect this to the GPS. Mahir's going to send us directions on how to get to the hotel he and Maggie are staying at. Keep the jammer going. The Masons made the news."

"What?" Becks glanced at me in confusion as she connected the ear cuff to the GPS. The GPS unit beeped and began to display its "loading" screen.

"Mom has a broken arm. Dad has some broken fingers. Think they tripped and fell after we left the house?" I gripped the wheel harder than necessary, resisting the urge to slam my foot down on the gas and race my anger away. "The fucking CDC, Becks. My parents called the fucking CDC and said we'd be waiting for them, gift-wrapped and unsuspecting, and when we weren't there, the fucking CDC showed their disappointment."

"You can't be sure it was the CDC."

"That's what the blogs are saying. They're calling it a training exercise. As in, 'The CDC decided to train their employees on beating the crap out of my parents.'" My fingers clenched even tighter. "Those fuckers. They had no right."

"Ahead, turn left," said the GPS.

Do it, said George.

I turned left.

"This is insane," said Becks. "What the hell is going on here? What did we *do*?"

"Honestly? I don't know anymore." Something in my face must have told her to let it be. Becks shook her head, settling in her seat. After a moment's hesitation, she drew one of her pistols, resting it against her thigh below the window's sight line. If someone decided to use us for a "training exercise," they weren't going to find us as off guard as they might have liked.

The GPS led us through a maze of side streets to what looked like a relatively major road, one that led us away from downtown and toward the less densely populated residential areas. The buildings took on a dilapidated look as we crossed from one zone into the next . . . and then, abruptly, began to improve, until we were passing well-maintained mini-mansions surrounded by high fences instead of tenement apartment buildings. Some of them even had their own private gatehouses. The convenience stores and their kin were replaced by upscale grocery stores, fancy salons, and dry cleaners whose signs boasted zero-contact door-to-door service. There were no blood tests on the corners; instead, men on motorized scooters patrolled the sidewalks, running checks on anyone who wanted to get out of a vehicle.

More tellingly, as we drove deeper into the clearly wealthy part of town, people began appearing on the sidewalks. Some of them were walking small dogs, like Maggie's teacup bulldogs, or the more traditional pugs and Pomeranians. Others had cats on leashes. We even passed a couple with one of those bizarre tame Siberian foxes trotting at their heels, its bushy tail low and its triangular ears pricked forward as it scanned its surroundings for danger.

"This can't be right," said Becks, watching the fox slide out of view. "Check the directions."

"These are the directions Mahir gave me. Maybe they're hiding in someone's attic. I don't know. Wherever they are, they're going to be trying to stay unobtrusive."

"In two hundred yards, you have reached your destination," announced the GPS.

I looked ahead. "Oh, fuck."

"You have *got* to be kidding," said Becks.

In front of us loomed the elegant, fenced-in shape of a luxury resort. It looked like it was large enough to host the entire Republican National Convention, assuming anything as gauche as politics were ever allowed to pass its pristine white gates. The guardhouse in front was staffed by four men, their concierge uniforms somehow managing to go perfectly with their assault rifles. Two of them moved out to the street, motioning for me to stop the van.

"There's no way we can reverse fast enough," said Becks. "They have to have cars."

"Or they'd just shoot the windows out." I set the brake. "It was nice knowing you."

"Same here."

The men took positions on either side of the van, one next to my window, one next to Becks's window. The one next to mine raised a white-gloved hand and knocked, deferentially.

Forcing a smile, I lowered the window. "Hi," I said. "What seems to be the problem?"

"No problem, Mr. Mason. We've been expecting you." The man produced a handheld blood-testing unit while I was still gaping at him. "If you would please allow me to verify your current medical state, I would be delighted to explain." On the other side of the van, his companion was making a virtually identical speech to Becks.

"Uh." I stared at him for a moment before focusing on the most disturbing part of that statement. "You've been expecting us?"

"Oh, yes. Miss Garcia contacted the front desk after you called." The man kept smiling. It was starting to make me nervous. "We're thrilled to have you joining us."

"Uh . . . huh." I took the testing unit, pressing my thumb down on the pressure plate. "Did she threaten your lives, by any chance? Tell you you'd never work in this town again? Cry?"

The man actually laughed. "Oh, no, nothing like that! She simply asked us to meet you at the gates, and to assure you that the Agora Resort is a completely confidential retreat for those who may be in need of more . . . confidence . . . in their security."

"Wait—did you say the Agora?" Becks leaned into my field of vision, her right hand still outstretched as she pressed her thumb to her own blood-test unit. "This is the Agora?"

"Yes, Miss Atherton." The man frowned, although his overall air of polite readiness to serve remained. "You've heard of us?"

"My mother stayed here once, when she was younger. She was a Feldman before she got married."

"Ah!" said the man, suddenly all smiles again. "Of the New Hampshire Feldmans?"

"Yes."

"It's a pleasure to have another member of the family with us. I hope we can live up to whatever fond memories she may have shared with you." He deftly plucked the test unit from my hand, holding it up to show the green light that had come on at the top. "You are, as expected, clean. Welcome to the Agora, Mr. Mason. I, and the rest of the concierge staff, am pleased to serve."

"Um, thanks?" I looked from Becks—who was being shown her own clean test unit—to the concierge, not bothering to conceal my confusion. "What happens now?"

"Now you enter. A valet will take your van"—he paused as my hands tightened on the wheel—"or not, as you prefer. Your party is waiting for you in the lobby." He stepped back. His partner did the same, and the gates in front of us swung slowly open.

Becks put a hand over mine. "It's okay," she said. "I've heard of this place."

"So?"

"So I wouldn't have if my mother hadn't stayed here. You need so many zeroes in your bank account to get in that there are *presidents* who never stayed here." Becks pulled her hand away. "They believe in discretion above pretty much all else. Now let's go."

"You're the boss." I started the engine.

Becks smirked. "I like the sound of that."

"Yeah, thought you might."

Getting past the valet without ceding the keys was easier than I'd expected. Every place I'd ever seen that was even remotely like this had been staffed by people who were so desperate for tips that they'd do anything to guarantee them—as long as "anything" didn't involve coming close enough to actually touch another human being. There's a commonly held belief that people who work in the hospitality industry are less paranoid about strangers than the rest of us. I'd almost been able to buy it, until I stayed in a few hotels and saw how careful the staff was to avoid touching the guests. It was almost funny, except for the part where it was so damn sad.

George theorized once that the people who worked in hospitality were even *more* afraid of other human beings than the average man on the street. "This way they never get attached to anyone," she'd said. "People come and go. They don't stay long enough to become anything but names on a ledger. There's no sense of loss when there's nothing to lose."

The Agora was disturbingly different. The valet's smile when I said I'd rather park myself seemed sincere, and the garage maintained for self-park vehicles was large, spacious, and well lit, with emergency doors located every fifteen feet along the walls. The bellhop who opened the hotel's main door for us was also smiling, and kept smiling even when it became apparent that our days on the road didn't leave us exactly minty fresh. And neither of them held out a hand for a tip.

"This is weird," I muttered to Becks, once I was sure we were far enough past the guy for my comment to go unheard.

"This is wealth," she replied, and slapped her palm flat on the test sensor that would open the airlock separating the outer ring of the hotel from the main lobby. I did the same. The doors swished open a second later, allowing us both to step through.

"Welcome, Mr. Mason. Welcome, Miss Atherton," said a polite female voice. "The Agora recommends that you make use of our lavish guest facilities. A hot bath has already been drawn in your rooms. We're glad that you're here." The door on the other side of the airlock slid open, and the main lobby was revealed for the first time.

Now that's just overkill, commented George.

"You took the words right out of my mouth," I said, and followed Becks out of the airlock.

The Agora lobby was decorated in shades of white and blue. It looked like the interior of the world's most expensive glacier. A piano was tucked away into one corner, half blocked from view by tall plants with broad green leaves and trumpet-shaped blue flowers. The sound of the unseen pianist's playing echoed through the room, soft enough not to be distracting, yet somehow unpredictable enough to make it clear that there was a live person at the keys. The front desk was set just to the side of a curved flight of stairs leading to the second floor.

Maggie and Mahir were standing near the center of the lobby, talking quietly. They looked around when the airlock door slid shut behind us. "Shaun! Becks!" exclaimed Maggie, the volume of her voice seeming inappropriate in this overly rarified atmosphere. "You made it!" She started toward us at a trot, Mahir following behind somewhat more slowly.

"Uh, yeah. We did," I said, transferring my staring to Maggie. "You look . . ."

"Like the heir to Garcia Pharmaceuticals," she said, and smiled. "You like?"

"Uh . . ."

Maggie was wearing a tailored blazer over a white lace shirt, no bra, and pants that could have been applied with a spray can. Maybe they were—they've been doing some incredible things with memory polymers in the last few years, and I know canned clothing was one of the things being worked on. Her normally curly, normally braided brown hair was both loose and straight, falling down her back like it had developed its own private gravity. Again, maybe it had. The ways of the obscenely rich are alien to me. Her makeup was elaborate enough that I was certain she hadn't done it herself.

At least she was still wearing sensible shoes, rather than teetering on a pair of impractically high heels. I've heard them called "fuck-me pumps" in some of the pre-Rising media. These days, we call them "get-you-killed heels." I think it's a little more appropriate.

"It's Shaun, Maggie, and you're a girl," said Becks, coming to my rescue. "He has no idea what the safe answer is, and so he's going to vapor lock until you change the subject. Hi. It's good to see you. You look wonderful." She stepped forward, sweeping the head of the After the End Times Fictionals into a hug, which Maggie gladly returned.

Mahir caught my eye and smirked. "Hallo, Mason."

"Hey, Mahir." I shook my head. "Looks like we've both been having an interesting time. I'll see your luxury hotel, and raise you one zombie bear."

"I can see that this is going to be a deeply enlightening evening." He put a hand on my arm. "I've been following the feeds about the Masons. Two of our juniors are covering it, due to the connection to our site's founders. How are you holding up?"

It took me a second to realize that by "our site's founders," he was referring to me and George. "Oh, okay, I guess. Totally out of my mind, but that's normal. Should we be hanging around down here?"

Maggie disengaged from Becks, glancing my way. "Our rooms are on the third floor. Did the Agora tell you about the baths?"

"That depends. When you ask 'did the Agora' tell us, do you mean—"

"The hotel."

"That's what I was afraid you were going to say. Yeah, it told us."

"Good." Maggie looped one arm through Becks's and one arm through mine, tugging us across the lobby toward the elevators. "Let's get you cleaned up and into something that doesn't smell like road funk, and then we can sit down for dinner and to discuss our plan of attack for tomorrow."

"Road funk?" I asked.

"Plan of attack?" Becks asked.

Tomorrow? George asked.

"Your timing is impeccable, as always," said Mahir, moving to walk alongside the three of us. "Tomorrow morning we will finally be accomplishing our goal here in the city of Seattle."

"What do you mean?" asked Becks.

Maggie freed an arm long enough to push the elevator "call" button and leaned even closer, whispering conspiratorially, "We're here to meet the Monkey, remember?"

The elevator arrived with a loud *ding* and Maggie stepped inside, waving for the rest of us to follow. After exchanging a look with Becks, I did.

"I think I preferred the zombie bears," I muttered.

"That's just you, Mason," she said, and started laughing. Maggie and Mahir joined in. There was an edge of hysteria to the sound, like they were laughing to hold back the dark. I stood there, feeling the elevator gaining speed beneath us, and held my silence as we rose higher, and closer to the future.

I was never a "poor little rich girl." I had a lot of money, sure, but I also had parents who loved me, and who balanced the urge to give me everything I wanted with instilling me with a strong sense of personal responsibility. I never thought of my money as a burden. The only burden was the way it made people look at me. That was what I couldn't stand, and that's the reason I chose to go into the field I went into. I was good at being a Fictional. I was never that good at being a spoiled brat.

There are things money can't buy. People who love you, a job you're good at, a sense of personal respect . . . those are on the list.

—From *Dandelion Mine*, the blog of Magdalene Grace Garcia, July 31, 2041. Unpublished.

Buffy was complaining today about how we need a new transmitter for the van, and we can't afford it right now. She wants us to ask the Masons for a loan. She doesn't seem to understand that having parents who are in the media business doesn't mean we can turn to them for every little thing we need. Sure, they'd probably give it to us, but we'd be giving up something a lot more valuable. We'd be giving up our independence. All it's going to take is one loan, and they'll have the leverage they need to start worming their way into our business. They want it. I *know* they want it.

And I am not going to let them have it.

—From *Postcards from The Wall*, the unpublished files of Georgia Mason, originally posted on July 31, 2041.

Seventeen

"Georgia."

The word was distorted enough to seem unimportant. I didn't bother trying to respond. I was lying on something soft, it was pleasantly dark, and if people wanted to talk to me, they could knock themselves out. Nothing said I had to *answer*.

"She's unresponsive."

"I expected she might be. Let's assume she's awake, and put her back under for now."

"Are you sure? The strain to her system—"

"We need to finish this."

A needle slid into my arm. The sensation was sharp enough to break the haze, replacing soft darkness with sudden concern. I opened my eyes, peering into a blur of light. There were figures there, wearing medical scrubs, with clear plastic masks over their faces. That just made me more concerned. What were they doing that might splash them with my bodily fluids?

"Doctor—" The speaker sounded alarmed. Whatever I was supposed to do, opening my eyes apparently wasn't on the list.

"I see her. Increase the midazolam drip—I want her *out* until we're done." The taller of the two figures bent toward me. "Georgia? Can you hear me?"

I made a sound. It was faint, somewhere between a gasp and a groan.

It was apparently enough. "Increase that dose *now*, Kathleen," snapped Dr. Kimberley, her features becoming visible through the plastic as she leaned closer. She raised one blue-gloved hand, brushing my hair away from my face. "Don't try to move, Georgia. This will all be over soon."

That's what I was afraid of. The room was getting dark around the edges, hard lines turning into soft blurs as whatever they were pumping into me started taking effect. I tried to yell at her, to demand to know what she thought she was doing, but all that emerged was a faint squeak, like a hinge that needed to be oiled.

Dr. Kimberley smiled. "There you are, my dear. Just rest. It will all be over soon." Then she pulled her hand back, and once again, the world went away.

There was no sense of time in the darkness. But Shaun was there, somehow, and he held my hand, and we sat together in the black, and everything was fine, forever and ever and ever.

Or until his hand slipped out of mine, and the blackness began to fade, and I realized my temporary peace had been just another drug-induced lie. Fury flooded through me. How dare they keep playing with me this way? It wasn't right. It wasn't fair. It wasn't—

"Georgia."

Again, the word was blurred and warped by what felt like an immense distance. This time, I forced myself to strain toward it, struggling to open my eyes. Nothing happened. Frustrated, I tried to respond, and again, managed to make only the faintest squeak.

That seemed to be enough. "She's awake, Doctor. Not fully responsive, but recovering."

"Good." I heard the squeak of wheels rolling across a tile floor, followed by the soft compression of a body settling into a chair. "Georgia, this is Dr. Kimberley. I know you're confused, and you may not have an easy time moving, but if you can, please squeeze my hand."

Squeeze her hand? I wasn't even *touching* her hand. Furious, I managed to squeak again.

"Kathleen is getting something to make you feel better, but I need you to work with us. Please squeeze my hand." Her voice was measured, patient; the voice of a doctor who knew you wanted to trust her, because she was the hand that held the scalpel. "You've been under for about seven hours."

Under? Under *where*? I was becoming more aware of my body, which was lying flat on a padded surface. My head was somewhat higher than the rest of me, probably to help my breathing. I strained to focus, clenching my fingers in the process. They hit something yielding.

"Very good!" Dr. Kimberley sounded pleased. The something was pulled from my hand. "Kathleen, inject the solution into her IV line and pass me the stimulants. It's time for our Miss Mason to fully rejoin the living."

I squeaked in fury. If Shaun were here, these people would have been knocked on their asses so fast—

And then a familiar voice spoke, startling me out of my anger: "Is she all right?"

I froze, inasmuch as my current condition distinguished that from my efforts to move. Dr. Kimberley didn't appear to notice. "Yes, Mr. Vice President. The procedure was a success. Barring complications, I'm expecting her to make a full recovery."

"Good." A hand touched my forehead. I strained to open my eyes. "I'm so sorry you've had to go through all of this, George. Now do what you do best. Break this fucking thing wide open, and let the pieces fall."

I moaned. It was the best I could do.

Rick pulled his hand away. "They'll miss me if I stay gone any longer. Pass a message through my office if there are any complications. I want to know immediately. Do you understand?"

"Yes, sir," said Dr. Kimberley.

Sudden pain lanced through me, radiating out from a point somewhere near my heart. I couldn't speak, but I could scream, and scream I did, arching my back away from the mattress beneath me until it felt like I was making a perfect half circle.

"She's convulsing!" shouted Dr. Kimberley. "Trauma cart, *now*!"

Her voice began to slip away at the end, blurring into the general chaos as the dark reached out its tendrils and twined them around me once more. An alarm blared. I screamed again, so hard it felt like something tore inside my throat, and then the world fell away, leaving me to plunge into the black. There was no peace there this time, only pain, pain, *pain*.

Panicked voices in the dark, overlapping with each other: "—losing her, I don't know why, she's—" "—must have missed one—" "—check behind her collarbone—"

And then there was only the dark, so all-consuming it devoured even the pain, and the voices didn't matter anymore. And then there was, for a time, blessed nothing. Nothing at all.

"Georgia."

The third time my name called me out of the dark, it didn't have any blurred edges or comforting distance. It was near, immediate, and spoken with perfect clarity. I groaned, suddenly aware of my body as a part of my consciousness, and of my consciousness as something distinct from the dark.

"... what?" I whispered. Even that much motion triggered a hundred more realizations. I had a mouth; I could speak. My lips were dry, my throat was aching. That was the only pain, at least for the moment.

I was alive.

"How do you feel?" Dr. Kimberley sounded honestly concerned. I've spent enough of my life dealing with doctors to know when they're pretending to care, and she wasn't pretending. The edges of her words—still Welsh-accented; the masks, it seemed, were off for good—were soft and weary, like she hadn't slept for days.

"Water," I whispered.

"You're not dehydrated, but your throat will be dry. We've been feeding you via a tube for the past three days. It was removed about an hour ago. If you can open your eyes, I can give you some water. That's the bargain, I'm afraid. Responsiveness for water."

I opened my eyes. Light lanced into them like knives, and I quickly closed them again. There was a tap against the bridge of my nose as Dr. Kimberley settled something there.

"That will block the worst of it," she said. "I'm afraid we didn't have the equipment to keep reminding your retinas of light. They'll adjust if you give them a little time."

"What . . . where am I?" I opened my eyes again. This time, the disposable UV-blocker Dr. Kimberley had given me kept the worst of the light from reaching me. The doctor herself was standing in front of my bed, a glass of water in her hand.

"You're still in the Seattle CDC; we've been able to loop footage and falsify results to make it look like you're in my primary lab, but we haven't had any way to remove you from the premises. Not that we could have done so anyway, given the givens." She leaned forward, holding the glass to my lips and tilting it until I could take a few tiny, carefully measured sips. "Slowly, Georgia, slowly. You don't want to aspirate this."

I pulled my head back, coughing a little, and asked, "Why can't you just say 'don't breathe the water' like a normal person?"

"Because I'm a doctor, and they teach us never to use little words where big ones will do." Dr. Kimberley pulled the glass out of my reach. That made me focus on more of the room around us. It was packed with medical monitoring equipment, including an IV that was still anchored to my arm. I looked at it with disgust.

"What *is* all this?"

"It's what's been keeping you alive while we waited for the toxins to finish working their way out of your system." Dr. Kimberley put the glass down atop one of the machines before taking a seat in the chair next to my bed. "Gregory showed you your replacement, did he not?"

"Yes," I rasped.

"Then you'll have seen that they were tailoring her to their requirements. They did the same with you, my dear, although they left your mind basically alone—small mercies, and all of that. They needed you for display. The rest of you was free game."

"And that's why you drugged me?" I was too tired to sound as indignant as I felt. I still gave it my best shot.

"Yes." Dr. Kimberley nodded. "Have you ever heard of the sea wasp jellyfish? It's one of the many nasty surprises lurking in our world's oceans. This one comes from Australia, and has a sting capable of killing an adult human in minutes if untreated."

"So?" I whispered.

"The nice people responsible for making you wanted to be sure nothing akin to what is happening right now would succeed, and they implanted biological explosives at strategic points within your body. They were to burst, given the correct set of stimuli, releasing sea wasp venom into your bloodstream. The only circumstance under which death would not be instantaneous would be one in which the toxins were released while a full medical team was standing by, ready to counteract the poison."

The darkness was starting to make sense. I swallowed, trying to make my voice a little less unsteady as I said, "You could have warned me."

"No, I'm afraid we couldn't have. Some of the devices were set to trigger at specific key words that would inevitably have come up, if only because you'd have seen us dancing around them and demanded to know why." Dr. Kimberley patted my hand. She wasn't wearing gloves this time. Her skin was cool. "We removed eight venom packs from your intramuscular tissue, along with two trackers and a microchip identifying you as CDC property."

That managed to annoy me all over again. "You mean they *tagged* me? Like a dog?"

"It's not a bad comparison, sadly. If you ever made it out of this facility, they wanted to be able to track your movements, and to prove you were who—and what—they said you were. All that's been removed, and your incisions have mostly closed over. You should be fine after another day or two." A small frown crossed her face. "That doesn't leave us much time. I have custody of you for a week. We've already used up three days with your decontamination and recovery. We can move forward now that you're awake, but I'd hoped to have longer."

"What she isn't saying is that you nearly died three times," said Gregory. I looked toward his voice. He was standing in the doorway, a tray in his hands. "The first operation taxed your system enough that the remaining venom packs began to rupture. We got those out, only to find that we'd managed to miss one."

"And the third time?" I asked. It was hard not to smile, even with the things he was saying. I hadn't realized how much I needed to see a familiar, believably friendly face.

"Your heart just stopped. We still don't know why."

"But we did manage to get it started again; there's no reason to frighten the girl," said Dr. Kimberley sternly. "Now, Georgia, I'm sure that you must have questions—"

"Who are you, what are you doing, and how the fuck are you planning to get me out of here?" I pushed myself into as close to a sitting position as I could manage, using the pillows that had been supporting my head to support the rest of me instead.

Dr. Kimberley sighed. "And apparently, we'll be having question time now, rather than after you've put something solid in your stomach. I really am Dr. Kimberley; 'Shaw' was my mother's maiden name. My first name is Danika. I trained at Oxford, and then later with the Kauai Institute of Virology, under Dr. Joseph Shoji. I was recruited to the EIS six years ago. I've been undercover with the CDC for the past five years. I've been on the Shelley Project since it started. You're the first Georgia Mason to make it this far."

"The Shelley—oh, come *on*. They named the 'let's clone a reporter, it'll be fun' project after Mary Shelley? Couldn't they at least have gone with Herbert West or something?"

"I didn't get a vote," said Dr. Kimberley, looking faintly amused. "Gregory here is one of our best men."

"Dr. Gregory Lake, at your service," said Gregory. "I'm primarily a field epidemiologist, but I came here when Dr. Kimberley called for backup. I'm glad I did. The situation was more advanced than her reports led us to believe."

"It's not my fault they don't allow me access to the subjects until they reach the stage where the tests I'm supposedly here to run become necessary," said Dr. Kimberley, an edge of irritation in her voice. "Half the subjects went from lab to slab without darkening my door."

"Yeah, this is the sort of conversation that makes me feel really, really good about my prospects." I slumped against the pillows. "So what, you're the clone rescue squad?"

"Not quite." Dr. Kimberley leaned forward, resting her elbows on her knees. She looked at me gravely. "Georgia, we're here because we need your help."

I blinked at her, glancing at Gregory. He had the same solemn look on his face. The urge to laugh bubbled up inside my chest. "You need *my* help? I've been *dead* for the last . . . I'm not even sure. Not to mention the part where I'm not actually who I think I am, just close enough to her that I probably qualify as clinically insane. What can I possibly do to help you?"

Dr. Kimberley and Gregory exchanged a look. He cleared his throat and said, "Things have gotten worse since you died. Shaun Mason is currently unreachable, following a rather unpleasant incident at the Memphis CDC, in which he remains a person of interest. He—"

"Wait—Memphis? Is Dr. Wynne okay?" Dr. Joseph Wynne worked out of the Memphis office. He was one of the first CDC employees I'd ever met who seemed to genuinely care about people. Without him, we might have died in the desert between Oklahoma and Texas.

"Dr. Wynne was killed during the incident. It's still unclear what his role was—the CDC insists he was a martyr, but the EIS has reason to believe otherwise." Catching the stricken look on my face, Gregory continued reluctantly. "Dr. Kelly Connolly was also found dead in the Memphis CDC."

"Which was surprising when you considered that she'd been killed several weeks previously, in a robbery gone awry," interjected Dr. Kimberley. "Once we started analyzing video footage of your brother's team over the weeks leading up to the incident, we found a surprising number of shots including a blonde woman whose facial features mapped quite well with Dr. Connolly's. Perhaps she didn't die before that day in Memphis after all."

"What are you saying?" I asked.

Dr. Kimberley motioned for Gregory to bring the water over again. "I'm saying things are much worse than you knew at the time of your passing."

"That wasn't me," I said, almost sullenly. I'd just been drugged and cut open without my consent. I was feeling entitled to a little balkiness. Gregory held the glass of water up for me to sip, and I did, gratefully. The feel of the liquid coating the back of my throat may have been the sweetest thing I had ever experienced.

"No, you're right; it wasn't you," said Dr. Kimberley. "But it *was* you at the same time. You're a bit of a paradox, my dear girl, and possibly the only ace our side has left to play. We need you to be Georgia Mason, just as much as the other side needs for you not to be. We need you to think like her, we need you to act like her, and we need you to *be* her. We would never have made you. I like to think the EIS still has marginally more of a soul than that. Now that you exist, forgive us, but we *will* use you to our best advantage."

I coughed. Gregory pulled the glass away. "What do you think you're going to use me *for*? I won't betray Shaun for you."

"We never expected you would. Your loyalty is one of the things that makes you useless to Dr. Thomas and his ilk." Dr. Kimberley's lip drew back in a sneer. "That man's never understood the virtue of loyalty."

"Right." Moving my left arm felt like one of the hardest things I had ever done. Somehow, I managed, raising it to rest my hand against my forehead. "So you're the good guys. You're just going to find a way to set me free so I can run off and join Shaun, and we can blow this conspiracy open and go live happily ever after. Is that it?"

"I wouldn't have put it quite like that—" began Dr. Kimberley.

I looked to Gregory. "Is she stupid, or does she think I am? Because I know a line of bullshit when it's being fed to me."

"Florida has been declared a Level 1 hazard zone," he replied.

"W-what?" I managed, after that seeming non sequitur had been given a moment to sink in. "That's impossible."

"An insect vector for Kellis-Amberlee was swept over from Cuba by a tropical storm, and deposited along the length of the United States Gulf Coast. We've lost more than just Florida, but that's the only entire state to be designated Level 1. So far."

"Wait. Are you saying—"

"This isn't a natural mutation. These mosquitoes are three times the size of anything we've seen before—the perfect size for transmitting Kellis-Amberlee. Isn't it a little odd that they didn't appear until right after a major break-in at the CDC?" Gregory looked at me calmly. "The purpose of the EIS is tracking, containment, and eradication of infectious diseases. At this point, we consider the CDC a form of infectious disease. So yes, Georgia, we really are going to find a way to free you to find your team—what's left of them—and tell them what you know."

"It may not tilt the balance fully in our favor, but it will help," added Dr. Kimberley. "Your death was too well publicized, and you're too well made. There's no way you can be written off as a hoax once you get to the proper people. And if you can't find the proper people, we'd be happy to provide them."

I sighed. "Is this all just one big political ploy to seize control of the CDC?"

"Do you really care if it is?" asked Gregory.

Trying to think about this was starting to make my head hurt. I decided to try another approach. "Did I hear Rick? I remember waking up and hearing him here."

"You did," said Gregory. That was a surprise. I'd been half expecting them to lie. "He was able to sneak away to meet with us. I'm sorry you weren't awake during his visit."

"Vice President Cousins has been very concerned about you," added Dr. Kimberley. "He's the one who approached the EIS about infiltrating this project. He was able to get my security clearance improved—that's how we could pull off this little ruse in the first place."

"Not that it's going to do us any good if you don't recover fast enough for us to break you out of here," said Gregory. He turned to look at one of the monitors. "Your system is still stressed from all the excitement. You need to get some sleep."

"Sleep is the last thing I want," I objected. "I want to know what the hell is going on."

"And that's why you need to sleep." Gregory smiled a little, holding up an empty syringe. "I'm afraid you don't have all that much choice in the matter. I added a little something to your IV line. We'll see you in a few hours."

"What—?" My eyes widened. "You bastard."

"My parents were married."

"You could have ... could have asked me ..." My voice was already slowing down. I didn't know whether it was psychosomatic or just very well timed, but either way, I was *pissed*.

"You would have said no," said Dr. Kimberley, standing.

"Damn ... right ... I ... " I lost my grasp on the sentence as the dark reached up to take me. This time it was softer, and less menacing. That didn't mean I had to like it, but when it became apparent that fighting wasn't going to do me any good, I let go and let it pull me under.

The fourth time I woke, no one was calling my name, and no one else was in the room; I was alone in my little half-folded hospital bed, with a yellow blanket pulled up around my shoulders. I was so used to CDC white that the color was almost shocking. I pushed myself into a sitting position with shaking arms, letting the blanket fall away. My white pajamas were gone, replaced by a set of pale blue surgical scrubs. More color. After so long in a world without it, even those little splashes were enough to make me feel disoriented.

After I was sure I was steady, I swung my feet around to the floor—my bare feet. A momentary panic lanced through me as I realized my gun was gone. I grabbed the bedrail, intending to stand, and paused as I saw the gun resting on the bedside table. I picked it up, hand shaking slightly, and relaxed as the weight of the gun confirmed that it was loaded. They hadn't left me defenseless after all. I tucked it into the waistband of my scrubs, checking twice to be sure the safety was on before I tightened my grasp on the bedrail, took a deep breath, and stood.

I didn't fall. That was a start. There was no immediate pain, although most of me was sore, and various parts of me ached in an irritated way that made me think of feeding tubes and catheters. Necessary evils, but not things I really wanted to dwell on.

There was a door on the far side of the room. I focused on it as I let go of the bedrail and started to shuffle forward, slowly at first, but with increasing speed as my confidence came back. The soreness actually began to fade a little as I stretched the muscles in my legs and back. Maybe most of it was from lying still too long.

I made it to the door without incident and grasped the knob, honestly expecting it to be locked. Instead, it turned easily, and I stepped out of my small recovery room into what looked like the central lab. Dr. Kimberley was there, reviewing test results with two of her technicians. All three of them turned toward the sound of my door opening.

For a moment, the four of us remained where we were, blinking at one another. Dr. Kimberley was the first to recover. "James?"

"On it, Doctor," said the technician, and stood, hurrying over to a small specimen refrigerator. He opened the door and produced a familiar red and white can, which he carried over and offered to me. "It's good to see you awake."

I took the Coke without a word, popping the tab and taking a long drink. The soda burned the soreness in my throat. All of them watched me. No one spoke.

I lowered the can.

"The first thing I will do—the *first* thing—is have myself checked for tracking devices," I said, directing my words at Dr. Kimberley. "If we find anything, I don't work with you people. I don't give you anything. You'll need to shoot me and start with another clone, and hope you can get away with it twice. Clear?"

"As crystal," she said, nodding. "We're playing fairly. Not because we're innately fair, but because at this point, it's in our best interests to do so . . . and it's the only thing left that distinguishes us from the other side."

"All right, then. How much time do we have?"

"Still three days. You were only out for a few hours this last time—long enough to let us do the last of the post-op cleanup work."

"Yeah, don't ever do that again. If you're going to knock me out,

I need to know before it happens." I took another drink of Coke. "I need an Internet connection, shoes, and another soda."

Dr. Kimberley smiled. "I think all those things can be arranged."

"Good." My can was almost empty. I finished it before returning Dr. Kimberley's smile. "Let's have ourselves a revolution."

We've reached Seattle in one piece. It was a little touch-and-go for a while there, but now here we are, and Maggie has somehow managed to hide us by going the opposite of underground. Money. Is there anything it *can't* do?

We're about to leave to see the Monkey, the man who can supposedly make identities that fool anyone and everyone in the world. That makes this Maggie's last hurrah; when we're done here, she's heading back to Weed, back to her bulldogs and her grindhouse movies. I'm going to miss the shit out of her, but I'm also glad, in a way.

At least one of us is going to make it out of this shitstorm alive.

—From *Adaptive Immunities*, the blog of Shaun Mason, August 1, 2041. Unpublished.

—

There are days when I wake up and realize I no longer know the man in my mirror. Who are you, with your graying temples and your two-hundred-dollar haircut? Who are you, in your fancy suit, with your vast political power that does you no good when it really matters? Who are you, with all those ghosts in your eyes?

Seriously, you asshole. Who the fuck are you, and why are you looking back at me whenever I look into my own eyes? What good will it be for a man if he gains the whole world, yet forfeits his own soul? It's on days like this that I really want to know.

I wish I could explain to them why I let this happen. I wish I could tell them what it was for. And I wish I thought, even for a second, that they were going to forgive me . . .

—From the private journal of Vice President Richard Cousins, August 1, 2041. Unpublished.

Eighteen

The polite voice of the hotel roused me from my bed shortly before sunrise. I sat up, blinking in disorientation at the opulent room around me—it would have been a suite in any other hotel—before I remembered where I was, swore softly, and got moving.

My clothes were scattered near the bathroom door, under the panel with the light controls. I'd spent almost ten minutes the night before just playing with them, cranking them up to mimic natural sunlight for the seasonally depressed, shifting them into the UV spectrum for the sake of people with retinal Kellis-Amberlee. In the end, I'd gone to sleep with the black lights on and the white-noise generator turned to full. It was almost like being back in Berkeley, before everything changed.

I hadn't slept that well in a year. Being woken, even gently, felt like a betrayal.

There'd been no discussion of how we'd be getting to the Monkey's: We just assembled at the van, like all of us being together again was the way things were supposed to be. Mahir got into the front passenger seat, balancing his tablet on his knee. Maggie and Becks took the back, and in the rearview mirror I could see Becks sitting sentry, watching out the rear window for signs of pursuit.

"Where to?" I asked, as I buckled my seat belt.

"I've got the directions," said Mahir, and held up the tablet, showing me a black window with a blinking green cursor in the upper right corner.

I blinked. "What the fuck is that?"

"Our map." He lowered the tablet, swiping a finger across the bottom to make the keyboard appear. He typed the words "find Monkey" with quick, efficient taps before pressing the ENTER key. The cursor dropped to the next line.

Maggie was peering over the seat at us. I frowned at the tablet, which Mahir was watching with absolute focus. Minutes ticked by.

"Okay," I said finally. "This is officially stupid. In case you were wondering whether it had the 'Shaun thinks this is stupid' seal of approval, it does. Is there a plan B?"

"Yes." Mahir held up the tablet, showing it to me again. A second line of text had appeared beneath his, with the cursor blinking on a third line now.

EXIT GARAGE, it said.

"You've got to be fucking kidding me," I grumbled, and started the engine.

"It's based off a pre-Rising computer game," said Mahir. "So primitive it's invisible to most monitoring systems." He began typing. "At the end of the drive, wave to the guards and turn left. You'll come to an intersection with a 7-Eleven. When you get there, turn right."

"Fucking. Kidding. Me," I said.

At the base of the driveway, we all waved to the guards as we waited for the gate to open. They waved back, apparently accustomed to strange behavior from their eccentric, wealthy clientele.

"Are you sure this is necessary?" I asked, still waving.

"If the directions say to do it, we do it," said Maggie. "That's what everyone says. If you don't listen to the Monkey, he doesn't meet with you."

"Let's hope the directions don't tell us to shoot a man in Reno just to watch him die," I muttered, and pulled out onto the street.

The directions did not tell us to shoot a man in Reno just to watch him die. They did tell us to drive down dead alleys, only to turn around and go back the way we'd come; to drive in circles through residential neighborhoods, probably setting off dozens of security alerts; and to get on and off the freeway six times. It was incredibly annoying. At the same time, I had to admire the Monkey's style. None of the neighborhoods we drove through had gates or manned security booths. None of the freeway exits we used required blood tests. We might be driving like idiots, but we were driving like idiots without leaving a definite record of where we'd been, or why we'd been there.

We were crossing a bridge that actually floated on the surface of a lake—thankfully, the Monkey hadn't requested we do anything stupid, like drive into the lake; I would have refused, and then I might have had a mutiny on my hands—when Mahir looked up, eyes wide. "Shaun?"

"What?" I asked. "Are we being followed?"

"No. The directions . . ." He cleared his throat, looked at the screen, and read, "'Turn on your jamming unit. Tune it to channel eight, or these instructions will cease.' We don't have a jamming unit, do we?"

"Actually, funny story—hey, Becks!" I looked at the rearview mirror. She turned, the reflection of her eyes meeting mine. "Put the jammer's batteries back in and turn it on, will you? The text-based adventure wants us to get scrambled."

"On it, Boss," Becks called, and put down her gun.

I hadn't wanted us to kill the jammer in the Agora parking garage—no matter how upper-crust they were, there were bound to be *some* things that would upset them. We'd settled for checking it for obvious bugs and removing the battery pack before heading into the hotel. Now I was glad we'd taken that approach. If the Monkey knew we had the jammer, he would probably have been pissed if we'd killed it.

"This guy must think he's the goddamn Wizard of Oz," I muttered. "I don't like being spied on."

"We're off to see the Wizard," chanted Maggie, in a gleeful singsong voice.

"Before you start killing people with joyous abandon, you might like to know that the next batch of directions has arrived," said Mahir dryly. "Maggie, please don't antagonize him; he's had a hard week, and he's liable to bite."

"Spoilsport," said Maggie.

"Thank you," I said. "Where are we going?"

"At the end of the bridge, turn right," said Mahir.

There was no joking around after that. Whatever test we'd been taking, we'd apparently passed, because the directions sent us along a straightforward series of increasingly smaller streets, until we were driving down a poorly maintained residential road in one of the oldest parts of Seattle. This was a million miles from the cultivated opulence of the Agora, or even from the reasonably well-maintained Berkeley streets where I grew up. This was a neighborhood where half the houses burned years ago and were never rebuilt, and where the remaining homes were surrounded by the kind of ludicrous fencing that was popular immediately after the Rising, when people were frantically trying to protect themselves from the next attack.

"People still live in places like this?" asked Maggie. Her levity was gone. She stared out the window with wide eyes, looking baffled and horrified at the same time.

I shrugged. "Where else are they gonna go?" The question sounded rhetorical. It wasn't. There were patches like this in almost every city, tolerated despite their sketchy adherence to the safety requirements, because there was nowhere else to put the people who lived in those slowly collapsing houses. Eventually, they'd all be condemned and razed to the ground. Until that day came, people would do what they always had. They would survive.

"Take the next driveway on the right," said Mahir. "To be more specific, it says 'Turn right at the serial killer van.'"

"You mean the big white one that looks like it was set on fire at some point?"

"One presumes."

"One right turn, coming up." I leaned on the wheel, sending us bumping down a driveway that was, if anything, even less well maintained than the street. It felt like my nuts were going to bounce all the way up to my shoulders. I gritted my teeth, clenching my hands on the wheel as I steered us to a stop in front of the one house on the cul-de-sac that looked like it might still be capable of sustaining life. "Now what?"

"Erm." Mahir looked up. "Now you and I are to put our hands on the dashboard, and Maggie and Rebecca are to put their hands behind their heads."

"What?" demanded Becks.

"That's what it says—oh, wait, there's another line. 'Do it, or else Foxy will shoot you until you are very, very, very, exceedingly dead.'" He frowned. "That sounds unpleasant."

"Yeah, and it'll hurt, too," said a chipper female voice. It sounded like it was coming from the speaker on Mahir's tablet. He and I exchanged an alarmed look. The tablet chirped, "Hi! Look in front of you!"

We all looked toward the windshield.

There was a short, slim woman standing in front of the van. The top of her head probably wouldn't have come higher than my shoulder. That didn't really matter. The assault rifle she was aiming at the windshield more than made up for any lack of size.

"Ah," said Mahir. "I believe we've found the right place."

"That, or we've found the local loony bin." I put my hands on the dashboard. "Everybody do what she says. We're going to go along with this for now."

"Good call!" chirped the tablet.

"Mason—" said Becks.

"Just chill, okay? They knew we were coming. Let's do things their way and see what happens."

One by one, the rest of my team did as we'd been told. Becks was the last to move, sullenly putting her gun down and lacing her fingers behind her head. She glared at me in the rearview mirror the entire time.

Once we were all in position, the girl with the gun half walked, half skipped over to the van, stopping next to the driver's-side door. She beamed through the glass, blue eyes wide and bright as a kid's on Christmas morning. Her hair destroyed any illusion of childishness, despite her size. Most kids have bleach-blond hair these days, a sign that their parents are properly respecting security protocols. Her hair was so red it was almost orange, and only the last six inches had been bleached, ending in about an inch of inky black, like the tipping on a fox's tail.

She tapped the barrel of her gun against the window, gesturing for me to open the door. I did so, moving slowly in case she decided to take offense at the fact that I was moving at all.

"Hi!" she said, once the door was open. She removed her right hand from the gun stock long enough to reach over and tap the skin behind her ear, presumably turning off the transmitter she'd been using to speak through Mahir's tablet. "I'm the Fox. Welcome to the Brainpan."

"Uh," I said slowly. "Nice to meet you?"

"Oh, that's probably not true," she said, still with the same manic good cheer. "Why don't you come inside? The Cat baked bread this morning, and I don't think it's poisoned or anything! Also, leave your guns in the car, or I'll not only kill you, I'll fuck up your corpses so bad that even DNA testing won't be able to figure out who you were." She flashed us one last, bright-toothed smile and started walking backward down the path to the porch. She kept her gun leveled on us all the way. Only when she reached the porch did she turn, bounding up the stairs and vanishing through the open door.

"Oh, great," said Becks, in a faint voice. "I was wondering how we were going to fill our daily quota of bat-shit crazy."

"Maybe we can make quota for the rest of the month." I unbuckled my belt and slid out of the van. Once I was clear, I removed the guns from my waistband, setting them on the seat. "Everybody drop your weapons and come on. We came to them. We may as well play by their rules."

"Yes, because allowing the crazy people to set the rules is absolutely always the way to ensure one's survival in a hostile situation." Mahir managed to sound almost amused, even though he scowled as he removed his own pistol from the holster beneath his arm.

"Thanks for the vote of confidence," I said amiably. He had the good grace to look abashed. I leaned back in through my open door and punched him in the arm. "Don't worry. The lunatics have been running the asylum around here for a long time. We'll fit right in."

Becks had to shed six guns before she got out of the van, and even then, I was reasonably sure she was holding back at least a couple of knives. Maggie didn't need to remove anything. That made me grimace a little.

She really isn't field ready at all, is she?

"No, she's really not," I murmured, and slammed the van door.

The four of us walked together down the broken concrete pathway leading to the Brainpan porch. As we got closer to the house, I started spotting the security enhancements and architectural tweaks hidden among the general disorder and decay. All of them were subtle, and from what I could see, all of them were designed to be effective. That meant they were recent. If they'd been done immediately post-Rising, when most of the improvements—such as they were—were being made to this neighborhood, they would have been flashy. These had no flash at all. They weren't here to show off how secure the house was. They were here to secure it.

"Look," I said, elbowing Becks in the side before nodding toward a camera mostly hidden beneath one of the shingles edging the roof.

She followed my gaze. "Not very well concealed."

"Yeah, but it's also a dummy. You know, for dummies." The Fox bounced back into the open doorframe, beaming at us. "If you think that's the only camera, you're a dummy, and I get to shoot you."

"That's an entirely reasonable and understandable mechanism for judging one's guests," said Mahir smoothly. "Might we come inside now?"

"Oh, sure. Just take off your shoes. The Cat gets a little crazy when you track mud on her floors." She disappeared back into the house.

Becks and I exchanged a look. "I'm not sure what's worse," she said. "The fact that she just implied someone else might be crazy, or the fact that everyone here has a name that starts with the word 'the.'"

"Just pretend they're all comic book villains and it starts to make sense." Maggie took off her sandals, swinging them casually from one hand as she climbed the porch steps and entered the house.

"I'm Batman," deadpanned Mahir, and followed her. Becks was half a step behind him, and I brought up the rear, looking back over my shoulder for signs of pursuit as I stepped inside. There were none. For better or for worse, we were alone with the people we had come to find.

I expected the door to swing shut itself as soon as I was over the threshold. Instead, it remained open until an aggravated female voice shouted, "Shut the damn *door*!" from somewhere at the end of the hall.

I shut the door.

It took a moment for me and Becks to undo the laces on our boots. Mahir and Maggie waited for us to finish, and we walked down the short entry hall to the living room together.

The house was constructed on one of the pre-Rising open-space models, with the living room, dining room, and kitchen essentially blending together to form one large space. There were multiple windows, which must have provided a lot of natural light before they were sealed up and boarded over. Now they were just plywood rectangles set into the walls, barely visible behind the banks of computer equipment and monitor screens. The place looked like a combination of a server farm and a college student's dorm room, with one big exception: It was scrupulously clean. There might be a futon on the floor, but there were no pizza boxes or takeout containers; there was clutter, but no trash. It managed to be sterile and lived-in at the same time.

"Bizarre," muttered Becks.

"*Awesome*," I countered.

"Expensive, so don't touch anything," said a voice. I turned toward the kitchen, where a brown-haired woman was standing, arms crossed, a stern expression on her face. She was wearing jeans and a tank top, and her hair was cropped short, leaving nothing for a zombie mob to grab hold of. She looked more like a normal human than the girl from the driveway, who was now sitting on the counter, drumming her heels against a cabinet. Somehow, that made her more difficult to trust. Nothing that looked normal in this place could possibly be what it seemed.

Mahir had turned along with the rest of us. He recovered quickly, stepping forward and offering his hand. "I'm Mahir Gowda. It's a pleasure to—"

"You're not here to meet me," said the brunette, in the same disapproving tone. "No one comes here to meet me. You're here for the Monkey. Well, he's not sure he wants to talk to you just yet. Who sent you?"

"No one sent us. We came—"

"Whoops! Wrong answer!" The Fox was suddenly holding a pistol in each hand. I hadn't even seen her draw. "Somebody told you who to look for, and somebody told you where to look. So who sent you?"

"Alaric Kwong. He said the Monkey was the best in the business," said Becks.

The brunette blinked. Then, to my surprise, she smiled, a little wistfully. "Alaric? Really? You're the people he's been working with?"

The four of us stared at her for a moment. Slowly, I nodded. "Yeah. He's part of my crew. I'm Shaun Mason, After the End Times."

"I know you," she said, smile fading as fast as it came. "I'm the Cat. You've met the Fox."

"'Met' is a word," I agreed. The Fox lowered her guns. "Do we pass the security check?"

"For the moment." The Cat turned, picking up a bread knife from the counter. "Why did Alaric send you?"

We could have tried for diplomacy. We could have tried for plausible deniability. In the end, that seemed like too damn much trouble, and I did what Georgia taught me to do: I went for the truth. "There's a good chance we're going to need to run for the border pretty soon, since the CDC is trying to kill us—"

"—we think," Becks interjected.

"Right, we think. Anyway, they probably released bioengineered death mosquitoes and accidentally wiped out the Gulf Coast trying to get us, so they're a little pissed right now. That means we need IDs the CDC won't be watching for."

"Why?" asked the little redhead, guilelessly.

I hesitated. I could give the answer we'd been giving everyone else—so we could get out, so we could run and escape and live—or I could tell the truth. I looked toward my team. Mahir was still watching the two women, the redhead drumming her heels, the brunette slicing obviously home-baked bread. Becks and Maggie were watching me, waiting to see what I would say. I took a breath.

"Mahir needs a new passport to get him into Canada, so he can get back to Europe alive. Becks needs an identity that can get her out of the country, wherever it is she wants to go. Alaric needs IDs for him, and for his sister, Alisa. We're going to get her out of Florida. Maggie—"

"Is paying for all this," said Maggie.

The Cat turned to me, knife still in her hand. Raising an eyebrow, she asked, "And what about you? What are you planning to get out of this deal?"

"Assuming this dude is as good as Alaric thinks he is, I'm going to get an ID that doesn't set off any alarms. I'm going to stay low until we finish finding the people who killed my sister. And then I'm going to walk right in their front doors and shoot them in their fucking faces."

"I like this one," said the Fox, giggling. "He's funny."

Maggie was staring at me, clearly aghast. Becks and Mahir, on the other hand, didn't even look surprised. Becks looked a little sad; Mahir just looked accepting, like he'd been waiting a long time for those words to leave my lips.

Seeing them like that made me feel slightly ashamed, and more determined than ever to set things right. I all but glared at the Cat. "So? Are those reasons good enough for you people, or do we need to find someone else to help us?"

"You're doing this out of a suicidal need for revenge, even though it may not change anything," said the Cat coolly.

"Yeah." I shrugged. "Pretty much."

You're an idiot, muttered George. I ignored her.

"Okay," said the Cat.

I blinked. "What?"

"I said okay. The Fox likes you, and I think you're a suicidal idiot with friends who will pay to let you kill yourself in an interesting fashion. She"—she gestured toward Maggie with her knife—"can give us obscene amounts of money without thinking about it, and the other two are nonoffensive enough not to matter. Besides, you work with someone that I owe a favor."

"Who?" I asked.

"Alaric Kwong." She smiled at our expressions. "He doesn't know I ended up here. Probably break his heart if you told him. I may as well pay him back by passing you through."

"A favor? For what?" asked Becks.

The Cat smirked. "I broke up with him when our Quest Realm guild was in the middle of a raid, and then I kept making him heal me without answering any of his whiny whispers about why, Jane, why would you break up with me, I looooooooove you. So we'll get you your IDs. Cost is fifty thousand each, up-front, before you leave here today . . . and a favor."

"A favor?" Becks frowned, suddenly suspicious. Given how on edge she'd been since we arrived, that wasn't much of a transition. "What kind of favor are we talking about here?"

"Nothing you'd lose any sleep over. We need you to break into the local CDC building and drop a little something off for us," said the Cat. She resumed slicing bread.

"Define 'a little something,'" I said. "We're not blowing anything up. That's their game, not ours."

"Nothing like that. Their main storage facility isn't online. We want access. So we have a pressure-point hotspot that we just need you to get into the proper place and switch on. Then you come back here and get your shiny new identities, and with them, the warm satisfaction of knowing we're going to screw the CDC over in some fun ways that you don't need to know anything about." She put her knife down, resting her hands on the counter as she looked at us calmly. "Do we have a deal?"

Looking into her calm, cold eyes, I realized the Fox wasn't the only crazy person living in this house. She was just the one who had the honesty to wear her crazy on her sleeve.

"Yeah," I said. "We have a deal."

. . . all attempts to culture a live infection in blood samples taken from Subject 139b have failed. More interesting, we induced amplification in a white-tailed deer, and injected it via dart with a serum derived from Subject 139b's blood. The deer showed signs of improvement before dying of massive cerebral hemorrhage. The necropsy was inconclusive. Unfortunately, I think we'll need to try this with a human subject before we can be sure of anything. My team is scouring the area for freshly infected individuals; thus far, we've had no luck.

No reports of mosquito-borne Kellis-Amberlee have come in from any of my sources in California, Arizona, or Nevada. It's possible that we may be able to dodge this bullet. I don't think so; we haven't dodged any of the ones that came before it. But I'm starting to believe that there may be an answer. All I need is a little more *time.*

—Taken from an e-mail sent by Dr. Shannon Abbey to Dr. Joseph Shoji at the Kauai Institute of Virology, August 1, 2041.

Well, that's that, then. We're all going to die.

Charming.

—From *Fish and Clips*, the blog of Mahir Gowda, August 1, 2041. Unpublished.

Nineteen

Dr. Kimberley's technicians didn't have any street clothes in my size. They did manage to find me a pair of hard-soled slippers, which weren't quite the shoes I'd asked for, but were several thousand times better than the socks I'd been wearing since I woke up.

Better yet—best of all—they brought me a computer. A sleek, hard-shelled little laptop, which Gregory set in front of me with the top closed. I reached for it. He pulled it back. Only a few inches, but far enough to make it clear that I needed to listen before I was going to get my hands on the machine.

"You have a connection, and a guest log-in routed through one of the administrative offices," he said. "We can't spoof it forever, but we should be able to get you about twenty minutes without raising any red flags. Please don't run any open searches on phrases that might get the attention of our firewall."

"Like what?" I asked. "Governmental corruption? Conspiracy to defraud the American people? Cloning?"

"Yes," he said, without a trace of irony. "That's a good initial list of things to avoid. Don't log into any e-mail accounts with your name on them. Don't—"

"I promise I've used other people's networks before, and I've never managed to get anyone arrested when I wasn't trying to," I said, and reached for the laptop again. "We're all trying to trust each other here. For me, the last step to trusting you is seeing that I have a clear connection. For you, the last step to trusting me is seeing that I won't abuse it. So I guess we both start getting what we want when you let me have that computer, huh?"

Gregory chuckled and pushed the laptop toward me. "You're definitely feeling better if you're trying to use logic against me."

"That's me. Only rational when I'm not being cut open and dissected for the amusement of others." I took the laptop, breathing slowly through my nose to keep my hands from shaking as I opened it. The screen sprang to life, displaying a stark white background with the CDC logo in the center. I let my fingers rest against the keys, breathing unsteadily out. "Oh, wow."

"Maybe we only trust you because we don't have any other choice, but we *do* trust you, Georgia." Gregory touched my shoulder, causing me to look up. He smiled. "Let's try and earn it from each other."

I nodded. "I'll do my best," I said. And then I bent my head and started to type, and Gregory didn't matter anymore.

His warning about avoiding my e-mail was smart, if unnecessary: Anyone who's never worked professionally in Internet news would probably assume the first thing a journalist would do was go for their inbox. He was right, in a way. He was also wrong. All the public-facing e-mail addresses—the ones that fed into the customary webmail interfaces—were basically dummy accounts, feeding their contents into the true inboxes behind the After the End Times firewall system that Buffy had designed. The only time we ever needed to use those boxes directly was when we were somewhere that didn't allow for logging all the way into the system. Even if I only had twenty minutes, I had plenty of time to make it that far.

The first place I went was an online game site, the sort of thing that's been killing productivity in offices everywhere since the first computer was invented. Somehow, I wasn't surprised when the browser autofilled the URL after I'd entered only the first three letters. Not even the CDC is immune to the lure of brightly colored graphics and simplistic puzzles. The site presented a list of options, all with cute, easily marketed names and icons designed to catch the eye. I scrolled to the bottom.

"What are you doing?" asked Gregory.

"Not all computers have shell access these days, and any site that's obviously designed to be secure might as well have a big red label on it, flashing 'Oh, hey, look over here; people do things they don't want you to know about when they're over here,'" I said. The last icon on the list of games was a comparatively drab cartoon atom. I clicked on it. "So we have back doors, for those times when we need to get in, but don't have access to the normal equipment."

"And one of your back doors involves a game site?"

"Buffy designed their security." I smiled as the "loading" bar appeared on my browser. "Buffy designed a lot of people's security. She hid things all over the damn Internet."

"Well, I wish she were here," said Gregory.

"Yeah. So do I." The menu appeared, giving a list of options. I clicked a set of five that would have resulted in an unplayable game if I'd actually been trying to play, and hit start. The screen froze.

"Did it crash?" asked Gregory.

"Are you going to watch over my shoulder the whole time I'm online?"

"Yes. We're still in the 'earning trust' phase, remember?"

"Right. No, it didn't crash. This is what's supposed to happen." I tapped the space bar twice. "If I were a casual player who'd just chosen a bad set of options, this is where I'd reload and try again. Since I'm not, this is where we wait."

"Wait for what?"

"Wait for that." The browser flickered and vanished, replaced by blackness. A log-in window appeared, floating in the middle of the screen.

USER NAME? it prompted.

NANCY, I typed.

"Nancy?" asked Gregory.

"Remember how I said Buffy did our security programming? Well, Buffy was a pre-Rising media nut."

ADDRESS? prompted the window.

1428 ELM STREET.

There was a longer pause this time as the program controlling this particular back door checked my responses against the list. The pause wasn't necessary. It was one more trick programmed by our former professional paranoid. If I touched the keyboard before I was prompted, it would not only kick me out, it would lock this door until someone who was already inside the firewall decided it was safe to open it again.

Finally, the prompt asked, WHY DID YOU MOVE OUT?

Of the eight possible questions it could have asked, that was the one I'd been hoping for. I wasn't sure I remembered the answers to any of the others. I typed, BECAUSE A DEAD SERIAL KILLER WITH KNIVES FOR HANDS MURDERED MY BOYFRIEND.

The pause this time lasted less than a second. WELCOME, GEORGIA MASON appeared on the screen, and vanished, replaced by the After the End Times logo.

"That log-in won't work again for six months," I said, trying to make the comment sound casual. I probably failed, but it didn't matter as much as making sure I got my point across. "Buffy knew her business."

"Remind me—why wasn't she working for the CIA? Or better yet, for us?" Gregory dragged a chair over and sat down where he could watch my screen. Oddly, it made me feel more at ease, rather than making me feel spied on. There's almost always been someone watching over my shoulder while I worked. It was usually Shaun, but that didn't change the way Gregory's presence calmed me down.

"You guys didn't offer her enough opportunities for bad poetry, porn, or bad poetry about porn." I clicked the link that should have taken me to the staff directories. Instead of opening, it flashed a red "restricted" warning at me. "Crap."

Gregory frowned. "You're kidding, right?"

"About the poetry and porn? No. She was a genius. We all knew she'd been scouted by at least one of the alphabet soup agencies. I wouldn't be surprised to find out she'd been scouted by all of them." I glared at the screen. "I'm not kidding about this stupid firewall, either. They didn't close the loopholes into the system, but they locked down the staff directory. Who does that? Purge it all, or allow for the occasional spontaneous resurrection!"

"Most people who come back from the dead can't type, you know."

"Right now, I don't *care*. Let me try something else." I moved my mouse to the administrative panel for the forums. If anything was going to stop me, it would have done so on the first layer, when I accessed the full member list. Nothing pinged. "Oh, jeez. They let Dave do the purge, didn't they? He never finishes everything on the first go."

"David Novakowski?" asked Gregory, sounding suddenly hesitant.

I glanced toward him. "Yeah. Why?"

"I'm sorry to tell you this, but . . . "

Something in the way his voice trailed off told me what he didn't want to finish his sentence. My eyes widened. "Dave's *dead*? How the hell is Dave *dead*? He was the most careful Irwin I ever met!"

"There was an outbreak in the location of your team's new headquarters. It's unclear exactly why he did what he did, but he chose to remain behind after the quarantine sirens began ringing. He was still inside the building when it was sterilized."

"By 'sterilized,' do you by any chance mean 'carpet-bombed'?"

Gregory looked away.

Pressing my lips into a thin line, I looked back to the computer. The After the End Times forums were open in front of me like some sort of a miracle, with their threads and board titles looking so familiar that it was like I'd never left. It didn't matter that I didn't recognize even a quarter of them—that could happen when I spent a weekend in bed with a migraine and let Mahir take forum duty for me. What mattered was that they were *there*. I scrolled to the bottom of the screen, and closed my eyes for a moment from sheer relief.

The moderator's forum was listed. If there had been any changes to my profile following the purge of my core system access, the forum would have turned invisible, marking me as one more end user. I crossed my fingers, opened my eyes, moved the mouse to the appropriate icon, and clicked.

The forum opened without a pause. I started scrolling down, barely aware that I was crying. According to the admin script at the bottom of the page, only two users with mod privileges were currently online. One was me. The other was Alaric.

"What are you doing?" asked Gregory.

"Sending up a flare," I said. I opened a private message window and tapped out, ALARIC ARE YOU THERE? NEED TO CHAT ASAP, DO NOT HAVE MUCH TIME.

I hit enter.

"Georgia—"

"Just give it a second."

A message appeared in my inbox less than fifteen seconds later. HOW DID YOU GET THIS LOG-IN? THIS IS NOT FUNNY. LOG OFF RIGHT NOW OR I WILL CONTACT THE AUTHORITIES.

I grinned. "Oh, good. He's pissed."

"That's *good*?"

"Yeah, that's good. If he's pissed, he'll want to know who I am so he can have someone to be pissed *at*. That means he'll talk." I hit REPLY, typing, BUFFY GAVE ME THIS LOG-IN THE DAY WE WENT LIVE. ALARIC, IT'S ME. IF YOU DON'T BELIEVE ME, OPEN A CHAT. I CAN PROVE IT.

Gregory looked dubiously at my screen. "Let me guess. The goal here is to make him *really* mad."

"Kind of, yes. Alaric thinks better when he's mad—he doesn't second-guess himself nearly as much." I was speaking from a flawed model and I knew it: Not only had Alaric been alive while I wasn't, giving him time to adapt and change, but I was working off memories extracted from a dead woman's mind and implanted in my own. Even the way I thought about myself—half "me," half "her"—told me I couldn't trust my own judgment where the reactions of others were concerned. And that didn't matter, because my judgment was the only thing I had.

That was a depressing thought. I was trying not to dwell on it when a light blinked at the bottom of my window, signaling an incoming chat request.

"I don't want to sound like I'm rushing you, Georgia, but we can keep this window active for another ten minutes at best."

"That should be all I need." I opened the chat window. THANKS FOR TALKING TO ME, ALARIC. I APPRECIATE IT. HOW HAVE YOU BEEN?

The response was immediate, making me think it had been more than half typed before I said anything. YOU'D BETTER LOG OFF THIS SYSTEM RIGHT NOW AND NEVER COME BACK. YOU'RE JUST LUCKY MY BOSS ISN'T ONLINE, OR YOU'D BE SORRIER THAN YOU CAN IMAGINE.

DO YOU MEAN MAHIR OR SHAUN WHEN YOU SAY THAT? It was common knowledge that Mahir was my second; he was almost certainly also my replacement. I WOULD BE MORE AFRAID OF SHAUN, PERSONALLY. MAHIR MAY GET ALL PISSY AND BRITISH AT YOU, BUT HE DOESN'T HIT. IT'S ME, ALARIC. IT'S GEORGE. LICENSE AFB-075893, CLASS A-15. THE FIRST TIME WE MET IN PERSON, YOU BROUGHT ME A CAN OF COKE TO SHOW YOUR RESPECT, BUT YOUR HANDS WERE SHAKING SO HARD THAT IT EXPLODED EVERYWHERE WHEN I OPENED IT. SOME CAMERA JOCKEY FREAKED OUT, AND WE WOUND UP IN DECON FOR THREE HOURS. REMEMBER?

There was a longer pause before his answer appeared—at least in part, I was sure, because my reply wasn't what he was expecting. Finally, two words flashed on my screen: Georgia's dead.

I took a deep breath. Then, more slowly than before, I tapped out my answer.

ARE YOU REALLY GOING TO SIT THERE, POST-ZOMBIE APOCALYPSE, AND TELL ME THE DEAD NEVER COME BACK?

"Five minutes, Georgia."

"Hold on." I stared at the screen, willing Alaric to reply. Seconds ticked by, making me feel like my time had been wasted—maybe worse than wasted. If he thought I was an imposter, and told Shaun . . .

How?

I was so relieved I actually laughed as I typed, CLONING. THE CDC HAS BEEN A NAUGHTY, NAUGHTY GOVERNMENT ORGANIZATION. NEED TO GET A MESSAGE TO SHAUN. IS HE THERE? I regretted the question as soon as I sent it. If he still didn't believe me . . . Hurriedly, I typed, DON'T ANSWER THAT. IF YOU HAVE A WAY OF REACHING HIM, TELL HIM I AM BEING HELD AT THE SEATTLE CDC. I AM WORKING WITH THE EIS. I NEED AN IMMEDIATE EXTRACTION. I AM IN DANGER. PLEASE CONFIRM.

Again, seconds ticked by. I was still crying. I wiped my cheek viciously with one hand, watching the screen, praying to a higher power I didn't believe in for some sort of miracle. Alaric was a Newsie. Even if he didn't believe I was who I claimed to be, there was a chance he'd be interested enough in the idea of me to chase the story. If he did that, I might have a chance.

Finally: WHY SHOULD I BELIEVE YOU?

"Oh, thank God, he's asking something easy," I muttered, and typed, EITHER I'M THE REAL THING, A TRAP, OR A GREAT STORY. FIRST OPTION, YOU NEED TO SAVE ME. SECOND OPTION, YOU NEED TO FIND OUT WHO'S TRYING TO TRAP YOU. THIRD OPTION, YOU NEED TO GET YOUR FACTS STRAIGHT BEFORE YOU GO PUBLIC. PERSONALLY, I THINK I'M ALL OF THE ABOVE. In case that wasn't good enough, I added, BESIDES, IF THERE'S ANY CHANCE I'M THE REAL DEAL, AND YOU DON'T GO AFTER IT, SHAUN WILL NEVER FORGIVE YOU.

Gregory's watch beeped. He looked at it and winced. "You need to log off *now*. IT has started scanning the wireless connections in this part of the building. Nothing indicates that this isn't random, but—"

"Better safe than sorry. I get that." Quickly, I typed, GOT TO GO—SECURITY IS LOOKING OUR WAY. TELL SHAUN YOU HEARD FROM ME. HE'LL BE SO PISSED HE'LL COME TO FIND THE FAKE AND BUST ME OUT INSTEAD. PLEASE, ALARIC. BELIEVE ME. I AM BEGGING YOU.

I hit ENTER and logged off. Gregory snatched the laptop as soon as I pulled my hands away from it. He flipped it over, ejecting the battery pack with a motion too smooth to be anything but practiced.

"I'll be right back," he said, and then he was striding out of the room, the battery in one hand, the laptop in the other. I stayed where I was, slumping ever lower in my seat, my eyes fixed on the space where the computer had been.

For just a moment, I'd been able to reach the outside world. I'd been able to tell someone what was happening—and whether he believed me or not, Alaric *listened*. He *knew*. I had put my hands on the keys, and even without the muscle memory of the body I was born in, they'd known what to do. Maybe I could still be Georgia Mason after all. As long as I could still tell the truth . . .

"Rise up while you can," I whispered. Then I slumped in my seat, put my head down on my arms, and sobbed until the tears ran out.

Mahir are you there?

Mahir I need you to reply RIGHT NOW. It's important or I wouldn't be trying to break radio silence.

Mahir, PLEASE. If you're ignoring these messages because you think I'm fighting with Dr. Abbey or something, PLEASE. I NEED TO TALK TO YOU. I can't talk to Becks or Shaun until I talk to you.

MAHIR GODDAMMIT YOU ANSWER ME RIGHT FUCKING NOW.

. . . fuck.

—Internal chat log, user AKwong to user MGowda, August 1, 2041.

We have removed all tracking devices and self-destruct triggers from the subject, who continues to self-identify as "Georgia Mason." She was made aware of the realities of her situation by Dr. Lake before we reached this phase, and her psychological progress has been nothing but encouraging. I believe she will remain stable in the long term, providing we are able to secure her release. My team can keep her isolated for a few days more; Dr. Thomas and his lackeys are distracted with the final preparations to awaken her replacement.

This has crossed a line. This experiment has always been both disgusting and morally questionable, but for the first time, it has become obscene. She's a real person. She knows who she is, even if she is only that person because of us. She thinks, she feels, and she wants to go home.

How did we ever come to this?

—Taken from a message sent by Dr. Danika Kimberley, August 1, 2041. Recipient unknown.

Twenty

We left the Brainpan and returned to the Agora. Breaking into the CDC in broad daylight would take a stupid plan and render it actively suicidal—not something I was in a hurry to do, all indications to the contrary aside. Besides, even if it had been full dark, I would have insisted on going back to the resort. There was no way we were going to take Maggie into the field with us. Not for something like this.

She was silent during the drive, almost shrinking in on herself as she listened to Becks and Mahir arguing about the best ways to bypass CDC security. She'd been a part of this team almost from the beginning, but that time was coming to an end, and we all knew it. When this was over, if she was still alive, she wouldn't be one of us anymore.

I parked the van in the Agora garage and twisted around to face her. "Maggie, I—"

It was too late. She was already out of the van and on her way to the airlock door. I froze where I was, not sure what I was supposed to do.

"Let her go."

For a moment, I thought the voice was Georgia's. Then I lifted my head and saw Becks looking at me.

"She's made her choice. That doesn't mean she feels good about herself. Let her go. We can talk to her when we get back."

If we get back, said George.

"Yeah," I said, answering them both, and unfastened my seat belt.

We didn't talk as we followed Maggie's path to the airlock. The lobby was empty when we arrived. Somehow, that wasn't much of a surprise. We didn't discuss our next move. We just split up, each of us heading for our own room to do whatever it was we had to do in order to feel like we were ready. If you can ever feel ready for something like this.

Becks and I hadn't had much time to get unpacked—or much with us to unpack—but there was enough that it took me about fifteen minutes to get everything together, double-checking the ammo in every gun and the straps on every holster. I even retied my boots. It never hurts to be overprepared. Then I stopped, looking at the empty room, and closed my eyes.

"This is all I'm going to leave behind," I said aloud. "No apartment. No belongings. No family. Just a hotel room that won't remember me tomorrow."

"I'll remember you." Georgia's hand on my shoulder was gentle. I started to turn toward her. "Shhh. Don't open your eyes. Just come with me." She tugged me to the bed, pushing on my shoulder until I sat. "Now you're going to get some rest."

"George—"

"Don't argue. You don't do well on sleep dep. You never have. Now, go to sleep. You have hours to kill before the sun goes down."

She was right. I knew she was right, just like I knew she wasn't there; she was the part of my mind that gave a damn about keeping the rest of me alive. I still took an unimaginable amount of comfort from the feeling of her hand on my shoulder as I fell backward on the bed, eyes still closed, gear still on, and let myself drift off into sleep.

My dreams were full of screaming. I saw my team die half a dozen times, in half a dozen ways. Oddly, that helped, because every time I saw one of them get killed, I saw something else that wouldn't work for getting us into the building alive. We were going to need to be careful, and quick, and never hesitate.

The light in the room was dimmer when I finally opened my eyes. George was gone, but that didn't matter; she'd be back, and soon. She always came back..

I went to the bathroom, splashed some water on my face, and then began the final preparations to depart. I was loading my pockets with clips when a speaker hidden somewhere in the room chimed, and the voice of the Agora said, "Mr. Mason, I apologize for the interruption, but Mr. Gowda has been trying to reach you for the past fifteen minutes. I didn't want to wake you. Will you accept the call?"

"If I don't, he'll probably wind up coming down here to yell at me," I said, still working. "Hell, I'm surprised he hasn't already. I'll take it."

"Thank you." The Agora went silent, followed by another chime.

"Shaun?" It was Mahir this time, sounding worried. Business as usual, in other words.

"Hey, Mahir. What's up? Aren't you like, three doors down? This takes 'lazy' to a new level, don't you think? Then again, I just spent the whole day asleep, so who am I to talk?" I couldn't fit any more clips in my pockets. That was a bummer. I picked up my tablet, clipping it to my belt. There was one nice thing about this particular suicide mission: We'd downloaded floor plans for all the major CDC installations as part of our research weeks ago, right before we followed Kelly into the Memphis office and got her killed. Seattle was a major enough office that we had pretty good blueprints. It didn't show any secret tunnels, but it had the public areas. At least we wouldn't be lost while we were rushing off to our deaths.

There was a time when that thought would have made me uneasy, rather than reassuring me. It's amazing what has become comforting since the start of the Ryman campaign.

"Alaric tried to get in touch with me."

My head snapped up. No one respects radio silence like a Newsie. It's practically one of their sacred creeds, right alongside "protecting your sources" and "off the record." "Did he say why?"

"No, and that's why I'm concerned. The message he left was basically 'you know this matters, or I wouldn't be doing it,' over and over. I already tried dialing one of his burn phones."

"And?"

"There's no response. I've left a message and sent an e-mail to one of Dr. Abbey's encrypted addresses, but—"

"Do you want to stay here and keep trying to reach him while Becks and I go to the CDC?"

"What? No." Mahir actually sounded offended. "I didn't come this far to be left sitting on the stands when things are finally getting interesting. I do intend to return to my career once I'm no longer a wanted fugitive, and the more I can learn, the better my prospects will be."

"You're a natural-born snoop, Mahir," I said, and picked up my pack. "You ready to blow this taco stand?"

"Have you ever even *seen* a taco stand?"

"Sure. There was one right next to campus. Are you ready to *go*, Mahir?"

He sighed, attempts at levity dismissed in an instant. "Yes. Much as I'm afraid of what's to come, I rather do believe I am."

"Good. Meet me in the hall."

"Shall do." There was no dial tone, but something about the shape of the silence filling the room told me that he'd hung up. I slung my pack over my shoulder and turned to head for the door. I didn't look back. There was nothing there to see.

Becks's room was between Mahir's and mine. I had barely finished knocking when her door swung open. "Yes, Mason?" she asked.

"You ready to go?"

"As ready as I'll ever be. I've been waiting on you." She was dressed almost exactly like I was: a charcoal-gray T-shirt, camouflage pants, combat boots, and way too many weapons to be on her way to a tea party. Her hair was slicked back in a tight, no-nonsense ponytail. This wasn't an expedition intended to be filmed and sold by the download. This was serious work.

She raised an eyebrow at my assessing look.

"Something wrong?"

"No. Just thinking how much it sucks that we can't post any of this."

Her grin was sudden, the flash of white teeth there and gone almost before it had fully registered. "Someday this story is going to make us legends."

"Only if it doesn't make us dead," I shot back, and then winced, waiting for Georgia to say something. She didn't. I wasn't sure whether that was a good sign or not.

Becks looked at me with concern. She'd clearly seen the wince, and was waiting to see what it was going to mean. "Boss?"

"I'm good. Come on." I turned to head for the elevator, waving for her to follow me. With barely a moment of hesitation, she did.

Mahir met us in the elevator lobby. "Are we ready?" he asked.

"That is a question for the sages, not for us, Mahir," I said. "But we're going either way, so what the fuck does it matter, right?"

He took that answer in stride. None of us said anything as we got into the elevator and rode down to the lobby. The concierge smiled at us politely, like journalists stormed through his hotel every day. I waved, and we walked on, to the van.

I had unlocked the doors and was about to get inside when Becks caught my elbow, saying urgently, "The jammer."

"...shit." If the Masons could use that thing to track us—still unproven, but still likely—then so could other people. The Monkey's people had known we had it. That made it a liability if we were going somewhere sensitive, like, say, the CDC. "Got a hammer?"

"I've got a better idea." She picked up the jammer, dropping her backpack on the passenger seat, and turned to walk back toward the hotel.

I blinked. "Mahir? You want to logic that one out for me?"

"The concierge is supposed to be the hotel's private on-call miracle worker," said Mahir, hoisting himself into one of the rear seats. "Presumably, she's gone to ask him if he has access to an industrial-grade furnace of some sort."

"Rich people are weird," I said, and got into the van.

Becks returned about five minutes later, looking smugly pleased. She hopped into her seat, pushing her backpack to the floor, and slammed the door before announcing, "The staff of the Agora is more than happy to dismantle any unwanted professional equipment we may have, and can promise the utmost discretion in the destruction of the individual components."

"Is there anything money *can't* buy?" I asked.

Immortality, said George.

I grimaced and started the van.

The Seattle branch of the CDC wasn't technically in Seattle at all; it was across the lake, in Redmond. The facility was located on part of what used to be the main Microsoft campus, before the Rising demonstrated every possible flaw in their architecture. The CDC bought the site when the rebuilding of the area was getting underway; it was viewed as a major coup, since at the time, having a CDC installation nearby was seen almost as a magical talisman against further infection. That hasn't changed much in the last twenty years. People would rather live near the CDC than in areas with good schools or excellent hospitals. The CDC will keep the zombies away.

I chuckled as I drove, largely because laughter stood a chance of keeping me from screaming. Becks kept herself busy cleaning and double-checking her guns, while Mahir monitored the GPS. The only conversation consisted of directions, given quietly and with calm efficiency, like we were going to be graded on how fast we got there. The Cat's instructions included the location of a secure parking garage formerly connected to a grocery store. The store was long gone, but the garage remained, free-standing and abandoned. With the CDC so close, regular patrols checked the area for signs of zombie infestation. We'd be safe there, as long as the roof didn't collapse on us.

No one was in sight as we turned off the road and into a back alley that led to the old employee entrance to the parking garage. I parked in the darkest corner I could find, despite the fact that every instinct I had told me to avoid those shadows. Our headlights didn't catch any motion. I still signaled for the others to stay quiet as I turned off the engine. It ticked for a few seconds before stilling into silence.

Nothing moaned or shuffled in the darkness. We were alone. "Clear," I said.

"This place gives me the creeps," complained Becks. "Is there a reason we keep winding up in places that should have stayed in their horror movies?"

"I guess I just know how to show a girl a good time." I opened my door, sliding out of the van. My boots crunched on the broken glass and gravel covering the pavement.

"Then what are you showing me?" asked Mahir.

"I'm not sexist. I can show a guy a good time, too." I looked between them. "You all cool?"

"I'm cool," confirmed Becks.

"I haven't been 'cool' since arriving in this godforsaken hellhole you persist in claiming is a civilized nation. I am, however, ready to go violate a few more laws," said Mahir. "I believe at this point we're simply waiting on you."

I'm ready when you are, said George.

"I thought you were supposed to keep me out of trouble," I said, not caring that Becks and Mahir would hear me. We were long past the point where I could get any mileage out of pretending not to be crazy.

I gave up.

"Well, folks, even the girl who lives in my head says it's time to go, so we'd better get moving. According to the directions, we have a quarter-mile to go before we even hit the fence."

"Which means total silence and trying not to fall into any unexpected holes," said Becks dryly. "This *isn't* my first rodeo."

"No, but it's mine, so I appreciate the repetition," said Mahir. "Is the fence likely to be electrified?"

"Yes, but that's what these are for." I held up a pair of rubber clips. "They'll bridge the current and let us cut through the wire. We'll have to leave them behind when we run, but at least we'll be *able* to run."

Mahir eyed the bridgers. "Buffy's work?"

"Dave's." I smiled a little. "He'd love this shit."

"He'd already be halfway to the fence," said Becks.

"Whereas we still need to get moving," said Mahir. "Is there anything else I should know about the area?"

"Lots of blackberries, very little ground security according to the Cat's schematics; they don't patrol all that much. Once we're inside—"

"We run, we keep our heads down, and we pray."

"I do love it when you have a concrete plan, instead of making it up as you go along," said Becks dryly. She pulled a pistol from her belt. "Let's move."

The Seattle night seemed surprisingly bright after the darkness of the parking garage, the moon and the distant glow of streetlights providing more than sufficient light. Mahir lagged at first, but found a pace that kept him between me and Becks, all three of us tromping over the broken ground as quickly and quietly as we could.

The quarter-mile between the van and the CDC was mostly open fields. We hunched over as we crossed them, running low through the tall grass. No floodlights came on to mark our trails, and no alarms went off that we could hear. Arrogance was working in our favor once again—the CDC's, not ours. They'd been heroes since the Rising, and anyone who tried breaking into one of their installations wound up on trial for treason, if they were lucky. We'd always come in via legitimate entrances, whether we were supposed to be there or not. It had been so long since their external security was tested that they weren't prepared for a small group of people who really wanted to get inside.

The fence was only a few yards farther away than I expected; our map was accurate, if not precise. That was a good sign for the rest of the job. I tossed one of the bridging cords to Becks, jerking my chin toward the fence. She nodded, and we approached together, waving for Mahir to stay back. He didn't argue.

I told you he was a smart guy when I hired him, said George.

I held up one finger toward Becks. She nodded, holding up two fingers of her own. When we were both holding up three fingers, we leaned forward and snapped the bridging cords into place. A bright blue spark arced through them, and the air was suddenly filled with the hot, burning tang of ozone. Becks squeaked, and all the hair on my arms stood on end.

Slowly, I reached forward and wrapped my fingers through the links of fence between the cords. Nothing happened. Our bridge was successful; the current was no longer routing through this patch of fencing. I gestured for the others to come closer and pulled a pair of wire cutters out of my coat pocket.

It took only a minute, maybe less, for me to cut through the fence separating the Seattle CDC from the abandoned fields behind it. Then we were onto the manicured expanse of their lawn, running for the building, waiting for the sirens to start going off.

They never did.

I never thought of myself as a coward before all this. I actually thought I was kinda brave. Choosing to live in the middle of nowhere, where I could be attacked at any moment. But I was lying to myself. I was never brave at all.

I also wasn't nearly as stupid as the people I love tend to be. So I suppose that's something to reassure me as I wave from the window while they all march off to die. God, Buffy, why did you have to hire me? I could have worked for some other site. I would never have gone through any of this. And if you had to hire me—if God insisted—why did you have to go off and leave me to deal with all of it alone?

—From *Dandelion Mine*, the blog of Magdalene Grace Garcia, August 1, 2041. Unpublished.

Hey, George. Check this out.

—From *Adaptive Immunities*, the blog of Shaun Mason, August 1, 2041. Unpublished.

Twenty-one

Either Dr. Kimberley and her team were monitoring me or their timing was uncannily good, because no one came into the room until I was done crying. I was drying my tears on the sleeve of my shirt when two of the technicians stepped through the door, arguing with each other in low, urgent voices. Neither of them looked in my direction.

"Hi," I said, just in case they didn't know I was there.

"Hello, Miss Mason," said the female technician, waving. I still couldn't see her face, but I recognized her voice. Kathleen. "Is everything all right?"

"I don't know if I'd go that far, but things have been worse." I stood, the muscles in my calves protesting the movement. I'd been sitting still for too long. Everything had started to stiffen up. "Ow, damn." I bent double, kneading the muscle of my left calf with both hands.

That's probably why the first bullet missed me.

The shooter was using a silencer. There was a muted bang, too soft to be a proper gunshot, and the technician who entered with Kathleen staggered back, slamming into the wall. A red stain was already spreading across the chest of his formerly pristine white lab coat. He looked down at it before raising his head and looking at me, mouth forming a word he couldn't quite push all the way out into the world. It was George.

It took the sound of his body hitting the floor to make me start moving. In my experience, once a person goes down, they don't *stay* down for long, and when they get back up, they tend to be more interested in eating the flesh of the living than they are in finding out who shot them. I darted forward, grabbing Kathleen's wrist and yanking her away from the body.

"Come on!" I shouted.

"What?" She looked toward me, eyes wide and terrified. "George—"

"Is dead! Now, let's get out of here before he decides to wake up and make *us* dead, too! I've been dead; you wouldn't enjoy it!" I dragged her toward the door on the opposite side of the room, somehow managing to babble and shout at the same time.

The second shot was as quiet as the first. Kathleen suddenly collapsed, the dead weight of her body pulling her hand out of mine. I turned, looking back at her, and at the hole in the middle of her forehead like a third, unseeing eye. Unlike George, she wouldn't be rising. A shot to the head kills humans and zombies the same way: stone dead.

Suddenly aware of how exposed I was—and how *alone* I was—I drew my own gun and ran out of the room as fast as my legs would carry me. Gregory was in the hall outside, running toward the room that I was running away from.

"They're both dead!" I shouted. "What's going on?"

"We're blown!" He put on a burst of speed, closing the distance between us. He grabbed my wrist, turned, and ran back the way he'd come, hauling me the way I'd been hauling Kathleen right before she was shot.

Sick terror lanced through me as I struggled to keep up. "Is it my fault?"

"Not unless you called down a full security team while you were trying to get through to the outside world." Gregory didn't slow down. "Save your breath. I don't know how long we're going to need to run."

I didn't answer. I just ran. Terror had my body flooded with enough adrenaline that I wasn't in danger of falling down from a cramp in the immediate future. That was the good part. The bad part—aside from the unidentified shooter or shooters—was that I wasn't out of shape so much as I had never been *in* shape. My mind remembered hours of exercise, both in the gym and in the field. My body had less than two months of experience. Not the sort of thing that builds endurance. My lungs were already starting to burn, signaling worse things to come.

A door slammed open ahead of us, and Dr. Kimberley appeared, signaling frantically with one hand. The other hand was out of sight. "This way!" she hissed. Her normally perfect hair was in disarray, and there were spots of blood on the sleeve of her lab coat. Whether it was hers or someone else's, I couldn't tell.

Gregory changed angles, still hauling me along. She stepped to the side, letting us run past her into the narrow hall on the other side of the door. As soon as we were through, she stepped back and pulled her hand away from the sensor to the left of the doorframe. The door promptly slammed, the light above it switching from green to red.

"Report," she said briskly, turning toward the wall. She pried open what looked like a section of paneling to reveal a control panel. Not looking at us, she started typing.

"At least two shooters, at least three technicians down."

"Kathleen and George," I panted. I slumped against the wall, bracing my hands on my knees. There was blood on my slippers; Kathleen's blood. I kicked them off, shuddering. "They're both down."

"Dammit." Dr. Kimberley kept typing. "They've been with me for years—how many people do we still have in there?"

"Seven," said Gregory. I didn't like the resignation in his voice. "At this point, they're locked in with two armed hostiles and at least one risen infected. Sorry, Danika, but I think we have to call this mission compromised."

"And it was going so *well*," she said, with a note of mock peevishness. She stopped typing and pressed her palm against the control panel's testing pad. "Do we know how they made us?"

"James didn't report for his shift. Given the timing, we have to assume he was a mole, and had been waiting for the opportunity to report back. We've been too busy for the last several days for anyone to sneak away unnoticed."

"Remind me to punch myself in the mouth for agreeing to take anyone who didn't come with me from the Maryland lab," said Dr. Kimberley. She pulled her hand away from the test pad. "They haven't changed the biometrics yet. I'd move back if I were you."

Not being a fool, I straightened and took a step backward. Gregory and Dr. Kimberley did the same. A metal shield dropped from the ceiling between us and the door, slamming down with enough force that it was easy to picture anything caught between it and the floor getting smashed flat. "Decontamination procedures initiated," announced a calm, robotic voice. "Decontamination commencing in ten . . . nine . . . "

"Run!" shouted Gregory. He grabbed my hand and we were off again, racing down the hall. Dr. Kimberley pulled up next to us, her high-heeled shoes swinging from her left hand. That was smart of her. She would never have been able to keep up with them on.

An alarm blared, drowning out the calmly counting voice of the security system. I barely heard Gregory swearing. My heart skipped a beat as I saw the red lights clicking on all along the hall in front of us.

"Dammit, Danika! You triggered a full lab decon!"

"I did no such thing! Someone's playing silly buggers with the security protocols!" She sounded frantic. I didn't blame her. I wasn't sure what a full lab decon entailed, but I knew enough about CDC procedures to know it wouldn't be anything good.

Gregory snarled something I couldn't quite make out. It sounded profane, whatever it was. He let go of my hand, apparently trusting me to run on my own, and began removing his lab coat. He didn't slow down. I stumbled a little, but kept running, aided by Dr. Kimberley's hand on my back.

"Here!" Gregory turned, now running backward as he thrust the coat into my hands. "Danika! Give her your shoes!"

"Right!" Dr. Kimberley shoved her shoes at me. I took them without thinking about what I was doing. "If you make it out of here, get in touch with Dr. Joseph Shoji. He'll help."

"What are you talking about?" I demanded. "We're all getting out of here!"

Gregory smiled sadly. "No," he said. "We're not." Then he stopped running, grabbing my arm and jerking me to a halt as he pulled the ID card from his pocket. He swiped it over the sensor pad of the nearest door, which slid immediately open.

"Override," said Dr. Kimberley approvingly. "Nice one."

"I thought so," he said, and shoved me through the open door. Another of those metal shields slammed down a split second later, shutting them both from view. It was thick enough that it also cut off the sound of the alarms, leaving me in a sudden, almost shocking silence. I stared at the blank wall of steel in front of me for several precious seconds as I tried to process what had just happened.

There was a full decontamination cycle starting on the other side of that wall. And the only two people I knew were on my side were on the other side of it.

Okay, see the problem here? It's one of scale. That's all. It's like math. Evil math. Take five bloggers, split them into three groups, and scatter them along the West Coast of the United States. Impose a radio silence. Start the apocalypse. Now, if Blogger A starts trying to contact Blogger B, using a secure DSL connection from Lab X, how long before Blogger A has a full-blown nervous breakdown?

Just wondering.

—From *The Kwong Way of Things*, the blog of Alaric Kwong, August 1, 2041. Unpublished.

RISE UP WHILE YOU CAN.

—Graffiti from inside the Florida disaster zone, picture published under Creative Commons license.

Twenty-two

"This isn't right." Becks watched the door, pistol drawn. "There should be more security."

"Maybe there's something going on." I kept most of my attention on my phone. I had a scanner running, checking for security frequencies that might give away our location. "Mahir? How's it looking?"

"The booster should be online in a few more seconds." He was on his back on the floor, using magnetic clasps to affix the Cat's equipment to the bottom of a server rack. "I still feel odd about this whole thing. I think this is the first actual *crime* I've committed for you people."

"We'll put it on your résumé," Becks said dryly.

"And we're good." Mahir pushed himself away from the server rack and stood, dusting off his still-immaculate pants. "That should work until they find it. Which will be never if that woman is half as good as she believes herself to be."

"Let's say she's half as good as Buffy was, and assume that means she gets about a year." I lowered my phone. "There's still no security activity in this part of the building. We're either clean to evac, or they're setting up an ambush."

Becks snorted. "Let me guess what you're going to say next. 'There's only one way to find out.'"

"Sounds about right," I agreed. "Let's get out of here."

The light above the door turned yellow just as we started to move. "There has been a security breach," announced a calm female voice. "Please proceed to the nearest open lab and await instructions. There are currently no confirmed contaminants. Please proceed to the nearest open lab and await instructions. Remain calm. Please proceed to the nearest open lab . . ."

The three of us turned to look at each other.

"Okay," I asked. "Who touched the bad button?"

The door slid open. We stopped looking at each other in favor of looking at it.

"Is that good, bad, or horrible?" asked Mahir.

"Don't know, don't care," said Becks. "Let's move."

Finding the correct server room had put us deep enough in the building that we couldn't just bolt for the exit. I gestured for Becks to exit ahead of me. She nodded understanding, suddenly all business, and left the room with her pistol held at waist level. I motioned for Mahir to go after her, and I brought up the rear. It wasn't as cold a move as it might have seemed from the outside. Becks was well equipped to handle herself, Mahir needed the cover, and I . . .

I was the most expendable one here.

We made our way through the halls, ducking out of sight whenever we heard footsteps, and avoiding any room with a red light above it. Becks went around each corner first, signaling us to follow once she was sure the next hall was clear. I would remain behind just long enough to be sure we weren't being tailed. It was slow. It was nerve-racking. I would actually have preferred a zombie mob. At least you can shoot those.

We all wound up standing together at a T-junction, identical halls stretching out to the left and right. "I . . . I can't remember which way we turn here." Becks sounded horrified. "I don't know which way to go."

"You go that way." I pointed left. "I'll go the other way. If you find the exit, wait there; I'll catch up. If you don't, turn around."

"Shaun—"

"Still in charge," I said amiably, before turning and jogging down the right-side hall. They didn't follow me. They were smarter than that.

The hall was deserted. I kept going, looking for the outer wall. My attention was so tightly focused that I didn't hear the woman who was running barefoot down the next hall until she came whipping around the corner and ran straight into me.

I staggered backward, barely managing to keep my balance. She did much the same, ducking her head for a moment in the process—long enough for me to register that she was wearing doctor's scrubs and a lab coat, but no shoes or socks. Her hair was short-cropped and dark brown, where it wasn't bleached in streaky patches.

Then she looked up, and my heart stopped.

"George?" I whispered.

"Shaun?" Her voice was unsteady, like she wasn't sure how she was supposed to be using it. We stared at each other, neither of us seeming to be quite sure of what we were supposed to do next.

Then she grabbed my hand and shouted, "Run!"

"Impossible" is something that stopped having any staying power when the dead started to rise. Trust me on this one. I'm a scientist.

—From the journal of Dr. Shannon Abbey, date unknown.

Every day I wake up thinking "We're all going to die today." Maybe it's weird, but I find that comforting. Every day, I wake up thinking "This is the day it ends, and we all get to rest."

That'll be nice.

**—From *Adaptive Immunities*, the blog of Shaun Mason,
August 1, 2041. Unpublished.**

GEORGIA: Twenty-three

I slipped the lab coat over my scrubs, dropping the shoes on the floor, where they landed with a clatter. I stepped into them, still moving on autopilot. There was no blood on me—it had all been on my slippers, and those were on the other side of the barrier. I was clean, and I was alone. If I was getting out of here, I was doing it under my own power. I took a deep breath, turned, and walked down the hall. It took all my self-control not to break into a run. Running would attract attention. I was one more person in scrubs and a lab coat, practically part of the landscape, and the last thing I wanted was to attract attention to myself.

Voices drifted down the hall ahead of me. Suddenly remembering my little gun, I dropped it into the lab coat pocket and kept walking. A group of unfamiliar technicians rounded the corner and walked right past me, barely seeming to register my presence. I really was invisible . . . until someone recognized me, anyway. That was going to happen sooner or later. I needed a plan, and "keep walking until you find the exit" wasn't going to cut it.

Rescue came from an unexpected source: the building's security system. "There has been a security breach," it announced. All down the hall, the lights changed color. Some turned red. Most turned yellow, followed by their associated doors sliding open.

"Please proceed to the nearest open lab and await instructions. There are currently no confirmed contaminants. Please proceed to the nearest open lab and await instructions. Remain calm. Please proceed—"

I stopped listening in favor of turning and walking toward the nearest open door, trying to look like I knew what I was doing. The first lab contained three anxious-looking orderlies. They were murmuring amongst themselves with their backs to the door. I stepped out of view as fast as I could, starting for the next open lab. It looked oddly familiar—oddly, because so many of the labs looked exactly like every other CDC lab I'd ever seen. I stuck my head into the room, scanning for signs of movement. There were none.

But there was a heavy black curtain covering the back third of the room. A faint blue glow seeped around the edges, casting shadows on the floor and ceiling. "No way," I whispered, and stepped all the way into the room. The door slid shut behind me. I barely noticed.

Why would they unlock this lab? Wouldn't they be too worried about the sanctity of their big bad mad science project to let people get near the tank? Then again, everyone who'd seen me had to know I was a clone. Maybe this was a wing where no one who didn't have the appropriate security clearances would ever set foot. I walked across the room, pausing barely a foot from that dangling curtain. Did I really want to know?

Did I really have a choice? I reached out, grabbing hold of the nearest fold of fabric, and pulled the curtain aside.

Subject 8c floated peacefully in her tank, asleep and unaware. The window to 8b's room was open. She was lying on her bed, headphones clamped over her ears. They were finishing her conditioning, implanting the subliminal memories they hadn't been able to extract from the original Georgia's damaged brain—or maybe just implanting the memories they'd crafted to *replace* the ones they chose not to salvage. Rage crawled up the back of my throat, chasing away the last of my fear. This was my replacement. This was the reason I'd been slated for termination. Their controllable Georgia Mason.

"Fuck that," I muttered, and turned to survey the lab.

I'm not the technical genius Buffy was. I'm not even on a level with Alaric or Dave. I am, however, the girl who grew up with the world's first Irwin for a mother, and a suicidal idiot for a best friend and brother. You can't do that without learning a few things the Irwins trade, including the art of improvising explosives. It's amazing how many of the things needed for a basic biology lab are capable of blowing up, if you're willing to try very, very hard, and don't much care about possibly losing a few fingers in the process.

No one came through the lab door as I mixed up my jars of unstable chemicals. That was a relief. I didn't want to shoot anyone. Not because I was concerned about their lives—I was getting ready to blow massive holes in the building; concern about a few gunshot wounds would have been silly—but because I didn't want to attract attention, and unlike our friend the sniper, I didn't have a silencer. Ripped-up rags provided the fuses I needed, and I found a box of old-fashioned sulfur matches in one of the supply cabinets. Some things will never stop being stocked, no matter how far science progresses.

When I was done, I had eight charges, none of which was going to be much good without a spark. I set two of them along the base of the tank and two more by the window of the room where 8b slept. I wanted to feel bad about what I was doing. I was taking their lives away from them, and they hadn't done anything wrong. Only it wasn't their life. It was mine, because I was the closest thing to Georgia Mason that they were ever going to get. Call me selfish, but if I was going to die, I was going to die knowing my replacement wasn't waiting in the wings.

I set the other four charges around the edges of the lab, where they would hopefully knock down a few walls and cause a little more chaos when they went off. Hell, it was worth trying, and it wasn't like I had that much left to lose.

"Here goes everything," I said, and lit the first match.

There's no guidebook to making fuses from the things you can scavenge out of a CDC lab. I had no idea how long they'd burn, or whether they'd burn at all; maybe my big boom would be nothing but a fizzle. I wasn't going to stick around to find out. After the third fuse was lit, I turned and sprinted for the door.

The locked door.

"Oh, *fuck*," I said. "This can't be happening. This *can't* be *happening*." I hit the door with the heel of my hand. "Let me out, you fucking machine!"

"Please clarify the nature of your request," said the security system.

"Uh . . . " I froze for several precious seconds before blurting, "The tank has been compromised. I need to get some sealant, now, or the experiment will be terminated."

"Please state the nature of the compromise."

"There's a break in one of the feeding tubes."

I was taking shots in the dark. There was a pause before the system said, "Please hurry. Movement is currently restricted due to security conditions." The door slid open.

I ran.

The halls were practically deserted. I paused long enough to kick off Dr. Kimberley's heels and kept running, heading for what I hoped would be one of the building's outer walls. I hit a corner and turned, hit another corner and turned again. The first of my explosives would be going off at any second. I had to run, or else—

I was so focused on running that I didn't look where I was going. I whipped around a corner and slammed straight into the man who was running in the opposite direction. We both staggered backward, my head going down as I tried to recover my equilibrium.

He spoke first. "George?"

"Shaun?" I stared at him. He stared back. I wasn't sure what I wanted to do first—scream, cry, or hug him until the world stopped spinning. I had to settle for the fourth option. Darting forward, I grabbed his hand and shouted, "Run!"

Thank God for habit. Shaun didn't hesitate. He followed my lead, letting me tow him down the hallway and around the nearest corner, where two more familiar faces were waiting.

Shaun pulled me to a stop, saying, "We need to get out of here."

Becks and Mahir stared at me in abject disbelief. They were clearly taking my appearance the way I'd expected Shaun to take it: with surprise, and no small amount of anger. A few seconds passed while none of us said anything. Then Becks reached for her gun.

"There isn't time to shoot me!" I said. I didn't let go of Shaun's hand. I didn't know what he was doing here or how he got in, but if I was going to die, I was going to do it holding on to him as tightly as I could. "This place is about to blow. Do you know the way out?"

"Why should we trust you?" she demanded.

Shaun's eyes widened. "Wait a second. You can *see* her?"

"Yes, Shaun, we can see her," said Mahir. He sounded more dazed than Becks, and less angry.

"I have no idea what that means, but if you don't trust me, we're all going to be dead before you can find out how I got here." I focused on Mahir. "Do you know the way *out*?"

Mahir looked at me for only a moment before making his decision. "This way," he said, and gestured for us to follow as he turned and stepped through an unmarked doorway. Shaun pulled me along with him, perfectly willing to accept my presence. Becks brought up the rear, and I knew without looking that she had a gun pointed at the back of my head. Shaun had trained her well.

The door led to a small storage room. A panel in the back wall was missing. I could see grass and the nighttime sky through the opening. Shaun pulled me along. I went without fighting.

We were almost outside when the explosions began.

This is not fucking possible. Do you hear me, world? THIS IS NOT POSSIBLE. I don't care if she fools Shaun and Mahir and everyone else, she's not who she's claiming to be. This sort of thing doesn't happen in the real world, and if we were living in a science fiction novel, good would triumph over evil a whole lot more often than it does.

I am going to find out who she is. I am going to find out what she's doing here. And then I am going to take great satisfaction in blowing her smug little imposter head right off her fucking shoulders.

—From *Charming Not Sincere*, the blog of Rebecca Atherton, August 2, 2041. Unpublished.

Genetic testing of the remains found in Lab 175-c confirms that they belonged to Georgia Mason. Perhaps if we had fewer Georgia Masons running around the premises, we could be sure our rogue killed herself in her efforts to escape. As we do not have any mechanism for confirming the identity of the deceased, and as the explosions caused too much damage to determine the number of Georgias to die in the ensuing fire, we must assume for the time being that Subject 7c is now loose.

Congratulations, ladies and gentlemen. We have successfully resurrected a woman with every reason to want us all dead. I hope you can feel good about this accomplishment. I certainly cannot. Please consider this my resignation. Further, please send someone to clean my lab, as I am about to get blood all over the walls.

Everything went so very wrong so very fast. I will not take the fall for this.

I hope you're happy.

—Taken from an e-mail sent by Dr. Matthew Thomas, August 2, 2041.

SHAUN: Twenty-four

She ran back the way I'd come. I ran with her, trying to wrap my mind around how *solid* her fingers felt. They were warm and strong and *right*, and I didn't care if it meant I'd finally snapped. I had her back. Crazy or not, I had her back, and there was no way I was ever letting her go.

We caught up with Becks and Mahir less than a minute later. They turned and stared when they heard my footsteps. "We need to get out of here," I said, skidding to a stop. They kept staring, but not at me.

They were looking at George. Scowling, Becks reached for her gun.

"There isn't time to shoot me!" said George, not letting go of my hand. Thank God for that. "This place is about to blow. Do you know the way out?"

I opened my mouth to relay what she'd said, but Becks cut me off. Still staring straight at George, she demanded, "Why should we trust you?"

It felt like the bottom dropped out of the world. "Wait a second. You can *see* her?"

"Yes, Shaun," said Mahir, sounding like he wasn't sure quite what was going on, but was certain he didn't like it. "We can see her."

"I have no idea what that means, but if you don't trust me, we're all going to be dead before you can find out how I got here." George looked at Mahir as she spoke. "Do you know the way *out*?"

For a moment, I thought Mahir was going to refuse to answer. Then he nodded, gesturing for us to follow. "This way."

I pulled George with me as I followed Mahir through the nearest doorway, still not willing to let go of her hand. Becks was right behind us. I didn't look to see whether she had her gun out. I didn't want to know how I'd react if she did.

The panel we'd removed on our way in was still off to one side, leaving our exit clear. It looked like security hadn't been through yet, probably because of whatever breach had the lights going wacky. That was a small blessing. George didn't say anything as we climbed through the hole, but she looked like she was torn between laughter and screaming when she took her first breath of outside air.

Becks was just stepping through the opening when the explosions began.

And thus, in a single moment, did my life go from unbearably strange, but still tolerable, to actively impossible. I am willing to allow that, once one lives in a world where science can transform mosquitoes into the harbingers of the apocalypse, the rules of our forefathers have, perhaps, ceased to apply.

That doesn't mean that the dead should walk. Not unless they're zombies, anyway. It's simply impolite, and I don't think we should stand for it.

—From *Fish and Clips*, the blog of Mahir Gowda, August 2, 2041. Unpublished.

Joey—

Not sure when I'll be able to reach you again. We've done it. She's loose. It wasn't quite like we'd planned—someone leaked what we were doing, and we lost half the techs—but it worked, and she's on the run. I'm going to be off the grid for a little while. Keep the lines open. God willing, Georgia Mason will be reaching out to you soon, and when she does, I want you to be ready to help her in any way that you can.

This may end soon. Pray to God it ends as well as it can.

—Taken from an e-mail sent by Dr. Danika Kimberley to Dr. Joseph Shoji, August 2, 2041.

GEORGIA: Twenty-five

Shaun didn't let go of my hand once after he had it—not while we were climbing through the hole in the wall, and not when the explosions started. It was like I was the lifeline he'd been looking for. I wasn't going to object. I *knew* he was the lifeline I'd been looking for, and no matter how improbable his presence was, I wasn't going to let go of him until I absolutely had to.

Concussive booming sounds came from the building behind us as we ran. They followed a definite wave pattern, with a small crumping explosion followed by a cascade of louder, more enthusiastic booms. My little charges had managed to break through into something a lot more combustible—probably the formalin tanks. It's nice how many common chemicals are just looking for an excuse to explode.

We ran across a vast, manicured lawn, with evergreen trees standing between us and the fence. If there was a scheduled security sweep of the grounds, it had been canceled in favor of dealing with the explosions; no one stopped us or sounded any additional alarms as we fled.

"If this is anything like Portland, emergency services should start responding to the alarms any minute now!" shouted Shaun, glancing back over his shoulder at the others. "Extra confusion is good, but extra eyes won't be! Keep running!"

"Shaun—" began Becks.

"Talk later! Flee now!"

I didn't say anything. I was struggling just to keep up. No matter how much this body looked and felt like the one that I remembered, it wasn't, and it simply wasn't equipped for this sort of situation. Maybe it would be one day—assuming I survived that long—but right now, it was all I could do not to fall over and wait for someone to come along and shoot me.

Our path took us to a hole in the fence that looked like it was created by using a pair of magnetic current-bridging strips to reroute the electricity before cutting the wire. Mahir went through first, followed by Shaun, who kept my hand even while I was struggling not to snag my lab coat on the fence. Slowing down made me realize how much my lungs hurt, and how much my *feet* hurt. I didn't want to risk looking at them, but I was pretty sure they were bleeding.

This wasn't the time for first aid. We needed to get as far from the CDC as possible. I straightened, catching my breath as best as I could, and let Shaun pull me back into a run.

We got lucky; any zombies in the area had been attracted by the sound of sirens, and left us alone as we ran. We made it out of the grass and onto the broken sidewalk before my toes caught on the curb and I fell, gravity and momentum conspiring against me for one horrible moment. My hand was yanked free of Shaun's, but not fast enough for me to catch myself. The landing knocked the air out of me—what little air had been *left* in me—and I wound up prostrate and wheezing, trying to find the strength to get back up again.

"Are you okay?" asked Shaun. He sounded concerned, but calm. Too calm; scary calm, like he wasn't surprised to see me in the least.

I was still trying to get enough air to answer when the grass rustled, Becks and Mahir jogging up behind us. There was a click—the sound of a pistol safety being released.

"Move and you die," snarled Becks, tone leaving no room for

argument. I froze, stopping everything but my efforts to breathe. "Now who the fuck are you, and what are you doing here?"

"She fell," said Shaun, sounding wounded. "Dude, what's your damage?"

"It's all right, Shaun," said Mahir, who sounded as calm as Becks was angry. "Let her deal with this. You just stay right there."

"What's my damage? What's my *damage*?" Becks laughed, a short, brittle sound that made the hair on the back of my neck stand on end. "I want to know what the hell game she thinks she's playing. That's all."

"I'm not playing a game, Becks," I said, voice muffled by the fact that I was talking into the pavement. "Can I get up before I try to explain myself?"

"Hold on," said Shaun. Now he just sounded perplexed. Not being able to see people's faces was starting to get to me. "I realize things were a little crazy in there before, so I was sort of willing to blow it off and all, but are you telling me you guys can actually *see* her?"

"What?" I said, lifting my head slightly. Becks didn't shoot me. That was something.

"We can both see her, Shaun," said Mahir wearily. He was panting from the run, although not as much as I was. "I don't know who this woman is, but she's no ghost, and no hallucination. We can see her perfectly well."

"And if she doesn't start talking soon, we can see her bleed," said Becks. She nudged my leg with her toe, snapping, "Well? Identify yourself."

"*Please* can I get up first?" I asked. "It'll be easier for us to understand each other if I'm not talking into the street."

There was a pause as some consultation I couldn't see took place behind me. Finally, Becks said, "Fine. Get up. But if you so much as twitch funny, you're going back down, for keeps. Understand?"

"I understand." I pushed myself to my hands and knees, wincing as gravel and chunks of pavement bit into my hands. It was worse when I actually stood, pressing my bloody feet down on the ground.

Shaun took a half step forward, reaching out to help me with my balance. Becks switched her aim to him.

"Don't," she said, very softly. "Don't make me."

He stepped back, putting his hands up. "Okay, Becks, don't worry. I'll stay right here."

"Thank you."

"Thank you all," I said. My hair was sticking to my forehead in sweaty, matted clumps, and the wind was cold on my cheeks. I hurt, I was possibly going to get shot in the next few seconds, and I'd never been so happy to be alive. I glanced at Shaun, reassuring myself that he was really there and really real, before looking back to Becks and Mahir. "I understand you're probably confused and upset right now. I was, too, when all this started. But I swear, it's me."

"There is no 'me,'" snarled Becks. Her eyes narrowed. "What the fuck kind of stunt is this? Plastic surgery? Natural lookalike so we wouldn't be able to find the scars?"

"Cloning and experimental memory-transfer techniques," I said. That was enough to stun Becks into a momentary silence.

Not Mahir. He drew his own gun, aiming it at my chest. "What's your name?"

"Georgia Carolyn Mason."

"What's your license number?"

"Alpha-foxtrot-bravo, zero seven five eight nine three." I rattled off the number without hesitation, glad it wasn't one of the things stored in the fuzzy area of my memory. "I was issued my provisional B-class license on my sixteenth birthday. That license number was bravo-zulu-echo, one nine three two seven one. It was retired when I tested for my A-class license. I did that when I turned nineteen."

"What's my name?"

"Mahir Suresh Gowda. Your license was issued by the Indian consulate in London, so it's about ninety digits long and comes with diplomatic immunity and what are you *doing* here? Aren't you supposed to be on a different continent, objectively observing our problems?"

He snorted. "Well, my boss went and got herself killed, so it seemed I was needed on a more local level."

Becks recovered from her brief silence, asking, "If you're George, what's wrong with your eyes?"

I touched the skin below my left eye, grimacing. "Freaky, isn't it? Again, cloning. The scientists who grew me couldn't induce a specific reservoir condition. When they tried, they caused spontaneous amplification in the clones unlucky enough to be their test subjects. I guess it got pretty expensive, so they stopped trying before they got to me."

"Makes you a pretty lousy copy," said Becks coldly.

"I know." I dropped my hand back to my side. "I'm the show model, to prove that they can make a realistic copy of a person. I wasn't supposed to get out. The clone they were planning to send to you was surgically altered to look like she had retinal KA."

"The clone they *were* planning?" asked Mahir.

I smiled. I couldn't help myself. "She was in the lab where I planted the initial explosives. You wouldn't have wanted her anyway. She was programmed to betray you."

"And you weren't?" demanded Becks.

"If I have been, I don't know about it," I said.

"This is impossible," said Mahir.

"This is insane," said Becks.

"This wasn't my idea," I countered.

Shaun cleared his throat. "This is starting to make my head hurt, and that's probably not a good sign. Does somebody want to explain to me exactly how the CDC managed to bring George back from the dead?"

"They didn't," said Becks. "This woman is *not* Georgia."

"Yes, I am," I protested. "I know it's unbelievable, but it's true."

Mahir frowned. I knew that look. It was the look he got when something presented him with a really interesting problem to solve. "We'll not come to any conclusive decisions standing out here," he said. "Miss, if you'll allow us to search you for weapons—"

"And scan her for tracking devices," interjected Becks.

"Yes, of course. Search you for weapons and scan you for tracking devices, and if you come up clean, we can take you back to the hotel where we're currently quartered and try to sort this out."

I let out a breath I'd only been half aware of holding. "I have a gun in the pocket on the right-hand side of my lab coat. It's loaded, but the safety's on."

Becks stepped forward, sticking her hand into my pocket with more force than was strictly necessary. She pulled out my gun and stepped back, stowing it in her belt. I felt instantly less clothed. "Got anything else?"

"Not that I'm aware of. If there are tracking devices on me, I don't know they're there. They're probably subcutaneous." I shook my head. "The EIS would have removed any of those that they found, but that doesn't mean they found them all."

Becks sneered. "We'll just see. You picked the wrong team to try infiltrating, lady, and as soon as we find out who you really are, I'm going to kick the ever-loving crap out of you."

I smiled slightly, relief fading into a mellower look of generalized exhaustion. "See, that sort of thing, right there, is why I missed you guys so much." I glanced at Shaun. "Becks is with you, instead of working with the betas now? Good call."

"Becks is in charge of the Irwins," he said. Then he frowned. "Shouldn't you already know that, if they've sent you here to infiltrate us?" His tone was turning belligerent. He was starting to get angry. That was bad.

"They didn't send me, Shaun. I *escaped*," I said. "The one they wanted you to find would have a better cover story."

"This is all academic," said Mahir. "Whether or not she's really Georgia—"

"She's not," said Becks.

"—she's here, and we're going to have to contend with her, one way or another."

"At least we won't have any issues with the law if we need to shoot her." Shaun looked at me coldly. "She's already dead."

Seeing that look on his face hurt more than almost anything else in the world. "I'm not dead anymore, Shaun. I swear to you, it's me. Please believe me."

He suddenly lunged forward, grabbing my shoulders and turning me to fully face him. Becks started to moved toward us. Mahir grabbed her upper arm, stopping her. I barely noticed. I was too busy staring into the eyes of the man in front of me, the eyes I'd been waiting to see since the moment I woke up. They were looking at me with such *anger*. I'd seen that look on his face before, but never directed at me.

"Who are you?" he demanded, voice pitched low. The pain in it hurt almost as much as the anger in his eyes. My poor, poor Shaun...

"I'm Georgia," I whispered. "I'm not anyone else, and that means that I'm her."

He looked older, like he'd lived through more than just a year without me. His eyes searched my face, finally settling on my hairline. "Why haven't you dyed your hair?" he asked.

"The doctors responsible for my care didn't give me the opportunity. I would have, if they'd let me." I would have given myself retinal Kellis-Amberlee, just so I'd feel less like a stranger in my own skin. I would have done a lot of things.

"Can you prove to me that you are who you say you are?" He didn't let go of my shoulders. "Is there anything, *anything* you can do that will make me believe in you?"

He wanted to believe; I could see it in his eyes, a deep ache buried under the pain. That was why he couldn't let himself do it. There's no such thing as miracles, and when the dead rise, they don't look in your eyes and say their names. Maybe in some other world, but not this one.

I took a slow breath, casting another glance toward Becks and Mahir. Then I looked back to him and said, "There's only one thing we never wrote down. You know what it was."

"Do you?"

"I do, but, Shaun, I don't know if—"

"Prove it, right now, or I swear to you, I will shoot you myself."

"You have no idea how much I've missed you," I said, and leaned in and kissed him. His hands tightened on my shoulders, his whole body stiffening against mine as he realized what I was doing.

And then he started kissing me back.

That was the one thing we never wrote down—the one thing we *couldn't* write down, because no file or server is ever totally secure, and it would have gotten out. No one would have cared that we weren't biologically related, or that we'd gone in for genetic testing when we turned sixteen, just to be absolutely sure. No one would have cared that we didn't trust anyone else enough to let them be there while we slept. No. The media loves a scandal, and we'd been raised as siblings in the public eye. It would have destroyed our ratings, and then the Masons would have destroyed *us*, for blackening the family name.

There were a few people who'd guessed over the years. I'm pretty sure that Buffy knew. But we never, *never* wrote it down.

He squeezed my shoulders so hard it hurt. I didn't pull away, and after a few seconds, his hands relaxed and he pulled me to him, returning the kiss with a frightening hunger. I grabbed his elbows and pulled him closer still, until it felt like we were pressed so closely together that there was no room for anything to come between us. Not even death. We were home.

I didn't pull away until my lungs started burning. His hands dropped from my shoulders and he opened his eyes, staring at me. I stared back. Slowly, he reached out with one shaking hand and brushed my bangs away from my forehead.

"Georgia?" he whispered.

I nodded.

"How—?"

Mahir cleared his throat. "Unbelievable as I find all this—and believe me, I *do* find it unbelievable—this is, perhaps, not the best place to go into it. CDC security will find the hole we created sooner or later, and we've been standing here long enough that I feel it will be sooner. If everyone agrees, we should remove this reunion to a safer location."

"I still say we shoot her," said Becks.

I glanced at her, frowning. "Has she always been this bloodthirsty?"

Shaun kept staring at me. It was like there was nothing else in the world. Somehow, I understood the feeling. "I may have taught her a few things."

"If we're going to move, we should move," said Mahir. There was a core of cold efficiency in his voice that hadn't been there a moment before. "Shaun, you're unfit to lead the remainder of this mission. Becks, I outrank you. Georgia . . . " He faltered, realizing what he'd just said. "Miss, whoever you are, you are not currently a part of our structure. As that makes me the senior staff member here, I hereby command the rest of you to *move*."

I smiled at him. I couldn't help it. "Thanks, Mahir. I missed you, too."

Shaun grabbed my hand, starting to walk. I went with him, only wincing a little as my battered feet hit the ground. Mahir and Becks followed us, Becks never putting her pistol away. I didn't care. She wasn't going to shoot me now; not without getting the story of who I was and what I was doing with them. She was a Newsie for too long to throw away a lead like that once the heat of the moment had passed.

We didn't talk as we made our way across a decrepit parking lot to an even more neglected-looking garage. There was nothing we could say that wouldn't confuse matters further. Shaun and Becks produced flashlights from their pockets, clicking them on and using them to light the way into the darkness of the parking garage. I stopped when I saw what their beams had illuminated, a grin spreading, unbidden, across my face.

"You still have the van," I breathed. "I was afraid that after . . . well, after what happened, that the decontamination would have been too expensive." And that he wouldn't have wanted to keep it after he killed me in it.

"I had to replace all the upholstery, but I wasn't willing to lose the frame," said Shaun. "We spent too much time there for me to give it up that easily."

Tears welled up in my eyes. Becks took one look at my face before she snorted, snapped, "Let's get the fuck out of here," and went storming over to the van.

"She's not always like this," said Shaun.

"I've got a feeling she will be for the next few days," I said, and let him lead me to the van.

All four of us had to submit to a blood test before the locks would disengage. I held my breath until mine came back clean and the doors unlocked. Becks opened the back and pulled out what looked like a modified metal detector wand. "Spread," she ordered me.

I knew better than to argue with an Irwin who had that look on her face. I pulled away from Shaun, who let go of my hand with obvious reluctance, and assumed the position used by air travelers since the birth of the TSA. She ran the wand along my arms, legs, torso, and back, scowling a little more each time it failed to beep. Then she passed it to Mahir, who repeated the process. I had to admire their thoroughness, even though I knew that a false positive—or worse, an accurate one—would probably result in my getting shot in the head.

Finally, Mahir lowered the wand. "She's clean," he said. Becks scowled.

Shaun, on the other hand, grinned like he'd just been told that he was now uncontested king of the entire universe. He tossed Becks the keys. She caught them automatically. "You're driving," he informed her. "I'm riding in back with George."

She muttered something before getting into the driver's seat. I didn't need to hear it to know that it wasn't complimentary. I also didn't have the energy to worry about it just then. Shaun helped me into the back of the van, where he sat down on the floor, opening his arms to me. I climbed into them willingly, nestling myself as closely against him as anatomy and the space around us would allow, and closed my eyes.

I fell asleep listening to the sound of his heart beating. I have never slept that well in my life, and I may never sleep that well again.

Book IV

Reservoirs

Okay, that's it. No more Mister Nice, Heavily Armed, Really Pissed-Off Journalist.

—Shaun Mason

The dangerous thing about truth is the way it changes depending on how you're looking at it. One man's gospel truth is another man's blasphemous lie. The dangerous thing about people is the way we'll try to kill anyone whose truth doesn't agree with ours. And the dangerous thing about me is that I've already died once, so what the fuck do I care?

—Georgia Mason

Miss me?

—From *Images May Disturb You*, the blog of Georgia Mason, August 2, 2041. Shared internally only.

Yes.

—From *Adaptive Immunities*, the blog of Shaun Mason, August 2, 2041. Shared internally only.

SHAUN: Twenty-six

The Agora guards were all smiles as they came out to meet us. "Welcome back to the Agora," said the one next to Becks's window, holding out a blood testing unit. "If you would be so kind—"

"We're going to need a fourth kit," I said, craning my neck to see the window from between the seats. George was still asleep, curled up against me with her fingers locked in the fabric of my shirt.

"Or we could just let them shoot her," said Becks sweetly.

Mahir put his hands up before I could say anything. "There will be no shooting of anyone who tests cleanly. Can we please get a fourth testing unit?"

"Of course, sir," said the guard, looking unflustered. Apparently, people drove up with battered, dirty women in CDC scrubs all the time.

"George." I shook her shoulder. She didn't respond. I shook her again, harder this time. "Georgia. Wake up."

"Problems, Mason?" asked Becks.

"Nothing I can't handle," I said. Leaning down until my mouth was only a few inches from George's ear, I said, "If you don't wake up *right now*, I'm going to get a bottle of water from the travel fridge. I will then pour it down your back. You won't enjoy it, and I won't care. Just in case you were wondering."

Her eyes opened. I had the time to think, almost academically, that my crazy was useful after all—all those hallucinations got me used to the idea of a Georgia without retinal KA, and now I actually had one. Then she smiled, and all thoughts went out the window except for holding on to her and never, ever letting go.

"You have no idea how much I've missed you threatening me awake." She untangled her fingers from my shirt and sat up, looking around the van. She stiffened when she saw the armed guards looking through the windows, patiently waiting for us to get our shit together. "Shaun? Where are we?"

"At our hotel. It's a long story. Can you sit up and let them run a blood test?" Seeing the look of alarm in her eyes, I added quickly, "This place has security that would have given Buffy, like, spontaneous orgasms for *days*. They're not going to share their results. They just want to know that we're all clean before they let us through the gates."

"If you say so," she said warily.

"Promise." I kissed her forehead before opening the van's side door. Another guard was waiting there, this one holding a testing unit in each hand. I gave him a smile. He didn't give it back. "My man! Is it time to prove that we're not planning to eat the other guests?"

"We have a strict policy of non-cannibalism here at the Agora," he replied, holding the tests toward us. His eyes flicked toward George's bloody feet, noticing and acknowledging them, but he didn't say a word. If we wanted to engage in dangerous behaviors, we could, as long as it didn't result in our bringing infection past their gates. It was an attitude I could definitely respect.

"We're good with that," I said, and leaned over to take one of the tests. George did the same with the other. "On three?"

A flicker of a smile crossed George's face. "On three," she agreed. "One."

"Two."

Neither of us said "three." Instead, we each reached out and placed our right index fingers on the test unit in the other's hand. The guard didn't say anything; again, if we wanted to be crazy, it wasn't his problem, as long as we were clean.

We didn't look at the lights. We just looked at each other. There were tears at the corners of George's eyes, and I wouldn't have been surprised to learn that she wasn't the only one. If she failed this, I wasn't going to shoot her again. I wasn't—

"Thank you, Mr. Mason, ma'am." The guard leaned forward, pulling the test units from our hands before either of us could react. I turned, and saw the green lights gleaming at the top of each small white box. He smiled genially. "We're pleased to have you back. Miss Garcia has been alerted to your arrival, and to the presence of your guest. One of our attendants will meet you at the door with slippers for the young lady. Please have a pleasant stay at the Agora."

"See? Cake." I turned to look toward the front. The windows were back up; Becks and Mahir had apparently passed their own tests while I was distracted.

"It's not going to last," said Becks. Her eyes met mine in the rearview mirror as she started the engine. "We just showed up with a woman who looks like she's been kidnapped from a lab, and is basically a walking hot zone right now, with those feet. This isn't cool."

"Maybe not, but what else was I supposed to do?"

"This discussion is not going to end well," said Mahir sharply. "We're going to go inside, meet with Maggie, and decide what happens next. No one gets the deciding vote. Am I understood?"

"It is *so* good to see you," said George. She got up onto her knees, half kneeling as she looked through the windshield at the hotel. Her eyes widened. "Where are we? Hill House?"

"Whatever walks here walks in the presence of a large, well-trained staff ready to attend to your every need," said Mahir. "As the gentleman said, welcome to the Agora. It's a resort of a kind, for people whose monthly allowance puts my annual income to shame."

"You let Maggie choose the hotel, didn't you?"

"Don't answer that," said Becks. "Until we know what's going on, we're not telling you anything more than we have to. I'm pretty sure this place is expensive enough that they'll dispose of a body for us if we ask them."

"The privileges of wealth." George sank back to the floor. She gave me an anxious look, and I took her hand, squeezing it. The solidity of her was still the most amazing thing I'd ever felt.

"It's going to be okay," I said.

"Maybe," she replied.

None of us said anything after that. Becks drove up the long driveway to the parking garage, where the valet waved us through the open gate, apparently remembering our preference for self-parking. Becks got out first. By the time I opened the van door, she was already there, pistol out, covering us.

"I think it says something deeply disturbing about me that I find this comforting," said George, wincing as her cut-up feet hit the cool cement of the garage floor.

"That's Becks. Always ready to offer a helping headshot." I restrained the urge to pick George up and get her feet away from the ground. I needed to let her walk on her own. She'd never forgive me if I didn't.

"I thought I learned from the best," said Becks. She stayed where she was, letting us step away from the vehicle. It was clear she intended to follow us to the door, rather than risking George getting the drop on her. Oddly, it wasn't only George who found her paranoia comforting. Knowing there was someone behind me, ready to shoot if something started to go wrong, made me a lot more comfortable letting George take my hand, even though it would keep me from getting to a gun as fast as I might need to.

Mahir walked on my other side. He didn't say anything. He didn't need to. The worried, faintly disapproving look on his face said volumes.

True to the concierge's word, a man in the hotel uniform was waiting by the airlock with a pair of fluffy blue and gold slippers in one hand and a matching robe in the other. He held them out to us as we approached, saying, "The management is thrilled that you're here, but would prefer that you not distress the other guests."

"What?" I asked blankly.

Mahir cleared his throat and nodded toward George. I turned, looking at her.

There were stains on the sleeves of her once-white lab coat. Some were clearly chemical; others could have been blood. Some of the stains on the cuffs of her pants were definitely blood, as were the streaky smears on the tops of her feet. The fact that she was dressed like a medical professional would just make those little spots more terrifying for most people. We trust doctors because we have to. We never forget that they're the profession with the highest day-to-day risk of infection.

George looked down at herself, clearly coming to the same conclusion. "Thank you," she said, reaching out to take the robe and slippers. Putting them on made her look less disheveled, and oddly younger; the robe was at least three sizes too large, and hung on her like a shroud. She tied the robe around her waist, sleeves all but swallowing her hands, and flashed a quick, professional smile at the attendant. "It's great."

"Welcome to the Agora, miss. We hope you'll enjoy your stay." He bowed before turning and stepping into the airlock. I was pretty sure any charges associated with the robe and slippers would be appearing on our master bill, and would be hefty enough to make me choke. Good thing none of us were ever going to see the price tag for this place.

Once the attendant was clear of the airlock, George and I stepped inside. A little more of the tension went out of her shoulders as soon as we were past the first layer of glass, like even that thin barrier took us farther from her captivity. I couldn't reach her hands, swaddled as they were in layers of plush terry cloth, so I squeezed her shoulder instead.

The smile she flashed my way was a lot less professional. "You can keep doing that forever," she said quietly.

"Planning on it," I said. Then the door was sliding open in front of us, and we left the airlock together, letting it begin a new cycle as Becks and Mahir were processed through.

George looked around the Agora lobby with a cool, calculating curiosity, like she was assessing the whole place for acoustics, security, and exit routes—the three most important functions of any space as far as a journalist was concerned. Every move she made just convinced me a little more that she was who she said she was. I knew I wanted to believe her, which put me at a disadvantage, but . . . if she'd been off in anything but the superficialities of her appearance, I would have been the first to notice. So far, she was doing everything right. That meant she was either the real thing, or an unbelievably good fake.

Please be the real thing, I prayed, to no one in particular.

Only one of us can be real, replied the quiet voice of my inner Georgia.

I stiffened. She'd been quiet for so long that I'd almost started thinking of it as a transition. George dies, she moves into my head. George comes back to life, she moves out again. It was simple. Straightforward.

Impossible. You don't recover from going crazy just because the thing that made you that way is magically undone. If the human mind worked like that, we'd be a much saner species.

"Shaun?" George looked up at me, frowning. "You okay?"

For a horrible moment, I didn't know which of them I was supposed to respond to. Then Maggie stepped out of the elevator lobby, eyes wide. She was back in her normal clothes, a heavy cable-knit sweater over a long patchwork skirt, and her hair was braided into a semblance of control. She started toward us, her gaze never moving away from George's face.

"Shaun?" she said, when she was close enough to be heard without raising her voice. "What is this?"

"That's a complicated question," I said honestly. The airlock door slid open behind me, and footsteps marked Mahir and Becks falling into a flanking position, Mahir to my left, Becks to George's right.

"Hi, Maggie," said George.

Maggie stiffened. "She sounds like—"

"That's because she is," I said.

"Maybe," said Mahir.

"Probably not," said Becks.

"We should go upstairs," said Maggie, eyes still locked on George's face. "This sounds like the sort of thing that shouldn't be talked about in the lobby."

"That's probably a good idea," I agreed.

Maggie led us back to the elevator lobby, not looking to see whether we would follow. She knew we would. George freed her hand from the layers of terry cloth and reclaimed mine, sticking close to my side as we walked. I clung back just as fiercely. Becks and Mahir brought up the rear, and none of us said a damn thing, because there was nothing we *could* say. This was too big, and too impossible, and too important to crack open before we were secure.

"My room," said Maggie, once we'd reached the floor where the four of us—five of us, now—were staying. "It has the most space."

"Wait—more space than *my* room?" I asked. "How is that possible? You could call the room I'm staying in an apartment and not get busted for false advertising. I think there's someone living in the closet."

Maggie cracked a very small smile. "My father owns a share in the Agora. When I stay here, I get a specific room."

"Wealth hath its privileges," said Becks, with none of the faint disdain that so often colored her voice when she talked about money.

Then again, she was normally talking about money in the context of her own family, and she didn't like them. Maggie's money must have been somehow less offensive by dint of not belonging to the Athertons.

"Yes," agreed Maggie, without irony. She led us all the way to the end of the hall, where a single door was set in a stretch of wall that could easily have played home to three doors leading into rooms the size of mine. Even that didn't prepare us for the size of the room on the other side.

Becks put it best: "Holy shit. That's not a bedroom, it's a ballroom."

"Also a living room, dining room, kitchen, and a bathroom with a private hot tub," agreed Maggie, holding the door open for the rest of us. "The hot tub seats eight, in case you wondered. According to my mother, I was conceived in a suite very much like this one, but thankfully, on a different floor. I'm pretty sure she told me that so I'd never have sex here, ever."

"Did it work?" I asked, curious despite myself.

She closed the door behind Mahir. "No. I brought Buffy here to celebrate when she first got the job working with the two of you. She wasn't the first, and she won't be the last."

"And we are now officially getting too much information," said Becks. "Thank you."

"No problem. Can I get anyone anything before we start going over exactly how we've managed to shatter the laws of nature today?"

George cleared her throat, looking a little embarrassed as she said, "I don't suppose you have any Coke on hand, do you?"

That was the best thing she could have said. Maggie blinked, looking briefly surprised. Then she smiled. "I do. Shaun? Same for you?"

"Coffee for me, actually," I said.

"Coffee? Really?" Maggie's surprise only lasted a few seconds. "Coffee and Coke, got it. Becks? Mahir?"

"Nothing for me," said Becks.

"Tea, please," said Mahir. "I have the feeling this is about to become one of those days wherein there is no such thing as too much tea."

"You're not alone there," said Maggie. "Go ahead and sit down. I'll be right back." She vanished through a door near the entrance, presumably heading into the kitchen to get the drinks.

George walked over and sat down on one of the room's two couches, burying her hands in the pockets of her robe. She slumped there, looking tired and frail. George was always smaller than me, but she'd never been skinny like this before. It was a little disturbing.

You're willing to accept that I might come back from the dead, but you're upset because I haven't been eating enough? What should I be eating, the flesh of the living?

"Be quiet," I said automatically.

George looked up. "Nobody said anything."

Shit. "Uh . . ."

"It's been difficult for all of us since Georgia passed," said Mahir, in a voice stiff enough to sound starched. He took the seat next to George, presumably so I couldn't. I could respect that, even as it annoyed me. She was, after all, claiming to be my dead sister, resurrected, and I had just demonstrated, openly, that I was crazy.

"Come on, asshole. Let's sit." Becks took my elbow and led me to the other couch, where she pushed me into a sitting position. She sat next to me, resting her pistol on her knee.

"You don't normally call me asshole without provocation," I noted.

"You don't normally act like one," she responded.

George looked between the two of us before turning to focus on Mahir. "I'm sorry about that," she said. "I mean, no one means to die, but . . . I'm so sorry." She hesitated before asking, "How much of this was our fault, Mahir? How many people died because we wouldn't stop telling the truth?"

Mahir's eyes widened. I think that was the moment when he started to let himself think that maybe believing her was an option. "I don't know," he said. "Quite a few, I'm afraid."

"Yeah." She sighed, glancing at Becks and me before returning her attention to Mahir. "Rick was at the CDC a few days ago."

"What?" Becks half stood. "You little bi—"

"Rebecca, sit *down*," snapped Mahir. It wasn't a request.

Becks sat.

George blinked, looking bemused. "Okay, does someone want to explain that?"

"We haven't been able to get through to Rick for a while," I said. "We're pretty worried, especially given everything that's been going on. If he was at the CDC, you're saying he knows what's going on and he just doesn't care. That's sort of a big deal."

"No." George shook her head, expression hardening into that old, familiar look of burning journalistic fervor. She wasn't a scared, bruised-up girl who might or might not be who she claimed to be. She was a reporter, and she had a story she needed to tell. "He's been helping the EIS. I think he was there because he *does* care, and something's been stopping him from getting to you."

"What are you talking about?" demanded Becks.

"She was about to politely offer to wait for me to come back before she explained," said Maggie, walking back into the room. She had a tray of drinks in her hands. It was embossed with the Agora logo, and looked like it was made of solid silver. Considering everything else around us, I would have been almost more surprised if it wasn't.

"Sorry, Maggie," said Becks, looking faintly abashed.

"It's okay." Maggie made her way around the room, starting with Mahir, who got a white ceramic mug and saucer. George got two cans of Coke, both cold enough to have drops of condensation on their sides. By the time Maggie reached me with my coffee, George already had the first of those cans open, and was taking a long, desperate drink.

Maggie leaned close as she handed me my coffee, cutting off my view of George. "If she isn't who she says she is, she can never leave this room," she murmured. "You understand that, don't you, Shaun?"

I nodded minutely. "I do."

"Good." She straightened again, walking over to an open chair and sitting with the tray, and her own cup of tea, in her lap. "So can I get the recaplet of what happened after you left here? I doubt we have time for the whole episode."

"We broke into the CDC through the back fence," I said. "We got inside just fine, managed to plant the bug and everything, but then we got turned around."

"You are in a maze of twisty little passages, all alike," said Mahir, and laughed for no apparent reason.

"Uh, yeah. Anyway, we split up. Becks and Mahir went one way, I went the other way. And then this lady comes running around a corner and slams into me, and it's, well . . . " I indicated George with my free hand. "Honestly, I didn't think she was really there until everyone else started saying they could see her, too."

"That's understandable," said Maggie, not unkindly.

"Yeah. So she says we have to get out fast, because the building is about to blow up. We get out fast. The building blows up. And then Becks starts threatening to shoot her in the head, we sort of negotiate a temporary peace, and we wind up back here, with you, having coffee." I took the first sip of my coffee and moaned. "Really fucking *good* coffee. What did you do, Maggie, sacrifice a bellboy to the coffee gods?"

"Not this time," she said, and sipped her tea before turning surprisingly sharp eyes on George. "What's your side of the story?"

George took a breath. "Do you want the long version or the short version?"

"Let's take the version somewhere in between. Mahir's never going to be satisfied with the short version, and Becks will probably start shooting people if you go for the long version."

"True," said Becks. "To be honest, I'm tempted to start shooting people right now."

"I missed you, too, Becks," said George. She took another drink of Coke for courage, and said, "I woke up about a month ago—maybe a little bit more; I don't really know, since they never let me have a calendar—in a CDC holding room. A man named Dr. Thomas said I'd been in recovery for a while, and that things were going to be better now. But my eyes were wrong, and my muscle tone was wrong, and the tattoo on the inside of my wrist was gone. I asked if I was a clone. He confirmed it."

Becks scoffed.

To her credit, George ignored her, and continued. "One of the orderlies, Gregory Lake, was actually an EIS doctor assigned to infiltrate the facility. He's one of the people who got me out. He told me I'd been created from a combination of electrical synapse recordings and implanted information. I'm supposed to be a ninety-seven percent match to the original Georgia Mason." She looked toward me. "I'm not her, and I am, all at the same time."

"So you're not really her, and we can shoot you now, right?" asked Becks.

Mahir shook his head, frowning. "No."

"What?" Becks gave him a wounded look. "Why not?"

"I've read some of the memory recovery studies. It arose from research aimed at assisting brain damage victims." His frown deepened. "We're nothing but electrical impulses stored in meat. If you can measure and codify those impulses, you can transcribe what a person remembers."

But I was dead, said George. *How could they measure my thoughts if I was dead?*

Whether I liked it or not, it was a good question. "George was dead," I said. "So how does that work?"

"Kellis-Amberlee keeps turning the electricity in the body *and* brain back on after the point of death," said Maggie. We all turned to look at her, even George. She shrugged. "Raised by pharmaceutical magnates, remember? Kellis-Amberlee really improved our understanding of the human brain, because it won't let the brain die. It turns back on again and again, trying to keep thinking. Only the virus starts getting in the way of those electrical impulses. It scrambles them. The body can't translate what the brain wants anymore, and so the virus just takes over."

"If the CDC's built a system for recovering the electrical impulses from an infected brain, cleaning out the static and then implanting them in a new mind, it's entirely feasible that they'd be able to accomplish what you're claiming." Mahir looked thoughtfully at George.

"I'm the closest match they ever made," said George. "That's why they decanted me. I was their show pony. I think they were planning to sell the tech that made me. Immortality for the highest bidder."

Every eye in the room went to Maggie. She blinked, and then slowly shook her head. "No way. My parents wouldn't do something like that, even if they could afford it."

"Are you sure?" I asked.

"Yes. I am." Her tone was firm, cutting off further discussion.

George bit her lip. "Anyway. I wasn't supposed to be here."

"You keep saying that, but how do we know you're not lying?" asked Becks. "Maybe you're telling the truth, only the ninety-seven percent Georgia died at the CDC, and you're the Judas."

"It's a possibility," George agreed. "I guess we'll just have to wait and see whether I'm consumed by the urge to betray you. Thus far, no urges."

"No one is betraying, or shooting, anyone right now," said Mahir firmly. "Please continue your story."

"Gregory said he wanted to get me out, but we'd need to find a way to do it. If we weren't careful, things could get ugly. He had another associate in the facility, working undercover with the CDC. She said her name was Dr. Shaw, but then after they managed to get me away from my handlers, she started calling herself Dr. Kimberley. She—"

"Dr. *Danika* Kimberley?" Mahir sat up a little straighter.

"Yeah." George blinked at him. "You know her?"

"She's an epidemic neurologist, specializing in infections that alter the behavior of the brain—including Kellis-Amberlee." He frowned, focusing on George. "Describe her."

"Tall, white-blonde hair, really blue eyes, looks sort of cold. She wore incredibly stupid shoes." Her face fell. "She gave them to me when she told me to run."

"And she had a Scottish accent?" asked Mahir.

George frowned. "Welsh, I think. She never told me where she was from."

Mahir nodded like she'd just passed some sort of test. "They got you away from your 'handlers.' Then what?"

"Then they drugged me and operated on me without my consent." Her lips thinned. "Guess the people who made me wanted to protect their investment. They had some lovely surprises implanted in my muscle tissue, designed to release neurotoxins when they decided they were done with me. I guess that seemed more humane than taking me behind the building and shooting me. Have I mentioned recently that I hate science?"

"You didn't need to," I snarled. The urge to go back to the CDC, find some survivors, and start punching them in the face was almost too strong to be denied.

Down, boy, said George.

"Oh, good. I hate science. That operation is probably why you couldn't find any trackers when you scanned me. The EIS doctors took those out, too."

"Or maybe the CDC always thought there was a chance the EIS would smuggle you out, and they wanted to be sure they couldn't get any useful information out of you," said Maggie quietly. Again, every eye in the room went to her. She reddened. "It makes more sense than 'and then we implanted really expensive biological bombs in somebody instead of using a bullet.' She was a booby trap. Just not for us."

"I wish that didn't make sense," muttered George.

My scowl deepened, while Mahir looked quietly relieved. Every word she said made her story a little bit more believable. That didn't make me happy about it.

Becks ignored my obvious unhappiness as she leaned forward and addressed George. "So where does Rick come into all this?"

"I was in recovery—still pretty drugged—when he came into the room. I couldn't open my eyes, but I heard his voice. He said . . ." She faltered, and took a long drink from her Coke before she continued. "He said he was sorry I'd had to go through all this. And he told me to do what I did best."

"What's that?" asked Mahir.

George looked at him. "He said to break this fucking thing wide open and let the pieces fall."

"Ah. And after that?"

"I told the EIS I'd only cooperate if they let me get online. So they got me a connection, and I managed to use one of the back doors into the secure server to talk to Alaric."

"Which one?" asked Becks.

"The Elm Street entrance."

Maggie laughed, once, sharply, and was silent.

George continued. "We were supposed to talk about evacuating me after that, but . . . something went wrong." She looked down at her soda. "Someone started shooting. I saw two of the orderlies go down. Gregory and Dr. Kimberley and I ran. They shoved me through a quarantine door as it was closing. I managed to get into an empty lab and set some charges. I mostly just wanted to create a distraction so I could try to sneak out in the chaos. Instead . . . well. That's where Shaun came in."

"I see." Mahir turned, looking toward me. "Well?" he asked.

"You know my vote," I said.

Becks scowled. "I don't like this."

"I didn't ask if you liked it. It's a horrible perversion of the laws of nature, we're doubtless to be struck down by the divine, should the divine ever bestir itself to remember that we're here. As we're still periodically having a zombie apocalypse, I doubt that's going to happen any time soon. Now what's your answer?"

Becks looked at George. Then she turned and looked at me. "I believe her," she said finally. "If she's not Georgia, she thinks she is. It's better that we keep her close."

I could have cheered. Instead, I looked toward Maggie, who smiled.

"This is the sort of thing that happens in comic books," she said. "I'm in."

"Thank you." Mahir turned back to George. "It's good to have you back. Disorienting and terrifying, and you'll forgive me if I don't rush to embrace you, but . . . good. Now, how would you feel about breaking this fucking thing wide open, to see where the pieces fall?"

George finished her first can of Coke and put it aside before opening the second. The carbonation hissed into the silence. Then she spoke: "What else am I supposed to do?"

Shannon—

Danika was just in touch with me. Please provide the nearest safe meet-up point. I am en route to you. We need to talk. The endgame is beginning, and you're going to need all the assistance you can get if you're going to make it through this in one piece.

We all are.

—Taken from an e-mail sent by Dr. Joseph Shoji to Dr. Shannon Abbey, August 3, 2041.

They got her out. Kimberley and Lake . . . they got her out. She's alive, she's intact, she's clinically sane, and she's *out*.

Peter still doesn't know what I've done, or what I'm going to do. But history will remember him as a president worthy of the name, and not another in the long line of crooks and monsters to have held the position. He will be known for who he was, and for what he did, and for what he sacrificed. All of them will. If that means history must also remember me as a monster, well . . .

So be it.

—From the private journal of Vice President Richard Cousins, August 3, 2041. Unpublished.

GEORGIA: Twenty-seven

After some discussion, we—meaning "Maggie and Mahir," who were the only ones still considered completely rational; the rest of us were treated as compromised, to one degree or another—decided the best course of action was to stay at the Agora long enough to recover, and then head out. Mahir also pointed out that we were better off keeping the van under cover for at least a few hours, in case it had been seen leaving the vicinity of the CDC. So we were staying put. I wasn't inclined to argue. The last few hours were starting to catch up with me, and I wanted nothing more than a dark corner I could curl up in until the urge to start shaking went away.

After a bit more discussion, Becks reluctantly agreed that I wasn't likely to go crazy and kill Shaun without setting off the hotel security system, which meant the two of us could do our recovery in the same hotel room. "The Agora takes the safety of its guests very seriously," Maggie assured her. "There are so few blood tests because the biometric monitoring system is so advanced. If either of them is in medical distress, the guards will be alerted within seconds."

"Nice place," I said approvingly. "I didn't even know this was here."

"That's the point." Maggie smiled, still looking somewhat

uncertain. "Is there anything I can have sent up to the room for you?"

I bit back my first answer, waiting a few seconds to be sure that it was what I wanted to say. Oh, well. In for a penny, in for a pound. "Can I get some clean clothes, a pair of sunglasses, and a bottle of the darkest brown hair color you can find?"

Most of the uncertainty went out of Maggie's smile. "We can do that," she agreed. "Shaun? Do you want to show Georgia to your room? I'll call the front desk and have things sent up." She gave me a measuring look. "I think the biometrics from the door will give us her size."

"Thank you," I said. There wasn't time to say much more—Shaun was making hasty farewells as he grabbed my hand and started hauling me toward the door. Mahir was still saying good-bye when the door slammed shut behind us, leaving us alone in the hall.

I expected Shaun to say something then. He didn't. He just kept pulling me along, walking briskly back toward the elevators. I glanced at his face and decided to give it a minute. He'd survived me being dead for over a year. I could survive him being silent for a little while. Still, my feet hurt, and even the soft carpet wasn't helping all that much. I was relieved when he finally pulled me to a stop in front of a door that looked like every other doorway in the hall.

There was a small green light just above the peephole. It blinked twice when he gripped the door handle. Then the door swung open, revealing a room that looked like the younger sibling of Maggie's room. I had to blink twice before I realized the dimness wasn't only because he had the curtains drawn; the overhead lights were set to UV. It was the kind of change that used to be second nature to both of us, making sure the lights in our hotel rooms wouldn't give me migraines that left me incapable of doing my job.

Shaun let me enter first. He pulled the door closed as he stepped inside and said roughly, "The bathroom's through there. You can change the lights if you want to. I don't mind."

"No. No, this is . . . this is good." There were no signs that he'd been in this room before, except for the curtains and the lights. I turned to face him. He was watching me, a deep, anxious hunger in his eyes. "I'm real, Shaun. I'm not going anywhere."

"What did you give me for my eighth birthday?"

"A black eye, because you said girls couldn't be Newsies."

"How did we meet Buffy?"

"Online job fair."

"Who was your first boyfriend?"

I had to smile at that. "You were. Also my second, and my third, and every other number you can think of. You can keep asking questions as long as you want, Shaun, but I'm only going to get ninety-seven percent of them right. It's up to you whether that makes me real or not."

"I missed you." He raised a hand, touching my cheek so gently that it made my heart hurt. I put my own hand over it, forcing his fingers flat against my skin. He sighed. "You *died*, George. I shot you, and you *died*."

"No. You shot Georgia Mason." He winced, but didn't pull his hand away. I forced myself to keep going. If I didn't say this now, when we were alone for the first time, I was never going to say it. And I had to say it. "You shot a woman whose DNA profile I share. I have ninety-seven percent of her memories. I remember growing up with you. I remember my first blog post. I even remember dying. I remember everything, right up until you pulled the trigger."

"George . . ."

"I remember thinking I was the luckiest woman in the world, because you were there to do it. But those memories aren't only mine. Do you understand?"

"You're Georgia enough for me," he said, finally pulling his hand away. "Neither of us is perfect anymore."

I nodded. Fine, then. If this was who I was going to be, then I was going to be her. "You saved me."

Shaun dipped his chin in what would have been a nod, if he'd raised his head again. Instead, he kept looking down at the floor, slow tears beginning to make their way down his cheeks. "I wanted to die with you."

"You didn't." I grabbed his hand again, squeezing his fingers. "You kept going. And now I'm back, and we get to finish this thing together."

He raised his head, looking at me anxiously. "What if you get hurt again?"

"We can't start living in 'what if,' Shaun. If we do that, I might as well have stayed dead." I smiled a little. "Is there a first-aid kit? I want to get some sealant on my feet."

"What? Oh!" He straightened, focus returning almost instantly as he realized he had something he could *do*, rather than standing around worrying until Mahir came back and said it was time to go. "This way."

He led me to the bathroom, where a search of the medicine cabinet yielded a first-aid kit that could have put some hospitals to shame. I sat on the edge of the bathtub while he wiped my feet off with a wet cloth, then sprayed them with a fast-drying layer of wound sealant. It would act as an artificial skin, porous enough to let my wounds heal, but thick enough to prevent infection. I'd used the stuff before, although never on quite such a large area. It's amazing how big the bottoms of your feet can seem when you've managed to run all the skin off of them.

He wrapped my feet in a layer of gauze once the sealant was dry, just in case. I didn't ask him to stop. I just watched him work, studying the tension in his shoulders and the new strands of gray at his temples, visible even through the bleached-out streaks of almost-blond. I saw the moment when that tension turned into decision, and was prepared when he straightened up, leaned forward, and kissed me.

There have been times when I wondered how people didn't put

the pieces together. How many so-called siblings share hotel rooms after puberty, much less share bedrooms with a door connecting them? We never dated. We never went to school events with anyone but each other. We never did any of the normal social things, and yet people still assumed we were on the market, not that we'd been off the market before we even knew what the market was.

We were still in the bathroom ten minutes later when someone knocked on the front door. The voice of the hotel said politely, "Mr. Mason, your request from the front desk has arrived. Would you like to claim it now, or would you prefer that it be left for your convenience?"

Shaun pulled away from me, cheeks flushed. "Uh . . . " he said. Then, more coherently, he said, "I'll be right there. Thanks." He got up, leaving me sitting where I was as he walked out of the room. I'd expected being alone to make me nervous, but it did the opposite. For the first time since the CDC decided to bring me back, no one was watching me. I was genuinely free.

Low voices came from the hall, followed by the sound of the door closing. Shaun reappeared, a brown paper bundle in one hand and a bottle of hair dye in the other. "What do you want to do first?" he asked.

I smiled.

An hour later, I actually felt like myself again. My hair was damp and dark brown, sticking to my ears and forehead as it dried. The clothes Maggie requested were perfect, if two sizes smaller than I would normally have worn—black slacks, a white button-down shirt, and a black blazer with pockets for my audio recorder and notepad. I didn't have either of those at the moment, but just having the pockets made me feel better. Even the shoes fit. My eyes were the only things that didn't look right, and that was what the sunglasses were for. Once I put them on, I looked like I'd been sick for a while, but I didn't look like a clone.

I looked like Georgia Mason.

Shaun apparently thought so, too. When I put the sunglasses on, he stopped talking and just stared at me. Finally, in a quiet, reasonable tone, he said, "If it turns out that this is all some crazy, impossible hoax, and you're a fucking android or something, I'm going to kill us both."

"Cloning is crazy enough for me, so I'm good with that," I said. "Can we kill a bunch of other people first?"

"Yeah," said Shaun, and smiled. "We can."

"How much of this is our fault, Shaun? How much . . . how many questions did we ask that we should have left quiet? People are dying." I walked over to the bed, sitting down on the edge of the mattress. "Do we own this?"

Shaun barked a short, humorless laugh. "The people who started all this shit own it. We just made it happen a little faster. I think . . . enough of it is ours that we have to fix it if we can."

"We can."

"God, I hope so." He sat down next to me, taking my hands. "This is what you missed. Your post got out—you know that—and it changed a lot of things, and nothing, all at the same time. It's part of why Ryman got elected. You made it pretty clear he wasn't playing on Tate's team. It probably doesn't help that Tate went all bad movie villain when I cornered him."

My eyes widened. "When you what? Shaun—"

"Just listen, okay? See, after you . . . after I . . . I had to leave the van. Steve—you remember Steve, from Ryman's security detail? Big fucker, looked like he could stand in for the entire Brute Squad?"

"Please don't tell me Steve died," I said.

"No, he's fine. Still writes me sometimes, or did, before we had to go off the grid. See, Steve and I broke quarantine to get to Ryman . . ."

The story he told was crazy and impossible and enough to break my heart. I'd always known that Tate was bad, but Shaun was the one who confronted him, and got fed a line about restoring America to its roots through fear and control. Tate martyred himself. It might have worked, too, if he hadn't martyred me first.

Shaun buried me and tried to move on, but the world wouldn't let him; the world never does. Instead, he wound up neck deep in conspiracies and craziness. Dave died. Kelly Connolly died. Dr. Wynne turned out not to be an ally, but one more crazy man out to change the world into what he thought it should be. The longer Shaun talked, the more I realized that the only allies we had were the ones we shared a website with.

I only stopped him twice: once to ask about the reservoir conditions, and once to make him repeat, several times, that he'd been bitten and hadn't amplified. Crazy as it might sound, that was the part I had the most trouble believing. The additional details on the insect vector for Kellis-Amberlee just left me cold. Maybe mankind was going to lose the war against the living dead after all—and this time, it might not be because someone dropped a vial.

Eventually, Shaun stopped talking. Then he reached up and removed my sunglasses, putting them beside me on the bed. "We could run," he said. "You and me. Head for Canada, or something. The others could finish this without us. You know they would."

"And we'd never forgive ourselves," I said. "We finish this. And if we survive, somehow, through some miracle . . . then we run. You and me, and anywhere they won't find us."

"It's a date." He leaned back, reaching for the phone.

I blinked. "What are you doing?"

"Calling room service. I don't want you to blow away if there's a stiff wind."

I laughed and hit him without thinking about it. That brought a totally sincere smile to his face before he turned away to deal with placing our order. Less than fifteen minutes later, two massive bowls of chicken cacciatore were delivered to our door, along with a six-pack of Coke and a piece of tiramisu the size of my head. My stomach growled when I saw the food, and I realized that I was genuinely hungry for the first time in a long time.

The only thing I wanted more than food was access to the Internet, which Shaun provided as soon as our dinner was just memory and crumbs. My laptop wasn't at the Agora—why would it be?—so he let me borrow his, both of us stretching out on the bed with our backs to the headboard, my shoulder pressing into his chest as I began doing the most important thing I could possibly do.

I began catching up on the news.

Working as a professional journalist meant years of learning to absorb as much information as possible in as short a time as possible, since failure to stay on top of current events could easily result in posting a story that had no relevance at all. I was always a little slower than most of my contemporaries, because I was always so damn careful to check and double-check my facts before I put my name behind them. Oh, I had my op-ed blogs—*Just the Wind* when I was a teenager on a provisional license, and *Images May Disturb You* once I was old enough to go full-time—but those were thoughts. Opinions. Ideas. It was the articles I put on the main site that really mattered, and those were the things that needed me to do my research.

Using After the End Times as my start point, I pulled up the archives, going all the way back to the day after I died. Shaun's posts from that period were a jumbled mess; half the time, I wasn't even certain they were written in English. Mahir and Alaric did most of the real reporting, following the rest of the Ryman campaign with a clinical detachment that told me everything I needed to know about the depth of their grief. Shaun wasn't the only one who'd been hurting. And the headlines rolled on.

Ryman elected in a landslide vote, stuns voters by choosing Richard Cousins as his replacement vice president! The Democratic candidate, Susan Kilburn, is so devastated by her loss that she takes her own life! Ryman takes the White House!

Shaun Mason goes quietly crazy, while his staff scramble to cover up the cracks in his facade. Maggie Garcia moves into Buffy's place, and does a good job, especially considering the circumstances. Shaun cedes his position to Rebecca Atherton, letting her run the Irwins while he runs deeper into the damaged recesses of his own psyche. Mahir continues shaping the site into a force for the truth, doing as much as he can to stand against the tide of ignorance and corruption.

CDC researcher Kelly Connolly is shot in a robbery gone wrong! Downtown Oakland is sterilized following an outbreak, resulting in the tragic death of thousands, including reporter David Novakowski! An insect vector for the Kellis-Amberlee virus appears along the Gulf Coast, killing millions more! The members of the After the End Times core team are wanted in conjunction with potential bioterrorism, and should be reported if seen! Ryman grieves for his wounded nation!

The CDC decides to raise the dead. Someone tells a whole lot of lies, and someone else makes sure the world will believe them.

Everything goes wrong.

The effort of filtering the headlines for the truth hidden beneath them—the truth hidden between the lines, in the places where it was less likely to be seen—left my head pounding. I slumped backward, letting my head rest against Shaun's shoulder.

"I couldn't have done it," I said, closing my eyes.

"Done what?"

"What you did. Kept things going. I wouldn't have—*couldn't* have—done it. I would have fallen apart."

"I *did* fall apart," he noted, in a tone that was almost comically reasonable. "I went nuts. I've been talking to you since Sacramento, and you've been talking back."

"I thought it might be something like that. You never did do 'alone' very well."

"Neither did you."

"That's why I would have killed myself by now."

Silence fell, and stretched out for almost a minute before Shaun said, "Well, then, I guess it's a good thing I'm the one who got out of Sacramento, huh? Which is kind of funny if you stop to think about it."

I put the laptop aside on the bed and pushed myself up, twisting around to look at him. "What are you talking about?"

"Dr. Wynne died because Kelly—the Doc, that's what I called her while she was with us—stabbed him with a scalpel while he was in the middle of a big-time bad-guy soliloquy. I mean, I don't know if there's an Evil Fucker 101 class that they all take, but between him and Tate, I'm about ready to slap the next person who wants to tell me about his evil plan." Shaun's eyes were haunted. "The Doc was a good person. Maybe the only good person left in the CDC. I don't know. I never had time to find out."

I thought of Gregory and Dr. Kimberley, both of whom had chosen the EIS over the CDC. "Maybe you're right," I admitted.

"Anyway, before Dr. Wynne died, he as good as said that whoever shot you wasn't *aiming* for you. The needle was supposed to be mine." He brushed my hair away from my cheek. "You were supposed to shoot me, not the other way around. Then Tate would give you his big bad guy speech, and you'd think it was over, because you believed in black and white."

My stomach felt like a solid ball of pain. "They knew how to beat us."

"Yeah. But the cold equations fucked them up, because the math doesn't care. They subtracted the wrong half of the equation, and I've been kicking them in the ass ever since. For you." He looked at me earnestly. "I was doing it all for you."

I sighed, folding my hand over his before I scooted closer. "I know."

Some time later—once the laptop had been put back on its charger, and the "do not disturb" light had been lit on the door—we slept, both sprawled on top of the covers. Shaun kept one arm around me as we drifted off, clinging like he was afraid I'd vanish before he woke up. I've never been the world's cuddliest person, and that didn't seem to be one of the things that dying and coming back had changed, but for once, I didn't mind. Anything that kept me from waking up and thinking I was back in CDC custody was okay by me.

We'd been asleep for a few hours when a gentle chiming noise filled the room, followed by the voice of the Agora saying, "I do hope you've enjoyed your rest. Miss Garcia would like to remind you that you have an appointment that cannot be rescheduled."

"Huh?" I sat up, wiping the sleep from my eyes with one hand and fumbling for my sunglasses with the other. It's amazing how quickly habits reassert themselves, even when they're not really needed anymore.

"She means it's time to go see the Monkey." Shaun leaned over to grab his shirt off the floor before sitting up.

"The who?"

"I'll explain on the way. Come on."

Having just the one set of clothes made getting dressed to go substantially easier than it used to be. Not that I ever spent that much time thinking about what to wear, but when you own ten identical pairs of black pants, you sometimes have to spend a few minutes figuring out which ones are clean. We were both ready in half the time it would have taken before I died. Shaun led the way to the door, where he paused, looking back at me.

"I was tired of being a haunted house," he said. "Thank you for coming home." Then he stepped out into the hall, not leaving any space for my response. Maybe that didn't matter. Maybe this was one of those things that didn't need to be responded to. I followed him out of the room. The door swung shut behind me, the locks engaging with a muted "click."

Mahir, Maggie, and Becks were already in the lobby, standing near the entrance to the airlock. Mahir paled when he saw me, looking for all the world like he'd just seen a ghost. In a weird way, I guess he technically had.

"Everything fit?" asked Maggie, as we walked into conversational distance.

"Like a dream," I said. "Even the shoes are perfect. Thank you. You have no idea how good it feels to be *dressed* again. They wouldn't even let me have a bra while I was under observation."

Maggie shuddered at the thought of that indignity. Becks kept eyeing me, expression not giving away what she might be thinking about the whole situation.

"We were thinking you might not feel completely clothed just yet," said Mahir, shaking off his shock. He dipped a hand into his pocket, pulling it out with the fingers curled around some small object. "If you would be so kind?"

Blinking blankly at him, I held out my hand. He dropped an ear cuff into it.

It was a small thing, barely weighing a quarter of an ounce, but it felt like the heaviest, most valuable thing in the entire world. I raised my free hand to my mouth, suddenly doubly glad for the familiar screen of my sunglasses. They would keep everyone else from seeing the tears in my eyes.

"Oh, God, Mahir, thank you." I blinked the tears away as firmly as I could. More rose to take their place. "Thank you so much."

"It only has three numbers in its address book," said Becks, tone still tight with suspicion. "Tap it once for Shaun, twice for Mahir, and three times for me. *Don't* try to reprogram it. There's a safety lock on the controls. You mess with the directory, the whole thing will short out, and we'll know."

"I wouldn't dream of it," I said. "Seriously, thank you all. You have no idea how much this means to me."

Maggie smiled. "I think I might have a bit of a clue."

I smiled back before reaching up and delicately affixing the ear cuff to the shallow outside curve of my ear. It pinched the skin in a way I remembered from high school, back when I started wearing the portable contact devices on a regular basis. I'd have raw spots and blisters for at least a week while I got used to it. And I didn't really give a damn.

"If we're all prepared to wander gaily off to our dooms, we should really get moving," said Mahir, tearing his eyes away from my face. "I'm sure our gracious hosts would prefer the doom not find us early."

"You are always such the little ray of golden sunshine, Mahir, you know that?" Shaun grinned. "Let's roll."

Joey—

What the fuck do you mean, "Danika was just in touch with you"? Danika hasn't been in touch with anybody in *years*. She's still on crazy safari in the crazy jungle, looking for the crazy magical herbal cure to the walking dead. Seriously, that woman is so much crazy crammed into a small space that she's practically a crazy singularity. Have you been sticking your dick in the crazy singularity? Because that's how you catch the really *good* social diseases.

My coordinates are attached. They're good for another four days. Then I'm cutting bait and we're getting ourselves to higher ground. The floods are coming, my friend. Try to disengage from the crazy long enough to get the fuck out of their way.

—Taken from an e-mail sent by Dr. Shannon Abbey to Dr. Joseph Shoji, August 3, 2041.

I'm not sure which is worse: the fact that Shaun was willing to accept this woman as his dead sister, or the fact that I'm beginning to believe it might be true.

Georgia Mason had a certain way of reacting to things—a kinesthetic language, rather than a verbal one. It wasn't the sort of thing you could fake without years of practice. If this woman is an imposter, she hasn't had years . . . and she moves like Georgia. She has all the little ticks and twitches down cold. When she came out of that elevator dressed, with those sunglasses on . . . I was ready to call her Georgia and ask what we were going to do next. And that's not a good thing.

If she's the real deal, then awesome, the laws of science have been twisted even further away from what they were intended to be. Bully for the laws of science. And if she's not the real deal . . .

If she's not the real deal, I'm pretty sure she's going to get us all killed.

—From *Charming Not Sincere*, the blog of Rebecca Atherton, August 3, 2041. Unpublished.

SHAUN: Twenty-eight

There was no handy text-based adventure game to guide us back to the Brainpan, which meant I had to drive, since I was the one who'd driven us there the first time. I didn't appreciate being separated from George. I've never been clingy—codependent, sure, according to every psychologist I've ever talked to, but not *clingy*. That didn't mean I appreciated having her out of arm's reach now that she was alive again.

The need to have her where I could touch her would fade, given time. I was sure of it. Or at least I hoped I was sure of it, and not just lying to myself.

You've had a lot of practice lying to yourself, commented Georgia. She didn't sound angry. Just resigned.

"Quiet," I mumbled.

Maggie, who was sitting in the passenger seat, gave me a sidelong look but didn't say anything. I appreciated that. I had absolutely no idea what I would have said in return.

In the back of the van, Mahir and Becks—mostly Mahir—were quizzing George, trying to feel out the limits of what she knew. She fielded most of their questions without hesitation. I stopped breathing a little bit every time they asked her something and she didn't answer right away, waiting for the sound of Becks taking the safety off her gun, but George recovered every time. If there were questions she wasn't going to get right, they weren't the kind of questions the two of them would think to ask.

I didn't care what answers were hidden in the three percent of herself she'd lost by dying and coming back to life again. She'd already given me all the answers I needed.

Maggie surreptitiously hit the button to seal the doors as we drove through the neighborhood leading to the Brainpan. Her worried glances out the window confirmed the reason why. Even after visiting and surviving once, the decay of the buildings disturbed her.

"It'll be okay, Maggie," I said. "I doubt anyone lives here except the crazy people we're on our way to visit. And sure, they may decide to shoot us and store our bodies in the freezer or something, but at least that's a normal thing, right?"

She muttered something in sour-sounding Spanish before saying, "It was never normal before I started traveling with you."

"See? It's like I always say. Travel is broadening."

Maggie showed me a finger.

I clucked my tongue. "Really? You're going to flip me off? I mean, jeez, Maggie. In the last twenty-four hours, I've broken into the CDC—"

"Again," called Becks from the backseat. "Don't forget Portland."

"—okay, point, broken into the CDC *again*, which, PS, kind of blew up while I was still there, seen my sister come back from the dead, and had a *lot* of coffee. It's going to take more than a middle finger to upset me."

Maggie raised both hands, backs to me, and showed me two fingers.

I nodded agreeably. "Much better. Hey, look! There's the serial killer van!" It seemed a little odd to use a burned-out pre-Rising van as a landmark, but it made a certain amount of sense. In a neighborhood as decrepit as this one, you couldn't exactly use paint colors or house numbers to navigate, and saying "turn at the house that looks like it was painted to blend in with viscera" would probably inspire even less confidence than "turn at the serial killer van."

"Goodie," said Maggie.

"You don't *sound* excited."

"That's because I would rather be home, with my dogs, writing porn," she said.

I glanced over at her. "Soon you will be."

She didn't have anything to say to that.

The van bumped and jounced down the driveway to the Brainpan. I parked outside the garage and killed the engine, waiting.

George poked her head up between the seats. "Is there a reason we're just sitting here?"

"Yes."

"And that reason would be . . . ?"

"The house is full of crazy people who would love an excuse to shoot us in one or more of our extremities—probably more—so we're going to wait in the car until they tell us we're allowed to go inside." Said aloud, it sounded even more ridiculous than it really was. That wasn't enough to make me move.

"Crazy people like that one?" asked George, pointing toward my window.

I turned.

The Fox was perched in one of the half-dead trees still clinging to the soil around the edges of the yard. She'd somehow managed to become almost unnoticeable, despite her tricolored hair and rainbow leg warmers. She raised one hand in a jaunty wave when she saw us looking her way. Then she jumped easily down to the cracked dirt of what used to be lawn, sauntering toward the van.

I had the driver's-side window rolled down by the time she reached us. My hands were resting on the dashboard, clearly visible.

"Hi!" she said, peering past me to George. There was a large gun in her hands. I was reasonably sure it hadn't been there when she jumped out of the tree, and I knew I hadn't seen her draw it. My conviction that this woman was not just crazy, but very, very dangerous, grew. "What's your name? You weren't here before."

Georgia looked at her coolly. The sunglasses helped. She was better at maintaining a neutral expression when her eyes couldn't give her away. "Georgia Mason, journalist. You are?"

"Me?" The Fox blinked at her, then cocked her head. "I'm Foxy. I used to be called Elaine, and everything was boring, and I was sad all the time. But things are better now. I wouldn't ask that question again, if I were you."

George frowned. "No? Why not?"

"Oh, because if you ask it where the Cat can hear you, she'll tell me I should shoot you in the head a couple of times to teach you not to pry. And then I'll probably do it, because she makes the best cookies, and I don't like remembering that I used to be someone who was sad." The Fox said this as if it were entirely reasonable. In her scrambled little head, it probably was.

I broke in before George could say anything else. "Foxy, we've finished the errand we agreed to do. Can we come inside and talk about what happens next?"

"Oh, sure." The Fox smiled, taking two short hop-steps back from the van. "Come on in. I bet the Cat's going to be thrilled to see you!"

Behind me, I heard Becks mutter, "Only if she's got a really good idea for ways to skin people alive."

"You heard the lady, gang," I said, hoping the Fox hadn't heard that. If she had, it didn't seem to have bothered her. She was rocking back on her heels and looking at the sky, with the gun still in her hands and pointing at the car. I was pretty sure her crazy wasn't an act, but her clueless definitely was. "Let's get ourselves inside."

"Don't forget to leave your weapons, or I get to shoot you all," said

Foxy blithely. "I'll start with the shouty girl. She probably needs shooting more than all the rest of you combined."

"I do believe she likes you, Rebecca," said Mahir.

"Shut up," snarled Becks, and began disarming.

The Fox turned and wandered toward the house, apparently dismissing us. George, meanwhile, grabbed my shoulder and demanded, "Are we *actually* going to get out of this van without any weapons?"

"That would be the plan." I removed both guns from the waist of my jeans, putting them on the dashboard. George gasped a little. I paused, really *looking* at the guns for the first time in a long time. "Oh. I guess this one's yours, isn't it?"

"She can get it back *after* we finish dealing with the happy neighborhood psychopath brigade, okay?" said Becks, dropping three clips of ammo onto the floor. "Right now, I want to get in, get what we came for, and get the hell out of here. Seattle is not a good place for us to be anymore."

"Tell me something I don't know." I opened the van door. Still looking unsure about the whole thing, George followed Mahir out the side door. Maggie walked around the van to meet us, and the four of us waited as patiently as we could for Becks to finish disarming.

"What are you carrying, an armory?" I called.

"I'm prepared," she shot back, and slid out of the van. Part of the reason it had taken her so long was revealed; she had already unlaced her combat boots, making them easier to remove. Seeing the understanding in my expression, she smirked. "See? Prepared. You should try it some time, Mason. You might discover that you like it."

Mahir snorted. "And swine may soar. Now come along."

"Yes, sir," said Becks, in a lilting, half-mocking tone. She was still chuckling as we walked toward the house.

I dropped back, letting Mahir and Maggie lead George as I asked Becks quietly, "You okay? You're all . . . chipper . . . all of a sudden."

She shook her head. "I'm not, really. I feel like I've been put through seven kinds of emotional wringers in the last year, and I can't even begin to imagine how you feel right now. Thing is? It's not going to change, and it's not going to stop, and it's not going to go away. The dead are coming back to life, and this time, they want to give us a piece of their minds instead of taking a piece of ours away." Becks nodded toward George, who was walking up the porch steps. "The more I talk to her, the more I think she's for real. That's terrifying. That's my whole life, falling down, because my parents are the kind of old money that funds politicians who fund places like the CDC, and now the CDC is bringing back the dead, *again*. So no, I'm not okay. I just don't have the energy left to be miserable about it all the damn time."

"So you're in a good mood because it's easier?"

"Yeah." Becks gripped the crumbling remains of the banister, holding it as she started going up the stairs. "You went crazy because it was easier. So what's so bad about deciding to stop scowling for the same reason?"

I didn't have a good answer. I shrugged and followed her into the house. The others were waiting for us there.

Once we had all removed our shoes, we proceeded into the living room. George hung back to walk beside me, our hands not quite touching. Her presence was almost reassuring enough to make up for the fact that none of us were armed.

The Cat was sitting on one of the room's two couches, feet up on the coffee table and a tablet braced against her knees. The Fox was nowhere to be seen. I honestly couldn't have said whether or not that was a good thing.

"You know, I did *not* think we would be seeing you again," said the Cat, not looking up from her tablet. Her fingers skated across the screen with the grace of an artist, making connections in some pattern I couldn't see. "If there'd been a bet, I would have lost."

"We're here for our IDs," said Becks. "We did our part."

"Oh, I know. I knew as soon as the bug started transmitting. They've been naughty, naughty boys and girls there at the CDC. They're going to be very sorry when they get the bill for this. Killing people, cloning people, arranging outbreaks . . . it would have been so much cheaper if they'd settled their debts in a civilized manner."

I went cold. Grabbing blindly for George's hand, I asked, "What do you mean, 'the bill'?"

The Cat looked up. For a moment, the smug, almost alien look on her face told me exactly where her nickname had come from. "We're free operatives, Mr. Mason. You can't blame me for taking my money where I can get it."

"It was you." Mahir's voice was tinged with a dawning horror. I turned to look at him. He was staring at her, the white showing all the way around his irises. "One thing always seemed a little off to me when I reviewed the tapes we managed to recover from Oakland. Dr. Connelly was traveling on one of *your* ID cards. She should have been safe. She should have been untraceable. So how is it the CDC tracked her less than two hours after she arrived? And why did they lose track of her after that first ID was consigned to the fires?"

"I don't know," said the Cat. "Why don't you tell me? You're the journalists. You're supposed to be the *smart* ones."

"Wait." Becks turned toward Mahir. I didn't like the edge in her voice. "Are you telling me this woman got Dave killed?"

"If you answer that question, you don't get your new identities. Think about that." The Cat looked back down at her tablet, seemingly unconcerned. "You came here because you wanted a free pass out of your lives. You committed an act of treason because you were willing to do whatever it took to get that free pass into your hands. Are you going to let something that happened in the past come between you and getting what you paid for?"

"I guess that depends on whether getting what we paid for is going to get an airstrike called down on our heads," I said.

Then a small, perplexed voice spoke from the stairs: "Kitty, what did you do?" I looked toward it. The Fox was descending from the second floor. The look on her face was almost childlike in its confusion, like whatever was going on was so far outside her experience that it verged on impossible. "Did you do another bad thing? You know what Monkey said he'd do if you did another bad thing. You remember what he did to Wolf."

"Go back upstairs, Foxy," said the Cat calmly. "Watch a movie in your room. I'll bring cookies later."

The Fox frowned. "You're not answering my question."

"That's because I don't have to answer to you."

"No, but you do have to answer to me." We all turned toward the new voice, Becks reaching for a gun she didn't have. Her hand hovered in the air next to her hip for a moment, and then dropped back to her side.

The man who had emerged from the short hallway behind the kitchen looked at us mildly, like he had groups of strangers appear in his living room every day. Then again, maybe he did, considering his line of work.

"Mr. Monkey, I presume?" I said.

"No, no, Mr. Monkey was my father." His voice was vague enough that I couldn't tell if he was joking or not. "You must be the journalists."

"Yes, we are," said Mahir. "Are you the gentleman in charge of this establishment?"

"Not sure anybody really runs the Brainpan, but I guess it's down to me." A certain sharpness came into his eyes as he surveyed our motley group, belying his earlier vagueness. "Now what am I going to do with you?"

The Monkey was average-looking to the point of being forgettable almost while I was still looking at him. Caucasian male, average height, average weight, features that were neither ugly nor attractive, brown hair with bleach streaks, just like every other man on the planet who cared more about functionality than vanity. No one's that forgettable without working at it. We were probably looking at the result of years of careful refinement, possibly including some plastic surgery. This was a man who never wanted to stand out in a crowd. He could disappear into the background before you even realized he was there. In its own way, he was as terrifying as the Fox. At least there, you'd probably see the crazy coming.

Or not, said my inner George. *Remember the front yard.*

I bit back my response to her and smiled at the Monkey instead. "You're going to give us our fake IDs, whip up another one for my sister here, and send us on our merry way?"

"Monkey!" The Fox shoved her way through our group, all but flinging herself into the arms of the unassuming man. "Kitty did a bad thing, she *did*, she didn't say she did, but she didn't say she didn't, either, and that means she did!"

"I did *not* follow that," said Becks.

"The Cat killed Dave," said Maggie. There was a low menace in her tone. I didn't like it. I knew how the rest of us would act if we decided this would be a good time to lose our shit. Maggie . . . I had no idea. I'd never seen her really flip out. Suddenly that seemed like a genuine possibility.

"Who?" asked the Monkey. He stroked the Fox's head with one hand as he looked at us, waiting for an answer. She snuggled into his arms, posture half that of a lover, half that of a pet. "I don't remember anyone by that name."

"He wasn't one of your clients," Maggie practically spat. Mahir put a hand on her shoulder, preemptively restraining her. She ignored him, eyes locked on the Monkey. "You made a new identity for a woman from the CDC. Kelly Connolly."

"You used the name 'Mary Preston,'" interjected Becks.

"Ah!" The Monkey smiled. He wasn't forgettable when he did that. For a moment, his face pulled itself into a configuration that was handsome enough to explain how he was able to shack up with two attractive, if psychologically damaged, women who did his bidding without complaint. "That was a tricky piece of work. I don't usually do that much image replacement for a simple death-and-rebirth routine, you know? It was a challenge. I like challenges."

I spoke before I had a chance to think better of it, saying, "Yeah, well, that challenge came with a tracker that led the CDC right to her, and hence, right to us. They bombed the whole block. It destroyed our offices and killed one of our staffers."

The Monkey's smile faded, replaced by a frown. "That's not possible. I don't place trackers in my IDs. It would damage my reputation among my primary clientele, and I've spent quite some time building it up."

"The reputation, or the clientele?" asked George.

"Both." The Monkey squinted at her. "Aren't you supposed to be dead? I remember your face from the news feeds—and from the CDC records I've been reading all morning. Fascinating stuff."

"I got better," she said.

"We're losing the thread here," I said, wanting to divert the Monkey's attention from George. Somehow, he struck me as the kind of guy who'd love to take her apart, just to be sure she was a clone and not a cyborg or something. "We planted the bug at the CDC for you. We want our papers."

"You killed Dave," said Maggie, not budging from her core point.

I was starting to feel like there were at least three conversations going on, and I wasn't directing any of them. "Can we all settle down for a minute? Please? It's getting sort of hard to figure out what's going on here."

"No, it's pretty simple," said the Monkey mildly. "You exchanged currency and services for a set of false identities that could potentially get you out of whatever trouble you've managed to get into—which I have to say, is extremely impressive trouble, especially given where you started. You don't trust me or my girls, but you didn't have anywhere else that you could go for this sort of service. I understand that. I've worked hard to keep down the competition."

The Fox pulled her face away from his chest long enough to look over her shoulder and inform us solemnly, "That's part of my job."

"I'm sure it is," I said. "You look like you do it very well."

She offered a hesitant smile, and then turned to nestle back against the Monkey. He stroked her hair and said, "Now, you're also having a crisis of . . . call it faith . . . because you've decided I was somehow responsible for the death of your friend. I assure you, it's not the case. Not unless he was trying to establish himself as one of my competitors."

"He was a journalist," said Becks quietly.

"So he wasn't trying to set himself up as the competition. Huh." The Monkey looked toward where the Cat still sat calmly, fingers skating over the surface of her tablet. "Cat? Does what these people are saying have any merit?"

"Mmm-hmm," she replied. She didn't raise her head. She might as well have been responding to a question about whether she wanted soup for dinner.

The Monkey frowned, a flicker of irritation crossing his face. He pushed the Fox gently away from him. "Look at me while I'm speaking to you."

The Cat still didn't look up.

"*Look* at me." The Monkey's annoyance was entirely unmasked now. He didn't look forgettable at all. "Jane. Put it down, look at me, and tell me what you did."

"That's not my name." The Cat finally took her eyes off the screen. Her lips were pressed into a thin, hard line as she raised her head and glared at him. "My name is *Cat*."

"Your name is scared little girl who couldn't deal with all the boys who only wanted you for your body, but wished you'd put your brain in a jar so that they could fuck you and be smarter than you at the same time. Your name is 'I took you in when you said you wanted out.' Your name is 'you came to me.' I *own* you. Now what. Did you. Do?"

Carefully, like she was in no hurry at all, the Cat put her tablet aside. She stood and strolled over to us, stopping barely out of the Monkey's reach. "You took the man from the CDC's money. You said you'd build him the perfect disappearing girl—one who'd never set off any red flags or raise any alarms. And then you went into your damn workshop, like you always do, and you left me alone with Princess Crazy-Cakes here"—she gestured toward the Fox—"to entertain your client until he got bored and went away. He didn't get bored. He knew how you worked. He was waiting for you to leave."

"What?" The Monkey glanced at the Fox. "Why didn't you tell me about this?"

She sniffled. "Kitty told me to go outside and play with the crows. We found a dead squirrel. I set it on fire."

"Kids these days," said Becks dryly.

The Monkey ignored her. His attention swung back to the Cat. "What did you do?"

"He offered me a hundred thousand dollars to plant a tracker in her state ID. You know how easy it is to bug those things. Just swap out the RFID chip for one that broadcasts what *you* want it to broadcast, and you're in business."

"You're supposed to refer all business decisions to me," he said in a low, dangerous voice.

"You would have said no."

"Yes, I would. That isn't how we do business."

"Maybe it isn't how you do business, Monkey, but times are changing, and you're not changing with them. There are a lot of people out there offering services we aren't. We need to stay competitive."

"And that means going behind my back and getting half of downtown Oakland bombed?"

The Cat shrugged. "They only took out half."

The Fox paused, a thought almost visibly struggling across her face. "Is this why you told me I should put things in their shoes?" she asked.

"Hold up there," I said. "Whose shoes? What things?"

"Don't freak out," said the Cat. "They were tracking devices for the CDC to follow, so they'd be able to take out the horrible bastards who broke into their facility. They must have been too busy to come after you until you'd ditched the shoes. You got lucky."

"That, or we were staying at the Agora," said Maggie. "Best security screening technology on this side of the state. No matter how much those trackers were broadcasting, they wouldn't have gotten through the shields."

"I haven't changed my shoes," said Becks slowly. She looked at me. "Have you?"

"No."

The Cat stared at us. Then she pointed at the door and started shouting, "Out! Get the fuck out of here! You have to leave!"

"What's going on?" asked the Fox.

For a moment, I felt almost bad for her. Sure, she was crazy and homicidal, and probably the most dangerous person in the room, but she was also the one who had the least responsibility for her own actions. She needed to be taken care of, and the people she'd chosen to do that had used her as a weapon. That wasn't her fault.

And it wasn't my problem. "Kitty did a bad thing," I informed her. Looking back to the Cat, I said, "Well? Turn them off already."

The Cat licked her lips, eyes darting from me to the Monkey as she said, "I can't."

There was a moment when it felt like the world stood still, all of us considering the meaning of her words. Then Becks shouted, with all the authority of an Irwin in a field situation, "The van! Get to the van, get armed, and get Maggie out of the line of fire!"

"*Just* Maggie?" I asked.

She smiled thinly. "Georgia Mason always knew how to defend herself." Then she was off and running, heading for the front door.

The rest of us followed her. George didn't complain as she ran, even though it must have been painful—the dressings on her feet were designed to deal with light walking, not a full-out sprint. She just gritted her teeth and kept going.

We left our shoes where they were. If they were bugged, they were more of a liability than a little barefoot running.

I could hear the Cat and the Monkey yelling at each other when we hit the front door, although I couldn't tell what they were saying. I wasn't aware that the Fox was following us until she took hold of my hand and asked, "Is this going to be *very* bad?"

Mahir and Becks were trying to pry the door open. The security system had clearly engaged once we were all inside, and it just as clearly didn't want to let go again. I exchanged a glance with George before looking back to the Fox. "Well . . ."

The sudden shriek of alarms stopped me from needing to figure out the rest of that sentence. Metal sheets slammed down over all the windows, and red lights came on at the tops of the walls, flashing almost fast enough to qualify as strobes. The Fox yelped, yanking her hand out of mine. As she clamped her hands over her ears, I saw that she was holding a nasty-looking sniper's pistol. At least she came prepared.

Becks kicked the door viciously before turning and jogging the few steps back over to me. "I'm going to go punch our host in the face until he lets us out of here," she said.

"Punch the woman instead; she seems to deserve it more," said Mahir. He walked back to where I was standing. "We're proper trapped now. Probably all going to die here. I'd say it was nice knowing you, but as you've effectively ruined my life, it almost certainly hasn't been."

"What he said," said Maggie.

"Aren't you sweet?" George was frowning at the door, looking thoughtful. "Hey, George? You planning something, there?"

"A place like this . . . Mahir, remember when we did the report on the clone organ farmers? The ones who were so used to getting raided that they almost treated it as a reason not to bother washing the windows?"

"Yes!" Mahir's eyes lit up. "They knew they'd be caught in a death trap if they ever let themselves be taken unaware—"

"—and so they never set up a headquarters without at least three escape routes." She turned to the Fox. "How do we get out? All our weapons are outside."

The Fox brightened, lowering her hands. "I have weapons!"

"We know you do, but we need *our* weapons. Please. How do we get out of here?"

"Oh." The Fox thought for a moment. Finally, she said, "This way," and trotted back toward the living room. Lacking anything better to do, we followed.

As we rounded the corner, we were greeted with the fascinating sight of Becks slamming the Cat rhythmically into the wall while the Monkey looked calmly on. "You're a feisty one," he said. "Do you have a boyfriend?"

The Cat wailed. Becks slammed her into a wall again.

"Last guy I was interested in turned out to be an incestuous necrophiliac," she said. "So no, not currently dating, and definitely not doing any more shopping in the 'sociopath' category. Now tell her to open the doors."

"She can't do that," said the Monkey. The Fox trotted past him without pausing; he turned to watch her go. "Foxy? What are you doing?"

"Opening the garage!" she called back cheerfully, before pulling a picture off the wall to reveal the control panel it had been concealing. She slapped her palm against it, and the light above the nearest door went from red to green.

A look of horror spread across the Monkey's face as he realized what she was doing. He lunged for her, one hand stretched out to grab her shoulder. "No! Don't! That's not—"

It was too late. The door swung open, revealing a garage packed with servers and computer terminals, and a garage door that was slowly rolling upward. As it rose, it exposed the men who were standing in the driveway between us and the van, their rifles trained on the house. They were all wearing hazmat suits, with rebreathers covering their mouths and noses.

"Oh," said the Fox. "Oopsie." Then she slammed the door.

The gunfire started a split second later.

Oh, don't worry. You don't need to tell *Alaric* what's going on. You don't need to tell *Alaric* who was in our system claiming to be Georgia Mason, or why the Seattle CDC is on CNN, in flames, or whether you're all still alive. *Alaric* likes sitting around with his thumb up his ass, waiting to find out whether he's got a bunch of funerals to not attend, since he's still under house arrest with the paranoid mad scientist brigade.

Assholes.

—From *The Kwong Way of Things*, the blog of Alaric Kwong, August 3, 2041. Unpublished.

Upon reflection, I must note that I have, in fact, had better days.

—From *Fish and Clips*, the blog of Mahir Gowda, August 3, 2041. Unpublished.

GEORGIA: Twenty-nine

None of this made any sense, and none of Shaun's explanations had done anything to help the situation. Not that it mattered. As soon as people started shooting, I stopped needing to understand and started needing to react. I ducked, grabbing Maggie's hand—she was the one with the least field experience, at least as far as I remembered—and dragging her around the corner into the living room. They'd need to shoot through more walls to get to us here.

"Shaun!" I shouted, hoping I'd be heard over the gunfire. "Get the hell out of there!"

"The wall's holding for now!" Shaun shouted back. Mahir rounded the corner, taking up a position on the other side of Maggie. He flashed me a wan smile.

My hand went to my waist, habit telling me that when I was dressed, I was also armed. There was nothing there but my belt. "Dammit, Shaun! If you don't have a secret escape plan, you need to make the crazy people give us guns!"

The woman they called the Cat shouted, "We don't let strangers go armed in this house!"

"Sort of a special circumstance, don't you think?" I demanded.

There was an answering burst of gunfire from the hall, followed by the sound of the door slamming. Someone who actually *had* a weapon must have opened the door, taken a shot at our attackers, and closed the door again. "I think everybody should have *lots* of guns!" said the cheerful, faintly lunatic voice of the little redhead. "Monkey, can we? Can we please give everybody guns?"

"Yes, Monkey, please?" asked Shaun. He backed into view, not joining our cluster against the wall, but getting farther away from the door to the garage. "We promise not to shoot up any more of your shit than is strictly necessary."

"Fascinating as diplomacy is, perhaps *during a firefight* is not the time?" Mahir sounded frantic, like he was the only one taking things seriously.

Shaun gave him a startled look. "Dude, chill. We're fine until they shoot through the door."

"Then we're fine for another ninety seconds," said the Monkey. "Foxy, give them guns."

"Yay!" The redhead ran to the other side of the living room. She opened what I'd taken for a coat closet, exposing enough weaponry to outfit a good-sized tabloid. Shaun whistled.

"Okay, I'm in love," he said.

"Fickle, fickle heart." I started for the open closet, the others following. This whole situation seemed faintly unreal. We were trapped in a decrepit-looking private home while a small army tried to shoot their way in. The fact that they hadn't already succeeded told me this place had some pretty good armor plating under the peeling paint. The people who lived here were concerned, but not panicked. That made it a little too easy to be casual about things, like there was no way we could get hurt.

We could get hurt. I'd already died once. That sort of thing tends to teach you that no one is invincible.

"Here!" The Fox handed me a revolver, and gave Shaun a semi-automatic handgun. She kept passing out guns, grinning like a kid on Christmas morning. "We're going to shoot them reeeeeeal good, so it's important everybody be ready to look their best!"

Shaun and I exchanged a look, his expression making it clear that he understood what was going on about as well as I did—which was to say, not at all. Somehow, that didn't make me feel any better.

The Monkey and the Cat joined us at the closet, both of them taking weapons of their own. The Cat glared at us the whole time, like this was somehow our fault.

"This is what's going to happen now." The Fox was suddenly calm, like having a group of armed men firing on her house was what it took to bring out her saner side. "We're going to go out the back door. We're going to circle around the side of the house. And then we're going to shoot those fuckers until they stop squirming. Any questions? No? Good. Follow me."

"I'm not sure which is worse," muttered Shaun. "The fact that we're following the crazy girl, or the fact that she sounds so damn happy about it."

"I'm going to go with 'the fact that we don't have a choice,'" said Becks. "Maggie, you're in the middle."

"Yes, I am," said Maggie, putting herself behind Becks and Shaun, and in front of me and Mahir. We followed the Fox, with the Cat and the Monkey bringing up the rear. I had the distinct feeling we were being used as human shields. Not that it mattered. There were men with guns outside, and as long as the Cat and the Monkey weren't shooting us in the back, I didn't care where they walked. I already knew we couldn't count on them.

We reached the Fox as she was prying the last sheets of plywood off the back door. Shaun stepped in and helped her finish, revealing a pre-Rising sliding glass door that had been boarded over for good reason.

"This place was a death trap," I muttered.

Mahir shot me a half-amused glance. "Was?" he asked.

It felt odd to be laughing during a firefight. Then again, if you can't laugh when you're about to die, when can you? The sound of gunfire covered any noises we might make, at least until we left the house.

The back porch had been reinforced at some point, more structural improvement concealed by a veil of cosmetic decay. The seemingly rotten wooden steps had no give to them at all. The Fox slunk through the knee-high grass as quietly as her namesake. I tried to emulate her, failing utterly as the gravel beneath the grass bit into my already injured feet. The best I could manage was not making any more noise than was absolutely necessary as I followed the rest of the group to the corner.

Once we were there, the Fox turned, smiled at the rest of us, sketched a curtsey clumsy enough to seem entirely sincere, and bolted back the way we'd come.

The Monkey realized what she was doing before the rest of us did—he knew her better than anyone, except for maybe the Cat, who had already locked her free hand around his elbow. He tried to run after the Fox as she pelted up the porch steps and back into the house. The Cat held him back.

"No," she hissed. "Do that, and this was for nothing."

He turned to look at her, a cold anger burning in her eyes. "Don't think I'll forgive you."

The Cat didn't say anything.

The sound of gunshots from the front of the house suddenly took on a new, more frantic timbre, accompanied by the distant but recognizable sound of the Fox's laughter. At least someone was having a good day. Shaun looked back to me.

"There's no plan B," he said.

I nodded. "I know."

There was no one left for us to run to, and nowhere to run except the van. That meant we had to take the opportunity the Fox had created for us, no matter how insane that opportunity seemed. Shaun looked to Becks, making a complex gesture with one hand. She nodded, picking up on his unspoken command. I felt a flush of jealousy. Just how close had they gotten while I was dead, anyway?

I forced the feeling away. It was none of my business, and even if it was, this wasn't the time. The Fox was still laughing, but it had a pained edge to it, like she was running out of steam. It was now or never. Being occasionally suicidal, but not stupid, we chose now.

It wasn't until we were running around to the front of the house that I realized the Cat was no longer with us. The Monkey was running alongside Mahir, but his . . . whatever she was . . . was gone. The Fox was still shooting from the kitchen window, keeping the majority of the team in the driveway occupied through sheer dint of being impossible to ignore. Either her aim was incredibly good or she was using armor-piercing bullets; five of them were already down, leaving another nine standing. Part of me was pleased to see that they'd considered a bunch of journalists enough of a threat to send fourteen armed CDC guards to take us down. The rest of me wished they'd been willing to settle for a sternly worded cease-and-desist-letter.

Journalism must have been very different before people resolved so many of their conflicts with bullets.

The men from the CDC were so busy shooting at the house that we made it halfway to the van before they noticed us. Three more of them went down in the interim. I was starting to think we might make it when the Fox screamed, a gasping, quickly cut-off sound, and the gunfire from the house stopped. The Monkey froze, face going white. Then he screamed and rushed toward the driveway, opening fire as he ran.

The guards who were still standing turned toward the sound of gunfire. "Oh, sh—" began Shaun, and then they were firing on us, and there was no time left for conversation.

Maggie and Mahir hit the ground, leaving Becks, Shaun, and I to return fire. Fortunately for us, the guards were distracted by the Monkey's suicide charge; he took down two of the six remaining men before going down in a hail of blood and bullets. That left four standing, all with more firepower and better armor than we had. Our next step didn't need to be discussed. We stopped firing, raising hands and weapons toward the sky. If we were lucky, they'd want prisoners they could question even more than they'd want bodies they could bury.

Luck was with us. The man at the front of their ragged little formation signaled for the others to stop firing. He held out one hand, palm facing us, and then gestured toward the ground, indicating that we should put our guns down. We knelt to do as we were told. It might have ended there, except for one crucial detail:

The Fox hadn't been trying for headshots.

My hand was still on my borrowed revolver when the first of the downed guards lurched to his feet and grabbed for the still-living man beside him. His chosen victim screamed and started firing wildly. His commander shouted for him to stand down, but it was too late; panic had already set in. Four men suddenly finding themselves surrounded by nine potential zombies weren't going to listen to orders anymore.

Grabbing my gun from the ground, I ran full-tilt for the van, trusting the others to follow me and praying the zombies would be so busy going for the accessible prey that they'd let us by.

There were no bullet holes in the van. That was something. Becks and I reached it first, ducking behind the bulk of it while she fired at the guards and I fumbled with the door. The blood test cycle to open it had never seemed so long. Mahir reached us as I was waiting for the door to finish processing, leaving only Shaun and Maggie in the open—and Maggie was still on the ground, not moving.

"Oh, fuck," I breathed. The lock disengaged. I jerked the door open, motioning for the others to climb in. Mahir promptly clambered over the driver's seat and into the back, bypassing the blood test.

Becks shook her head, digging a set of keys out of her pocket and tossing them to me. "I'll cover you! Now hurry!"

"On it." I slammed the door, shoved the keys into the ignition, and started the engine, hitting the gas hard enough to send Mahir sprawling. Becks waited until she was clear and then opened fire on the guards, living and dead alike.

Driving was another thing I didn't have the muscle memory for anymore, even if I intellectually understood the process. I barely managed to skid to a stop in front of Shaun and Maggie, the tires digging deep divots in the lawn. Mahir opened the side door and hopped out, helping Shaun lift Maggie inside. The entire front of her blouse was bloody.

"Is she breathing?" Mahir demanded.

"Yes," said Shaun. "First-aid kit, *now*." He slammed the door. "George, get Becks."

Becks had taken cover behind a half-fallen pine tree that listed at a severe angle across one side of the tiny courtyard. She was firing at the two guards who remained standing, but their attention was more focused on their formerly dead compatriots, who were still attempting to take them down. I pulled up next to her and she grabbed the passenger-side door, waiting impatiently for the lock to release.

"Oh, God, there's so much blood," moaned Mahir. I didn't let myself look. I needed to focus on getting us out of here alive.

The door opened. Becks climbed inside. I looked back toward the house and saw the Fox waving weakly from the window, blood running down the side of her face. She had what looked like a remote control in one hand. Becks looked that way, and her eyes widened.

"Oh, fuck," she breathed. "Georgia, *drive*."

I hit the gas.

We were all the way to the end of the driveway when the house exploded.

The edge of the explosion caught us, hot wind buffeting the van. The frame was weighted to make it harder to tip us over, but even so, it was a struggle to maintain control of the steering wheel. In the back, Maggie screamed. That was almost encouraging. If she was screaming like that, they hadn't managed to puncture a lung, and with two Irwins playing field medic, she might be able to hold on long enough to get us—

I had no living clue where we were going, and no one else was available to take the wheel. "Where am I going?" I demanded.

"Take us back to the Agora!" shouted Shaun. "Just tell the GPS to retrace the last route we took. It can guide you from—aw, fuck, Becks, keep the pressure on, will you?"

Wincing, I turned on the GPS, tapping the screen twice to make it show me the way back to the Agora. A red light came on above the rearview mirror as the GPS began scrolling the names of streets. "Shaun, I'm getting a contamination warning up here."

"That's because Maggie's bleeding all over the fucking van!"

"Still showing clean here," said Mahir. His voice was tight, verging on panicked. "Becks, how's her breathing?"

I took a deep breath and tightened my hands on the wheel, trying to focus on the road. Maggie was shot, not bitten. Her blood would be a problem, especially if she ran out of it completely, but as long as no one else had open wounds on their hands . . . or on their legs . . . or anywhere else . . .

We were fucked. We were thoroughly and completely fucked, and all we had to show for it was a bunch of corpses and a house that wasn't even there anymore.

As if he had read my mind, Shaun called, with manic cheerfulness, "Don't stress out about it, George. Things could be worse!"

"*How*?" demanded Becks.

"We could still be wearing shoes full of homing devices!"

For the first time since she'd been shot, Maggie spoke: "I am going to . . . kill you . . . *myself*, Shaun Mason." Her voice was weak, but it was there. If she was talking, she couldn't be too far gone.

Shaun laughed unsteadily. "You do that, Maggie. You get up and kick my ass just as soon as you feel like you can manage it."

She mumbled something in disjointed Spanish, voice losing strength with every word.

"This would be a good time to drive a little faster, Georgia," said Mahir. His tone was utterly calm. I recognized that for the danger sign it really was. Mahir only sounded that serene when he was on the verge of panic, or getting ready to pounce on some fact that every other reporter to look at a story had somehow managed to miss. That detachment was the way he handled the things that otherwise couldn't be handled at all.

I pressed my foot down on the gas, envying that cool veil of calm. It was all I could do not to start hyperventilating as we blew through downtown Seattle, slowing down only when the lights forced me or I had to take a turn. I doubt I could have done it under pre-Rising speed limits, back when they worried more about pedestrian safety than they did about getting people from point A to point B as quickly as humanly possible. I was still running the very edge of "safe driving" when the GPS signaled for me to slow down; we were approaching our destination.

We were approaching our destination in a vehicle that was essentially a traveling biohazard zone. "Guys?" I asked. "Now what am I supposed to do?"

Maggie mumbled something. It must have made more sense to the people around her, because Mahir spoke a moment later, saying, "When we reach the gate, roll down your window but do not attempt to put any part of your body outside the car. Tell them Maggie is injured—use her full name—and that we need immediate medical assistance. The Agora has protocols that will take it from there."

"Do those protocols include a full tank of formalin with our names on it?" asked Shaun. Nobody answered him. He sighed. "Yeah, I figured as much."

The Agora gatehouse was in front of us. I slowed, finally stopping the van as the guards approached. The urge to slam my foot down on the gas and go racing off to anywhere else was overwhelming . . . and pointless. Driving away wouldn't make things any better.

I rolled down my window when the first guard reached the van, careful to stay well away from the opening. "We have an injured hotel guest," I said. "She was shot."

The guard's expression of polite helpfulness didn't falter. "Would you like the address of the nearest hospital with field decontamination capacity?" he asked.

"I'm sorry, I said that wrong. Magdalene Grace Garcia is in the back of this van, and she has been shot. We need immediate medical assistance." I hesitated before adding, "Please."

The effect Maggie's name had on the man was nothing short of electric. His expression flickered from politely helpful to shocked to narrow-eyed efficiency in a matter of seconds. "Drive through the front gate and follow the lighted indicators next to the road," he said. "Do not attempt to leave your vehicle. A medical team will meet you at your destination." Almost as an afterthought, he said, "Please roll up your window."

"Thank you," I said. He stepped away, and I rolled the window up before putting my foot back on the gas. The gate opened as we rolled forward, and bright blue lights began flicking on next to the driveway, indicating our route.

The lights followed the obvious path to the Agora for about a hundred yards before branching off, leading us down a groundkeeper's road that had been cunningly surrounded by bushes and flowering shrubs, making it almost unnoticeable if you didn't know it was there—or weren't following a bunch of bright blue lights. I kept driving, inching our speed up as high as I dared. The road led us around the back of the Agora to a separate parking garage with plastic sheeting hanging over the entrance.

I took a breath and drove on through.

The garage was brightly lit, and already swarming with people in white EMT moon suits, their hands covered by plastic gloves and their faces by clear masks. I managed to kill the engine before they started knocking on the van's side door, but only barely. The door slid open, and suddenly the van was rocking as EMTs poured through the opening.

Someone knocked on my window, making me jump. I turned to see another of the EMTs looking through the glass at me. I lowered the window. "Ma'am, please leave your vehicle and prepare for decontamination," he said, voice muffled by his mask.

A chill wormed down my spine. The idea of going through decontamination—of going through *any* medical procedure, no matter how standard—was suddenly terrifying.

The others were climbing out of the van. Mahir and Becks were already in front of the van, being led along by more EMTs. I knew Shaun would wait for me as long as he could, unwilling to let me out of his sight if he didn't have to. That was what it took to spur me into motion. I didn't want Shaun getting sedated because I wasn't willing to get out of my seat.

One of the EMTs grasped my upper arm firmly as soon as my feet hit the asphalt, not waiting for me to shut the door before he began pulling me toward the building. I didn't resist, but I didn't help him, either, letting my feet drag as I looked frantically around for Shaun. He was being led toward the building by another of the EMTs. He broke loose as soon as he saw me, ignoring the way his EMT was shouting as he ran in my direction.

"Shaun!"

He stopped in front of me. There was blood on the front of his shirt, but his hands were clean. Either he'd been wearing gloves, or he'd somehow managed to avoid touching Maggie. Given what I'd heard from the back, that seemed unlikely. He'd played it smart. For once. "Are you okay? Are you hurt? Things were so hectic back there, I didn't have time to—"

"I'm fine, but I think you're scaring the locals."

"What?" Shaun looked over his shoulder, seeming to notice the EMTs for the first time. They were all holding pistols now, and those pistols were aimed in our direction. Smiling cockily, Shaun waved.

I doubt any of them saw the hollow fear behind his eyes. I doubt anyone but me would even have realized it was there. "Hey, fellas. Sorry to frighten you like that. I just have a thing about being separated from my sister. Makes me sort of impulsive."

"Makes you sort of *insane*," I corrected, without thinking. Then I winced. "Shaun . . ."

"No, that's pretty much true." Four more EMTs walked by us, carrying a stretcher between them. A clear plastic sheet covered it, Maggie visible underneath. A respirator was covering her face. I just hoped that meant that she was still breathing, and that she still stood a chance of recovery.

"Sir, ma'am, you need to come with me now." I glanced toward the EMT holding my arm. He looked at us sternly through his mask. "I understand your concern, but we need to clear and sterilize this area."

Shaun's eyes widened. "Our van—"

"Will be returned to you once it has been decontaminated. Now please, sir, you both need to come with me."

Shaun and I exchanged a look. Then we nodded, almost in unison. "All right," I said. "Let's go and get decontaminated."

The EMT led us out of the garage and into the building. Metal jets emerged from the ceiling as we stepped into the airlock, beginning to spray a thin mist down over the area. The smell of it managed to sneak through the closing doors, tickling my nose with the characteristic burning scent of formalin. I shuddered. Nothing organic was going to survive that dousing.

"We're going to need to replace the rug again," commented Shaun.

I glanced at him, startled, before starting to laugh under my breath. I couldn't help it. He looked so sincere, and so annoyed, like replacing the rug was the worst thing that had happened to us in a while. Shaun blinked, his own surprised expression mirroring mine. Then he started laughing with me.

We were both still laughing when the EMT led us out of the airlock and into the Agora Medical Center. My laughter died almost instantly, replaced by a feeling of choking suffocation. White walls. White ceiling. White floor. The EMTs looked suddenly hostile behind their plastic masks, like they had been sent by the CDC to take me back.

"George?" Shaun's voice was distant. "You okay?"

"Not really," I replied. I turned to the startled EMT who had led us inside. "Do you have a room with some color in it? I have a thing about white." It made me want to curl up in a corner and cry. A phobia of medical establishments. That was a fun new personality trait.

Working at the Agora had apparently prepared the man for strange requests from people above his pay grade—which we, traveling with Maggie, technically were. "Right this way, miss," he said, and turned to lead us away from the rest of the action. I felt a brief pang of regret over letting us be separated from the others, but quashed it. The EMT assigned to work with me and Shaun wasn't one of the ones who was needed to help Maggie, or he wouldn't have been with us in the first place. Me having a panic attack over the white, white walls wasn't going to do anything to help anyone.

The EMT led us to a smaller room where the walls were painted a cheery yellow and the chairs were upholstered in an equally cheery blue. We didn't need to be told that this was the children's holding area. The testing panels on the walls and the double-reinforced glass on the observation window cut into the room's rear wall made that perfectly clear.

Oddly, the window made me feel better, rather than setting my nerves even further on edge. It was honest glass, letting the observed see the observers without any subterfuge. If it had been a mirror, I think I would have lost my shit.

"If you're feeling better now, ma'am, sir, I would very much appreciate it if you'd let me begin the testing process."

Shaun and I exchanged a look, and I jumped a little as the blood on his shirt fully registered. Maggie wasn't dead when she was bleeding on him. That didn't mean her blood couldn't potentially carry a hot viral load.

"Please," I said.

"Sure," said Shaun, sounding oddly unconcerned. I frowned at him. He mouthed the word "later," and gave me what may have been intended as a reassuring smile.

I was not reassured.

The EMT produced two small blood test units, using them to take samples from our index fingers. No lights came on to document the filtration process. Instead, he sealed the kits in plastic bags marked "biohazard," nodded as politely as a bellhop who'd been doing nothing more hazardous than delivering our luggage, and left the room. The door closed behind him with a click and a beep that clearly indicated that we had been locked in.

Shaun looked at me. "You okay?"

"No." I shook my head. "Is Maggie going to be okay?"

"I don't know." Shaun folded his arms, looking at the closed door. "I guess we'll find out soon enough."

"Yeah. I guess we will." We stood there in silence, waiting for the door to open; waiting for someone to come and tell us how many of us were going to walk away alive.

When Maggie went down ... fuck.

Maggie was one of the first people Buffy hired after we said "sure, we want a viable Fiction section." She's never been anything but awesome. She took us in when we had nowhere else to go; she took care of us when we would have been frankly fucked without her. She's been our rock. If Mahir is the soul of this news team—and I'm not an idiot, I know that when George died, the mantle went to him, and that's cool, because I never wanted it in the first place—then Maggie is the heart. And when she went down today, the only thing I could think was "Thank God it was her. Thank God it wasn't George. I don't think I could survive that happening again."

George being back is a miracle, and it's also what's going to mean this all ends bad, because I'm not thinking straight anymore. I lived without her once. I can't do it again.

Fuck.

—From *Adaptive Immunities*, the blog of Shaun Mason, August 4, 2041. Unpublished.

Madre de Dios ... Mother Mary, hold me closely; Mother Mary, love me best. Mother Mary, treat me sweetly. Mother Mary, let me rest.

I have never hurt this much in my life. Morphine is supposed to make the hurting stop, but instead, it shunts the pain to the side, like a houseguest you never intended to keep. It isn't in your face, but it's there, using the last of the milk, leaving wet towels on the bathroom floor . . .

This hurts. I am alive. The two balance each other, I suppose.

This was supposed to be Buffy's revolution. It was never supposed to be mine.

—From *Dandelion Mine*, the blog of Magdalene Grace Garcia, August 4, 2041. Unpublished.

SHAUN: Thirty

I don't know how long they left us in that room. Long enough that George was pale and freaking out a little by the time they came back, even though she was trying pretty damn hard to hide it. I watched her anxiously, not sure what I was supposed to do. She'd never had a problem with hospitals before. Then again, I guess being brought back from the dead and used as a CDC lab rat would fuck up just about anybody.

The delay may have put George's nerves on edge, but it helped settle mine. When those bullets started flying . . . there was a time when that would have elated me. With George in the field, all it did was make me sick to my stomach. She could have been hit. I could have lost her again. *Again.* And I couldn't even grab her and hold on until I stopped feeling sick, because there was blood on my shirt. If it was hot, even touching her could kill her. I should never have grabbed her hand. I should have stayed away from her and observed proper quarantine procedures. And I *couldn't*.

It was sort of ironic. I couldn't catch the live form of Kellis-Amberlee because I'd managed to catch the immunity from her, and now that she was back where she belonged, she didn't have that same protection. Even when I was safe, she wasn't.

"I hate the world sometimes," I muttered.

"What?" George stopped staring at the wall, turning to look at me instead. She removed her sunglasses, rubbing her left eye with the heel of her hand. "Do you think we'll find out what's happening soon?"

"I hope so." I sighed. "All that for nothing. We didn't get the damn IDs."

"Didn't those people send you to the CDC?"

"Yeah, they did."

"So it wasn't for nothing." George shrugged, trying—and failing—to look nonchalant as she said, "It got you me."

I was still trying to find a response for that when the door opened and the EMT who had escorted us inside stepped through. He was wearing clean scrubs, and the plastic face mask was gone. We both turned to face him, waiting for his verdict.

"We apologize for any inconvenience the delay may have caused. Miss Garcia required immediate attention," he said. "If you'd come with me, I'd be happy to take you to your party."

"Does that mean we're cool?" I asked.

The EMT nodded. "Yes, Mr. Mason. You're both in fine health. Your internal viral loads are well within normal safety perimeters. Now if you would please come with me?"

"Right." George looked faintly ill. "Back to the white rooms."

"Hey." She looked my way. I smiled at her. "I'm here. It's all different now."

"Yeah." George returned my smile before turning to the EMT. "Lead the way."

We followed him back to the hall where we had first entered. The sound and motion that had been my only real impression of the place was all gone now, replaced by cool, sterile peacefulness. If it hadn't been for the airlock looking out on the garage, I would never have realized it was the same hall. George kept her eyes locked straight ahead, looking like she was going to be sick at any moment. I just hoped no one would see her and take that for a sign of spontaneous amplification. Another fire drill was the last thing that we needed at the moment.

She relaxed a little when we passed through a sliding door and into a hall where the walls were painted a pale cream yellow. Interesting. It was just the white that bothered her. I made a mental note to punch the next CDC employee I saw in the face.

"Mr. Mason, Miss Mason, at this point, I do need to ask that you proceed through these doors," the EMT indicated two doors in the wall to our right, one marked "Men," the other marked "Women." "There will be clean clothes available for you to wear while yours are being sterilized."

I glanced at George. "You going to be okay with this?"

She laughed unsteadily. "If I can't handle a basic sterilization cycle, I may as well give up and go back to the . . . go back to the place where you found me right now. I'll be fine."

"Okay." I risked reaching out and squeezing her hand before stepping through the appropriate door.

The room on the other side was small and square, and—to my relief—tiled in industrial gray. I could have kissed whoever was responsible for that particular decorating choice. As long as the women's side was decorated the same way, George might not flip out. As expected, there were no windows, and a large drain was set in the middle of the floor. The door I'd arrived through was behind me. Another was on the wall directly in front of me.

"Hello, Shaun," said the pleasant voice of the Agora. "Welcome back."

"Thanks," I said, hauling my shirt off over my head. "Where do you want me to put my clothes?"

A hatch slid open in one wall. I hadn't even been able to see the outline of it in the tile. "Please place your clothes in the opening to your left. I promise they will not be damaged in any way by the cleaning process. We are only interested in your comfort and well-being."

"Great." I finished stripping before shoving my clothes, shoes and all, through the hatch. I held up my pistol. "What do you want done with the weapons?"

"Please place them in the same location. They will be separated out before the cleansing process begins."

"Right." I wasn't happy with that answer. I didn't see another way. Automated sterilization systems can get mean when they feel like protocol is being violated, and no matter how nice the Agora was programmed to be, refusing to give up my weapons would qualify as violating protocol. I placed them in the opening with everything else, barely pulling my hand back before the hatch slammed closed again.

"Thank you for your cooperation, Shaun," said the Agora. "Please move to the center of the room and close your eyes. Sterilization will commence once you are in the correct position."

"On it," I said. I moved to position myself directly over the drain, closed my eyes, and tilted my face toward the ceiling. The water turned on a second later, raining down on me from what felt like half a dozen differently angled jets. I didn't open my eyes to find out.

Sterilization follows the same basic protocols no matter where you are or how high class a place pretends to be. First they boil you, then they bleach you, then they boil you again. If the powers that be could get away with dipping us all in lye, they'd probably do it, just to be able to say that one more layer of "safety" had been slapped on. The Agora was nicer about it than it technically had to be; the hot water lasted almost thirty seconds, followed by eight seconds of bleach, and then a citrus-scented foam that oozed down from more jets in the ceiling. Sterilization *and* a shower.

Twice, the Agora instructed me to change positions or turn, letting the bleach, hot water, and cleansing foam cover every part of me. The hot water jets were repeated three times; the bleach was only repeated once. Guess I was dirtier than I was potentially diseased.

Finally, the water turned off, and the Agora said, "Thank you for your cooperation."

"Didn't you say that, like, five minutes ago?" I opened my eyes. The door in front of me was open, revealing an antechamber that looked like the locker room of a really upscale gym.

"My range of programmed responses is wide, but sometimes, repetition is inevitable," said the Agora patiently. "If you would like to register a complaint—"

"That's okay," I said, cutting the hotel off midsentence. "Thanks for the scrub. Do I get pants in the next room?"

"Yes, Shaun," said the Agora.

"Awesome," I said, and proceeded on. The "pants" were drawstring cotton, purple with the Agora logo over the hip, like they were advertising a high school pep team. The bathrobe that went with them was a few shades darker, with the same logo. I pulled everything on, checked to be sure the ties were tight, and stepped out the door in the far wall.

George was waiting in the hall, tugging anxiously at the sleeves of her own bathrobe. Her feet were bare, the legs of her sweatpants pooling over their tops, and her sunglasses were gone. Without a medical condition to make them mandatory, she could have them confiscated at every sterilization checkpoint we encountered. Another EMT was standing nearby, using that weird gift that some people in service industries seem to possess, and basically blending into the furniture.

I ignored her, focusing on George. "Hey," I said. "All clean?"

"All clean." She sighed, giving up on tugging her sleeves into place. "Do you think that after we see how Maggie's doing, we can get me a can of Coke?"

"We can get you a *gallon* of Coke," I said.

"Good." She looked to the EMT. "Where to now?"

"This way," said the EMT. She started down the hallway and we followed, only lagging by a few steps. The hall ended at a pair of sliding glass doors, which opened to reveal a small but well-appointed hospital waiting room. There was even an admissions desk, with a woman sitting behind it, tapping away at her computer.

"The Masons are here for Miss Garcia," called the EMT, as she led us past the desk. The other woman nodded, looking up with a smile. Her fingers kept moving the whole time, and her eyes snapped quickly back to the screen.

"Do you get many medical emergencies here?" asked George.

"The Agora is proud to provide hospital services to our guests, both past and present," said the EMT. "We have patients most days, seeing our private doctors. It offers a guarantee of privacy and discretion that is unfortunately not present in many more public hospitals."

"Better care for rich people, right?" I said. "Figures."

George didn't say anything. She just looked thoughtfully around as we followed the EMT past a row of unlabeled doors, finally pausing at one that looked like all the others.

"A moment, please," said the EMT, and pushed the door open, vanishing inside. Only a few seconds passed before she pushed the door open again, this time holding it to let us through. "Miss Garcia will see you now."

"Awesome," I said, and stepped past her into the room. I stopped dead just past the threshold, too stunned to speak.

George ducked in behind me. After a few startled seconds, she said, "Remind me to come here the next time I decide to get hurt."

"You and me both," I said.

The halls of the Agora's medical center might look like the ones you'd find at any other upscale hospital, but the patient rooms were something completely different, at least if Maggie's was anything to go by. The walls were painted a warm amber, and there was actual carpet on the floor—easy-clean industrial carpet, sure, but a world of luxury away from normal hospital tile. The only medical equipment in sight was a flat-screen display that flickered periodically between images, apparently doing the work of multiple monitors.

Maggie was lying in the middle of a comfortable-looking bed with a wine red comforter and more pillows than anyone needs, sick or not. She was too pale, especially for her. An IV was connected to her left arm, and there were sensor patches on her collarbones, but apart from that, she could have been taking a nap. Mahir was sitting to one side of the bed; Becks was standing near the wall. They both turned to look at us.

There was a moment of awkward silence before Mahir said, "If Maggie were awake and mobile, this is doubtless the point where she would leap to her feet, announce how worried she'd been, and run to embrace you. Please forgive me if I choose to take all that as written, and move straight to asking what the bloody hell we're meant to do now."

I nodded. "Forgiven. How is she?"

"The bullet went clean through. That's about the only good thing I can say about it." Becks didn't look at Maggie as she spoke. She didn't really look at us, either; her gaze was fixed on the wall, preventing anything uncomfortable, like eye contact. "Several of her internal organs were damaged, and her liver was nicked. She lost a lot of blood."

"But she didn't amplify," I said.

"No. She's going to be fine. They're transfusing her with scrubbed plasma and filtering as much of the viral load out of her bloodstream as they can, but she never started to amplify."

"What Rebecca isn't saying is that Maggie came very, very close to crossing that line, and she can't be moved." Mahir dropped his head into his hands, voice muffled as he said, "She can't be moved, and you can't stay here. This is a disaster."

"No, it's not," I said. For a moment—just a moment—I wished the George who only existed in my head would speak up and tell me what to say. Then I glanced to the George who was standing beside me, alive and breathing and as lost as the rest of us, and the moment passed. "Maggie can't be moved, but she'll be safe here. The Agora would never let anything happen to her, and she wasn't involved with the actual break-in at the CDC, so it's not like she can be accused of anything more criminal than letting herself get shot."

"Harboring fugitives," said Becks.

"Criminal negligence—she should never have left the van," said Mahir.

"Being a journalist," said George. The rest of us turned to her, startled. She shook her head, expression grim. "I read as much of the last year's site archive as I could before we left to get shot at. Whoever's running this game, they don't like journalists, and they're not discriminating between the branches. To them, a blogger's a blogger."

"She's right," whispered Maggie.

Mahir raised his head. Becks whipped around to face the bed. Maggie's eyes were still closed, but there was a tension in her that hadn't been there when we entered the room, a tension that spoke of consciousness.

"You know . . . they're targeting the bloggers," whispered Maggie. Every word seemed heavy, like it was being dragged out of her. "Martial law in Florida. Arrests all over the country. They're . . . hiding something."

"Hey. Hey. Don't try to talk, honey. You need to save your strength." Becks moved to crouch down next to Mahir. Looking at the three of them, I felt suddenly left out, like they had formed a unit I wasn't meant to be part of. Then George touched my elbow with one hand, the sort of quick, subtle contact that had always been the limit we allowed ourselves in public, and I realized they'd formed their unit because they understood—probably before I did—that they were never really going to be a part of mine.

I was always going to be a haunted house. The only difference was that now my ghost wore flesh and held me when I needed her. Somehow, that made it better . . . but it didn't stop the realization from hurting.

"No. Need to talk." Maggie struggled to open her eyes, managing a single blink before they closed again. "Shaun, you have to . . . you have to take Georgia and go. Go back to Dr. Abbey. She'll know another way to hide you."

"What about you?" I asked.

The ghost of a smile flitted across her face. "I am going to lie here until I can feel my toes. And then I'll ask the concierge to call my parents so I can tell them that the CDC is being naughty."

Mahir actually laughed. "Well, that'll certainly complicate things in our favor."

"You have to stay with her," said Becks.

"What?" Mahir twisted to face her, eyes narrowing. "I don't believe I heard you correctly."

"I'm staying out of this," I murmured to George. She nodded, not saying anything.

"One of us has to stay here and make sure Maggie keeps breathing until her parents get here—and that if she stops, there's someone ready to tell them the real story." Becks grimaced. "Sorry, Maggie."

"It's okay," Maggie said, another ghostly smile crossing her face. "Medical family, remember? I don't kid myself about things like this." The smile faded, replaced by a grimace. "Could've done without getting shot, though."

"And I'm volunteered to remain behind precisely why?" Mahir demanded.

"Shaun's crazy, Georgia's a clone, and I'm prepared to shoot them both if they so much as look at me funny. Whereas you have virtually no field experience, and have never shot someone you care about."

"I've had field experience," said Mahir.

"Was any of it voluntary?" asked George.

He grimaced. "No," he admitted. "But I don't care one bit for being the one who gets sidelined. It seems that's always what you lot do right before you kick off the endgame. Remember Sacramento?"

"Bet I remember it better than you do," said George quietly.

Mahir grimaced again. "I'm sorry. But you take my point."

"Yeah," I said. "You lived. You're staying here, Mahir, and Becks is coming with us. You'll like Dr. Abbey, George. She's probably clinically insane, but she's good people, and that's harder to come by than sanity these days."

Maggie made a thin choking sound that made us all freeze, until we realized she was trying to laugh. "You people," she whispered finally. "You still think any of this is a choice. Get out of here. Get in your van, and get out of here, and finish it. Do you hear me? *Finish it.*" This time, she managed to force her eyes open for almost five whole seconds, glaring at us. "Finish it, or I swear, I will die, and come back, and *haunt* you."

"I've had enough of being haunted," I said. "We'll finish it. But only because you asked so nicely, Maggie."

"I can live with that," she said, eyes drifting closed again. "Now go 'way. I want to sleep. Can't do that with all you reporters here staring at me."

Mahir stood, pausing long enough to glare at me before he stalked out of the room. Becks walked back to Maggie, bending to kiss her on the forehead. Then she followed Mahir, leaving me and George alone with Maggie.

"Let's go," I said.

"Wait," whispered Maggie.

We froze.

"Tell her to come here."

I glanced at George, who stared back at me, eyes wide and somehow helpless. I nodded. She sighed, nodding back, and walked over to Maggie.

"I'm here."

"Closer."

George leaned down until her ear was next to Maggie's mouth. Maggie whispered something, expression as urgent as her voice was weak. George hesitated before replying, "I understand. And yes. I promise."

"Good," said Maggie, loud enough for me to hear. "Now go."

George walked away from the bed, looking unsettled. She didn't pause before leaving the room. I followed her, grabbing her arm before she could head for the admissions desk, where Mahir and Becks were speaking with the EMT.

"Hey," I said. "What did she say to you?"

George turned to face me, her eyes meeting mine with a directness that her sunglasses had always prevented before. "She said that if I'm even a little bit Georgia Mason, I'll kill myself before I'll let the CDC use me to hurt you more than they already have. And I agreed.

"I *think* I'm mostly me, Shaun. I really do. But I know that mostly isn't entirely. If there's any chance I'm less myself than I think I am—if I feel even the slightest bit like I might be slipping—I will take myself out of the picture." Her smile was humorless. "I won't be the one who stops you from avenging me."

There was nothing I could say to that.

We think we have an idea where she's been, if not where she's going. There was an explosion in one of the supposedly deserted neighborhoods; police found evidence of a massive amount of computer equipment there. It's possible she and her friends were trying to buy themselves new identities when something went wrong. How things went wrong, I don't know. We thought we'd removed all the tracking devices from her body. If we didn't . . .

If we didn't, you may have to prepare yourself for the idea that all of this was for nothing. There's nothing we can do now but wait and see what happens next.

—Taken from a message sent by Dr. Gregory Lake to Vice President Richard Cousins, August 5, 2041.

Alaric took less than kindly to the message that Maggie had been injured and I was remaining behind to tend her while the others returned to the lab. I didn't mention Georgia. There's complicating matters, and then there's blowing up Parliament just so you can make a few adjustments to the seating chart. He'll find out soon enough.

Please God we all get out of this alive. Please God Maggie gets better. I want to go home. I want to see my wife again.

I want this all to be over.

—From *Fish and Clips*, the blog of Mahir Gowda, August 5, 2041. Unpublished.

GEORGIA: Thirty-one

We left the Agora shortly after sunset, when the cleanup crew declared the van road-serviceable and unlikely to infect and kill us all. Shaun took the wheel, since Becks wasn't willing to let me drive. She said it was because I didn't have a license; from the way she refused to meet my eyes while she was saying it, I suspected it was more an issue of her not quite trusting me yet. I couldn't blame her. If I'd been in her position, and someone I'd already buried had come back . . . yeah. It was a miracle any of them trusted me at all. A miracle, or the kind of madness that was going to get us all killed.

With no real idea where we were going, and nothing I could do to help, I contented myself with pulling up the site archive on the local server and reading as we drove down the length of Washington State and into Oregon. This was a slower, more careful read than my earlier looting for information; I could take the time to really absorb what I was looking at, rather than just clicking the next report as quickly as possible. There was even a link to the site's financials. I was somehow unsurprised to see that Shaun had maintained ownership of my files, and was using them to finance a large percentage of the site's overhead. I was one of the higher-profile journalist deaths since the Rising. That made me fascinating, and made my previously unpublished op-ed pieces lucrative, even when they'd been written to parallel events that happened years before. That's the human race. Always willing to slow down and look at the train wreck.

Becks kept watch from the passenger seat while Shaun drove. The route he chose involved a disturbing number of frontage roads and narrow trails that were basically glorified footpaths. He drove them like they were familiar, and after everything that he and the others had been through since I died, they probably were. I stopped reading and leaned back in my seat, closing my eyes for just a moment, missing the familiar ache I used to get whenever I forced myself to look at a brightly lit computer screen for too long. I never thought I'd miss having retinal KA, but now it was just one more thing about my life that I was never going to get back.

This was my fault. I was the one who pressured Shaun into agreeing to follow the Ryman campaign, and together we'd strong-armed Buffy into going along with us. If I'd just been willing to work my way up through the ranks the way everyone else did, taking it one step at a time instead of rocketing straight to the top—

Then someone else would have died in my place, and in Buffy's place, and someone else's brother would be the one making this drive. This was all going to happen eventually. The only thing that made us special was the thing that has distinguished one journalist from another since the first reporter found a way to distinguish gossip from the real headline story: We were the ones on the scene when everything went down. We weren't better. We weren't worse. We were just the ones standing in the blast radius.

Everything that happened from there was inevitable.

That didn't absolve us of blame—there's always blame when the wrong stories get told and the wrong secrets get out—but even if we weren't innocent now, we were then. We really believed in what we were doing. It wasn't our fault that we were wrong.

I drifted off reading Alaric's analysis of the political situation after Ryman's election—situation normal, all fucked up, with some interesting developments in the regulation of larger mammals and a few changes to the rules for determining hazard zones, but nothing earth-shaking—and woke to see the first rays of false dawn painting the edge of the sky in shades of pollution pink and caution tape gold. Becks was driving. Shaun was asleep in the passenger seat, his head lolling back and his mouth hanging slightly open. He looked exhausted.

Becks must have heard me stirring. She glanced at the rearview mirror, her reflected eyes meeting mine, and raised one eyebrow. That was all she needed to do; the message couldn't have been easier to understand if she'd posted it on the front page of our news site.

I nodded. I understood, and I wasn't going to hurt him. Not if I had any choice in the matter.

My mouth felt like the ass-end of a Tuesday morning. I cleared my throat and asked, "Where are we?"

"Oregon. We're almost there."

"There where?"

"Shady Cove."

I paused, trying to convince myself I'd heard wrong. It didn't work. Finally, I demanded, "*What*?"

Shaun didn't flinch. Becks replied, "Shady Cove, Oregon. Our friend Dr. Abbey has a lab there. Right now, anyway. She'll probably move it soon. Possibly after she demands that we let her dissect you."

"In Shady Cove."

"Yes."

"But there's nothing *in* Shady Cove." Shady Cove, Oregon, was on the list of cities abandoned after the Rising, when the economic cost of rebuilding was determined too great to balance out the benefits. We'd take it back someday, when the great march of progress demanded we leave the dead with no country of their own. Until then, Shady Cove would stand empty, just like Santa Cruz, California, and Truth or Consequences, New Mexico, and Warsaw, Indiana, and a hundred other towns and cities around the world.

"That's why she has her lab there," said Becks curtly, before leaning over and snapping the radio on. Further conversation was rendered moot by the sound of a pre-Rising pop star informing us, loudly and with enthusiasm, that she was a rock star.

Shaun jerked upright, eyes open, hand going to the pistol at his belt. "Wha—"

"Settle, Mason. We can't all be as polite as the wakeup call at Maggie's fancy-ass hotel," said Becks, turning the radio down again now that its purpose had been achieved. "We're almost there. I need you on watch."

"Right." Shaun ground the heels of his hands against his eyes, wiping the sleep away. This time he finished the process of drawing the pistol from his belt, flicking off the safety. Once he was done, he twisted in his seat, shooting his old, familiar, who-gives-a-fuck? grin in my direction. "Sleep well?"

"Like a rock," I said. I almost said "like the dead," but realized he might not take that well. Like it or not, Shaun was going to be a little sensitive about that sort of thing for a while. Possibly forever.

"Good, because the good Doc's going to be real interested in talking to you." Shaun twisted back around to face forward, watching the darkened forest roll by outside his window. "She's a little hard to explain if you haven't met her. Hell, nobody explained her to me."

"I read the files."

"There's reading the files, and then there's the reality of a mentally disturbed Canadian woman throwing a live octopus at your chest so you can tell her whether exposure to Kellis-Amberlee has changed its reflex speed. Which, in case you wondered, doesn't happen. An octopus infected with Kellis-Amberlee is still fast, smart, and incredibly easy to piss off." Shaun shuddered. "All those suckers . . ."

"Wait. Octopuses aren't mammals."

Becks smiled coolly at me in the rearview mirror. "And that's why Dr. Abbey is difficult to explain to anyone who hasn't met her."

I sighed. "I'm not going to like this, am I?"

"Probably not," said Becks, and turned off the narrow dirt road we'd been traveling down, onto another, narrower, dirtier road. This one seemed more like a deer trail with delusions of grandeur than an actual thoroughfare, and the van shuddered and jumped with every bump and pothole. Shaun whooped a little, causing Becks to shoot him a wide-eyed look. He grinned unrepentantly back. I got the feeling that there hadn't been much whooping while I was away.

The dirt trail—I refused to dignify it with anything that sounded more maintained—emptied us onto a road that was just as decrepit, but had obviously been better, once upon a time. Chunks of broken pavement jutted up where the roots of the encroaching trees had managed to break through the surface. Becks swerved around them with practiced ease, and actually sped up, cruising through the dark like she'd driven this route a hundred times before. Judging by the calm way Shaun was watching the trees, she had.

The road ended at a large parking lot in front of a large, glass-fronted building that was probably originally some sort of government building or visitor's center. "Forestry center," said Shaun, before I could ask. "Welcome to Shady Cove."

". . . thanks." I shifted in my seat, putting my laptop to the side. "Is someone going to come out and meet us?"

"No, but you should probably count on lots and lots of people with guns waiting for us inside." Shaun shot me another manic grin. "Dr. Abbey knows how to greet visitors."

"With terror and intimidation?" I asked.

"Something like that," Becks agreed. She slowed down but kept driving, steering us into a covered parking garage attached to the back of the building. There were only a few vehicles already parked there, including—

I sat up straighter. "My bike!"

Shaun's grin softened, becoming sadder and more sincere. "You didn't think I'd leave it behind, did you?"

I didn't answer him. I couldn't speak around the lump in my throat. As soon as Becks parked the van I opened the door and climbed out, heading for my bike in what I hoped looked like a reasonably nonchalant manner. Not that it made a damn bit of difference either way. There was nothing—absolutely nothing, including the sudden appearance of a shambler from the shadows, which thankfully didn't happen—that could have kept me away from my bike in that moment. I actually hugged the handlebars, I was so damn glad to see it.

Shaun and Becks followed, pausing long enough to get their duffel bags from the car. They stopped about eight feet away. Out of the corner of my eye, I saw Becks elbow Shaun in the side, mouthing the words, "Ask her."

He looked at her uncertainly before he cleared his throat and said, "Uh, George? Did you want to start the engine? Make sure I've been doing regular maintenance and all that good shit?"

"That depends." I stopped hugging the handlebars, straightening as I turned to face them. "Do you actually want me to check the condition of the engine, or do you want me to run my fingerprints against the ones in the bike's database?"

"The second one," admitted Shaun.

"Right. Did you engage the biometrics when you locked the bike?" He nodded. I sighed. "Fine," I said, and stuck out my right thumb, holding it up for both of them to see, before pressing it down on the pressure sensor at the center of the bike's dash. A blue light promptly came on above the speedometer. I held my breath, and kept holding it until the light turned green before shutting off entirely. "Biometrics disengaged," I announced. "Happy now?"

Shaun turned to Becks, grinning as he said, "Extremely. Told you she could do it."

Becks nodded slowly. "Okay. You got one right. Come on. Dr. Abbey knows we're here by now." She started walking toward the nearest door, not waiting for the two of us.

I took a deep breath before heading over to join Shaun. Maybe he'd been sure that I could trigger the bike's biometric lock, but I hadn't been. Identical twins don't have the same fingerprints. Why would clones?

Answer: because at least in my case, the clone was intended to pass for the original in every way possible, and that meant that if my fingerprints could be matched to my old body, they would be. I was just glad they'd taken the trouble with this body, given that it was never intended to see the outside of a lab.

Thinking about that too much made me feel nauseous. I shuddered and sped up a little, matching my steps to Shaun's. Becks was already at the door, her palm pressed against a blood test panel. The light above it turned green, and she opened the door, stepping inside. She waved before slamming it in our faces. I moved into position next, slapping my hand down on the panel. The light cycled and the door unlocked, letting me inside.

"Be right there," said Shaun.

I smiled at him and closed the door. "You know, for a black-ops virology lab, this place has pretty straightforward security," I said, turning to face the room.

"No, we don't," said the short, curvy woman standing next to Becks. She was wearing a lab coat, blue jeans, and a bright orange T-shirt, all of which paled a bit when taken together with the hunting rifle she had pointed at my chest. "We just take slightly different steps to enforce it."

I froze.

The door opened behind me. "Hey, Dr. Abbey," said Shaun.

"Hello, Shaun," said the woman. She had a faint Canadian accent. "Who's your friend?"

"Oh, right, you never met George, did you?" Shaun closed the door and moved to stand next to me. "Georgia Mason, meet Dr. Shannon Abbey, mad scientist. Dr. Abbey, meet Georgia Mason, living dead girl."

"He must be feeling better if he can make bad Rob Zombie jokes," said Becks.

"Feeling better doesn't mean sane, stable, or thinking clearly," said Dr. Abbey. Her eyes swept across my face, assessing me. "What do *you* think your name is, girlie?"

"Georgia Mason," I replied, relieved that she'd asked a question whose answer I already knew. "I'm a ninety-seven percent cognate to the original. Don't quiz me on my fifth birthday party and I'll be fine."

She raised an eyebrow. "You sure you should be telling me that?"

"I'm sure that if you're going to shoot me, you'll do it regardless of what I say now, and if you're going to study me, you're not going to shoot me regardless of what I say now, so I may as well be honest with you." I smiled despite the tension. "I like being honest."

"You brought me a mouthy clone," said Dr. Abbey, looking toward Shaun. "And here it's not even my birthday."

He shrugged. "I try to be thoughtful. How's it hanging, Doc?"

"Well, let's see. You went to get me mosquitoes. You didn't bring me any mosquitoes. Instead, you bring me a clone of your dead sister. So I'd say it's hanging pretty damn poorly right now." Dr. Abbey sighed, lowering her rifle. "Thank God you're not the only people I have to work with. Come on. There's someone here that I want you to meet."

She turned, starting to walk away. I followed, and got my first real look at her facility. I stopped, staring.

I'm not sure what I expected from an off-the-grid virology lab run by a woman with the fashion sense of a traffic cone. I certainly didn't expect a fully equipped, if somewhat quixotically designed, research facility. Racks of medical equipment, computers, and lab animals were everywhere I looked. The place seemed slightly understaffed for its size, but that was probably a function of its underground nature—it wasn't like they could advertise for staff on the local message boards. "Mad Scientist seeks Minions. Must be detail-oriented, well educated, and unconcerned by the idea of being charged with terrorism if caught." Just no.

As she walked, Dr. Abbey asked, "How's Maggie?"

"Gut-shot and cranky, but the doctors say she'll live," said Shaun. "Is there any news about Alisa?"

"You haven't been looking at the non-world shattering news feeds recently, have you?" Dr. Abbey paused to hang her rifle from a hook on the wall and said, "Alisa Kwong was removed from the Ferry Pass Refugee Center two days ago when well-known Internet journalists Stacy and Michael Mason made an eloquent plea for custody of the tragically orphaned girl. They ran their reports from just outside the interdicted zone, making it impossible to shut them down without causing a massive Internet shitstorm. So the feds gave them the kid. Alisa's been e-mailing Alaric constantly. He can't tell her where we are, but being able to communicate with her without worrying about the mosquitoes getting into the facility where she's being held is doing them both a world of good. We'll worry about getting her back when it's safe."

Her words were clearly directed at Shaun, who nodded, a serious expression on his face. It was still a little weird, seeing him look so grave about something that wasn't related to risking his neck or getting a good ratings share. His priorities had shifted while I was gone.

He shot me a look, a smile curving up one corner of his mouth. Well. Not all his priorities.

"This is impressive," I said. "Did you set this all up yourself?"

"Golly-gee, Miss Clone, no! The government used to set up surprise scientific research facilities all over the country, just so they'd be around for people to stumble into when they were needed. If you break a few jars, you'll probably find guns and bonus lives inside." Dr. Abbey's smile was closer to a snarl, leaving her teeth half bared. "We're here for your amusement."

I raised an eyebrow. "You could have just said 'yes.'"

"And miss the opportunity to see what you'd do if I called you stupid?" Dr. Abbey's smile faded. She grabbed a small testing unit off one of the shelves, lobbing it at me. I caught it. She nodded slightly, apparently taking a mental note of my reflexes. "Go ahead and get yourself another clean blood result while we're all standing here. I want a portable sample."

"Doesn't Shaun get one?" I asked, concerned. The unit was heavier than I expected, with no visible lights on the top.

Dr. Abbey actually laughed. "You mean he didn't tell you? The lucky boy's immune."

"Probably due to extended exposure to someone with a reservoir condition, which brings us back to you, Georgia." The man who walked up behind her was clearly of Asian descent, even if his accent was pure Hawaiian. He was wearing knee-length khaki shorts and sandals, which wouldn't do a damn thing to save him if we had to run. He had a round face, and a kind expression that put my teeth instantly on edge. I was quickly learning that no one who looked at me kindly was planning to do anything I'd enjoy. Call it the natural paranoia born of dying and coming back to life again.

Shaun's hand clamped down on my shoulder. "Dude," he said, voice radiating suspicion, "who the fuck are you?"

The stranger's smile didn't waver. "I'm Dr. Joseph Shoji. You must be Shaun. You know, I don't think this could have been engineered to go any better if we'd tried. I really had no idea how we were going to get the two of you into the same place, and then you go and manage to perform a rescue op—"

The rest of the word was cut off as Shaun let go of my shoulder, pushing me back a step, and lunged for Dr. Shoji. Becks and Dr. Abbey watched impassively as Shaun's momentum drove the two men backward, stopping only when Dr. Shoji's shoulders slammed into the nearest wall. I made a startled noise that was shamefully close to a squeak.

"You CDC asshole!" snarled Shaun.

"He's not with the CDC," said Dr. Abbey. Shaun didn't seem to hear her.

"Bets on the crazy boy," said Becks.

"Joey's pretty mean when you get him riled," countered Dr. Abbey.

I stared at them. "What are you two *doing*? Make them stop!"

"Sweetcheeks, there's only ever been one person who could make that boy do anything he didn't want to do, and she's ashes in the wind." Dr. Abbey's gaze was assessing. "You're close, but you're not sure you're good enough, are you? Now take that blood test."

"You're insane," I said, and started to move toward Shaun and Dr. Shoji.

"Isn't that what the 'mad scientist' after my name is meant to imply?" asked Dr. Abbey. Then she sighed. "Look. You can go along with what I'm asking, which isn't much when you stop and think about it. Or you can try to intervene in Shaun's attempt to throttle the life from my colleague—way not to fight back there, Joey—and I can have one of my interns shoot you where you stand. Pick one."

Cheeks burning, I muttered, "I am getting damn sick of scientists," and popped the lid off the testing unit. I slammed my thumb down on the panel inside, feeling the needles bite into my skin.

Dr. Abbey nodded. "Good. You can follow directions. That's going to be important." She placed two fingers in her mouth and whistled. On cue, an impossible terror came lumbering down the hall, jowls flapping, eyes glowing with menace.

I couldn't help myself. I screamed. It was a high, piercing sound, and I was ashamed of it as soon as it left my throat. It had the unexpectedly positive effect of stopping the terror in its tracks. The huge black dog cocked its head, looking at me. Shaun also stopped trying to strangle Dr. Shoji, twisting around to regard me with alarm.

"George? What's wrong?"

Mutely, I pointed to the dog.

"Oh." Shaun blinked, releasing Dr. Shoji's throat. The Hawaiian virologist took a hasty step away from him. "That's just Joe. He won't hurt you."

"He will if I tell him to," said Dr. Abbey, leaning over to pluck the test unit from my hand. She didn't bother with a biohazard bag. She just snapped the lid closed and tucked the whole thing into the pocket of her lab coat. "Joe, guard."

The dog sat, gaze remaining on me. Something in its posture told me it wouldn't regard ripping my throat out as the high point of its day, but it would do it all the same if Dr. Abbey gave the order. The idea of moving seemed suddenly ludicrous, like it was the sort of thing only crazy people did.

"You're a bit high-strung, aren't you?" asked Dr. Shoji, rubbing his throat and giving Shaun a sidelong look. "Have you considered the benefits of marijuana? Or at least reducing your caffeine intake?"

"Don't push it, Joey; he's had a long day," said Dr. Abbey.

"He just tried to strangle me."

"Yes, but he failed, which means we're still playing nice."

"Don't you touch my sister," snarled Shaun, seeming to remember that Dr. Shoji was there.

I sighed, reaching out to grab Shaun's elbow. "He's not one of the doctors from Portland. It's okay."

"I heard screaming—is everything okay out here?" Alaric emerged from one of the side rooms, showing an admirable lack of self-preservation—it takes a reporter, after all, to run *toward* the sound of screaming. Reporters and crazy people, they were the only ones who would be moving in a situation like this. So which one was I going to be?

"The dog startled me," I said, turning to face him. I tried a smile. It felt foreign, like it wasn't quite designed to fit my face. "Hey, Alaric. Long time no see."

Alaric stopped dead, blood draining from his face. Then, with no more ceremony than that, his eyes rolled back in his head and he hit the floor in a heap. The five of us stared at him. Even Joe the giant fucking dog turned his head to study the prone blogger for a moment before returning to the serious business of staring at me.

"Dude really needs to toughen up," said Shaun.

Becks sighed. "Or maybe we need to stop doing twelve impossible things every day. Are we all done waving our crazy flags around and proclaiming ourselves the Kings of Crazytown? Because I want to know what the new guy is doing here, and I want you to do whatever you need to do to prove that she"—she jerked a thumb toward me—"is close enough to legit that we can let Shaun keep her. I think he'll cry if we don't."

Shaun glared at her. Becks ignored him.

"If I may?" Dr. Shoji looked from Shaun to Dr. Abbey, and finally to me. "As I was saying, I work with the Kauai Institute of Virology. I've been consulting with their Kellis-Amberlee research division for the past seven years, which is fairly impressive, considering they think I'm on loan from the CDC."

I paused before saying slowly, "But you don't work for the CDC, do you?"

"No. I believe you've already met some of my associates, Drs. Kimberley and Lake? They spoke very highly of you, even before they were sure you'd be able to make it out of the facility. They certainly thought you were the most promising subject—forgive me for using that word; it's an ugly word, but it's the only one I have—to arise from Project Shelley. We were all rooting for you from the start." He was smiling again. It was such a *kind* smile. What was my life going to be like if I didn't trust people who looked kind?

Probably a lot like it was before, when I didn't trust anyone who wasn't on my team. "You're with the EIS."

"What?" said Becks.

"What?" said Shaun.

"That was quicker than I expected," said Dr. Abbey. She gestured toward Alaric, who was still lying on the hallway floor. "One of you, get him up. I don't want an intern coming along and shooting him before he can wake up and tell them he's not dead."

"Giant dog," I said.

She sighed. "Fine. Joe, *down*." The dog abandoned its watchful position, lumbering back to its feet and trotting to stand next to Dr. Abbey, tail wagging wildly. She placed a hand atop its head. "Happy?"

"Not really, but I'm not seeing much of an alternative here." I stepped closer to Shaun, still watching the dog warily. "Why is it *here*?"

"Joe is, like, a super-long story, and I'm a little more interested in the story that makes you meet Mr. Hawaii here and jump straight to him being with the EIS," said Shaun. "Does that mean he's working for the people who were holding you captive?"

"No," said Dr. Shoji. "It means I'm working with the people who helped her escape, and it means I'm here to make sure you get her where she needs to be—where you both need to be. The man who funded most of Project Shelley needs you. This is what he was hoping for all along."

"Who?" demanded Becks.

I didn't need to ask. A quiet certainty was growing in the pit of my stomach. Maybe it had been since Dr. Shoji showed up, and I realized that everything—*everything*—was connected, whether we wanted it to be or not. There was no running away from the past. Alive or dead, it was going to catch up with us in the end.

Alaric groaned, starting to stir. I looked at Dr. Shoji and said calmly, "Rick. He paid to bring me back, didn't he?"

"Yes," said Dr. Shoji. "And now he needs your help."

I sighed. "Right. Let's peel Alaric off the floor and get him up to speed, guys. I think we're heading for Washington D.C."

Oh, of course. Georgia isn't dead. Or, well, she was dead, but now she's not, because the CDC is running an underground cloning lab, and the best thing they could think of to clone was a dead journalist who was a pain in their asses when she was alive the first time. And ninety-seven percent memory transfer? That isn't science fiction, that's science lying-through-your-teeth. Either she's not as perfect as she thinks, or there have been a lot of scientific advances that no one's bothered to share with the rest of us.

And then I think . . . Kellis-Amberlee in mosquitoes. Someone killing all the people with reservoir conditions. Dr. Wynne trying to kill half the team. That Australian scientist. All that census data. All the things that don't add up, that never added up, that have been not adding up since before . . . well, since before Dr. Matras hijacked his daughter's blog and told the world the dead were walking. All the things that never added up at all. And I think. Well.

Maybe this isn't so impossible after all. And that scares the pants off me.

Thank God Alisa's safe with the Masons. And if that's a sentence that I can write without irony, maybe nothing is impossible anymore.

—From *The Kwong Way of Things*, the blog of Alaric Kwong, August 6, 2041. Unpublished.

Dear Alaric.

The people I am with, the Masons, say I should send this e-mail and tell you I promise I won't e-mail again for a while, because I won't be able to check mail and I don't want you to feel bad when you send messages that aren't answered. I can check e-mail again when we get back to Berkeley, but we aren't there yet.

Mr. Mason is nice, but he stares into space sometimes, and it scares me a little. Ms. Mason isn't so nice, I don't think, but she's trying hard, and I know that should count. Anyway, they said you sent them, and I should go with them, and they had pictures of those people you work with, the cute guy and the dead girl, and so I figured it would be okay. Please don't be angry. I needed to get out of there before the mosquitoes got in, and I was so scared, and you said you'd send someone.

Thank you for sending the Masons. I'll see you soon. I love you.

—Taken from an e-mail sent by Alisa Kwong to Alaric Kwong, August 6, 2041.

SHAUN: Thirty-two

The engines of the Kauai Institute's private jet hummed smoothly, just loud enough that we could be confident that we were still on the plane and not, I don't know, sitting in a really funky modular living room. It didn't help that we were practically alone on the plane. Becks and Alaric were sitting on one side, reading through the files Dr. Abbey had loaded onto their phones before we left. Dr. Shoji was at the front of the plane, monitoring the autopilot and giving us a little privacy in the last few hours before we landed. That left me and George, and she'd been asleep for the better part of an hour, head pillowed on her arm, mouth relaxed from its normal hard line to something softer and more vulnerable. I kept glancing over to make sure she was still there, but I couldn't look at her for more than a few seconds when she was like that. It felt like I was stealing something. George was never that vulnerable, not even for me.

According to the little trip monitor at the front of the cabin, we were approximately two hours outside of Washington D.C., where presumably, Dr. Shoji would find a way of getting us out of the private airfield we were aiming for without anyone getting shot in the head. If you had to fly, there were worse ways than hopping from one private airfield to another in a fully outfitted corporate jet. Of course, there were better ones, too. Ones that didn't mean we were going in essentially blind, on the word of a man who just happened to know the people responsible for cloning my sister.

I pinched the bridge of my nose and groaned. "Things were a lot simpler when all I had to worry about was what I was going to poke with a stick today," I muttered.

George didn't stir.

Becks looked up, waving a hand until she caught my attention. Then she beckoned me to their side of the plane. I shrugged and stood, picking up my half-empty cup of in-flight coffee before walking over to join them. The coffee was lukewarm. I didn't care. Just being able to drink it without feeling guilty made it the best cup of coffee in the world.

"What do we know?" I asked, plopping down next to Becks. She wasn't wearing her seat belt. Alaric was. That, right there, tells you most of what you need to know about both of them.

"The clone tech they used for . . . " Alaric cast an uneasy glance toward George, seeming to lose the thread of the sentence.

When several seconds ticked by without him continuing, I nudged him with my foot. Just a nudge, but he jumped like I'd kicked him. I sighed. "The clone tech they used to bring Georgia back," I prompted. "What do we know?"

"They force-grew her body with a lot of chemicals, a lot of hormones, a lot of radiation, and a lot of luck," said Alaric slowly. "It only worked because they didn't need to worry about getting a clone with cancer. She probably *was* cancerous by the time they finished maturing her, and they just let the Marburg Amberlee part of Kellis-Amberlee do the mop-up when she was exposed to the virus."

"She mentioned that she wasn't the only one," said Becks. "What I'm pretty sure she doesn't know is that she wasn't even one of ten."

I raised an eyebrow. "No?"

"Try more like one out of ten *thousand*, if you're starting from the zygote level and then moving up to full-on vat-grown humans. Most of them never made it out of their petri dishes. The ones that did . . . I don't understand half this science, except to understand that I don't like it. It was technically ethical, or would have been, if they hadn't been growing bodies with functioning brains, but the fact that the CDC can do this at all disturbs me." Becks shook her head. "I mean, what next? The military starts force-cloning soldiers?"

"Only if they feel like paying five million dollars for every functional model," said Alaric. "That's the cost of the cloning—the starting cost. It doesn't include the cost of the subliminal conditioning, the synapse programming—"

"Which is how she can actually *remember* things, like dying," chimed in Becks.

Alaric gave her a look that was half glare, half fond exasperation. "I would have gotten to that," he said. "But yes. The synapse programming is why she *remembers* things. And then there was the physical therapy to keep her muscles developing, the immunizations, the process of getting her to maturity . . . you're looking at thirty or forty million dollars of medical technology. Easy."

There was a pause while we turned to look at George. She shifted in her sleep, one foot kicking out a few inches before it was pulled back to nestle against the opposite ankle. I turned back to the others.

"Well, I hope they don't think they're getting her back," I said. "What else can you get out of those files?"

You want to know if I'm going to die again. Georgia-in-my-head was talking less and less the longer there was a living, breathing George for me to hold on to, but that didn't mean she was gone. It just meant my crazy was biding its time, waiting to strike when I was least prepared. You don't go that far past the borders of Crazytown and come waltzing out unscathed.

The worst part of it was that she—the dead girl's voice in my head—was right, because she was always right. I wanted to know if George was going to die. There was no way I could survive that twice.

Becks looked at me levelly. "She's stable, Shaun. Those doctors from the EIS took out the CDC fail-safes, and they couldn't actually build a human body that would self-destruct without help. The science isn't that good."

"Yet," said Alaric. He shook his head. "I believe in her now, Shaun. I mean, she's right when she says she's an imperfect copy—the Kellis-Amberlee kept turning her brain's basic functions back on, but there was a little bit more tissue loss every time. That doesn't mean she's not who she says she is. She never had the chance to become anybody else."

"God." Becks shuddered. "Headshots just became a hell of a lot more important to me."

I frowned, finishing off my lukewarm coffee before I asked, "Why?"

"Because Miss Atherton has just realized one of the things the CDC would prefer the population not be aware of." Dr. Shoji took the seat next to Alaric. "I hope you don't mind my joining you. When I realized you were finally getting around to discussing the science, I thought you might like the opportunity to question someone who used to be involved with it."

My eyes narrowed. "You mean—"

"No, no." He put his hands up, motioning for me to stay calm. "I left that part of my life behind a long time ago. There were some ethical lines I couldn't bring myself to cross, and at that point . . . I was still suited to work in the private sector—hence my work with the Kauai Institute—but I could no longer stomach the CDC."

"The cross-infection trials Kelly mentioned," said Alaric.

It took me a moment to realize what he was talking about. When we first got to Dr. Abbey's lab—what felt like a million years ago—we'd still been traveling with Kelly Connolly. In an effort to show us that the CDC wasn't all rainbows and roses, Dr. Abbey asked her about some cross-infection trials using prisoners who "volunteered" to be injected with multiple strains of KA. All of them died.

"Yes," said Dr. Shoji. "Those men and women died horribly, and they didn't have to. That was when I realized it had to end. I stopped working on things that we didn't need to do—and forgive me, Shaun, but finding a new way of bringing back the dead wasn't something that needed to be a priority. We'd already done that. It didn't work out well."

"It's cool," I said.

Slowly, Becks said, "Kellis-Amberlee 'raises the dead' by turning the body's electrical impulses back on. It's like a viral defibrillator that just keeps on working, and working, and working, until there's nothing left to work with. If they got a clean brain scan off of Georgia after you shot her, that means her brain was turned on at the time. They took their scans off a living brain."

Dr. Shoji nodded. "Yes," he agreed. "That's how the technology works. It was originally intended to be a treatment for Alzheimer's, a way of calling back memories that were still present, but had become . . . clouded, let's say. Misplaced somehow. Once we realized that it could be used on the victims of Kellis-Amberlee, there was hope that we'd be able to bring them back to themselves—that memory recall could be used as a form of treatment, that, combined with antivirals and proper therapy, they could be cured."

"So why didn't it work?" I asked.

"The virus didn't give up that easily. Nothing we did resulted in anything but agitation in the subjects. Some researchers, myself included, were concerned that we might actually cause the infected to become self-aware. People with rabies are aware that they've done horrible things. They simply can't prevent themselves from doing them. No one wanted that with Kellis-Amberlee, and so the project was suspended."

"Why didn't you publish?" asked Becks.

"For the same reason the government is shooting everybody with a reservoir condition," said Alaric. "If they let it get out that people are still thinking, no one's going to pull the trigger. And then there won't be anyone left to do the curing, because we'll all be zombies."

I frowned. "I'm not following."

"They're saying that once someone is infected, the virus takes over, but they're still in there." The engines might be soft, but they were loud enough that I hadn't heard George walking up until she spoke. I turned to see her standing beside me, hair still rumpled from sleep, sunglasses in her hand. She looked at Dr. Shoji and asked, "Do zombies think?"

"No," he said. "The virus does their thinking for them, thank God, because Alaric is right. If people stop shooting because they're afraid of committing murder, we're all going to die. But there's a chance—not a huge chance, but a chance—that zombies dream."

George nodded, leaning against the seat next to me. "That's what I thought you were going to say. How long before we land?"

"We have about an hour before we begin our initial descent into Washington D.C.," said Dr. Shoji. "How are you feeling?"

"Exhausted. I need a Coke."

I was never going to get tired of hearing those words. "I'll get you one," I said, standing. "I needed to get another coffee anyway."

She slid into my seat, flashing me a quick, grateful smile. Then she leaned forward, posture making it clear that she was asking Dr. Shoji a question. Probably more things about zombies thinking. Whatever it was, they would fill me in later.

I walked to the self-serve kitchenette at the back of the plane, pulling a can of Coke from the refrigerator unit before pouring myself a cup of blessedly hot coffee. There were wrapped cheese and turkey sandwiches in one of the cold drawers over the coffee machine. I took down three of those—one for me, one for George, and one for the first person who asked where their sandwich was. We needed to keep our strength up if we were going to go take on the United States government. Which was, by the way, insane.

You should know, said George.

I didn't reply. It felt weird, trying to reject that little inner voice when it was the only thing that had kept me even halfway functional in the months following the real Georgia's death, but I couldn't have them both, and given the choice, I'd take the George I could share with other people. That made her real. I needed real. I needed real to anchor me to the world, because otherwise I was going to slip right over the edge.

Going all the way crazy seemed a lot less appealing now than it had a few weeks ago. I used to view a total break with reality as a sort of psychological permission to spend the rest of my life—however long or short it happened to be—with George, and maybe even be happy. Having a living, breathing woman with her face made me admit that it wouldn't make me happy. The George in my head wasn't the real thing. Neither was the clone, if you wanted to get technical, but I've never been a technical guy. I needed Georgia in my life. I chose the one who was sitting in the cabin, waiting for her Coke.

Alaric had come around surprisingly quickly, after he finished yelling at us for not keeping him updated while we were in Seattle. Typical Newsie; he was less upset about the CDC raising the dead than he was about us not sending him regular reports. He'd spent about half an hour quizzing George on everything he could think of while Becks and I were getting us packed to go. She must have passed, because when he was done, he'd looked at me, said, "It's her," and started listening to her like she'd never died in the first place. If only it was going to be that easy for everyone.

"What did I miss?" I asked, walking back over to the group. George stuck her hand out as soon as I was close enough. I passed her the Coke and a sandwich, and was rewarded with a brief smile. She was wearing her sunglasses again, even though she didn't technically need them. We were all frankly more comfortable that way.

"Dr. Shoji was explaining the landing plan," said Becks. "We're going to set down at the Montgomery County Airpark in Maryland, and drive from there."

"The airport has been owned by the EIS since shortly after the Rising," said Dr. Shoji. "We've managed to resist all CDC efforts to buy it from us, and since we're still officially on the books as a functional organization, they haven't been able to simply take it. There's a ground crew waiting, and they've promised to have a vehicle ready."

"How are we going to get off the property?" asked Becks. "I don't suppose you're running a completely unsecured airfield less than fifty miles from the nation's capitol."

"We're good, but we're not that good," said Dr. Shoji. "You'll take a blood test when you deplane, and another when you exit the airport. Both will be performed on EIS equipment, and logged in our mainframe. If the CDC is tracking you by blood test results, they won't get anything from us. We stopped sharing all our data a long time ago."

"Isn't that illegal?" asked Alaric.

"Isn't human cloning illegal?" asked George. She opened her Coke and took a long drink before adding, "The CDC isn't playing by the rules anymore. Why should anyone else?"

"What a wonderful world we've made for ourselves." Alaric scowled, slumping in his seat. "I'm getting sick and tired of everybody double crossing everybody else. Can't something be straightforward?"

I raised my hand. "I'm just here to hit stuff."

Becks glared. The anger in her eyes was impossible to miss, no matter how hard I might try to pretend it wasn't there. "Don't you dare, Shaun Mason. You may have been here to hit stuff once, but things have changed since then, so don't you dare. You don't get to go back to pretending you're an idiot just because you have Georgia here to hide behind, you got me? I won't *let* you. Even if you try, I won't *let* you."

A moment of awkward silence followed her proclamation, each of us trying not to look at Dr. Shoji, who had just witnessed something that felt intensely personal, at least to me. That wasn't something that should have been shared with anyone outside our weird little semi-family.

Dr. Shoji clearly knew that. He stood, clearing his throat as he jerked his chin toward the sandwiches in my hand. "That's a good idea. You should all eat before we land. I don't know how much opportunity we're going to have to stop once we hit the ground. We can't risk any of you taking CDC-operated blood tests before we get to where we're going." That said, he turned and walked away, heading back toward the cockpit. In a matter of seconds, the four of us were alone again.

We looked at each other. Finally, Becks took a slow breath, and said, "Shaun, I'm sorry. I shouldn't have said—"

"It's okay." I shook my head. "It's true. I spent a lot of time letting George do the thinking for both of us, because I could get away with it. I've been doing all the thinking for a year now. I don't think I can stop. But that doesn't mean I want to do anything at this point beyond smashing things and shooting people and making sure this ends. You get me? This is going to end."

"No matter what?" asked Alaric, almost defiantly.

I turned to look at him. Out of all of us, he was the one who still had something to lose. His little sister was with the Masons. If he died, she'd wind up staying with them. There were too many orphans in the world to take one away from an apparently loving family. They'd probably be more careful with her than they were with us, but that didn't make them good parents, and that didn't make them good for her. Not in the long term.

"If you need to get out at any point, you get out," I said. "But aside from that? For me and George? Yeah, no matter what. If this doesn't end here, they're never going to stop coming for us. So it ends, or we end, and either way, I won't blame you for running."

"Thank you," said Alaric quietly.

"So what are we doing?" asked Becks. "What's the plan? Does *anybody* have a plan? Or did we just get on a plane with this guy and cross the country because, hey, at this point it was the only stupid thing we hadn't done?"

"Rick was involved with the program that had me cloned," said George. "Dr. Shoji is taking us to Rick. Rick wouldn't have done this if he didn't think it was absolutely necessary."

"Wow, you mean people *don't* arrange to have their dead friends brought back at huge financial and ethical cost just because they miss them?" asked Alaric dryly.

There was a pause, all four of us looking at each other wide-eyed. Then we all burst out laughing. Becks leaned forward, resting her elbows on her knees as she shook with laughter. Alaric sank back in his seat. George leaned sideways, her shoulder pressing into my hip, and tried to cover her mouth with the hand that wasn't holding her soda.

Becks was the first to get herself back under control. Straightening up, she wiped her eyes and grinned at Alaric. "Glad to see you're feeling up to being an asshole again, Kwong," she said.

Alaric half saluted. "Just doing my part for Assholes Anonymous of America."

"Somebody has to," I said. I sat down in Dr. Shoji's abandoned seat, tossing the last turkey sandwich to Alaric before taking a sip of my still-warm coffee. "So basically, we're going to hit the ground running."

"Do we ever do anything else?" asked Becks.

"No," said George.

I toasted her with my coffee. "And thank God for that."

Becks laughed again as she stood and made her way back to the kitchenette. Alaric started unwrapping his sandwich. I smiled one more time at George before unwrapping my own sandwich and taking a large bite. We needed to keep our strength up. I had the distinct feeling that not only would we be hitting the ground running, we were probably never going to slow down again. Our lives—all our lives—had been measured in calms between storms for a very long time. Even when we were dead, in George's case. Well, this was the last calm, and I was going to enjoy it while it lasted.

I've always lived my life—

No. That's a lie.

Georgia Carolyn Mason, b. 2016, in the final year of the Rising, d. 2040, during the Ryman campaign, always lived her life by one simple commandment: Tell the truth. Whenever possible, whatever it requires, tell the truth. This blog was for opinions and personal thoughts, because those, too, are a part of the truth. No one is truly objective, no matter how hard we try, and unless people knew where her biases were, they couldn't know when to read around them. Georgia Mason lived to tell the truth. Georgia Mason died to tell the truth. It's not her fault some people couldn't leave well enough alone.

I am not Georgia Mason. I am not anyone else. I am a chimera, built of science and stolen DNA and a dead woman's memories. I am an impossibility. These are my biases. These are the things you need to know, because otherwise, you won't be able to read around them. I am not her.

But my name is Georgia Mason.

And I am here to tell you the truth.

—From *Living Dead Girl*, the blog of Georgia Mason II, August 10, 2041. Unpublished.

Listen to the clone girl. She's got some pretty good ideas, and oh, right, if you so much as look at her funny, I'll blow your fucking face off. We clear? Good.

—From *Hail to the King*, the blog of Shaun Mason, August 10, 2041. Unpublished.

GEORGIA: Thirty-three

Despite Becks's dire predictions, no one shot us out of the sky. The computerized voice of the autopilot came on over the intercom as the plane touched down on the main runway of the Montgomery County Airpark, saying, "Welcome to Montgomery County, Maryland, where the local time is nine fifty-seven P.M. Thank you for flying with the Epidemic Intelligence Service. Please remain seated while the sterilization crew secures the plane. Any attempts to get up and move about the cabin will result in the immediate activation of security measure Alpha-16."

"Meaning what?" asked Shaun.

"Meaning the plane fills with knockout gas and we stay unconscious until somebody comes along and shoots us full of the counteragent," said Alaric. We all turned to stare at him. He shrugged. "While some people were taking naps and fucking around with their guns, I was reading the security information card. Well. Security information booklet. They take security seriously around here."

"They *are* the EIS," said Becks.

"Which has meant basically jack shit for the last twenty years," said Shaun.

"They saved me," I said. "They can secure us as much as they want."

That killed the discussion. We looked at each other, then toward the front of the plane. There was still no sign of Dr. Shoji.

"You know, if he was planning to double-cross us, this would be the best time to do it," said Shaun.

"If he was planning to double-cross us, wouldn't he have just crashed the plane somewhere over Iowa?" asked Alaric.

"Not if he wanted to live," said Becks. "And not if he wanted to dissect us. I mean, Shaun's immune, Georgia's a clone . . ."

"And I'm an asshole," said Alaric helpfully.

Everyone laughed nervously. There was a soft "thump" as the plane stopped rolling down the runway, followed by the sound of clamps affixing to the wheels and windows. This was one plane that wouldn't be flying anywhere until it was certified infection free. Blue antibacterial foam began cascading down the windows, blocking our view of the airfield.

"The foam they use to sterilize planes costs eight dollars a gallon," said Alaric. "It takes approximately two thousand gallons to sterilize a plane this size."

Becks gave him a sidelong look. "Why do you know these things? What inspires you to learn them?"

"It impresses the ladies," said Alaric. They both laughed. Shaun didn't. I turned to look toward the front of the plane, and waited.

The blue foam slowed from a torrent to drips and drabs, finally stopping altogether. A steady stream of bleach followed it, washing away both the remains of the foam and any biological agents foolish enough to think that hitching a ride on an EIS plane was a good idea.

"Overkill much?" muttered Shaun. I surreptitiously reached over and squeezed his knee.

Alaric must have heard him, because he held up the security information booklet and said, "If they had any reason to believe we'd flown through or over an active outbreak, they'd be rinsing the whole plane down with formalin. Twice. And we'd be praying the plane was properly sealed, since otherwise, we'd probably melt."

"It's just our way of saying 'thank you for flying EIS Air,'" said Dr. Shoji, shrugging on a lab coat as he emerged from the cockpit. His black T-shirt and shorts were gone, replaced by khaki pants and a loudly patterned Hawaiian shirt covered with purple and yellow flowers. I raised an eyebrow. He shrugged. "It's camouflage. I'm supposed to be the visiting director of the Kauai Institute of Virology—which is technically true, even if I'm not here on the business of the Institute—and this is what they expect. I'd wear shorts if I thought I could get away with it, but the CDC dress code forbids exposed legs. Something about caustic chemicals." He waved a hand, clearly unconcerned.

"Why are you up and moving about the cabin?" asked Shaun. "Not in the mood to get gassed because you had a cramp, thanks."

"Ah—sorry." Dr. Shoji produced a small remote from his pocket and pressed a button.

The "fasten seat belts" sign turned off, and the voice of the autopilot said, "We have finished external decontamination. Please rise and collect all personal belongings. An EIS representative will be waiting on the jet bridge to confirm your current medical condition and offer any assistance that may be required. Once again, thank you for flying with EIS Air. We appreciate that you have many choices in government-owned health services, and would like you to know that the EIS has always been dedicated to the preservation of the public health, above and beyond all other goals."

"Wow. Even the private planes have to say that shit," said Shaun.

Alaric stood, snagging his laptop bag from the overhead compartment as he asked, "By 'offer any assistance,' do they mean bandages or bullets?"

"I don't know." I stood, stretching, before retrieving my jacket from the overhead bin. I shrugged it on, checking to be sure my holster was covered. I probably wasn't legally allowed to carry a concealed weapon—my field license almost certainly expired after I died—but I wasn't going to tell unless someone asked me. "It probably depends on your test results."

"You are a ray of sunshine and I don't know how we got by without you," said Becks.

I nodded sympathetically. "I'm sure it was hard. But it's all right. I'm here now." Inwardly, I was ecstatic. She was acknowledging me in the present tense. She was admitting that, real Georgia or not, I was the one they had. And it felt wonderful.

"If you're done squabbling with each other, please follow me," said Dr. Shoji. He walked back to the plane door, where he opened the control panel next to the lock and pressed a button. There was a hiss as the hydraulics released, and the door slid open, revealing an airlock. I closed my eyes, shuddering.

We were going into an EIS facility. An endless succession of white halls and people dressed in medical attire rose behind my eyes. I pushed them aside. It wasn't like I had a choice. If I wanted to develop fun new phobias, however justified, I was going to deal with them. However I had to.

Shaun's hand was a welcome weight on my shoulder. "Hey," he said. "It's cool."

I opened my eyes and forced a smile, glad that my sunglasses kept him from seeing my eyes. He knew how scared I was if anyone did—I was still enough of the woman I'd been programmed to be to react in ways he recognized—but that didn't mean I needed to shove it in his face. "Cool," I echoed, and followed him into the airlock.

I was expecting to find men in cleanroom suits waiting for us with blood tests in one hand and guns in the other, ready to shoot if our results were anything other than perfect. It was a little odd that the EIS had a manned jet bridge, rather than using one of the safer, more convenient automated systems, but it was possible they hadn't wanted to attract the attention a major renovation would draw. They were trying to keep the CDC from taking them seriously, and being the kind of small, unassuming organization that still needs to process incoming passengers by hand would help with that.

I wasn't expecting to find a smiling woman with ice-blonde hair loose around her shoulders, wearing a lab coat over a blue tank top and jeans. She smiled when she saw us, the expression lighting up her face in a way that would have seemed impossible when I thought her name was Dr. Shaw and she was dancing to the CDC's tune.

"Hello, Georgia," said Dr. Kimberley. She looked to the rest of the group, assessing them each in turn. "Who are your friends?"

"Dr. Kimberley." I had the sudden urge to hug her—another point of deviation, as my memories were quick to inform me. I stiffened instead, rejecting the alien urge. "You made it out of the building."

"I did, barely; we were able to delay the cleansing sequence long enough to get into one of the incinerator shafts, and climb from there to the roof," she said. "Gregory is safe as well. We're both hopelessly compromised, but we'll find a way around that. We always do."

"Such is the life of the epidemiological spy," I said. I half turned to the others, gesturing to each in turn as I said, "Rebecca Atherton, Shaun Mason, and Alaric Kwong. The staff of After the End Times. This is Dr. Danika Kimberley. She saved my life."

"I'd say she was exaggerating, but she's not," said Dr. Kimberley. She looked toward Dr. Shoji, who was hanging back, waiting for us to finish. "Were there any issues?"

"None. Our flight plan was approved without a hitch. No mechanical troubles, and the plane was swept for transmitters before we left and three times during flight. We're clean."

"Thank God for that," she said fervently. She rummaged through the bag she had slung over one shoulder, producing five slim-bodied testing kits with the words EIS Official Use Only stenciled on their sides. She handed one to each of us and said, "We use these for internal testing, which means they don't upload to any servers but our own. If any of you come up positive, you'll be isolated for six hours before we make a final determination."

Becks paused in the act of opening her test kit. "What does that mean?" she asked.

"It means that if you have any chance of recovering from the Kellis-Amberlee amplification process, you'll have started to show signs by the end of that time. If you haven't shown any signs, we can either decommission you or retain you for further testing. We'd prefer to keep you, of course—undamaged live subjects are difficult to come by—but the choice would be yours, providing you made it before you finished amplifying."

"You should absolutely be on the Maryland tourism board," said Becks, and slipped her thumb into the kit.

There was a moment of quiet as everyone waited for confirmation that we were still among the legally living. Shaun watched the ceiling rather than watching the lights blinking on the test kits. Each set of lights blinked at its own tempo, analyzing the blood sample the kit had taken, looking for signs of seroconversion. One by one, they settled on a steady green. Clean. All of us were clean.

I elbowed Shaun in the side. "It's good," I said. "You can come down now."

"Huh?" He looked down, eyes fixing on the green-lit test kit in his hand. "Oh." He cast a quick sideways glance at my kit and visibly relaxed, some of the tension going out of his jaw.

Dr. Kimberley plucked the kit from his hand, sticking it into a small biohazard bag, which she then made disappear into the bag on her shoulder. The other kits went into a separate, larger biohazard bag, which she pushed into a chute in the side of the jet bridge. Then she smiled, not quite as brightly as when we first deplaned, and said, "Well. I suppose we'd best be moving along. Follow me."

She turned and walked away. I was almost disappointed to see that she was wearing sensible sneakers instead of the impractical heels she'd sported at the Seattle CDC. The heels must have been one more part of her cover as Dr. Shaw, and sneakers would be a lot easier to run in if there was an outbreak. Still, it was odd to hear her walking without the gunshot clatter of her shoes hitting the floor.

The jet bridge let out on a small pre-Rising room painted a merciful shade of yellow-beige. I'd never considered beige the color of mercy before, but anything was better than that dreaded medicinal white. Chairs lined the windowed walls, presumably to give passengers a view of the airfield. There was no one there, and the air smelled like disinfectant and dust. We might have been the only things alive in the entire building.

Alaric was the last into the room. The door closed behind him, locks engaging with a loud beep. Dr. Shoji moved to the front of the group, waving for the rest of us to follow. "Come along," he said. "The decontamination fumes can cause severe irritation if you stand too close."

"And of course a door that actually sealed would look too much like competence," muttered Alaric, and started walking faster.

Dr. Kimberley stepped back so that she was walking on my right. Shaun cast a suspicious look her way. She ignored it. "How do you feel?" she asked. "Any unusual pain or strange sensations in your hands or feet?"

"Hold on," said Shaun. There was a tightly controlled note in his voice that I recognized as dawning alarm. "What are you asking her that for?"

"It's okay, Shaun." I put a hand on his arm as we walked, trying to soothe him. Looking back to Dr. Kimberley, I said, "I'm tired a lot. I ache. Everything feels pretty much normal."

"You're achy because you're getting proper exercise, rather than the illusion of it," she said, nodding. "That will fade as your body comes into alignment with your idea of what it's capable of. I'd like to do a full physical, which there simply isn't time for, but if that's all you're experiencing that seems out of the ordinary, I'd say that you're entirely fine. Better than fine, really. You're alive."

"And she's going to stay that way," said Shaun.

Dr. Kimberley flashed a rueful smile his way. It was odd seeing her this emotive. Adjusting to her accent had been easier. "Let's hope you're the prophet in this scenario, rather than anyone with a more dire view of what's to come."

The hall ended at a pair of old-fashioned swinging doors. I frowned, studying them, but couldn't see anything that looked even remotely like modern security upgrades. They were just doors, unsecured, with no scanners or test units installed beside them. We stopped in a ragged line, all of us looking at those doors—all of us looking for the catch. There had to be a catch.

There was always a catch.

Dr. Shoji didn't seem to notice our dismay, and neither did Dr. Kimberley. They kept on walking, pushing those unsecured doors open to reveal an underground parking garage, and the big black SUV that was waiting at the curb.

There's a certain shape of car that just screams "I belong to a private security force." They're always big and black and solid-looking, with run-flat tires and bulletproof glass in the windows. And then there are the cars that belong to the Secret Service. The differences are subtle, but you can see them if you know what to look for. Wireless relay webbing built into the rear window, for those times when cell service is compromised. Thin copper lines through the rest of the glass, ready to be turned on and cut off *all* service, cellular or otherwise. The glass in a Secret Service car isn't just bulletproof, it's damn near indestructible. A group of Irwins who modeled themselves after a pre-Rising TV show called *MythBusters* managed to get hold of a decommissioned Secret Service vehicle a few years ago. They set off six grenades inside the main cabin. The explosions didn't even scratch the glass.

I once asked a member of Senator Ryman's security crew whether the Secret Service had a sign on the wall somewhere counting off the number of years since a sitting president had been eaten on their watch. He laughed, but he didn't look happy about it. I think I was right.

"I miss Steve," I said quietly, looking at the car.

"Me, too," said Shaun.

The passenger-side door of the SUV opened, and a big blond mountain of a man unfolded himself, straightening until his head and shoulders were higher than the car's roof. "It's good to be remembered," he said. "Shaun. Georgia."

Shaun's mouth fell open as a grin spread across his face. "Steve, my *man*! What the fuck are you doing here?"

"I could ask you the same thing. Last time I saw you, you were in no condition to be causing this much trouble." Steve turned his face toward me, expression unreadable behind his government-issue sunglasses. I hate it when people use my own tricks on me. "You, on the other hand, were in an urn. Because it was your funeral." His tone telegraphed what his expression didn't: He was deeply uncomfortable about my presence.

I shrugged. "Sorry. I guess I was just too stubborn to stay dead for long."

"Mad science," said Alaric. "What *can't* it do?"

Shaun shook his head, snapping out of his delight over Steve's appearance. "Sorry, man, I got distracted. Steve, this is Alaric Kwong, one of the site Newsies, and this is Rebecca Atherton, one of our Irwins."

"Call me Becks," said Becks. "Everyone else does."

"It's a pleasure to meet you," rumbled Steve. "If you'd all get in the car, please? I have instructions regarding your destination."

"I'm afraid this is where we leave you," said Dr. Shoji. "I'll see you again, but I can't arrive with you. That would be suspicious."

"And I'm on house arrest," said Dr. Kimberley. She smiled at Steve. "I couldn't even have come this far if we hadn't been sure of who was going to be coming to collect you."

"Always glad to help, Dr. Kimberley," said Steve. He opened the rear passenger door. "We need to get moving. The security changes at midnight, and it will be best if we're past the checkpoints before that happens."

"Where are we going?" asked Becks.

Steve didn't answer. He just folded his arms, and waited.

"Come on," I said, and started for the car. Working with Steve during the Ryman campaign taught me a lot of things about professional security. Chief among them was that once Steve made up his mind about something, that was the way things were going to go. He'd explain where we were going on the way.

Becks and Shaun followed me. Alaric stayed where he was, looking unsure. I waited until the others were in the car before turning on my heel and crossing back to him.

"What's wrong?"

"This seems a bit . . . convenient, don't you think?"

I surprised us both by laughing, a single, sharp expression of both amusement and regret. "This has all been 'convenient,' Alaric. They've been herding us since Seattle. Maybe before, I don't know. I wasn't with you to see the signs. At this point, what's one more leap of faith between friends?"

"Seems like it might be a long fucking way to the bottom," he said.

"So what?" I shrugged. "If we're going to fall, let's do it with style. Now come on. That's an order."

He blinked, and then smiled. "You're not my boss anymore, you know."

"Alaric Kwong, I will *always* be your boss. Now get in the damn car."

I followed Alaric to the SUV. He climbed in ahead of me, and I paused to wave to Dr. Shoji and Dr. Kimberley before getting in. Steve closed the door as soon as I was inside, and the locks engaged automatically. There were no handles inside. We wouldn't be getting out unless someone decided to *let* us out. Becks and Alaric had gravitated to the far back, leaving Shaun and me closer to the partition that separated us from the driver's cabin.

"Isn't this cozy?" said Becks. "If they fill this thing with gas and kill us before we know what's happening, I swear, the first thing my reanimated corpse eats will be your face, Mason."

"I'm pretty sure I could kick your ass even if we were all dead," said Shaun.

Becks shrugged. "You won't reanimate. It won't be a contest."

The two of them continued teasing each other, using sharp comments and verbal barbs as a way to keep calm. Irwins. They all have a few basic personality traits in common, and one of them is a strong dislike for being pinned in small spaces that they don't control. That sort of thing is a death trap most of the time, and Shaun and Becks were both well trained enough to know it. I ignored the bickering as much as I could, squinting at the black glass divider between us and the front of the car.

If I had still had retinal Kellis-Amberlee, I would have been able to see through that glass and tell who was driving the car. I would have had at least a little more information to use in determining whether or not we were being driven to our deaths. If you'd asked me before I died whether I liked my eyes, I would have looked at you like you were insane. Now that I was someone different, I missed their familiar limits and capabilities. Maybe it was just a matter of first-hand experience—Georgia Mason had it, and I didn't. Regardless of what it was, or wasn't, I kept squinting at the glass, wishing I could see what was on the other side.

I was still squinting at the glass when it slid smoothly downward, revealing the shoulders of Steve and our driver. Shaun and Becks immediately stopped sniping at each other, straightening. My shoulders locked, going so tense that it hurt. Shaun grabbed my hand where it was resting against the seat, squeezing until my fingers hurt worse than my shoulders did.

Steve twisted to look at us. "We're almost there," he said. There was an odd tightness in his voice, like he wanted to say something, but knew he couldn't get away with it. That tightness hadn't been there before, when we were at the EIS—when we weren't in the car.

Lowering my sunglasses enough to let him see where I was looking, I glanced toward the window. He shook his head. I tried again, this time slanting my gaze toward the dome covering the overhead light. Steve nodded marginally. We were bugged. I looked to Shaun, and saw him nodding, too. Everyone who'd come with me was a trained journalist. They all knew what that exchange had meant.

"Going to tell us where 'there' is, big guy, or do we get to try and guess?" Listening to Shaun trying to pretend that he was still the careless thrill seeker who'd signed up to follow the Ryman campaign was almost painful. That man was dead. As dead as the real Georgia Mason.

We were both pretending. We were just doing it in different ways.

"You'll know it when you see it," said Steve. "There are a few ground rules I need you to understand. I advise listening closely. Anyone violating the terms will be shot. Your bodies will never be found."

"Wow. That's . . . direct," said Becks. "What are they?"

"First, you will not broadcast or record anything that happens after leaving this car."

Yeah, right. "Will there be an EMP shield up to prevent it?"

"Yes, for broadcast, but we're trusting you on the recording." He smirked a little. "I managed to convince my superiors that you didn't need to be searched for recording devices, mostly by showing them the list of what we never managed to take off you when we were on the campaign trail. I suppose they don't want to be here taking your transmitters off until dawn."

"Got it, no recording," said Shaun. "What else?"

"Second, you will not in any way initiate physical contact with anyone who does not initiate physical contact with you."

"Shake a hand, get shot?" asked Alaric. When Steve nodded, he looked faintly ill. "This gets better and better with every day that passes."

From the look that crossed Steve's face, Alaric had no idea just how bad things had gotten. I filed the expression away for later. Whatever was happening here, Steve didn't like it. That could be useful.

"Third, you will ask questions only when given permission to do so."

We all stared at him. Telling a carload of reporters not to ask questions was like telling a volcano not to erupt; not only was it pointless, it was likely to end with someone getting hurt. Steve sighed heavily.

"These rules weren't my idea. I know better. Then again, you coming here wasn't my idea." He shook his head. "This is going to end badly. Please try to postpone that as long as possible." Steve pulled back, and the divider slid upward again, blocking the cabin from view.

"I want to punch someone," said Shaun conversationally.

"Do it with the hand that's currently crushing my fingers," I suggested. "You're endangering my ability to type."

Shaun let go of my hand, grimacing. "Sorry."

"Don't be sorry. Just be ready for whatever's coming."

"He didn't say anything about weapons," said Becks. "Bets that they're going to take our weapons away?"

"No bet," said Alaric. "These pig-fucking sons of diseased dock workers aren't going to let us out of this car armed."

I raised an eyebrow. "You're really enjoying the possibilities of the English language today, aren't you?"

"Just wait," said Becks. "When he gets really worked up, he swears in Cantonese. It's like listening to a macaw having a seizure."

Alaric glared at her. She grinned at him. And the car stopped moving.

All levity fled, the four of us assuming wary positions that made our earlier tension look like nothing. Shaun put one hand on my shoulder; the other, I knew, would be going to his gun. We'd started out among friends. Now we had no idea where we were.

The car door swung open, revealing the bulky shape of Steve. He stepped aside, letting us see the man who was standing behind him.

"Hello, Georgia," said Rick, smiling as he offered me his hands. "I know we've never actually met before, but I have to tell you . . . it's been a long time."

The concierge just came to tell me my parents have landed at the Seattle/Tacoma International Airport, and will be at the Agora in less than an hour. I look like hell. My hair doesn't even bear thinking about. But oh I am so glad they're coming.

Mahir and I have discussed what to tell them, and we've settled on the only thing they're likely to accept: the truth. He's pointed out (a few too many times) that they're in medtech, they have contracts with the CDC, and they could be on the wrong side. I can't find a way to explain that I don't care. If they're on the wrong side now, they'll change when they find out what happened—what that bad, bad side was willing to do to me.

I have hidden the truth from them for too long. It's time I started living up to the mission statement that Georgia Mason chose when she founded After the End Times. It's time for me to start telling the truth.

But ah, it hurts.

—From *Dandelion Mine*, the blog of Magdalene Grace Garcia, August 6, 2041. Unpublished.

The lab is very quiet.

I'm not sure that I like it anymore.

I miss you, Joe.

—From the private files of Dr. Shannon Abbey, August 6, 2041. Unpublished.

SHAUN: Thirty-four

Rick had more gray in his hair than I remembered. It would make him look distinguished in the right circumstances. At the moment, it just made him look old. He was wearing a tailored suit that probably cost as much as three rescue missions into the Florida hazard zone, and his shoes were shiny and tight. He'd never be able to run from a zombie mob in those shoes.

Then again, he wouldn't have to—not with two Steve-sized Secret Servicemen flanking him, each of them wearing their firearms openly on their belts.

"Rick?" George got out of the car. Her movements were jerky, like she wasn't sure what she was supposed to do. She grabbed the edge of the door as she stood. "What are you—?"

The question was cut off as the Vice President of the United States—our former colleague and one of the only bloggers to survive the Ryman campaign—swept her into a hug. She made a squeaking noise, clearly startled, and her arms stayed down, but she didn't pull away. For George, that was practically a passionate embrace.

Becks shoved against my hip. "Hey, Mason. Move out of the damn way."

"What?" I tore my eyes away from Rick and George. I hadn't realized I was moving, but I apparently had; I was standing, blocking

Alaric and Becks from getting out of the car. I stepped to the side. "Oh. Sorry about that."

"Sure you are." Becks stood, moving far enough to the side for Alaric to squeeze out, and eyed Rick suspiciously. "So that's Richard Cousins, boy reporter."

"Pretty sure we're supposed to call him 'Mr. Vice President' now, but yeah, that's him." Becks was already with After the End Times when Rick joined us, but they'd only met once, at Georgia's funeral. Rick had just been asked to stand with Ryman. He'd been in shock, and so had the rest of us.

Becks looked at him critically, finally saying, "I could take him."

"And I could take you," said Steve. "Let's not get into a pissing contest. We both know who'd come out the winner, so there's no point."

"Sometimes the contest *is* the point," said Becks piously.

Rick pushed George out to arm's length, eyes avidly scanning her face. That was going to keep him distracted for a few more seconds at least. The fact that George hadn't pulled away from him yet meant she wanted us to be studying something else—namely, our surroundings.

I turned to look around, not bothering to be subtle about it. Let Alaric and Becks be subtle; I'd play the happy buffoon, a role I've been practicing since I was a kid. People underestimate you if they think your only interests in life involve poking zombies with sticks and getting that perfect camera angle.

We were in an underground garage. There was a row of SUVs identical to the one that drove us from the airfield parked nearby, presumably waiting to be needed. The lights were smooth and clear, and the doors weren't just gated; they were sealed with metal sheeting that looked almost like blast protection. This place was locked down tighter than a bank vault.

Oh. Crap. Feeling like an idiot, I turned to Steve and said, "I've never been to the White House before. Do you think we'll get some of those cool souvenir key chains before we leave? I've wanted one of those ever since I saw a video of this one dude from Newfoundland using his to pop a zombie's eye out."

Spreading it a little thick, don't you think? asked Georgia.

I forced myself to ignore it and keep on smiling. Crazy doesn't go away overnight. Especially not crazy you've watered and tended yourself. But wow was this not the time to have an incident.

"I don't think this is a souvenir key chain kind of visit, but man, it's good to see you," said Rick. I turned to see him walking toward me, leaving George behind. He kept talking as he stuck out his right hand, clearly expecting me to shake it. "There were a few points where you went quiet, and I was afraid—let's just say I've had reasons to be worried about your welfare."

"Really?" I took his hand, squeezing his fingers until that big politician's smile he'd acquired somewhere started to look strained. "Because it seems to me that if you knew we were having problems, you could maybe have answered your fucking e-mail and helped us."

"No. I couldn't have." His smile died as he pulled his hand away. "And just so you're aware, if it were up to me, I would have stuck a bow on her and delivered her to your doorstep on your birthday. I never wanted things to be this way."

Dr. Wynne. Buffy. Rick. How many of the people we considered allies were never allies at all? "But they are," I said.

Rick sighed. "True enough." He turned, starting toward the sealed blast doors behind him. His Secret Servicemen continued facing forward, watching us with what I could only describe as suspicion. They were waiting for one of us to do something.

Instead, we just stood there. Finally, Alaric asked, "Are we supposed to go with you?"

"What? Oh. Yes." Rick waved for us to follow him. "Right this way."

"Blood tests . . . ?" asked Becks.

"We don't bother with the security theater here," said Steve. There was a deep disdain in his voice—less, I thought, for the lack of security in this garage, and more for the idea that the security everywhere else in the world was flawed.

And it *was* flawed. I used to believe in that level of security, in blood tests every ten minutes and checking your reflexes and response rates constantly. Even as an Irwin, I swore by following the rules. And then I met Dr. Abbey, who maintained the absolute minimum where security was concerned, and I learned that half the tests we take on a daily basis are useless. If you haven't been exposed or gone outside, what's the point of sticking another needle in your finger? Those tests didn't tell us anything we didn't already know . . . but they reinforced the idea that we had to be afraid, always, that our humanity was fleeting, maintained only by a constant web of government oversight.

Rick tapped out a code on the keypad by the blast doors and they slid open, revealing a hall that could have belonged in any government building I've ever seen. I'm not sure what it is that identifies their hallways, but there's something in the inevitable combination of beige, white, and green that just screams "seat of power." Mind, the Presidential Seal etched on the sliding glass doors that had been concealed behind the blast doors didn't hurt.

"You know, my mother always dreamed I'd wind up here someday," said Becks. "Pretty sure she wanted me to be First Lady, not a semi-hostage journalist on the run from a global conspiracy, but hey. At least I'm in the White House."

I laughed and started for the doors. They slid open at our approach, and, once again, there was no blood test required to get inside.

"Getting into the White House through any of the public entrances requires six blood tests and a retinal scan," said Rick as we walked. "If you're unable to successfully complete a retinal scan for any reason, you have to submit to whatever further testing security deems necessary. Refusal to be tested will result in your being removed from the premises."

"And shot," said George. "Correct?"

Rick looked uncomfortable. "It generally doesn't come to that."

"Mm-hmm." She had stepped through the doors a few feet ahead of me. She stopped there, waiting until we could walk on side by side. "What are we doing here, Rick?"

"You're here because . . . it was time for you to be brought up to speed." He kept walking, trusting the rest of us to follow. I'm sure the presence of three enormous Secret Service agents had nothing to do with his degree of confidence.

No, really.

The four of us stuck close together as we walked along the hall, George and me in the lead, right behind Rick, with Becks and Alaric behind us. Steve and the two unnamed agents brought up the rear. The driver of our SUV stayed in the vehicle when we went inside. Presumably, he or she had been left in order to park the car. This was all very well organized. I stepped a little closer to George, whose face was set in the grim mask that meant she was as uncomfortable as I was. That was good. I didn't want to be the only one who knew we were walking into a trap.

We stopped at an apparently blank wall midway down the hall. Rick gave the rest of us an apologetic look as he said, "This is where we have to take your weapons away. I'm sorry. It's just that we're about to go into some very secure areas, and I don't have the clearance to authorize you to go armed."

"You're the Vice President of the United States," said George. "If you don't have the clearance, who does?"

He didn't say anything. He just looked at her.

"Right." George sighed and removed the gun from her belt. Steve stepped up with a large plastic bin; she put the gun inside.

That was the cue for the rest of us to begin shedding our weapons. Alaric and George were clean in a matter of minutes. Becks and I took longer. The bin in Steve's hands was dangerously full by the time we finished.

"Can we get a claim check for those?" asked Alaric.

Steve snorted, expression darkly amused. "Unlikely."

"Just checking," said Alaric, unruffled.

"Thank you," said Rick. He pressed his hand against the wall. A light came on behind his palm, and the wall turned transparent—a trick I'd only seen once before, in the Portland offices of the CDC. There was an elevator on the other side.

Alaric whistled. "Where can I get me one of those?"

"First, get a six-billion-dollar security budget. After that, I'll put you in touch with the DOD," said Rick. The transparent patch of wall slid to the side as the elevator doors swished open, revealing a surprisingly industrial-looking metal box. This elevator could have been located in any dock or warehouse in the world, and yet here it was, in the White House. Rick beckoned us forward again. "After you."

"If this is a trap, someone's getting a very stern talking to," I said blithely, and stepped into the elevator. George was barely half a step behind me.

Of the three Secret Service agents, only Steve got into the elevator with us, leaving the other two behind after handing one of them the bin containing our weapons. The doors swished shut again as soon as Steve was through, and Rick opened a metal panel on the wall, revealing, for the first time since our arrival, a blood testing array. It had eight distinct panels, one for each of us, with two to spare.

"I thought you didn't do security theater," said George.

"This is just a precaution. We're going into a highly secured area," said Rick. "We all have to test clean before the elevator will move."

"Oh, great," said Alaric. "I wanted to hang out in a death trap today."

Becks elbowed him in the side as she pressed her thumb against the first testing square. The white plastic turned red behind her finger, remaining that color for a count of five before turning green.

Rick did the same with the next square, cycling it from white to red to green. Then he stepped back, looking at the rest of us.

"You're up," he said.

None of us were infected. The elevator chimed softly and began sliding downward, moving with a smooth efficiency that bordered on unnerving. I realized that the four of us were standing clustered together on one side of the elevator, leaving Rick and Steve on the other. Steve was watching the wall. Rick was watching us, a deep longing in his eyes.

Talk to him, said Georgia.

I glanced toward the George beside me, wincing a little when I realized she hadn't spoken. Still, it was good advice. I took a half step forward, focusing on Rick, and asked, "Rick, dude—what the fuck happened to you?"

"Do you remember how your sister used to say the truth was the most important thing in the world? That if we all knew the truth, we'd be able to live our lives more freely and with fewer troubles?" The elevator was slowing down. "It's funny, because she always seemed to forget that a truth you don't understand is more dangerous than a lie. Robert Stalnaker told the truth when he said Dr. Kellis was creating a cure for the common cold, and look where that's gotten us."

Robert Stalnaker was the muckraker—sorry, "investigative reporter"—whose articles on the infant Kellis cure resulted in its being released into the atmosphere, which led in turn to the creation of Kellis-Amberlee. If he hadn't decided to "tell the truth," we might not be in the pickle we're in now. No one knows what happened to Stalnaker during the Rising. Whatever it was, I hope it hurt.

"Robert Stalnaker made up a story to sell papers," said George. "And by the way, I'm right here. I can *hear* you."

The elevator stopped. Rick turned to her, looking faintly abashed, and said, "I know. I just . . . I saw you made, Georgia. I can't quite wrap my head around the idea of you knowing everything you knew, well . . . before."

"I don't, because I'm not the same girl," said George coldly. "You of all people should know that. You can't really raise the dead."

"Great. Even the clone master has issues with Miss Undead America 2041," said Becks. "This is really the guy who paid to have you resurrected, Georgia? Because so far, not impressed."

It was nice to see that my team's "us against the world" mentality extended to George. "So what is it you're saying here, Rick?" I asked. "Are you saying we're here to learn how to lie?"

"No," he said. Rick pressed his hand against the panel next to the elevator door. It slid open, revealing the featureless gray hall beyond. "You're here to learn why *we* have to lie, and why we can't let you run around telling the truth without consequences. It's time you learned the truth about Kellis-Amberlee." He looked back over his shoulder at us, and his expression was haggard, like he'd personally witnessed the end of the world. "I am so, so sorry."

Then he stepped out of the elevator, leaving the five of us—my team, plus Steve—behind. I looked at the others. "Did that creep anybody else out, just a little bit? Or was it just me who was getting the weird 'and then they found out he was dead all along' vibe?"

"This isn't good," said Becks.

"No, and it isn't getting any less creepy while we stand in this elevator arguing about it." George stepped briskly out to the hallway, where she stopped, turned, and looked at the rest of us. "Well? Are you coming, or am I going to go get the scoop of the century by myself?"

"I don't know about you guys, but I'm not letting the dead girl make me look like a wimp," declared Becks, and shoved her way past Alaric to exit the elevator. She stopped next to George, folding her arms. "Okay, three dudes hiding in the elevator while two girls are hanging out in the scary hall? You are now officially wimps. In case you were wondering."

"We can't have that." I put a hand on Alaric's shoulder, propelling him along with me as I stepped out of the elevator to join them.

Steve was close behind me. The elevator doors slid shut as soon as he was clear, and the light above them blinked off.

Someone to my left began applauding slowly. I whipped around, hand going for a gun that wasn't there, and found myself looking into the face of a man I hadn't seen in the flesh for over a year—not since George's funeral, which he made by the skin of his teeth. The others turned with me, some of them reaching for weapons they didn't have, others just staring.

It was George who managed to find her equilibrium enough to break the silence first. I guess after coming back from the dead, nothing else is going to seem like a big enough deal to knock you off balance for long.

"Hello, Mr. President," she said.

President Peter Ryman smiled. "Hello, Georgia."

Maggie's parents have arrived, or so I'm told—I haven't been allowed to see her since their plane landed, and for all I know, they've come, bundled her into their private jet, and gone, leaving me to settle an utterly astronomical bill. I do hope they take physical labor in exchange. Washing dishes should have us paid off in, oh, three or four hundred years. Give or take a decade or two. Nan will shout when she finds out I've become an indentured servant in America. Probably say it serves me right for being so damn stubborn, going off and leaving her alone.

Dr. Abbey sent an e-mail last night, saying the others were leaving her lab on another mission. She wouldn't say where, and my mail to her has started bouncing. Either she's blocked me, or she's changed addresses. Either way, we're cut off for the nonce, because none of my colleagues are answering their e-mail. And I alone am left to tell thee . . .

Damn. I thought I was done being the one who stayed behind to write the story down. Bloody journalists.

May they all come home safely.

—From *Fish and Clips*, the blog of Mahir Gowda,
August 6, 2041. Unpublished.

Michael and Alisa are at the gift shop near the front gate, getting her some clean T-shirts. We've been at Cliff's Amusement Park in New Mexico for two days now, and we're all starting to run out of clothes. It should be safe to head back to Berkeley soon. Right now, it's a media circus, and the only way we can avoid it is by acting like everything is normal. Alisa's been a good sport about things, thank God. It probably helps that after Florida, *nothing* looks dangerous to her.

She's a good kid. Even after everything she's been through, she's a good kid. Shaun and Georgia . . . they were good kids, too. Even after everything we put them through, they somehow managed to grow up to be good people. I don't know how that happened. I guess that makes sense, because I never really knew *them.* I never wanted to. I suppose that makes me a hypocrite, because now that they're grown and gone—gone for good, in Georgia's case—I'm proud of them.

I wish I'd been a better mother when I had the chance.

—From *Stacy's Survival Strategies,* the blog of Stacy Mason, August 6, 2041. Unpublished.

GEORGIA: Thirty-five

President Ryman was flanked by three Secret Servicemen of his own, along with a man I didn't recognize, but whose CDC-issue lab coat immediately made my heart start beating faster. I managed to hold my ground only by reminding myself that Georgia Mason—the original—would never show fear in the face of a man who wasn't holding a gun to her head, and maybe not even then. If I was going to deal with these people, I had to do it the way she would have done it. Nothing else was going to work.

"You don't seem surprised to see me," I said, tilting my chin up just enough to be sure my sunglasses would entirely block my eyes. I didn't want him thinking of me as a science project. I wanted him thinking of me as *Georgia*, and Georgia's eyes didn't look like mine.

"That's because I'm not," he said. He looked tired. None of his Secret Servicemen were familiar—the only familiar face I'd seen among the guards was Steve, and Steve would probably have a job until everyone who'd been on the campaign was dead and gone. There's something to be said for loyalty like his.

Shaun took a step forward, planting himself beside me, and all but glared at President Ryman. "You mean you knew about this cloning shit, too, and you didn't tell me? Don't you people think that sending me a note might have been a good idea?"

"No, they didn't," I said, as calmly as I could. It was surprisingly easy. Losing my temper wouldn't do any good, and I was starting to become accustomed to the idea that everyone in the world—except Shaun—was going to betray me. "I was never supposed to leave the lab."

Rick moved to join President Ryman. He met my eyes as he turned to face the rest of us. President Ryman . . . didn't. He looked away instead, and the set of his jaw said everything he wasn't saying out loud.

"You bastard," whispered Shaun. He started to take a step forward. I grabbed his elbow, stopping him.

"The last thing we need today is for you to assault the president," I said quietly. "Take a deep breath, and let it go."

"He was going to let them kill you."

"He let them make me in the first place. Let's call that part a wash, and see where he takes it from there." I kept watching President Ryman's face. He kept not meeting my eyes. "Why are we here, Mr. President? You never had to let us make it this far."

"Yes, I did." His head snapped around. For a moment, I saw the man I knew behind the beaten shadows in his eyes. He looked angry. Not with us—with the world. "I owed you this."

"Did you owe us this before or after you let your people call an air strike on Oakland?" asked Becks. "David Novakowski stayed behind when those bombs came down. He was an Irwin. A good one. He wasn't involved in your campaign because he was in Alaska at the time, but he would have liked you." Her tone was calm and challenging at the same time, daring him to give an answer she didn't approve of.

"The air strike on Oakland was called in response to an outbreak, and did not involve the president," said the man from the CDC. I managed not to cringe at the sound of his voice. "Consider your words before you make accusations."

"It was a pretty convenient outbreak, considering one of your people had just shown up, running for her life," snapped Shaun. "Don't try to bullshit us, okay? We all know we're not leaving this building alive. So there's no point in fucking with our heads."

"Shaun." President Ryman actually sounded offended. "Please don't make assumptions. You're absolutely going to leave here alive. At a certain point, it became inevitable that we'd bring you here to fully explain the situation."

"Does that point have anything to do with us having secure footage of a living clone of Georgia Mason running around Seattle?" asked Alaric. "I ask purely out of academic curiosity, you understand. I know you're going to lie through your teeth."

President Ryman sighed. "You don't trust me anymore, do you?"

"Have you given us a reason to?" I asked.

"You're alive, Georgia. I'd think that might be enough to buy me a little patience."

"You were planning to have me killed and replaced with a more tractable version. I think that explains a little crankiness."

The man from the CDC cleared his throat. "It doesn't matter who's angry with whom. You are here to have the true nature of the Kellis-Amberlee infection explained. With that in mind, I believe it's time we make you understand why you have been remiss in your lines of inquiry."

"Ever notice how people like to use five-dollar words when they know they're wrong?" asked Becks, of no one in particular.

President Ryman shook his head. "Arguing is getting us nowhere. This way." He gestured down the hall before starting to walk. His Secret Servicemen promptly moved to get behind us, making it clear that we'd be herded along if we didn't come on our own.

We went.

The hallway led to a room with walls covered by crystal display screens. Two of them were already showing the structure of the Kellis-Amberlee virus. Another showed an outline of a generic human body. Ryman walked to the large table at the center of the room and stopped, clearly unhappy, as he turned to the man from the CDC.

"I believe that, at this point, I must remind you that national security depends on your silence," said the man from the CDC. "Nothing said here can leave this room."

"Uh, *reporters*," said Becks. "Or did you forget?"

"Even reporters have things they care about," he said, with chilling calm. "Perhaps you feel immortal. Perhaps you consider martyrdom something to aspire to—a thrilling entry for your much-lauded 'Wall.' But you have a family, don't you? Rebecca Atherton, of the Westchester Athertons. Your youngest sister was married this past summer. Katherine. A very pretty girl. It's a pity they live in such a remote area."

Becks's eyes widened before narrowing into angry slits, filled with a murderous rage. "Don't you even—" she began.

"And you, Mr. Kwong. *Your* sister is your only remaining family. She's currently in the custody of Stacy and Michael Mason—not people renowned for their ability to keep children alive, when you stop to think about it."

For possibly the first time in my life, original or artificial, the urge to defend the Masons rose inside me. "You've made your point," I snapped. "We'll keep our mouths shut. Now do you want to explain what the hell is so important that you need to tell us your evil plan before you have us all shot?"

"It's not an evil plan, Georgia; it's the truth." With those words, President Ryman went from sounding weary to sounding utterly heartbroken. "You've become too associated with this whole situation, and that means we need you. You're the ones who tell the truth, and the ones who fell off the radar when things turned bad. People will believe you."

"Even when we're lying to them?"

His silence was all the answer I needed.

"Please sit," said the man from the CDC.

Grudgingly, I sat. The others did the same. Only the man from the CDC remained standing.

"The first thing you need to understand is that the KA virus, being manmade, bonds tightly to anything it encounters," he began, in the sort of easy, lecturing tone that all doctors seem to learn in medical school. Ignoring the tension in the room, he produced a remote from his pocket and pointed it at the nearest screen. The Kellis-Amberlee model displayed there began to rotate. "This tendency created the hybridized virus to begin with. And it is what has complicated our cure for the infection."

Shaun frowned. "Complicated your *search* for a cure?"

"No," said the man from the CDC calmly. "Complicated our cure." The model was suddenly surrounded by smaller, semi-spherical images that looked something like slides I'd seen of pre-Rising flu virus. They began attacking the larger KA virus, surrounding it before engulfing it entirely. "We've managed to create several treatments that work remarkably well, destroying the Kellis-Amberlee infection in nine out of ten afflicted."

We all stared at him, even Steve. It was Alaric who found his voice first, asking slowly, "Then why haven't you released it?"

"The Kellis-Amberlee virus has become so entwined with our immune systems that killing it kills them as well. Without a functioning immune system, the cured become targets for every opportunistic infection that comes along. None of our subjects have lasted long." The image on the screen reset itself, returning to the single Kellis-Amberlee virus, floating serene and undisturbed. "To put it in simpler terms: Kill the virus, kill the population."

"So why don't you just *tell* people that?" demanded Shaun. "We're not idiots!"

"Try telling Alexander Kellis that people aren't idiots," suggested the man from the CDC. "We cannot say 'there will never be a cure.' People need hope. The hope that someday, Kellis-Amberlee will be banished, and we will be free to resume the lives that we remember."

"Why?" asked Alaric. He shook his head slowly. "We can live with the virus. The reservoir conditions are proof of that. We can find a new status quo."

"One where anyone could become a zombie, anytime, and you don't dare shoot them because they might—*might*—recover their senses? This nation barely recovered from the Rising when the lines were clear and infection meant death. I doubt we could hold together as a people if we were told that recovery was an option." I was starting to hate the absolute calm of the man from the CDC's delivery. He continued to watch us coolly. "A cure may be impossible, but a solution *will* be found. A strain of the virus that doesn't generate anomalous reservoir conditions will be discovered, and will be used to standardize the tragically incurable condition that now informs our society. No one will ever need to know that a cure is not possible. No one will ever need to give up hope."

"No one except for all the people who would have recovered if you'd just failed to shoot them in the head," said Shaun. The bitterness in his voice was strong enough to worry me. I put a hand on his arm, praying that would be enough to keep him from doing anything stupid. "The ones who would have *gotten better*."

"Sacrifices must be made," said the man from the CDC.

Something in his tone provided the last piece I needed to fully understand what he was saying. "You want to infect the entire world with the same strain of the virus," I said slowly.

"Yes."

"You're going to need a better distribution method if you're planning to accomplish that. You can't be sure of everyone getting exposed the natural way."

For the first time, he looked uncomfortable. Alaric, meanwhile, was staring at him, mouth actually falling slightly open in shock.

Finally, Alaric said, in a hushed tone, "You built the mosquitoes?"

"'Built' is a strong word—" began Rick.

"They were never intended to reach the American mainland," said President Ryman.

I had heard that man speak with conviction a hundred times on the campaign trail; I had heard him make promises he damn well intended to keep. I had never heard him deliver a party line with that little sincerity. He wasn't lying. He might as well have been. "What happened?" I asked. "Was there a leak?"

"No," said Shaun, before anyone else could speak. "They let them go. They wanted to bury the news cycle, keep what happened in Memphis from getting out. Isn't that right?"

"The storm was an unexpected complication," said the man from the CDC. "The carrier mosquitoes were never intended to make it out of Cuba."

I was busy holding Shaun's arm, keeping him from doing anything we might regret later. I didn't think to grab Alaric. Neither did Becks. Before any of us had a chance to react, the normally nonviolent Newsie was launching himself at the man from the CDC, locking his hands around the taller man's throat and slamming him into the wall. The crystal display screen shook dangerously, but didn't fall.

"YOUR COMPLICATION KILLED MY PARENTS!" shouted Alaric, slamming the man from the CDC against the wall again. No one moved to pull them apart. "THEY WERE IN FLORIDA! YOU KILLED MY FAMILY TO BURY A NEWS CYCLE, BECAUSE YOU COULDN'T READ A FUCKING WEATHER REPORT!"

The man from the CDC made a strained choking noise, clawing helplessly at Alaric's hands. Still, no one moved to pull them apart.

Finally, wearily, President Ryman said, "It would make everyone's job easier if you would stop trying to actually *kill* him. I understand that you're angry. This isn't helping."

Becks glared at him as she stepped forward, putting her hands on Alaric's shoulders. He slumped, fingers still locked around the doctor's throat. "Let him go, Alaric," she said quietly. "It's time to let him go."

"They killed my parents," Alaric mumbled.

"They killed a lot of people. They even killed Georgia. But strangling this man won't bring them back, and he hasn't finished telling us everything he knows. Now let him go. It's time to let him talk. You can kill him later."

Reluctantly, Alaric let go. The doctor staggered away from him, coughing, one hand coming up to clutch at his throat like he was going to finish the job of strangling himself. Pointing at Alaric, he demanded, "Restrain that man!"

"Begging your pardon, sir, but no," said Steve. "I serve at the pleasure of the president, not at the whim of the CDC."

The man from the CDC glared daggers at him. President Ryman ignored him, turning to us. "The mosquitoes are a modified form of the species that carries yellow fever," he said. "They're purely artificial. They can't reproduce, and they can't survive in temperatures below a certain level. The loss of American life has been tragic. It will end when winter comes."

"They can't reproduce?" said Shaun incredulously. "That's your big solution? They won't fuck? Did none of you people ever see *Jurassic Park*?"

"It may take us years to clean out the zombie mobs left by the outbreak, but I assure you, the mosquitoes will not be a factor for long," said President Ryman. He met my eyes for an instant, and I almost recoiled from the pain lurking in his face. He was the president. He was the man at the head of this conspiracy—somehow, he'd gone from being Tate's patsy to the man in the position Tate once aspired to. And he looked like he was being tortured.

"Tell that to my parents," said Alaric. He sagged against Becks, glaring daggers at anyone who made the mistake of looking his way.

If he'd been armed, I think more than one person would have been in danger of dying.

Still clutching his throat, the man from the CDC said, "Regardless, you were brought here for a purpose. You will do as you're told, or you will not leave here alive."

"What purpose would that be?" I asked warily.

"You have a certain reputation for honesty," said the man from the CDC. "You will begin reporting the news as we present it, rather than reporting it as you see fit. By adding your voices to ours, we can hopefully control some of the more unpleasant rumors to have arisen since the events surrounding the most recent presidential election."

It was my turn to stare at him. Finally, I said, "You want me to *lie* for you."

"Oh, no," said the man from the CDC. "You know, I'm disappointed. I really thought you'd be smarter. I suppose the cloning process wasn't as reliable as we had hoped."

"No," said Shaun. He pulled his arm free of my hand. "You're already out of the game as far they're concerned. You said it yourself. The George I got was supposed to be the brainwashed agreeable one who thought they had the best damn ideas ever."

"Then why?" I asked.

President Ryman sighed. "Shaun, I'm sorry."

"No, you're not." Shaun glanced at me. The look on his face was enough to make me wish I'd never come back from the dead. "They brought you back so they'd have something they could use to make me do what they told me to do. They brought you back for leverage, so they could make *me* lie for them. You always told the truth, George. But I made people believe it."

"Oh." My voice was barely a whisper. It hurt to even force myself to speak that loudly. "Well, then it's over. We won't do it."

"Again, I thought you'd be smarter."

I turned to the man from the CDC. He was shaking his head, and holding what looked like a fountain pen in his hand. Shaun went rigid, barely seeming to breathe.

"You'll do what we tell you to do. If you choose not to, well. We'll have to find ourselves some replacement reporters, because you are all going to die."

Because we chose to tell the truth
(The cool of age, the rage of youth)
And stand against the lies of old
(The whispers soft, the tales untold)
We find ourselves the walking dead
(The loves unkept, the words unsaid)
And in the crypt of all we've known
(The broken blade, the breaking stone)
We know that we were in the right
(The coming dawn, the ending night).
So here is when we stop the lies.
The time is come. We have to Rise.

—From *Dandelion Mine*, the blog of Magdalene Grace Garcia, August 7, 2041.

The problem with people who have power is that they start thinking more about what it takes to keep that power than they do about what's right or wrong or just plain a bad idea. Here's a tip for you: If you're ever in a position to be making calls on right and wrong that can impact an entire nation, run your decisions past a six-year-old. If they look at you in horror and tell you you're getting coal in your stocking for the rest of your life, you should probably reconsider your course of action. Unless you want to be remembered as a monster, in which case, knock yourself out.

—From *Charming Not Sincere*, the blog of Rebecca Atherton, August 7, 2041.

SHAUN: Thirty-six

The pen in the doctor's hand—so much like the one Dr. Wynne used to kill Kelly in the Memphis CDC, what felt like the better part of a lifetime ago—was enough to make me go cold. I was immune to Kellis-Amberlee. None of the others could say the same. Especially not George, who made me immune, but didn't confer the same immunity on her own clone.

Do you think you could survive losing me again? asked her voice, sweet and low and somehow poisonous. She'd never taken that tone with me before. But why shouldn't she turn on me? I was replacing her, and doing my best to shove her away.

What kind of world were we living in, where the people we trusted to keep us healthy were the ones keeping us sick, and a man couldn't even depend on his own insanity?

I raised my hands defensively and said, "There's no reason for us to do anything crazy. Let's just settle down, okay?" Out of the corner of my eye I could see Becks restraining Alaric, keeping him from moving toward the now-deadly doctor. He wasn't with us in Memphis. We'd told him what happened, but he didn't really understand.

"It's a pen," said George.

It took me a second to realize that it was the live George who was speaking, not the increasingly malicious voice inside my head. I glanced her way, giving a quick, tight shake of my head. "We're all going to stay calm," I said, hoping she'd decide to listen. "Okay?"

George frowned before nodding slowly. "Okay." She put her own hands up, mirroring my defensive position. "I'm sorry. I spoke too hastily. We'll consider your proposal."

"Why don't I believe you?" asked the doctor. He glared at President Ryman. "I knew this was a terrible plan from the start. We should have arranged for an outbreak in their hometown as soon as the campaign was over. Wynne was soft on them, the old fool. Leaving them alone was his idea, not mine."

"That sounds less like 'soft on us' and more like sensible resource management," said Becks, pulling the doctor's attention back to her. I winced, but didn't try to stop her. She was keeping him from focusing on any one person. That was valuable. I just hoped it wouldn't get her shot.

"Put down the pen," said Steve. His tone was clipped, indicating that he, too, knew exactly what it was.

"No, I don't think so," said the doctor. "The agreement was simple: I would allow the president to bring his little coven of pet journalists here, and try to sway them to the side of reason. If it failed, they would be mine to dispose of. As I expected, it has failed."

"Who says she speaks for the rest of us?" The words sounded alien even as they left my mouth. *George, please, forgive me,* I thought. "I mean, come on, man. It was nice of you to let the science dudes grow me a replacement, but you could have just sent a card. She's a *clone*. She's not a real person. She doesn't get to be the one who gets the real people dead."

The man from the CDC paused, an uncertain look crossing his face.

I decided to press what little advantage I had. "I'm not going to pretend we're happy about this bullshit. I mean, dude, you killed Alaric's parents. That's pretty crappy, and it doesn't make us feel like playing nice. But that doesn't mean she speaks for the rest of us. You know she's not a perfect copy of my sister. You built a broken Georgia. Maybe you could've done a better job if she hadn't managed to get away from you—that happens a lot, doesn't it? Clones, mosquitoes, reporters. You've been running the country for like twenty years. Shouldn't you be better at this by now?"

"That's quite enough, son," said President Ryman. Turning to the man from the CDC, he said, "Put the pen down. They're willing to listen to what we have to say. Isn't that what we brought them here for? To sway them to the right way of thinking?"

I could see George out of the corner of my eye. She had her face turned toward me, jaw slack in the way that told me she was staring behind the dark lenses of her sunglasses. I was briefly, terribly grateful she'd chosen to keep wearing them. I wouldn't have been able to keep smiling if I'd been able to see her eyes.

She believes every word you're saying, whispered my internal George, sounding pleased and disappointed at the same time, like she couldn't decide which was better. *I bet she's said those same things to herself every day since she woke up. Not good enough. Not Georgia enough. Not* real. *And now you've confirmed it. Think she'll ever forgive you?*

That seemed like a less pressing question at the moment than whether I was ever going to be able to forgive myself. We had to survive before I could find out one way or the other.

George sniffled before saying, in a small voice, "If I'm not going to be a part of this decision, can I please go lie down? My head hurts. I don't understand what's going on." She sounded utterly pathetic. I had to bite back a sigh of relief.

Georgia's migraines were the one thing that ever got the Masons to let her out of public appearances when we were kids. Her eyes meant that sometimes, migraines just happened, and the best thing for her to do was lie in a nice dark place and wait for them to go away. I used to wonder why the Masons never noticed that she always seemed to have a migraine when we were supposed to go to the government orphanage where she was adopted—lucky her, she was found within driving distance of Berkeley. The Masons had to go all the way to Southern California to get me.

As far as I knew, she never once visited that orphanage. And if she was claiming a migraine now, she was faking it. She was playing along.

Slowly, the man from the CDC said, "If he feels we built him a, as he says, 'broken George,' he won't mind if I shoot her right now. We can always make him a better one."

I froze, every nerve I had screaming two contradictory commands—*save her, save her, don't let her die again* warring with *no, you can't, you'll all die if you try, and you can choose that for you, but you can't choose it for Becks and Alaric.* I had to let him pull the trigger. I couldn't let him. As soon as he started to tense his fingers I'd jump for him, and whatever came after that would be anybody's guess. I knew that, even as the sanest part of me was telling me it was the worst thing I could possibly do. Becks and Alaric knew it, too. They glanced my way, uncertainty in their eyes. I was the boss. I was the one they counted on to keep them safe. And that wasn't going to stop me from getting them both killed.

Rescue came from an unexpected quarter. Steve cleared his throat before saying, with professional calm, "If your hand so much as twitches, sir, I *will* be forced to shoot you. Intentionally beginning an outbreak in the presence of the president is considered an act of treason. Intent to commit an act of treason authorizes me to take whatever steps are necessary to prevent that act from being carried out."

"Now," said President Ryman again. "Your point is made. He didn't stop you. They'll listen to us. Put the pen *down*."

"Fine." Looking disgusted, the man from the CDC slid the pen back into the pocket of his lab coat. "You say the clone has no part in your decision making process. Prove it. Agree to distribute the news on our behalf."

"Please, can I go lie down?" whispered George.

I knew she was faking. The pain in her voice was still enough to make me want to put my arms around her and never let go, men from the CDC and Secret Service agents and government conspiracies be damned.

"You treat all your science projects this badly?" asked Becks.

"Of course not," said President Ryman. "Rick, take her somewhere. Calm her down, give her a glass of water, whatever it takes to settle her. We'll decide what's to be done with her when we finish sorting things out here."

"Yes, Mr. President," said Rick. He moved quickly, taking George's elbow before I could formulate a protest. "Come with me. I'll see if we can't find you something to make you feel a little better." If it had been anyone other than Rick, I would have stepped in. I wouldn't have had a choice. But it was Rick, and he used to be one of us, and so I didn't say anything. Steve followed after him, a hulking, defensive presence. He'd keep her safe if Rick couldn't.

George sniffled and let herself be led away. She didn't look back at me. Not once.

See? whispered the George in my mind. *She believed every word you said.*

"Shut up," I muttered, and grimaced, waiting to see what effect that would have on the already questionably stable nameless doctor from the CDC.

He didn't appear to have heard me. Instead, he watched as Rick led George away, waiting until they were out of sight before turning back to me. "My apologies if I seemed somewhat aggressive before," he said finally. "Had things gone as originally planned, this is the point where we would be presenting her to you—not this clone, perhaps, but one that was not, as you put it, 'defective.' She would be a gift, given in good faith, to show you that working with us is the right thing to do."

I wanted to tell him that if he'd reached the point where giving other people away like party favors was "the right thing to do," he was too crazy for me to want to work with him—and I know from crazy. I wanted to tell him they shouldn't have worked so hard to make a person when they cloned my sister, because an empty shell and excuses about brain damage would have been an awful lot easier for them to control. I didn't say any of those things. I guess I never went all the way crazy after all.

Instead, I did what I do best, and went on the attack. "If you wanted us to get this far, why did your men try to kill us in Seattle?" I asked. "I mean, not exactly 'hi, let's be besties' behavior, you know?"

"That was an unfortunate misunderstanding," said the doctor.

"A surprising number of your misunderstandings involve bullets and body counts," said Alaric. He was glowering. If I were the man from the CDC, I would've been considering a fatal accident for Alaric as a simple matter of self-preservation.

"There are automated security protocols that go into effect whenever we have reason to suspect industrial espionage—and it does happen, especially in a place like the CDC. Our discoveries are often quite lucrative. The theft of subject 7c was enough to activate those protocols."

"Subject 7c?" I asked blankly.

"Georgia," said Becks.

Once again, I weighed the merits of punching someone, and regretfully decided I couldn't afford the fallout. "Do those automated security protocols usually include pre-bugging our shoes? Because your dudes only found us by following the bugs we already had on us."

The doctor looked uncomfortable. "It is sometimes necessary to protect our investments through extra-legal channels. We had an . . . agreement . . . with certain elements of the local underground that, were they approached about an infiltration of our facility, they would ensure we could apprehend those responsible."

"And by doing it after a crime was committed, you avoided getting in trouble for working with the 'local underground,'" said Alaric, with grudging respect. "Slick. Stupid, but slick. Why bother screwing around? Why not just stop them from getting inside in the first place?"

For once, I had the answer the Newsie didn't. "Because a few break-ins keep everybody believing the CDC is at risk, and we never look too hard at the budget for security upgrades and growing new people in big tanks. All of which loops us back around to the thing we're not talking about here. *Why* did you clone Georgia? There are way cheaper ways to convince us that you're the good guys. And yeah, I know, I said 'leverage' earlier, and I meant it, only again, way cheaper ways to do it. You could have threatened my parents, my team . . ."

"But we couldn't get to your team if we couldn't get to you, and we knew that was a risk as far back as the campaign trail," said the doctor calmly. President Ryman looked away. "She wasn't the only one we were prepared to resurrect, although her death meant she was the best candidate. We were able to extract her brain almost immediately, and get to work while the Kellis-Amberlee virus was still working in her system. It's a fascinating behavior, considering how little of the brain the virus actually requires—" He must have seen the storm warnings in our faces, because he changed topics in the middle of the stream, saying, "She was to be leverage, as you've indicated, but she was also going to help us be sure you were getting the information we needed you to have."

"Manipulate the old media during the Rising, manipulate the new media to keep the world from finding out how much of this you engineered," said Becks. "How did you get the rest of the world to go along with it?"

"I'm not Tate," said the doctor acidly. "I don't need to convince you that I'm in the right. I'm here to present you with a choice. Work for us. Help us to shape the next twenty years. Or never leave this building again. It's up to you."

I looked at Becks and Alaric. They looked back at me. None of us said anything. I don't think any of us knew what to say.

Finally, Alaric asked, "You promise the mosquitoes are going to die on their own?"

"You have my word as a scientist."

I somehow managed not to snort.

Alaric continued. "And none of us are being charged with any crimes?"

"The reverse. Once we've worked things out to our mutual satisfaction, we'll announce that you've been added to the list of bloggers with White House press access. The only reason you weren't added before was out of respect for your loss." The doctor smiled. The expression seemed alien on his face. "I think you'll find that we can be very reasonable when you follow the rules and behave like rational people."

"And George?" I asked.

"You can keep her, if you can keep her in line and out of sight."

"My sister?" asked Alaric.

"Will be returned to your custody as soon as possible. She was fortunate to escape Florida."

Becks didn't say anything. Her family was more likely to be supporting the CDC than at risk from their actions.

"Well?" asked the doctor.

I opened my mouth, not quite sure what was going to come out of it.

"We'll do it," I said.

"Good," said the doctor. "I hoped you'd see sense. Welcome to the CDC."

You know what? Fuck it. Just fuck it. The Rising didn't manage to wipe out the human race, it just made us turn into even bigger assholes than we were before. Hear that, mad science? You failed. You were supposed to kill us all, and instead you turned us into monsters.

Fuck it.

—From *Adaptive Immunities*, the blog of Shaun Mason, August 7, 2041. Unpublished.

Testing. This is a test post to check formatting and be sure the files are uploading correctly. Test test test.

Is this thing on?

—From *Living Dead Girl*, the blog of Georgia Mason II, August 7, 2041. Unpublished.

GEORGIA: Thirty-seven

Steve was a constant, silent presence behind us as Rick steered me down the hall. It was weirdly like being back on the campaign trail, only I wasn't carrying a gun, Rick wasn't carrying a cat, and I was no longer sure who the good guys were.

On second thought, it was nothing at all like being back on the campaign trail.

The hall ended at a door that looked like real oak. Rick let go of me to press his palm flat against the testing panel next to the door. A small red light clicked on above it, oscillating rapidly between red and green before settling on green. It remained lit for less than five seconds. Then it clicked off, and the door clicked open.

"I'm going to be waiting for you on the other side," said Rick. "Do you trust Steve?"

It was an interesting question. If Ryman was no longer one of the good guys, I wasn't sure I trusted anyone. But of the people I didn't trust, Steve was one of the ones I distrusted the least. "We'll be fine," I said.

"I'll see you in a moment," said Rick, and opened the door. Part of me wondered what kind of awesome security procedures they'd have in place to prevent people from following each other through—always a risk, no matter how much the people who design the airlock systems try to keep it from happening. Some airlocks will gas you if you try to go through without getting a blood test. Somehow I doubted they'd use something that crude on a door that might be opened by the President of the United States. The rest of me understood that playing with the security system was something too stupid for Shaun to do, and that meant it was absolutely too dumb for me.

The door closed behind Rick, the little red light making another brief appearance before shutting itself politely off. "Cute," I said, stepping forward to press my hand against the testing plate. Needles bit into the skin at the point where each of my fingers joined my palm. That was an unusual spot for a test array. I took a small, startled breath, finally pulling away as the light turned green and clicked off. "That's my cue."

"I'll be right through," said Steve. He smiled encouragingly when I looked back at him, and I held that image firmly in my mind as I stepped through the door to whatever was waiting on the other side. Steve wouldn't have smiled while he sent me to my death. I might be a clone, and Ryman might be corrupt, but some things about a person's essential nature never change.

The door opened on a narrow hallway that looked like it was constructed hundreds of years before the Rising and never substantially redecorated. Rick was waiting. A relieved smile spread across his face when he saw me. "I was afraid you wouldn't come."

"What, you thought I'd go back to the nice man in the lab coat who was about to have me recycled?" I dropped the pretense of having a migraine, straightening and looking at him flatly. "You could have warned me what we were walking into."

"No. I couldn't have." The door swung open as Steve joined us in the hall. Rick switched his attention from me to Steve, asking, "Anyone following us?"

"Not that I saw," rumbled Steve. I raised an eyebrow. He explained, "This is one of the tunnels built during the Cold War, in case we needed to evacuate the capital. They probably wouldn't have been any use in a nuclear strike—a nuke's a pretty damn big deal—but there's one thing they do manage, quite nicely."

I nodded slowly, catching his meaning. "We're underground. No wireless transmission."

"We sweep this hall hourly for bugs. For the moment, we're in the clear." Steve looked past me to Rick. "You can proceed, Mr. Vice President."

"Thank you, Steve." Rick sighed, beginning to walk. "It really is good to see you."

"Most people just send flowers. Raising the dead is a little extreme." I matched my steps to his, watching him as we walked. "What's going on, Rick? What's *really* going on?"

"I meant it when I said that, if it had been up to me, I would have simply handed you over to Shaun as soon as you woke up enough to know yourself." A muscle in Rick's jaw twitched as he continued. "I will go to my grave knowing that I have been responsible for your death more than twenty times. Each time one of the clones of the original Georgia Mason was decanted I told myself, 'That's it. No more. If she's not real, we find another way.' But each time, I couldn't think of another way, and we needed you. *I* needed you."

"Why?"

"Same reason those people back there were hoping you'd play nicely with the other children—people associate your face with the truth. If you tell them a lie they want to believe, they won't question it."

"And the government can keep on killing people like me. People like your *wife*. God, Rick, is that really what you want?"

"No. That's what *they* want." Rick stopped at an unsecured door, pushing it open. Gregory was sitting at a terminal on the other side, with Dr. Shoji looking over his shoulder. I couldn't even be surprised. Rick kept talking: "I want you to tell the world the truth. I want you to blow it all to hell. People believe you. People believe *in* you, because of the way you died. They'll believe the truth even if they don't want to, as long as they're hearing it from you."

"I don't understand," I said.

"Hello, Georgia," said Gregory, looking up from the screen. "It's good to see you again."

"It was touch and go for a while there, but I pulled through," I said. "How about you?"

"Minor burns, concussion, and I won't be working with the CDC again anytime soon. That's all right. I was tired of them anyway."

"Good." I turned to Rick. "Now please. *Explain*. A huge global conspiracy has ruined my life—hell, has *ended* my life, and then started it over again, leaving me with probably the worst identity issues I could imagine—and they did it for what? So you could clone me and use me to sell ice to the Eskimos?"

"A huge global conspiracy has ruined your life. If it helps, they also killed my wife." Rick's smile faded like it had never been there at all. "I took Lisa's death for a suicide, because that's what they told me it was. I found out differently only when I saw her file. They did it because of what you saw back in that room—there is no cure for Kellis-Amberlee. There's never going to be a cure. There's just going to be a war with the virus, one we can't win, but can only adapt to. We can only survive it. And that's not acceptable to some people."

"So they're doing *this* instead?"

"It didn't start out like this, Georgia. It started out with good intentions—God, such good intentions. They thought they were taking steps to protect the country. In the end, no one noticed when protection turned into imprisonment, or when 'for the good of the people' turned into 'for the good of the people in power.' It was all baby steps, all the way."

"Aren't the worst things usually that way?" I asked. "So why's Ryman on their side now? Wasn't he supposed to be the good guy? The one we could depend on?"

Rick didn't say anything. He just looked at me, waiting. He didn't have to wait long.

"Emily," I whispered. "Emily Ryman has retinal KA."

"Which makes her an excellent candidate for an 'accidental' death if he stops playing along—and you're not their first clone. Just the first one that really replicates the person you were based on. If you'd been alive for the last year, you would have noticed that Emily rarely speaks in public. She just stands and smiles. Does that sound like the Emily Ryman you know?"

I stared at him in mute horror. Rick continued: "They replaced her the night after the inauguration, and now she and the children are hostages against the president's good behavior. He's in the same position you are. He's a perfect figurehead, because even people who believe all politicians are corrupt remember his association with you on the campaign trail—and they remember what happened to Rebecca Ryman. They believe in him, even if they don't realize it." Rick laughed a little, bitterly. "I think this may have been the plan all along. Tate was never going to wind up in power. Ryman was too good a puppet to pass up."

"I think I hate the human race," I said.

"There's the Georgia Mason we all know and love," said Steve. "Now the question is, what are we going to do about it?"

I paused. "You mean I'm standing in a room with the Vice President of the United States, a member of the Secret Service, and two renegade EIS scientists, and you expect the clone to make the decisions? See, this is why this country is in trouble all the damn time. The people running it are crazy."

"We just want to know if you'll help," said Dr. Shoji.

"And by help, you mean . . . ?"

"Will you do what you did in Sacramento?"

What I did in Sacramento was reveal Tate's dirty dealing and the fact that someone had been bankrolling him—but we never suspected the CDC, and so mostly, what I did was make sure Ryman got into power. That, and die. I knew they were asking me to tell the truth again, to tell it for them this time, but I couldn't help remembering the way it felt to know that I was coming to an end. It wasn't my memory, just a snapshot stolen from the virus-riddled mind of a dead woman, but that didn't make it feel any less real. I *died* in Sacramento. If I did what they wanted me to do, I could very well die again.

And if I was going to be the kind of person who valued her life more than she valued the truth, I wasn't going to be Georgia Mason at all. Unless I wanted to find someone else I was willing to be, this was what I was made for.

"We have to get Emily—the *real* Emily—away from the CDC, and get the kids out of here," I said slowly. "They're going to be civilians in a position to confirm my story. If I start posting while they're still hostages, they won't make it out of here alive."

Steve cracked his knuckles. "Don't worry about them. The First Lady still has friends in the Secret Service. We can extract the kids at any time."

"Dr. Shaw is organizing a team to extract the First Lady from the CDC installation where she's being held, and move her to a secure EIS facility near here," said Dr. Shoji.

"The EIS has been a busy little secret government organization." I looked levelly at Dr. Shoji. "If I do this, I need to know that we're not replacing one bad deal with another. What are your plans?"

"I don't speak for the EIS as a whole, and I can't see the future," he said. "But for the past ten years at least, we've been bleeding off the best recruits the CDC gets. We've been getting the members of your generation, the ones who want a solution that doesn't always involve a bullet. I think that corruption is a risk for every organization. Even ours. But we're going to be very busy for quite some time, just cleaning up the mess that's been made for us. If the EIS is going to go the way of the CDC, it probably won't be within my lifetime."

"Whereas the CDC is a bad deal right now," I said. "That's fair. But you realize that if I do this, if I get involved, and you ever, *ever* start to cross the line—"

"I can't promise what the future will be. All I can do is promise that the EIS will try to make sure we have one."

I nodded. "Fine. Steve, get the kids out of here. Dr. Shoji, do whatever you need to do to get them to safety, and make sure Dr. Shaw takes care of Emily. Does anybody here have a gun I can borrow? The Secret Service confiscated all of ours."

Rick blinked. "I was expecting you to ask for an Internet connection."

"Oh, I'm going to need one of those, too, once we get everybody back together, but first, we have a job that requires weapons." Steve unsnapped his sidearm and passed it to me. I accepted it before smiling coolly at Rick. "We need to go and kidnap the president."

"And here my mother said a job in medicine would be dangerous," said Gregory.

Rick didn't say anything. But slowly, with an expression of almost painful relief, he nodded.

I regret to inform you that we have lied to you. Last year, when most of the site went "camping," we were in actuality running for our lives, being pursued by no less an adversary than the Centers for Disease Control. Our flight began when Dr. Kelly Connolly, believed dead following a break-in at the Memphis CDC, arrived at our Oakland offices and asked for our help. The destruction of Oakland followed soon after. In the interests of concealing our location and activities, we were forced to present a cover story to the world. For this, on the behalf of the Factual News Division, I apologize.

We are not lying now. Please download and read the attached documents, which encompass everything leading up to our departure from Oakland. If they do not load, please visit one of our mirror sites. Continue trying. This is important. These are things you need to know.

We are telling you the truth.

—From *Fish and Clips*, the blog of Mahir Gowda, August 7, 2041.

The mosquitoes that swept from Cuba to the American Gulf Coast, resulting in the death of millions, did not arise naturally. They were genetically engineered by scientists in the employ of the CDC. Please download and review the attached documents for further details, including a full description of the life cycle of the modified yellow fever mosquito.

We are telling you the truth.

That will not bring my parents back to life.

—From *The Kwong Way of Things*, the blog of Alaric Kwong, August 7, 2041.

SHAUN: Thirty-eight

The man from the CDC kept on talking; to be honest, I had pretty much stopped listening. Alaric and Becks were paying attention and periodically asking questions that seemed at least vaguely connected to the things coming out of his mouth, so I figured no one would notice—or care—if I checked out for a little bit. As long as I didn't start to drool, they'd probably figure I was just being a big, dumb Irwin and letting the smart people talk. That's the useful thing about being a figurehead. Nobody cares if you're an idiot, as long as you're a useful one.

They're never going to give her back to you, murmured Georgia. There was a faint echoing quality to her words, and I knew that if I turned my head she'd be there, watching me, waiting for me to admit that she was right. That scared me almost more than the things she was saying. I used to welcome the hallucinations, viewing them as the only way I could see her anymore. Now . . . I knew I wasn't going to go un-crazy as fast as I went crazy. But the idea of being left alone with a voice in my head and the occasional delusional vision was suddenly terrifying. I got her back. Why the hell wasn't the world going to let me keep her?

You don't need to worry about their little replacement. The world will let you keep me, she said. *Just you and me, forever. That's what you said you wanted, isn't it? You volunteered to be a haunted house.*

"Shut up," I muttered, trying to keep my voice low enough that no one else would notice.

It didn't work. "What was that?" asked the doctor, attention swinging back around to me.

Uh-oh. "Uh . . . " I began.

"He talks to himself," said Becks, matter-of-factly. "I'm actually impressed that this is the first time he's done it. Just ignore him and keep telling us why immune response in babies is enough to cause reservoir conditions, but not enough to avoid spontaneous amplification when they cross the sixty-pound threshold."

"He *talks* to himself?" The doctor frowned at me like I had suddenly become an exciting new medical mystery. I wondered how he'd feel if he knew I was immune to the Kellis-Amberlee virus. He'd probably start asking whether he could dissect me—assuming he cared about asking. George had already proven that people were now a matter of crunch all you want, we'll make more. Maybe he already had Shaun II baking in one of their cloning tanks, ready for his triumphant decanting.

Fuck. That.

"Turns out being forced to shoot the one person in the world you thought would outlive you in the head sort of fucks with your sense of reality," I said coldly. "I mean, my choices were a nice, mellow psychotic break with talking to myself and the occasional voice in my head, or climbing the nearest cell tower and playing sniper until somebody came and gunned me down. I figured option A would be better for my long-term health, if not my sanity."

"And you still listen to him? You still do what he says?" asked the doctor, his attention swinging back to Becks and Alaric.

Alaric shrugged. "Sure. He's the boss."

"Fascinating." The man from the CDC shook his head as he turned toward President Ryman. "You see the power of trust? Once you believe a person won't mislead you, you keep believing it, even after you realize they've gone insane. This plan may actually work."

"Or maybe not," said George. "It's a little bit of a coin toss right now, if you ask me."

The doctor whipped around, eyes widening. "What are you doing?"

His reaction made me realize she was really here, rather than speaking into the dark inside my head. I turned to see George standing in the doorway, an unfamiliar gun in her hands. She had it aimed squarely at the doctor's chest. Rick was behind her, expression grim, standing next to a man I didn't recognize. Steve was nowhere to be seen.

"If you so much as twitch, I swear, I will shoot you," said George.

The doctor ignored her, reaching for his pocket. The sound of the safety clicking off was very loud. He froze. "You're making a mistake," he said.

"Maybe your mistake was focusing so hard on my replacement that you forgot to give me an off switch," replied George.

"No, they gave you one," said the stranger. "We just took it out before they had the chance to use it."

"Oh, right," said George. "Silly me. I always forget about the excruciatingly painful nonelective surgeries."

The doctor's eyes got even wider, if that was possible. "Dr. Lake?" he demanded, looking toward the unfamiliar man.

The stranger smiled, the expression bordering on a snarl. "I resign," he said.

"So this is mutiny." The man from the CDC slanted his eyes toward President Ryman and his remaining agents. "This is *treason*."

None of the Secret Servicemen were reaching for their guns, and the look on President Ryman's face wasn't shock or outrage—it was relief, like this was what he'd been waiting for all along. "You'd know about that, wouldn't you?" he asked. I'd never heard him sound so bitter. "Treason? That's something you at the CDC have been experts on for quite a while."

The man from the CDC's eyes widened in exaggerated shock. "I don't understand what you're implying, Mr. President."

"Emily's safe," said George. "The EIS has her. Steve's getting the kids out of the building. They can't hold your family over you anymore."

"Do you think it's that simple?" asked the man from the CDC. "We've had a long time to get to where we are today. You're making a large mistake. People have died for less."

"People have died for nothing," George shot back. "And no, I don't think it's that simple. But I do think you made one major tactical error when you invited us here."

The man from the CDC sneered. "What's that?"

"We're the ones that people listen to . . . and we're the ones who learned about backups from Georgette Meissonier." George smiled. "Anybody here who doesn't have six cameras running, raise your hand."

Not a single member of my team raised their hand. Becks grinned. Alaric smirked.

And the man from the CDC, perhaps realizing that he was finished, moved. Jamming his hand into his pocket, he pulled out the pen he'd been holding before, aiming it at the president. The Secret Servicemen shouted something, grabbing Ryman's shoulders. Not fast enough. There was no way they'd be able to get him clear fast enough. I didn't think. I just jumped, putting myself between the man from the CDC and President Ryman half a second before I heard the sound of Georgia's gun going off.

The man from the CDC froze, looking slowly down at the spreading red patch in the middle of his chest. The pen dropped from his hand and he fell, crumpling to the floor. The last sound he made was a hollow thud when his head hit the tile. It was almost comic, in a weird way.

No one was laughing. They were all staring at me. Becks had a hand covering her mouth, and Alaric looked like he was about to be sick. Only Georgia didn't look distraught; mostly, she looked confused. Lowering her gun, she asked, "What is that?"

I looked at the needle sticking out of my chest, anchored in the flesh a few inches to the right of my sternum. It hurt a little, now that I was thinking about it. It would probably hurt more once the adrenaline washed out of my system.

"Oh," I said, my words almost drowned out by the sound of one of the Secret Servicemen emptying his gun into the man from the CDC's head. "That's a problem."

You know what's awesome? Assholes who do all their research, and have all the pieces of the puzzle, and can't be bothered with anything that doesn't fit the picture they've decided they're putting together. You know. Idiots. The kind of stupid you can manage to achieve only by being really, really smart, because only really, really smart people can reach adulthood without having any goddamn *common sense.*

Seriously. Thank you, smart people, for being absolute idiots. I appreciate it.

—From *Adaptive Immunities*, the blog of Shaun Mason, August 7, 2041. Unpublished.

Kill me once, shame on you.

Kill me twice, shame on me.

Kill my brother? Oh, it's on. And you are *not* going to enjoy it.

—From *Living Dead Girl*, the blog of Georgia Mason II, August 7, 2041. Unpublished.

GEORGIA: Thirty-nine

Everyone stared at the needle sticking out of Shaun's chest, their expressions showing varying degrees of shock and horror. I put the safety back on my borrowed gun and slowly lowered it, shoving it into the waistband of my pants.

No one said anything. One of the Secret Service agents pulled President Ryman back, putting more distance between him and Shaun. I tried to force myself to swallow. I remembered being hit by a similar needle in Sacramento, although mine had been attached to a syringe. "Shaun?" I said, very softly.

"The CDC weaponized Kellis-Amberlee a while ago," said Shaun. He grimaced as he pulled the needle out of his chest. "Okay, fucking ow. Could we go with a slightly less ouch-worthy doomsday weapon next time? Not that I don't appreciate it failing to, you know, puncture my lung or something, but that stings."

"Put the needle down and step away from the president," said one of the Secret Service agents. His gun was in his hand, and from his tone, he meant business.

"Shaun . . . " said President Ryman.

"Oh, right. You guys didn't get the memo, did you? See, part of why they're so into killing the people with the reservoir conditions—like, you know, George, or your wife, or Rick's wife, who probably didn't kill herself, and isn't that a bitch?—part of why they're so into that is because of whatchamacallit—"

"Antibody transference," said Alaric. He relaxed as he spoke, some of the tension going out of his shoulders.

"Yeah, that. Turns out the reservoir conditions are sort of like, the middle step in us learning how to live with our cuddly virus buddies. People with reservoir conditions get better because they're making antibodies. And then people who spend a lot of time with those people get something even better." Shaun grinned at me. "We get to be immune."

"What?" said President Ryman.

"What?" said Gregory.

"Can I get a biohazard bag over here?" said Shaun. He grimaced again. "And maybe some gauze or something? This *really* stings."

"This is impossible," said one of the Secret Service agents. He leveled his handgun on Shaun. "Sir, we need to get you out of here."

"No," said President Ryman. We all turned to look at him, even Shaun, who still looked perfectly lucid. Conversion takes time, but he should have been showing some of the outward signs of infection after being shot with that large a dose of virus.

"Sir?" said the Secret Service agent.

"I said no. We brought these people here because we were looking for a Hail Mary. If they're going to give us one, we're not going to turn our backs on them." President Ryman's gaze settled on Gregory. "I'm sorry, son. I didn't catch your name."

"Dr. Gregory Lake, sir. EIS." Gregory produced a testing kit from his lab coat pocket, tossing it to Shaun. "If I may be so bold, this might help keep these nice gentlemen from shooting you before we can get out of here."

"Practical *and* prepared. That's what I like to see in a public servant." President Ryman turned to Shaun. "Shaun . . ."

"I know, I know. Prove that this isn't just preamplification crazy." Shaun sighed as he popped the lid off his testing kit. "You know,

George, if you'd just listened when I said I wanted to skip the presidential campaign and petition to go to Yellowstone instead, none of this would have happened." He stuck his thumb into the opening.

I managed to smile. It wasn't easy. "But imagine all the fun we'd have missed. Meeting Rick, that town hall in Eakl . . .

"Burying Buffy. Burying *you.* I would have been okay with missing the fun." The lights on his test unit seemed to be confused. They were flashing, returning to yellow over and over again. Finally, the green light stopped flickering, and the red and yellow began to oscillate, like the unit was trying to make up its mind. The Secret Servicemen drew their guns.

I could see what came next as clearly as if it had already happened. Blood on the floor; Shaun falling, and no handy CDC madmen to bring him back to me. "Stop!" I shouted, putting both my hands up in front of me. "It hasn't stopped yet!"

It *hadn't* stopped. The light was still flashing between red and yellow—and as I watched, the green came back into the rotation. The flash began holding there, a little bit longer each time. "Fascinating," murmured Gregory.

"You can't dissect him," I said.

"No, but can we have some blood? Say, a gallon? For starters?"

"We'll see." The light wasn't flashing red at all anymore; instead, it was flickering between yellow and green. Then the yellow cut out entirely, and it was just green, uninfected, *safe.* I let out a slow breath, only then feeling the terror that had been burning in my veins the whole time. Shaun was safe. Shaun was going to be okay.

Shaun was holding up the green-lit test unit with an expression of vague amusement on his face as he asked, "Well? Does that clear me? Or do I need to do a little dance, too?"

"A little dance is never amiss," said Alaric, straight-faced.

I started to move toward Shaun. Gregory grabbed my shoulder, stopping me. "Don't."

"What?" asked Shaun and I, in unison.

Gregory shook his head, not letting go. "He may be immune, but you're not. If the virus on his clothing is live, it could cause you to amplify."

"This gets better and better." Becks glared at the body of the man from the CDC. "I should have taken the headshot."

"Maybe next time," said Shaun.

"In the meantime, Mr. President, your wife and children are safe," said Rick. "We can get out of here. We can find a way to make this right."

"It's going to be a little harder than we thought."

The sound of Steve's voice was a surprise. We turned to see him standing in the door, with plaster on the shoulders of his formerly immaculate black suit and the bin holding our equipment in his arms.

"Steve?" said Shaun.

"The building is surrounded," said Steve. He moved to put the bin on the table. "I took the liberty of retrieving your weapons. We may be shooting our way out."

"Surrounded?" asked Becks, as she moved to rummage through the bin. "By what, political protestors?"

"No," said Steve. "Zombies."

"It's always zombies," complained Shaun. No one laughed. He frowned. "Tough crowd."

"What is it about you two and massive outbreaks?" asked Steve. "We were outbreak-free until you got here."

"Just lucky, I guess," I said. "Where's everyone else?"

"With Dr. Shoji. I doubled back when I saw the moaners on the lawn."

At least something was going right. The Secret Service agents with President Ryman looked stunned, although whether it was at the zombies or our flippancy, I couldn't have said. They weren't with us on the campaign trail. They didn't understand that this was how we coped.

"Can't we get out through the tunnels?" asked Rick.

"Only if you enjoy being zombie-chow," said Steve.

"The CDC is nothing if not efficient." Shaun took his gun from Becks, careful not to touch her hand. "Is there any route out of here that doesn't get us eaten?"

"We go through the parking garage to the covered motorway," said Steve. "We may still get eaten, but we'll have a better shot at getting out alive."

President Ryman was starting to look distinctly unhappy. Poor guy. Leader of the free world—and unwilling tool of an international conspiracy—one minute, potential zombie-food the next. "How did this happen?" he demanded.

"Our extraction of your wife may have trigged some alarms," said Gregory. "Between that and the situation here . . . the CDC is taking steps to resolve the matter. Congratulations. We are all expendable."

"Cheer up, everybody," said Shaun, and grinned—the grin of a manic Irwin getting ready to shove his way into danger. "This is going to be *great* for ratings. Let's go."

We went.

The past thirty years bear a startling resemblance to the Greek myth of Pandora when looked at clearly, in the light. A box that should not have been opened; a plague of pains and pestilences loosed upon the world; and, at the end, hope. Hope that we refused, for many years, to allow ourselves to look upon with unshadowed eyes. What were we afraid of? Were we afraid hope would prove another phantom, slipping through our hands like mist? Were we afraid something worse was hidden in its wake?

I think not. I think we were, quite simply, afraid to admit to hope because admitting to hope would mean admitting the world had changed forever. There is no return to the world we knew before the Rising. That world is dead. But as the Rising itself took such great pains to teach us . . .

Even after death, life still goes on.

—From *Pandora's Box: The Rising Reimagined*, authored by Mahir Gowda, August 10, 2041.

Look, Ma! I'm abducting the president! Aren't you proud of your baby girl now?

—From *Charming Not Sincere*, the blog of Rebecca Atherton, August 7, 2041. Unpublished.

SHAUN: Forty

We fell into a ragged formation with President Ryman at the center. Alaric was almost as well protected; he'd never passed his field certifications, and none of us was particularly enthused by the idea of him firing a gun in an enclosed space. The next ring was made up of Secret Servicemen—all of them except Steve, who was on the outer ring with me, Gregory, and the rest of my team . . . including Rick, who'd taken a pistol from one of the agents and was walking next to Becks. None of them objected to the vice president endangering himself. Either they were giving up, or they figured they'd be lucky if they managed to get any of us out alive, much less both of the elected officials.

"You people still know how to throw a party," he said nervously.

"Practice. Alaric!" I didn't turn to face him; my attention remained on the hall ahead of us. Steve was on point, since he was the one who actually knew the way, but I wasn't going to let him hit the first wave—if there was a first wave—alone. "How are you doing with bouncing a signal out of this loony bin?"

"I'm still trying to get a clean connection!"

"Well, keep trying. We need to get this footage to Mahir *before* we get ripped to pieces by the living dead."

"You're always such an optimist," muttered George.

I slanted a grin her way. "Like I said. Practice."

"Is that also where you learned to be such an asshole?"

"Yup. How'm I doing?"

"Good."

The halls were eerily silent. That would have been a good thing—moaning usually means you're about to become a snack food—but we didn't know whether or not the zombies were inside. Eventually, even the nervous banter stopped. The only sounds were breathing, footsteps, and the occasional soft beep as Alaric tried and failed to make a connection with the outside world. I wanted to be comforted by the fact that George and I were walking into danger together, but I couldn't manage it. I kept thinking about how fragile she was, how breakable . . . how easily killed. She might have gotten better the first time, but now? In a new body, with a new immune system that never learned to coexist with the virus? She'd die, and this time, the CDC wouldn't be standing by to miraculously resurrect her. She'd stay gone.

"Fuck," I muttered.

No one said anything. At a time like this, me talking to myself was the least of our worries.

Steve led us to a T-junction and paused. "We can't take the elevator back up to the public garage; we're going to need to use the private vehicle pool. It's the only way to be sure we haven't been compromised."

"It's too quiet," said Rick.

George grimaced. "Why do people say that? Wouldn't it be quicker to just ask if that noise was the wind?"

Something moaned down the corridor to our right. I sighed. "That wasn't the wind."

"No, it wasn't," said Steve tightly.

"But how—" began Alaric.

"Questions later, running now," said Becks.

We ran.

The Secret Servicemen fell back until they were running behind the rest of us, moving at that strange twisted half jog men use when they want to cover the ground behind them as they run. Becks and Rick moved to flank the noncombatants—Alaric was still frantically slapping his PDA, trying to get a solid connection even as we were fleeing for our lives—while George and I took the front, running close on Steve's heels.

The moaning behind us continued, now getting louder. The zombies were fresh; they had to be, if they were gaining on us that fast. "I hate the fucking CDC," I snarled.

"Save your breath!" George advised.

We ran.

The hall seemed like it might be endless, right up until the moment where we turned a corner, and it ended, terminating in a set of clear glass doors leading into an airlock. There was a red light on above the door.

"It's gone into security lockdown," shouted Steve. "We're going to have to check out clean one at a time."

One of the Secret Servicemen moved through the group to slap his palm against the testing panel. The other agents were close behind him, dragging a protesting President Ryman in their wake. His safety was their job; ours wasn't. And the moaning was getting louder.

The light turned green. The first agent took his hand off the testing panel and stepped through the now-open door, letting the airlock cycle around him as he stepped out into the parking garage. Nothing attacked him immediately. He turned back to the rest of us, signaling for the second agent to send the president through.

"Got it!" said Alaric, his delight sounding almost obscene, considering the circumstances. The rest of us stared at him. He held up his PDA. "Upload established. I'm transmitting."

"Finally," breathed George, a certain tension slipping out of her shoulders. "Get those files up as fast as you can."

"Working on it."

"Even death doesn't change your priorities, does it?" asked Rick, tiredly amused.

"Not really, no," said George. She grinned at him, gun still aimed toward the unseen zombies.

I could have kissed her. It would probably have been a good thing, since we were all about to be zombie-chow. Instead, I adjusted my position, calling over my shoulder, "A little speed in the carpool lane would be appreciated, guys. We've got incoming, and I didn't bring enough limbs to share with everybody."

"The system's cycling as fast as it can," said Steve reproachfully.

"Don't really give a fuck how fast the system is cycling. Just don't want to get eaten by zombies right after uncovering a mass conspiracy to deceive the American public. Seems a little anticlimactic, you know what I mean? Like getting empty boxes on Christmas morning."

"You got empty boxes?" asked Becks. "Lucky bastard. I always got *dresses*."

Alaric glanced up. "Dresses?"

"*Frilly* dresses," she said with disgust. "*Lacy* frilly dresses."

"Are all journalists insane, or did I just hit the mother lode?" asked Gregory.

"Yes," said Rick and George, in unison.

We were still laughing—the anxious laughter of people who know they're about to die horribly—when the first zombies came around the corner, and laughter ceased to be an option.

At least the sight of the zombies answered the question of where they came from. They were wearing White House ID badges, dressed in respectable suits and sensible shoes. Someone must have trigged an outbreak inside the building, opened the right doors, and let the feeding frenzy commence. Anyone who hadn't been caught by the initial infection would have been taken out by the first wave of actual infected.

I'll give my companions this: No one screamed. Instead, everyone but Alaric and Gregory braced themselves and opened fire, giving the people at the airlock time to cycle through. Alaric moved to put himself behind Becks and out of the line of fire, attention still focused primarily on the device in his hands.

"Forty percent uploaded!" he called.

"Not enough," muttered George, and fired. Her shot went wild. With a wordless sound of frustration, she shifted the gun to her left hand and used her right to pull off her sunglasses and throw them aside. She resumed her stance and fired again. This time, she didn't miss.

"Mr. Vice President!" Steve's voice was anxious. "Sir, you need to go through the lock!"

Rick didn't move.

"Go on, Rick," I said, firing twice more into the seemingly endless tide of zombies. "Get out of here. Go be important. If we don't get out, somebody who understands the news is going to need to interpret what Alaric's putting online."

Rick still didn't move. He fired again; another zombie went down.

"Go on, Rick," said George. "Mahir gets left behind, and you leave when we need someone to make it off the battlefield. That's how this story goes." She never looked at him. She just kept shooting.

Rick shot her a stricken look, and he went, turning and retreating toward the airlock. I stepped a little closer to her, closing a bit more of the distance between us, and kept shooting. We were all falling back now, just a little bit, just a few steps. There are people who'll tell you the worst place to be in an outbreak is a narrow tunnel with a limited number of exits. They're probably right. But a narrow tunnel with a limited number of exits is also the *best* place to be in an outbreak, because the zombies can only come at you so fast.

The airlock hissed. Rick was through. "Dr. Lake!" called Steve. "Come on!"

Gregory didn't need to be told twice. He turned and ran, vanishing from my range of sight. My clip clicked on empty. I ejected it and slapped a new one into place, twisting the stock until I felt the clip snap home. George repeated the process two bullets later. By then, I was firing again, covering the hole she made. We still worked together well, even if neither of us was really the person we used to be. Even if neither of us was ever going to be that person—those people—again.

"If this is crazy, I don't care," I said, and fired. Another zombie went down. We were losing ground fast now, and still they kept coming.

"Neither do I," said George, and kept firing.

"Alaric!" shouted Steve.

"Coming!" Alaric started forward, and froze, eyes widening as he looked at the screen of his little device. "There's no signal there. I almost lost the connection."

"Alaric, just go!" snapped George.

"I can't! I have to get these files up before somebody hits us with an EMP screen!"

Becks took two long steps backward, firing all the while, and snatched the device from his hand. "I can manage an upload as well as you can," she snarled. "Now *go*."

Alaric stared at her. "Becks—"

"*Go*!"

He turned and fled. The zombies were still closing. There were five of us left now. Me, George, Becks, one of the Secret Service agents—I still didn't know his name—and Steve, who was urging Alaric through the airlock as quickly as he could.

"You see the failure inherent in this model, don't you?" asked George. She fired; a zombie went down. They were closing in.

"What are you talking about?"

Becks groaned, the sound similar to a zombie's moan only in that it held no actual words. No zombie could have sounded that aggravated. "You can't shoot while you're going through the airlock. That means someone has to watch your back. One person to stand guard, one person leaving. Until eventually . . . "

"There's only one person left," I said, feeling suddenly numb. A zombie lurched forward. I put a bullet through its skull. It fell. "Fuck."

"It always comes down to the cold equations," said George.

"*Fuck*!" I fired again. This time, I missed.

"Next!" shouted Steve.

"Go," said Becks, nodding to George. "Both of you, go. You need to get out of here."

"We're not leaving you."

"You're not leaving him, either." The last of the Secret Service agents was running for the airlock. "You're not going to leave her, and she's not going to leave you. We can't ask your big friend to stay behind, not when he may be the most muscle we have left. That leaves me. Now get out of here." Becks held up Alaric's PDA with the hand that wasn't holding her gun. "We're at ninety percent. I'll make sure the news is waiting for you when you hit the surface."

"Rebecca—"

Becks shot me a venomous glance. "I don't have her nose for news. I don't have your total lack of regard for my own safety. What I have is a family that doesn't want me, and a job that I know how to do. And that job says I stand here and let you get out, because you're the ones who can do the best job telling this story. Now *go*!"

"Shaun, come on." George took a step backward, still firing.

"I don't want to do this," I said quietly.

So don't, said George, in the space behind my eyes. Her voice was soft, cajoling. She would never ask me to do something I didn't want to do. She would never try to convince me to leave a teammate behind.

She would let me die here, and take everything we'd fought and bled for with me.

"*Shaun*! Go!" shouted Becks. She shoved the PDA into her pocket, and called, "Hey, big guy! How sturdy are those doors?"

"Sturdy enough," rumbled Steve. "Georgia, come on."

"Coming." She kept shooting as she backed away, until she had to turn and press her hand against the test unit, and shooting ceased to be an option.

"Good." Becks dug her hand into a different pocket, producing a small round object that I recognized, after a few seconds, as a concussion grenade. "Then I'm taking no prisoners."

"You had a grenade in your *pocket*?" I asked, unsure whether to be impressed or horrified.

"Dr. Abbey gave it to me. She swore it was stable."

"Dr. Abbey isn't stable!"

"Doesn't matter now." Becks grinned, still firing. Gunpowder streaked her cheeks and forehead, mixed with sweat and cleaned in narrow tracks by the tears I wasn't sure she was aware of shedding. "Get out of here, Mason. We had a good time, didn't we? It wasn't all bad."

The zombies were getting closer all the time. I kept firing. "We had a great time. You were amazing. You *are* amazing."

"Same to you, Mason. Now go."

"Shaun!" shouted Steve.

I took a deep breath, fired twice more into the throng, and ran.

Steve and Becks covered me while the airlock cycled. By the time I was through, there was a distance of barely ten feet between the leading wave of zombies—slowed by bullets, sickness, and the bodies of their own fallen—and the airlock door. Steve was the next one through, Becks covering him by herself. She fired faster than I would have thought possible, and almost every shot was a good one. Still, she was outnumbered, and the zombies were nearly on top of her when Steve stepped out into the parking garage with the rest of us.

Becks stopped firing. She turned to face the glass, a smile on her face, zombies looming up hard and fast behind her. We couldn't hear them moaning anymore, or the sound her gun made when it hit the ground. She raised her free hand in a perfect pageant wave, seemingly oblivious to the hands reaching out to grab her hair. Then she went over backward, vanishing into the teeming river of infected flesh.

The blast came a few seconds later. There was no sound, only a sudden red rain as the detonation destroyed everything it came in contact with. There was nothing of Becks in that redness—there was everything of Becks in that redness—and so I let George pull me away from the flames that were beginning to consume the hall, leading me toward the motorcade idling in the middle of the parking garage. Alaric was standing next to the lead car. He was crying, silently but steadily, his eyes fixed on the flames now starting to show through the streaks of blood on the glass. The hall was burning. Depending on how many alarms had been disabled before the zombies were released, the whole building might go with it.

I put a hand on Alaric's shoulder. "She got the news out," I said.

He nodded. "I know."

"Good."

There was nothing else that anyone could say. We climbed into the waiting cars, pulled the doors shut, and drove away into the darkness.

This is where I'm supposed to say something mealymouthed and meaningless, like "we regret" or "we are sorry to say." That's what you do at a time like this. But the thing is, there was never anything meaningless about Becks. She was one of the most calculated people I ever knew—and I don't mean that in a bad way. She always knew her angles; she always knew where the light was. I guess in another world, she was probably Miss America or something, one of those women who lived and died by the light. But we didn't live in that world, and so she grew up to be something else.

Something better.

Rebecca Atherton was a reporter before she was anything else. She was a crack shot with any ranged weapon you've ever heard of, and a few you probably haven't. She was honest and she was faithful and she was strong and she helped me kill a zombie bear.

She's also dead. So this is where I say we'd better live up to her sacrifice, because there's nothing in the world that can ever replace her. Good night, Becks.

You told the truth.

—From *Adaptive Immunities*, the blog of Shaun Mason, August 8, 2041.

GEORGIA: Forty-one

True to Steve's word, the zombies came surging in as soon as the parking garage doors were open. Their grasping hands and gaping jaws were no match for an armored presidential motorcade. We mowed them down in droves, their viscera splattering the windshield until Steve activated the wipers and cleaned the gore away. It was surreal, like driving into a bloody red rain. The barrier between the front and back of the car remained down the whole time, which was a mixed blessing. We could see what was going on . . . but being able to see meant, in some way, that we couldn't look away.

Alaric, Shaun, and I had been hustled into the same car, along with Steve and Rick. President Ryman, the rest of the Secret Service agents, and Gregory were in the other car. Presumably, Gregory was giving directions to the nearest EIS safehouse. Maybe, if we were lucky, we'd even make it there in one piece.

I wasn't feeling lucky.

My phone rang shortly after we were clear of the parking garage and its signal-suppressing architecture. I clipped my ear cuff on and tapped it, saying tightly, "Georgia. Go."

"Did you just blow up the bloody White House?" demanded Mahir, loudly enough that everyone in the back of the car turned and looked at me.

"Yeah, Mahir. We kind of did. Although technically, that's not entirely true. Becks kind of did."

There was a pause as he thought through that statement. Then, slowly, he asked, "Georgia, did Becks . . . ?"

"Shaun was her immediate superior, so I believe he'll be making the official announcement, but I am sorry to say that, as of August 7, 2041, Rebecca Atherton's name has been added to The Wall."

Mahir breathed out slowly. Several seconds passed in silence before he said, "Maggie is doing better. She's taken to swearing at the nurses."

"I'm sure everyone will be glad to hear that."

"Georgi—"

"Yes?"

"Did you kill the president?"

I glanced toward the red-streaked windshield. We were through the last line of zombies, and I could see President Ryman's car ahead of ours. The whole back window was blocked out by blood and chunks of flesh. Decontamination of our vehicles was going to be a massive undertaking.

"No," I said. "We just kidnapped him a little. Technically, I suppose he kidnapped himself. I guess that's one for the courts."

There was a long pause before Mahir said, "I'm suddenly glad to have remained in Seattle."

"It's conveniently close to the Canadian border, in case you need to make a run for it. Mahir, I need you to gather all the betas and moderators we have—wake people up if you need to—and get them online. We're about to have a massive fire drill."

"What's that?"

"Hang on." I turned to Alaric. "Where did you upload those files?"

"They were set to upload to my private folder. Mahir has the administrative password." Alaric's voice was dull, like all the life had been leeched out of it. He didn't lift his head.

I relayed this to Mahir, adding, "I need you to download, listen, and sort through the data. Get as many of the Newsies on it as you can; start cutting the data into coherent chunks, minimal editing, no two files the same size or length. We're going to need to get them out without making them easy to suppress. Do not post anything until you receive my next transmission. I need you to match my information."

Shaun shook his head. "Times like this, I wish Buffy were here."

I put a hand over his, waiting for Mahir's response. It came quickly: "Georgia . . . what is this?"

"This is the end. This is the last story." I sighed and closed my eyes, leaning until my head hit Shaun's shoulder. I was suddenly tired. So tired. "This is where we tell the truth and get the fuck out of the way while the experts figure out what they're supposed to do with it."

"I'll download the files," said Mahir. He took a breath. "After I tell Maggie about Becks, that is. I have to tell her."

"I know."

"Godspeed, Georgia Mason."

"Same to you, Mahir. Same to you." I tapped my ear cuff without opening my eyes, cutting off the connection. "When this is over, I want to find a new profession. Something with fewer zombies."

"I could get behind that," said Shaun, pushing me gently away. I opened my eyes, giving him a startled look. He indicated his shirt, where a spot of blood marked the needle's entry point. "Still potentially hot. Sorry, but I'm not losing you again. Not over *laundry*."

The statement was so ridiculous that I actually smiled before sobering again. "We all checked out clean when we went through the airlock."

"Yup. I remain immune. Thanks for that. I mean, really. It sort of explains how I got out of so many close calls—and here I'd been attributing my survival to sheer awesomeness on my part—but I'm okay with that if it means I'm going to survive." Shaun looked toward Alaric. "You okay? Not hurt?"

"She's gone," Alaric whispered, voice barely audible above the sound of the engine. "Becks is gone. She was there, and now she's just gone."

I exchanged a look with Shaun before saying, carefully, "I know. I'm sorry."

"Will she come back? You came back. Will she?"

We exchanged another look. This time, it was Rick who spoke, before Shaun or I could say anything. "I'm sorry, Alaric. What we did with Georgia was unethical, and it would have been impossible if Shaun's shot hadn't left her brain essentially intact. We might have been able to replicate her body, but we would never have been able to re-create her mind."

"I'm sorry," I said again.

Alaric sighed—a shaky, shuddering sound—and said, "I knew you were going to say that. I just needed to hear it." He lifted his head, regarding us with tear-filled eyes. "This wasn't worth it."

"It never is," said Shaun.

We rode in silence after that, blindly following the lead car down twisting back roads and half-hidden residential streets. The motorcade wasn't running its lights, but it was still equipped with the transmitters that changed the lights in our favor and allowed us to dodge the random blood tests on certain streets. It was possible the CDC could also use those transmitters to track us. I put the thought out of my mind as firmly as I could. If we were being followed, there was nothing we could do about it. We were out of places to go.

It felt like we'd been driving for an hour or more when we made a sharp left onto a private driveway. We had gone barely ten yards when a steel gate slid shut behind us, and blue guiding lights clicked on along the sides of the road.

"Wherever it is we're going, I think we're just about there," I said.

"Think they'll have cookies?" asked Shaun.

"I think they're more likely to have full-immersion bleach tanks," said Alaric darkly.

"Your optimism is duly noted," said Steve. He cocked his head, apparently listening to something on his own earpiece, before adding, "Welcome to the EIS."

"So that's a 'yes' on both the cookies and the bleach," I said.

We followed President Ryman's car into a low parking garage that was better lit than the one we'd left. It was also substantially fuller. Dr. Shoji and Dr. Kimberley were standing in front of the doors to the main building, flanked on either side by orderlies with tranquilizer rifles. It said something about the past week that I found the sight extremely reassuring.

The car stopped, and one by one, we climbed out, squinting under the bright fluorescent lights. Shaun stood just out of reach, both of us turning to look toward our welcoming committee. Once everyone was out of both cars, Dr. Shoji stepped forward and said, "According to the news, there has been a terrorist attack on the White House, and both President Ryman and Vice President Cousins are missing, feared dead."

"Where is my wife?" asked President Ryman.

"The clone died in the attack. The original is inside," said Dr. Shoji. "She and the children are safe, and have been waiting for you. What do you intend to do?"

President Ryman paused before turning to me and smiling that faintly off-kilter smile I'd seen so many times on the campaign trail—the one that promised he'd do his best to change the world, if only we'd be patient with him while he figured out exactly how to do it. "I think it's time I gave a little State of the Union interview. If Miss Mason would be so kind?"

I nodded. "It would be my honor, sir."

"Great," said Shaun, clapping his hands together. "Let's go through decon, get in there, and change the world. And then? Cookies."

"Cookies," agreed Rick.

I started toward the door. Alaric grabbed my arm before I took my second step, stopping me. I turned, blinking at him.

"Was it worth it?" he asked.

"God, I hope so," I said.

He let me go, and as a group—reunited at last, for whatever good it was going to do us—we walked into the building.

RED FLAG DISTRIBUTION RED FLAG DISTRIBUTION
RED FLAG DISTRIBUTION
CREATIVE COMMONS LICENSE ALERT LEVEL ALPHA
SPREAD TO ALL NEWS SITES IMMEDIATELY
REPOST FREELY REPOST FREELY REPOST FREELY
FEED IS LIVE
TRANSCRIPTION FOLLOWS

[IMAGE: A woman who appears to be Georgia Mason (ref. The Wall, 6/20/40) stands in front of a podium bearing the logo of the Epidemic Intelligence Service.]

WOMAN: My name is Georgia Mason. My name is Subject 7c. I died on June twentieth, 2040, during the Ryman for President campaign. I was resurrected earlier this year by the CDC, using illegal and unethical human cloning technology. If you are viewing this video or reading a transcription on a download-enabled site, you can verify my DNA structure by downloading the file labeled "G. Mason genetic profile."

[DOWNLOAD FILE HERE.]

GEORGIA: I am here because the CDC wanted a more effective mechanism for lying to you, and believed I would provide a viable control for my brother, Shaun Mason, as well as serving a potential role as a mouthpiece for their version of the truth. I am here because I was not allowed to rest.

[IMAGE: The camera swings around to show Shaun Mason (ref. "After the End Times") holding a whiteboard on which the date 8/7/41 has been written.]

SHAUN: Listen to the dead girl. She's telling you what you need to hear.

[IMAGE: The camera returns to Georgia.]

GEORGIA: Before I died, I told you all that someone was trying to keep you afraid. Someone was trying to keep you from realizing that you were being controlled through unnecessary security and exaggerated fear. I begged you to rise. I begged you to stop them. Unfortunately, words are cheap, even today, and actions are expensive. I did not change the world by dying. All I did was die.

But you still have the opportunity to change things—and that opportunity is greater and more immediate than any of us could have known. Kellis-Amberlee is not the scourge we have been led to treat it as. It is a living thing, and like any living thing, it seeks to evolve, to find a balance with its hosts. Kellis-Amberlee has been trying to adapt to us, and we have been trying to adapt to it. But our government, believing that it has the right to decide for everyone, has not allowed that adaptation. They have been killing those individuals who represented our best chance of finding peace with this disease. For more information, download the file labeled "reservoir condition fatality rates."

[DOWNLOAD FILE HERE.]

GEORGIA: You may already be hearing reports that we are terrorists. That we have destroyed a part of the nation's capital, and either killed or kidnapped the president. These reports are untrue. One of our reporters, Rebecca Atherton, was killed in the process of rescuing the president from those same individuals who had me brought back from the grave—those same individuals who had me killed in the first place.

[**IMAGE:** At this point in the video recording, a five-second clip of Rebecca Atherton, filmed a year previous, plays. She is wearing khaki, her hair is loose, and she is shooting a zombie with a paintball gun. Each paintball appears to be filled with acid. She is laughing. Her face goes to still frame, and the image returns to Georgia.]

GEORGIA: And why did they kill me? Why did they arrange a set of circumstances that resulted in Rebecca's death, and the death of countless others? Because there are things they didn't want you to know. This is one of them: The virus is changing. I repeat, the virus is changing. But there are people who wanted to control those changes, no matter how many lives it cost. They believed that only by keeping us afraid could they keep us under control. But we have had time to learn and grow since the Rising. We are smarter now. We have adapted.

There are things we cannot tell you, because there are answers we do not have. But we have more information than we did, and please believe me when I say the information that is left unshared is only that which must be studied further before it is safe to reveal. The EIS will be working with the government to codify that information. In time, you will know everything.

The CDC's motivation for resurrecting me, as opposed to any of the others they could have chosen, was simple: They thought you would listen to me. They thought you would accept my words as truth. Let's prove them right. Believe me. Believe the contents of these files . . . and believe your president.

[**IMAGE:** President Peter Ryman walks into the frame, followed by Vice President Richard Cousins. Georgia Mason moves to the side, and President Ryman takes her place. Vice President Cousins stands to his other side.]

PRESIDENT RYMAN: I am speaking now, not only to the citizens of the United States of America, but to the citizens of the planet Earth. Because Kellis-Amberlee is a global issue, not a national one, and the conspiracy in which I have been engaged over this past year is thus also global in its scope. Ladies and gentlemen, I am here to tell you that I have been held against my will, with my family as hostages to ensure my cooperation. The individuals responsible for this have a simple goal in mind: to continue to forward their control of the American public through manipulation of the Kellis-Amberlee virus.

I regret to state that, during my time in office, I have approved immoral, unethical, and illegal scientific experimentation, resulting in the murder of both American and international citizens. I have signed papers approving the weaponization of Kellis-Amberlee. I was present when the decision was made to release a modified strain of mosquito capable of carrying the Kellis-Amberlee virus into the sovereign nation of Cuba. The fact that I did these things under duress does not absolve me, or ameliorate the nature of my actions. I have betrayed my country. I have dishonored my office. I have betrayed myself.

Read the files accompanying this report. Read the comprehensive articles I am sure these and other reporters will shortly present to you. Realize that you have been betrayed. Realize that you have been misled. And heed the words of a very wise woman, who spoke from a place of genuine need when she addressed you a year ago. My name is Peter Ryman, and I am begging you.

Rise up while you can.

DOWNLOAD ALL ATTACHMENTS? Y/N
TERMINATE LIVE FEED
RED FLAG DISTRIBUTION RED FLAG DISTRIBUTION
RED FLAG DISTRIBUTION
REPOST FREELY
RISE UP WHILE YOU CAN

Coda: Living for You

Rise up while you can.

—Georgia Mason

It's the oldest story in the world. Boy loves girl. Boy loses girl. Boy gets girl back thanks to the unethical behavior of megalomaniacal mad scientists who never met a corpse they wouldn't try to resurrect. Anyone coming within a hundred yards of my happy ending had better pray that they're immune to bullets.

—Shaun Mason

We did the best we could with what we had, and when what we had wasn't enough, we found ways to make it work. We told the truth, even when it hurt us, even when it killed us, even when it set the wolves at our doors. I can't speak for the dead. But I think the living will agree that anything we did, we did because we felt we had to. History will judge us. The future will decide whether what we did was right, or wrong, or without meaning. In the here and now . . .This is as close as we could get to an ending. The world goes on. Zombies or no zombies, political conspiracy or no political conspiracy, the world goes on.

I think I like it that way.

—From *Living Dead Girl*, the blog of Georgia Mason II, May 17, 2042.

Who wants to see me wrestle a zombie moose?

—From *Hail to the King*, the blog of Shaun Mason, May 17, 2042.

MAHIR: Forty-two

The phone rang at half-three in the morning, waking both Nan and Sanjukta from a sound sleep. Nandini glared as she levered herself from the bed and left the room, following our infant daughter's wailing. I swore, rolling over and grabbing my cell off the bedside table, bringing it to my ear before I was done sitting up.

"This had best be bloody important, or I'm letting my wife give you what-for," I snarled.

"Mr. Gowda, this is Christopher Rogers, from the All-Night News. I apologize if I woke you—I thought I had calculated the time difference between London and San Francisco correctly."

Smug bastard. I could hear it in his voice, the vague self-congratulatory tone of a reporter who thinks he's put his subject off balance. "How did you get this number?"

"Mr. Gowda, I have a few questions, if you don't—"

"I bloody well *do* mind. This is an unlisted number, and I know what you're calling about. You want to know where the Masons are, don't you?"

Silence greeted my question. That was a sufficient answer in and of itself.

"When will you people learn to *listen*? I don't know where the Masons are. No one knows where the Masons are. They disappeared after the management of the CDC was given over to the EIS. Last anyone saw of either of them, they were in an unmarked car heading God-knows-where."

That wasn't entirely true. The last time I saw them was on the border between the United States and Canada, when Steve handed them the keys to their own van, which was waiting for them on the Canadian side. They mailed back all the bugs the CIA had planted a week later, and they were gone.

It was true enough. Every version of their disappearance ended the same way, after all: and they were gone.

"Mr. Gowda, your site is still syndicating blogs provided by both Masons. We find it difficult to credit your continued insistence that you do not know their whereabouts."

"You little nit. They're using relays put in place by Georgette Meissonier. So far as I know, your FBI has been trying to unsnarl that woman's mad coding since before she died. What makes you think I could do it from here? I'm a reporter, not a computer technician."

Nandini came back into the room, Sanjukta held against her chest. She cast a glare at me, demanding, "Who is it?"

"Another reporter. I'm getting rid of him."

"Let me."

"Not sure he deserves that yet, dear." I turned my attention back to the phone. "My wife is about to take the phone off me. You'd best hang up, and never call this number again, or I'll have you cited for harassment. Surprisingly, your government takes quite an interest in my complaints."

Emily Ryman had taken her place beside her husband while pictures of her clone, killed during the attack on the White House, were shown to the world. President Ryman was found guilty of betraying the public trust. He was not found guilty of treason. He had been coerced, he had been afraid for the lives of his family, and he had been uncovering a treasonous group within his own government. He barely escaped being hailed as a hero.

Shaun and Georgia's reports had a great deal to do with that, and President Ryman's gratitude to the Masons had transferred to the site when they vanished. Having the President of the United States indebted to me had proven very useful in some situations—such as this one.

"Mr. Gowda, please. The people have a right to know."

"The people know everything they have a right to know, Mr. Rodgers. I'll be hanging up now." They didn't know there was no cure. Someday they would—someday we'd take back India, and a great deal more of the world beside—but not yet. The world wasn't ready. Too many shots would go unfired, and too many more would die in the blind hope that their loved ones would be among the saved. Recovering from the first Rising took us twenty years. It might take twenty more to reach the point where we could recover from the second one.

"Mr. Gowda—"

I hung up on his protests and stood, dropping the phone onto the bed. "I'm sorry about that. Let me take her. You get some rest."

"I hate that those people call here," she complained, placing Sanjukta gently in my hands.

I drew my infant daughter close, smiling down at her sleepy face, her dark eyes almost closed. Looking up, I said, "I hate it as well. They'll stop eventually."

Nandini snorted her disbelief and climbed back into the bed, rolling over to face the wall. Her breathing leveled out in minutes, telling me that she had drifted back to sleep.

Sanjukta was less obliging. I left the bedroom, walking slow circles around the living room as I waited for her eyes to close. "Would you like to hear a story, my love? It's about some very brave people and the way they tried to change the world."

I wasn't lying to that reporter when I told him I didn't know where Shaun and Georgia—the second Georgia—were. They sent their posts and articles via blind relay. They sent their very rare postcards much the same way. So far as I knew, they were somewhere in the vast empty reaches of Canada, making a life for themselves. Maybe they had come back into the United States to rejoin Dr. Abbey—a few of her letters had led me to believe she might have seen them, at least briefly—but I doubted those would ever be more than visits. The Masons had lived and died in the public eye. Now, finally, they were free of it, and they were living for themselves, rather than living for anyone else. I wasn't going to be the one to take that away from them.

Especially not now. They were clever to vanish when they did, while the world was still reeling from their final revelations. Things exploded not long after. The new director of the CDC, Dr. Gregory Lake, publicly redirected their research into reservoir conditions and possible vaccination paths, while privately redirecting it into spontaneous remission and transmittable immunity. Oversight committees were called, and arrests were made through all levels of several governments. The world slowly began to change as the people began, finally, to rise.

Maggie recovered, and remained with the site. Her parents even assisted in funding replacements for the equipment we'd lost, both to disaster, and when the Masons insisted on reclaiming their van. Alaric and Alisa moved in with her; Alaric and Maggie will be getting married in the spring, mirroring the ceremony into several virtual worlds for the sake of those of us who have had quite enough of the United States for now, thank you very much.

Alaric took over the Newsies; one of our more promising betas—another George, amusingly enough, although he goes by "Geo" to prevent confusion—took over the Irwins; and I? I took over the entire operation, with Maggie as my second. We work well together. Maybe it's not as flashy and exciting as it was during the Mason era, but it does well enough by us.

We changed the world. That's all the news can hope to do, I suppose.

The last postcard I had from the Masons came not a week before that reporter's early-morning call. It summed up the whole situation rather neatly:

"Still having a wonderful time. Still glad you're not here.

All our love—G&S."

Sanjukta sighed, drifting back into sleep. I kissed her on the forehead as I turned to carry her back to her own room, where I settled her down on the mattress of her crib. She fussed, but didn't wake.

I drew the blanket over her and backed out of the room, pausing in the doorway to whisper, "They may not have lived happily ever after. But they lived happily long enough."

And then I turned, and I went back to bed.

Acknowledgments

Well: here we are. The story of the Masons is finally told, and it wouldn't have been possible without the assistance of an amazing assortment of people. As before, they ranged from medical professionals who worked with both humans and animals to gun experts and epidemiologists. *Blackout* has been an incredible adventure to both research and write, and I am grateful to everyone who has contributed to its creation.

Michelle Dockrey once again lent her incredible eye for blocking to the action scenes and logistics to my work, improving the book beyond all measure in the process. Brooke Lunderville consulted on medical standards and processes, while Kate Secor not only edited, she tolerated endless dinners where I talked about horrible viral outbreaks over dessert.

The entire *Deadline* Machete Squad returned for this book, and I remain honored by their willingness to work with me to make sure it comes out mostly right. Priscilla Spenser and Lauren Shulz joined the Squad for the first time with this book, and did incredible work. Many thanks to them all, and to the endlessly patient, endlessly tolerant, absolutely wonderful staff of Borderlands Books, who have put up with more from me than any one bookstore should.

Most of all, on this volume, I must thank DongWon Song, my

editor, and Diana Fox, my agent. Both of them put in hours upon hours improving and refining the text. They are truly amazing people to work with. (Not to discount all the other amazing people at Orbit, both US and UK. A special thank-you must go to Lauren Panepinto for her amazing cover design. I am seriously amazed by the work she does.)

Finally, and once again, acknowledgment for forbearance goes to Amy McNally, Shawn Connolly, and Cat Valente, who put up with an amazing amount of "talking it out" as I tried to make the book make sense; to my agent, Diana Fox, who remains my favorite superhero; to the cats, for not eating me when I got too wrapped up in work to feed them; and to Tara O'Shea and Chris Mangum, the incredible technical team behind www.MiraGrant.com. This book might have been written without them. It would not have been the same.

Both the CDC and EIS are real organizations, although I have taken many liberties with their structure and operations. To learn more about the history of the EIS, check out *Inside the Outbreaks: The Elite Medical Detectives of the Epidemic Intelligence Service*, by Mark Pendergrast. (Thanks to Bill McGeachin for supplying my copy of this wonderful book.)

Rise up while you can.

extras

www.orbitbooks.net

about the author

Born and raised in California, Mira Grant has made a lifelong study of horror movies, horrible viruses, and the inevitable threat of the living dead. In college, she was voted Most Likely to Summon Something Horrible in the Cornfield, and was a founding member of the Horror Movie Sleep-away Survival Camp, where her record for time survived in the Swamp Cannibals scenario remains unchallenged.

Mira lives in a crumbling farmhouse with an assortment of cats, horror movies, comics, and books about horrible diseases. When not writing, she splits her time between travel, auditing college virology courses, and watching more horror movies than is strictly good for you. Favorite vacation spots include Seattle, London, and a large haunted corn maze just outside of Huntsville, Alabama.

Mira sleeps with a machete under her bed, and highly suggests that you do the same. Find out more about the author at www.miragrant.com.

if you enjoyed

BLACKOUT

look out for

COUNTDOWN

an ebook only Newsflesh novella

also by

Mira Grant

COUNTDOWN

"The Rising is ultimately a story of humanity at both its very best, and at its very worst. If a single event were needed to represent all of human history, we could do worse than selecting the Rising."

—Mahir Gowda

"People blame science. Shit, man, people shouldn't blame science. People should blame people."

—Shaun Mason

May 15, 2014: Denver, Colorado

"How are you feeling today, Amanda?" Dr. Wells checked the readout on the blood pressure monitor, his attention only half on his bored-looking teenage patient. This was old hat by now, to the both of them. "Any pain, weakness, unexplained bleeding, blurriness of vision . . . ?"

"Nope. All systems normal, no danger signs here." Amanda Amberlee let her head loll back, staring up at the colorful mural of clouds and balloons that covered most of the ceiling. She remembered when the staff had painted that for her. She'd been thirteen, and they'd wanted her to feel at ease as they pumped her veins full of a deadly disease designed to kill the disease that was already inside her. "Are we almost done? I have a fitting to get to."

"Ah." Dr. Wells, who had two teenage girls of his own, smiled. "Prom?"

"Prom," Amanda confirmed.

"I'll see what I can do." Dr. Wells took impatience and surliness as insults from most patients. Amanda was a special case. When he'd first started treating her, her leukemia had been so advanced that she had no energy for complaining or talking back. She'd submitted to every test and examination willingly, although she had a tendency to fall asleep in the middle of them. From her, every snippy comment and teenage eye roll was a miracle, one that could be attributed entirely to science.

Marburg EX19—what the published studies were starting to refer to as "Marburg Amberlee," after the index case, rather than "Marburg Denver," which implied an outbreak and would be bad for tourism—was that miracle. The first effective cancer cure in the world, tailored from one of the most destructive viruses known to man. At thirteen, Amanda Amberlee had been given at most six months to live. Now, at eighteen, she was going to live to see her grandchildren . . . and none of them would ever need to be afraid of cancer. Like smallpox before it, cancer was on the verge of extinction.

Amanda lifted her head to watch him draw blood from the crook of her elbow. Any fear of needles she may have had as a child had died during the course of her cancer treatments. "How's my virus doing?" she asked.

"I haven't tested this sample yet, but if it's anything like the last one, your virus should be fat and sleepy. It'll be entirely dormant within another year." Dr. Wells gave her an encouraging look. "After that, I'll only need to see you every six months."

"Not to seem ungrateful or anything, but that'll be awesome." The kids at her high school had mostly stopped calling her "bubble girl" once she was healthy enough to join the soccer team, but the twice-monthly appointments were a real drain on her social calendar.

"I understand." Dr. Wells withdrew the needle, taping a piece of gauze down over the small puncture. Only a drop of blood managed to escape. "All done. And have a wonderful time at prom."

Amanda slid out of the chair, stretching the kinks out of her back and legs. "Thanks, Dr. Wells. I'll see you in two weeks."

Daniel Wells smiled as he watched the girl who might well represent the future of mankind walk out of his office. A world without cancer. What a beautiful thing that would be.

Dr. Daniel Wells of the Colorado Cancer Research Center admitted in an interview this week that he was "guardedly optimistic" about having a universal cure for cancer by the end of the decade. His protocol was approved for human testing five years ago, and thus far, all subjects have shown improvement in their conditions . . .

May 15, 2014: Reston, Virginia

The misters nested in the ceiling above the feeding cages went off promptly at three, filling the air in the hot room with an aerosolized mixture of water and six different strains of rhinovirus. The feeding cages were full of rhesus monkeys and guinea pigs that had entered five minutes earlier, when the food was poured. They ignored the thin mist drifting down on them, their attention remaining focused entirely on the food. Dr. Alexander Kellis watched them eat, making notes on his tablet with quick swipes of his index finger. He didn't look down.

"How's it looking?"

"This is their seventh exposure. So far, none of them have shown any symptoms. Appetites are good, eyes are clear; no runny noses, no coughing. There was some sneezing, but it appears that Subject 11c has allergies."

The man standing next to America's premier expert in genetically engineered rhino- and coronaviruses raised an eyebrow. "Allergies?"

"Yes." Dr. Kellis indicated one of the rhesus monkeys. She was sitting on her haunches, shoving grapes into her mouth with single-minded dedication to the task of eating as many of them as possible before one of the other monkeys took them away. "I'm pretty sure that she's allergic to guinea pigs, poor thing."

His companion laughed. "Yes, poor thing," he agreed, before leaning in and kissing Dr. Kellis on the cheek. "As you may recall, you gave me permission yesterday to demand that you leave the lab for lunch. I have a note. Signed and everything."

"John, I really—"

"You also gave me permission to make you sleep on the couch for the rest of the month if you turned me down for anything short of one of the animals getting sick, and you know what that does to your back." John Kellis stepped away, folding his arms and looking levelly at his husband. "Now, which is it going to be? A lovely lunch and continued marital bliss, or night after night with that broken spring digging into your side, wishing you'd been willing to listen to me when you had the chance?"

Alexander sighed. "You don't play fair."

"You haven't left this lab during the day for almost a month," John countered. "How is wanting you to be healthy not playing fair? As funny as it would be if you got sick while you were trying to save mankind from the tyranny of the flu, it would make you crazy, and you know it."

"You're right."

"At last the genius starts to comprehend the text. Now put down that computer and get your coat. The world can stay unsaved for a few more hours while we get something nutritious into you that didn't come out of a vending machine."

This time, Alexander smiled. John smiled back. It was reflex, and relief, and love, all tangled up together. It was impossible for him to look at that smile and not remember why he'd fallen in love in the first place, and why he'd been willing to spend the last ten years of his life with this wonderful, magical, infuriating man.

"We're going to be famous for what we're doing here, you know," Alexander said. "People are going to remember the name 'Kellis' forever."

"Won't that be a nice thing to remember you by after you've died of starvation?" John took his arm firmly. "Come along, genius. I'd like to have you to myself for a little while before you go down in history as the savior of mankind."

Behind them in the hot room, the misters went off again, and the monkeys shrieked.

Dr. Alexander Kellis called a private press conference yesterday to announce the latest developments in his oft-maligned "fight against the common cold." Dr. Kellis holds multiple degrees in virology and molecular biology, and has been focusing his efforts on prevention for the past decade . . .

May 29, 2014: Denver, Colorado

"Dr. Wells? Are you all right?"

Daniel Wells turned to his administrative assistant, smiling wanly. "This was supposed to be Amanda's follow-up appointment," he said. "She was going to tell me about her prom."

"I know." Janice Barton held out his coat. "It's time to go."

"I know." He took the coat, shaking his head. "She was so young."

"At least she died quickly, and she died knowing she had five more years because of you."

Between them, unsaid: *And at least the Marburg didn't kill her*. Marburg Amberlee was a helper of man, not an enemy.

"Yes." He sighed. "All right. Let's go. The funeral begins in half an hour."

Amanda Amberlee, age eighteen, was killed in an automobile accident following the Lost Pines Senior Prom. It is believed the driver of the vehicle in which Amanda and her friends left the dance had been drinking, and lost control while attempting to make a turn. No other cars were involved in the collision . . .

June 9, 2014: Manhattan, New York

The video clip of Dr. Kellis's press conference was grainy, largely due to it having been recorded on a cellular phone—and not, Robert Stalnaker noted with a scowl, one of the better models. Not that it mattered on anything more than a cosmetic level; Dr. Kellis's pompous, self-aggrandizing speech had been captured in its entirety. "Intellectual mumbo jumbo" was how Robert had described the speech after the first time he heard it, and how he'd characterized it yet again while he was talking to his editor about taking this little nugget of second-string news and turning it into a real story.

"This guy thinks he can eat textbooks and shit miracles," was the pitch. "He doesn't want people to understand what he's really talking about, because he knows America would be pissed off if he spoke English long enough to tell us how we're all about to get screwed." It was pure bullshit, designed to prey on a fear of science. And just as he'd expected, his editor jumped at it.

The instructions were simple: no libel, no direct insults, nothing that was already known to be provably untrue. Insinuation, interpretation, and questioning the science were all perfectly fine, and might turn a relatively uninteresting story into something that would actually sell a few papers. In today's world, whatever sold a few papers was worth pursuing. Bloggers and Internet news were cutting far, far too deeply into the paper's already weak profit margin.

"Time to do my part to fix that," muttered Stalnaker, and started the video again.

He struck gold on the fifth viewing. Pausing the clip, he wound it back six seconds and hit "play." Dr. Kellis's scratchy voice resumed, saying, "—distribution channels will need to be sorted out before we can go beyond basic lab testing, but so far, all results have been—"

Rewind. Again. "—distribution channels—"

Rewind. Again. "—distribution—"

Robert Stalnaker smiled.

Half an hour later, his research had confirmed that no standard insurance program in the country would cover a nonvaccination preventative measure (and Dr. Kellis had been very firm about stating that his "cure" was *not* a vaccination). Even most of the upper-level insurance policies would balk at adding a new treatment for something considered to be of little concern to the average citizen—not to mention the money that the big pharmaceutical companies stood to lose if a true cure for the common cold were actually distributed at a reasonable cost to the common man. Insurance companies and drug companies went hand in hand so far as he was concerned, and neither was going to do anything to undermine the other.

This was all a scam. A big, disgusting, money-grubbing scam. Even if the science was good, even if the "cure" did exactly what its arrogant geek-boy creator said it did, who would get it? The rich and the powerful, the ones who didn't need to worry about losing their jobs if the kids brought home the sniffles from school. The ones who could afford the immune boosters and ground-up rhino dick or whatever else was the hot new thing right now, so that they'd never get sick in the *first* place. Sure, Dr. Kellis never *said* that, but Stalnaker was a journalist. He knew how to read between the lines.

Robert Stalnaker put his hands to the keys and prepared to make the news.

Robert Stalnaker's stirring editorial on the stranglehold of the rich on public health met with criticism from the medical establishment, who called it "irresponsible" and "sensationalist." Mr. Stalnaker has yet to reply to their comments, but has been heard to say, in response to a similar but unrelated issue, that the story can speak for itself . . .

June 11, 2014: Allentown, Pennsylvania

Hazel Allen was well and truly baked. Not just a little buzzed, oh, no; she was baked like a cake. The fact that this rhymed delighted her, and she started to giggle, listing slowly over to one side until her head landed against her boyfriend's shoulder with a soft "bonk."

Brandon Majors, self-proclaimed savior of mankind, ignored his pharmaceutically impaired girlfriend. He was too busy explaining to a rapt (and only slightly less stoned) audience exactly how it was that they, the Mayday Army, were going to bring down The Man, humble him before the masses and rise up as the guiding light of a new generation of enlightened, compassionate, totally bitchin' human beings.

Had anyone bothered to ask Brandon what he thought of the idea that, one day, the meek would inherit the Earth, he would have been completely unable to see the irony.

"Greed is the real disease killing this country," he said, slamming his fist against his own leg to punctuate his statement. Nods and muttered statements of agreement rose up from the others in the room (although not from Hazel, who was busy trying to braid her fingers together). "Man, we've got so much science and so many natural resources, you think anybody should be hungry? You think anybody should be homeless? You think anybody should be eating animals? We should be eating genetically engineered magic fruit that tastes like anything you want, because we're supposed to be the *dominant species*."

"Like Willy Wonka and the snotberries?" asked one of the men, sounding perplexed. He was a bio-chem graduate student; he'd come to the meeting because he'd heard there would be good weed. No one had mentioned anything about a political tirade from a man who thought metaphors were like cocktails: better when mixed thoroughly.

"Snozberries," corrected Hazel dreamily.

Brandon barely noticed the exchange. "And now they're saying that there's a *cure* for the *common cold*. Only you know who's going to get it? Not me. Not you. Not our parents. Not our kids. Only the people who can *afford* it. Paris Hilton's never going to have the sniffles again, but you and me and everybody we care about, we're screwed. Just like everybody who hasn't been working for The Man since this current corrupt society came to power. It's time to change that! It's time to take the future out of the hands of The Man and put it back where it belongs—in the hands of the people!"

General cheering greeted this proclamation. Hazel, remembering her cue even through the haze of pot smoke and drowsiness, sat up and asked, "But how are we going to do that?"

"We're going to break into that government-funded money machine of a lab, and we're going to give the people of the world what's rightfully theirs." Brandon smiled, pushing Hazel gently away from him as he stood. "We're going to drive to Virginia, and we're going to snatch that cure right out from under the establishment's nose. And then we're going to give it to the world, the way it should have been handled in the first place! Who's with me?"

Any misgivings that might have been present in the room were overcome by the lingering marijuana smoke and the overwhelming feeling of revolution. They were going to change the world! They were going to save mankind!

They were going to Virginia.

—

A statement was issued today by a group calling themselves "The Mayday Army," taking credit for the break-in at the lab of Dr. Alexander Kellis. Dr. Kellis, a virologist working with genetically tailored diseases, recently revealed that he was working on a cure for the common cold, although he was not yet at the stage of human trials . . .

June 11, 2014: Berkeley, California

"Phillip! Time to come in for lunch!" Stacy Mason stood framed by the back door of their little Berkeley professor's home (soon to be fully paid off, and wouldn't that be a day for the record books?), wiping her hands with a dishrag and scanning the yard for her wayward son. Phillip didn't mean to be naughty, not exactly, but he had the attention span of a small boy, which was to say, not much of an attention span at all. "*Phillip!*"

Giggling from the fence alerted her to his location. With a sigh that was half love, half exasperation, Stacy turned to toss the dishrag onto the counter before heading out into the yard. "Where are you, Mr. Man?" she called.

More giggling. She pushed through the tall tomato

plants—noting idly that they needed to be watered before the weekend if they wanted to have any fruit before the end of the month—and found her son squatting in the middle of the baby lettuce, laughing as one of the Golden Retrievers from next door calmly washed his face with her tongue. Stacy stopped, biting back her own laughter at the scene.

"A conspiracy of misbehavior is what we're facing here," she said.

Phillip turned to face her, all grins, and said, "Ma!"

Stacy nodded obligingly. Phillip was a late talker. The doctors had been assuring her for over a year that he was still within the normal range for a boy his age. Privately, she was becoming less and less sure—but she was also becoming less and less certain that it mattered. Phillip was Phillip, and she'd love him regardless. "Yes."

"Oggie!"

"Again, yes. Hello, Marigold. Shouldn't you be in your own yard?"

The Golden Retriever thumped her tail sheepishly against the dirt, as if to say that yes, she was a very naughty dog, but in her defense, there had been a small boy with a face in need of washing.

Stacy sighed, shaking her head in good-natured exasperation. She'd talked to the Connors family about their dogs dozens of times, and they tried, but Marigold and Maize simply refused to be confined by any fence or gate that either family had been able to put together. It would have been more of a problem if they hadn't been such sweet, sweet dogs. Since both Marigold and her brother adored Phillip, it was more like having convenient canine babysitters right next door. She just wished they wouldn't make their unscheduled visits so reliably at lunchtime.

"All right, you. Phillip, it's time for lunch. Time to say good-bye to Marigold."

Phillip nodded before turning and throwing his arms around Marigold's neck, burying his face in her fur. His voice, muffled but audible, said, "Bye-time, oggie." Marigold wuffed once, for all the world like she was accepting his farewell. Duty thus done, Phillip let her go, stood, and ran to his mother, who caught him in a sweeping hug that left streaks of mud on the front of her cotton shirt. "Ma!"

"I just can't get one past you today, can I?" she asked, and kissed his cheek noisily, making him giggle. "You go home now, Marigold. Your people are going to worry. Go home!"

Tail wagging amiably, the Golden Retriever stood and went trotting off down the side yard. She probably had another loose board there somewhere; something to have Michael fix when he got home from school and could be sweet-talked into doing his share of the garden chores. In the meantime, the dogs weren't hurting anything, and Phillip *did* love them.

"Come on, Mr. Man. Let's go fill you up with peanut butter and jelly, shall we?" She kissed him again before putting him down. His giggles provided sweet accompaniment to their walk back to the house. Maybe it was time to talk about getting him a dog of his own.

Maybe when he was older.

Professor Michael Mason is the current head of our biology department. Prior to joining the staff here at Berkeley, he was at the

University of Redmond for six years. His lovely wife, Stacy, is a horticulture fan, while his son, Phillip, is a fan of cartoons and of chasing pigeons . . .

June 12, 2014: The lower stratosphere

Freed from its secure lab environment, Alpha-RC007 floated serene and unaware on the air currents of the stratosphere. It did not enjoy freedom; it did not abhor freedom; it did not feel anything, not even the cool breezes holding it aloft. In the absence of a living host, the hybrid virus was inert, waiting for something to come along and shock it into a semblance of life.

On the ground, far away, Dr. Alexander Kellis was weeping without shame over the destruction of his lab, and making dire predictions about what could happen now that his creation was loose in the world. Like Dr. Frankenstein before him, he had created with only the best of intentions and now found himself facing an uncertain future. His lover tried to soothe him and was rebuffed by a grief too vast and raw to be put into words.

Alpha-RC007—colloquially known as "the Kellis cure"—did not grieve, or love, or worry about the future. Alpha-RC007 only drifted.

The capsid structure of Alpha-RC007 was superficially identical to the structure of the common rhinovirus, being composed of viral proteins locking together to form an icosahedron. The binding proteins, however, were more closely related to the coronavirus ancestors of the hybrid, creating a series of keys against which no natural immune system could lock itself. The five viral proteins forming the capsid structure were equally mismatched: two from one family, two from the other, and the fifth . . .

The fifth was purely a credit to the man who constructed it, and had nothing of Nature's handiwork in its construction. It was a tiny protein, smaller even than the diminutive VP4, which made the rhinovirus so infectious, and formed a ring of Velcro-like hooks around the outside of the icosahedron. That little hook was the key to Alpha-RC007's universal infection rate. By latching on and refusing to be dislodged, the virus could take as much time as it needed to find a way to properly colonize its host. Once inside, the other specially tailored traits would have their opportunity to shine. All the man-made protein had to do was buy the time to make it past the walls.

The wind currents eddied around the tiny viral particles, allowing them to drop somewhat lower in the stratosphere. Here, a flock of geese was taking advantage of the air currents at the very edge of the atmospheric layer, their honks sounding through the thin air like car alarms. One, banking to adjust her course, raised a wing just a few inches higher, tilting herself hard to the right and letting her feathers brush through the upper currents.

As her feathers swept through the air, they collected dust and pollen—and a few opportunistically drifting particles of Alpha-RC007. The hooks on the outside of the virus promptly latched on to the goose's wing, not aware, only reacting to the change in their environment. This was not a suitable host, and so the bulk of the virus remained inert, waiting, letting itself be carried along by its unwitting escort back down to the planet's surface.

Honking loudly, the geese flew on. In the air currents above them, the rest of the viral particles freed from Dr.

Alexander Kellis's lab drifted, waiting for their own escorts to come along, scoop them up, and allow them to freely roam the waiting Earth. There is nothing so patient, in this world or any other, as a virus searching for a host.

—

We're looking at clear skies here in the Midwest, with temperatures spiking to a new high for this summer. So grab your sunscreen and plan to spend another lazy weekend staying out of the sun! Pollen counts are projected to be low . . .

June 13, 2014: Denver, Colorado

Suzanne Amberlee had been waiting to box up her daughter's room almost since the day Amanda was first diagnosed with leukemia. Her therapist said it was a "coping mechanism" for her, and that it was completely healthy for her to spend hours thinking about boxes and storage and what to do with things too precious to be given to Goodwill. As the parent of a sick child, she'd been all too willing to believe that, grasping at any comfort that her frightened mind could offer her. She had made her lists long ago. These were the things she would keep; these were the things she would send to family members; these were the things she would give to Amanda's friends. Simple lines, drawn in ink on the ledger of her heart.

That was thought. The reality of standing in her little girl's bedroom and imagining it empty, stripped of all the things that made it Amanda's, was almost more than she could bear. After weeks of struggling with herself, she had finally been able to close her hand on the doorknob and open the bedroom door. She still wasn't able to force herself across the threshold.

This room contained all Amanda's things—all the things she'd ever have the opportunity to own. The stuffed toys she had steadfastly refused to admit to outgrowing, saying they had been her only friends when she was sick and she wouldn't abandon them now. Her bookshelves, cluttered with knickknacks and soccer trophies as much as books. Her framed poster showing the structure of Marburg EX19, given to her by Dr. Wells after the first clinical trials began showing positive results. Suzanne could picture that day when she closed her eyes. Amanda, looking so weak and pale, and Dr. Wells, their savior, smiling like the sun.

"This little fellow is your best friend now, Amanda." That was what he'd said on that beautiful afternoon where having a future suddenly seemed possible again. "Take good care of it and it will take good care of you."

Rage swept over Suzanne in a sudden hot wave. She opened her eyes, glaring across the room at the photographic disease. Where was it when her little girl was dying? Marburg EX19 was supposed to save her baby's life, and in the end, it had let her down; it had let Amanda die. What was the good of all this—the pain, the endless hours spent in hospital beds, the promises they never got to keep—if the damn disease couldn't save Amanda's life?

Never mind that Amanda died in a car crash. Never mind that cancer had nothing to do with it. Marburg EX19 was supposed to save her, and it had failed.

"I hate you," Suzanne whispered, and turned away. She couldn't deal with the bedroom; not today, maybe not ever.

Maybe she would just sell the house, leave Amanda's things where they were, and let them be dealt with by the new owners. They could filter through the spindrift of Amanda's life without seeing her face, without hearing her voice talking about college plans and careers. They could put things in boxes without breaking their hearts.

If there was anything more terrible for a parent than burying a child, Suzanne Amberlee couldn't imagine what it would be. Her internal battle over for another day—over, and lost—she turned away, heading down the stairs. Maybe tomorrow she could empty out that room. Maybe tomorrow she could start boxing things away. Maybe tomorrow she could start the process of letting Amanda go.

Maybe tomorrow. But probably not.

Suzanne Amberlee walked away, unaware of the small viral colony living in her own body, nested deep in the tissue of her lungs. Content in its accidental home, Marburg EX19 slept, waiting for the trigger that would startle it into wakefulness. It was patient; it had all the time in the world.

—

Amanda Amberlee is survived by her mother, Suzanne Amberlee. In lieu of flowers, the family asks that donations be sent to the Colorado Cancer Research Center . . .